Our Nig

Our Nig

Our Nig;

or,

Sketches from the Life of a Free Black,

In a Two-Story White House, North.

SHOWING THAT SLAVERY'S SHADOWS FALL EVEN THERE.

by "Our Nig."

VINTAGE BOOKS
A DIVISION OF RANDOM HOUSE, INC.
NEW YORK

This edition of
Our Nig
is dedicated in memory of
Pauline Augusta Coleman Gates (1916–1987)
and
Henry Louis Gates, Sr. (1913–2010)

Acknowledgments

Without the support and encouragement of John W. Blass-ingame, professor of history at Yale University and chairman of the Program of Afro-American Studies, I would not have been able to verify Harriet E. Wilson's identity in 1982. When one seemingly solid lead would fail, Blassingame suggested others. Only with the enthusiasm generated by our daily discussions about *Our Nig* was I able to persist in my search for this black woman writer. Blassingame's intelligent advice and his generosity are models of scholarly magnanimity, especially for his younger colleagues. This book, in many ways, is John's book.

David A. Curtis, director of research for the Yale Black Periodical Fiction Project, devoted several weeks in September and October 1982 to archival research in Massachusetts and New Hampshire, research that helped me to confirm and supplement the initial facts about Harriet E. Wilson I had gathered in the summer of 1982. David Curtis's contribution to the rediscovery of *Our Nig* is major.

Excellent research assistants who participated in this project include John W. Blassingame, Jr., Donna Dennis, Alexandra Gleysteen, and Timothy Kirscher. For their invaluable assistance I would also like to thank expressly: Jeanne Wells, Olivia Iannicelli, Lisa Fetchko, Irma Johnson, Paul Johnson,

Mike Saperstein, Kwame Anthony Appiah, Martha Clarke, Olufemi Euba, Richard Powell, C. Peter Ripley, Nina Baym, Barbara Johnson, Kimberly W. Benston, Jean Fagan Yellin, Robert Farris Thompson, Mr. Wilfred A. Leduc, Mrs. Helen Draper, Mrs. Nancy Schooley, Mrs. Eugene W. Leach, Sr., Elizabeth Alexander, Maria Fernandez-Gimenez, Denise Hurd, Mrs. Helen Leahy, Rev. David L. Clarke, and Robert Curran. Thirty-five students in my Yale College seminar Black Women and Their Fictions combed through forty periodicals, published between 1859 and 1861, for any mention whatsoever of the book or its author.

William French, of the University Place Bookshop, introduced me to *Our Nig* and to the controversy among booksellers about its authorship. An NEH Chairman's Grant, a research grant from the Menil Foundation, and a Prize Fellowship from the John D. and Catherine T. MacArthur Foundation facilitated my research. Carl Brandt, my literary agent, offered astute advice regarding the publication of the second edition of *Our Nig*. Steven Kezerian, associate director of public information at Yale University, helped generate national press coverage of the resurrection of *Our Nig* and introduced the project to Leslie Bennetts of *The New York Times*, whose sensitive article spread the word about the significance of Mrs. Harriet E. Wilson's pioneering novel.

When I published the first Random House edition, I thanked Accelerated Indexing Systems, a project of major scope for scholars in all fields who found themselves dependent upon public documents for verification of their subjects. AIS, I wrote in the acknowledgments to my first Random House edition, could well aid in the rescue of other literary figures from oblivion. Now, almost thirty years later, the digital revolution has made the sort of research that I conducted to find Harriet Wilson so much more convenient, because millions of public documents (such as census records, birth, marriage, and death certificates, tax records, entire runs of newspapers, etc.) are available online. Ancestry.com and Archives.com, among many others, make these records accessible in seconds, whereas thirty years ago, locating these same documents took weeks and months and was, accordingly, very expensive. The Internet has begun to revolutionize emerging fields such as African American studies, and more "lost" authors and their texts will be discovered as scholars avail themselves of these tools to knowledge, just as R. J. Ellis and I have done to complete further research about Mrs. Wilson and her text.

Erroll McDonald, my friend and classmate at Yale and my editor at Random House, made possible the publication of the first Random House edition of *Our Nig* in 1983. Gwendolyn Williams and Mariner Carroll typed various drafts of the manuscript of the first Random House edition.

For this new edition of *Our Nig*, R. J. Ellis and I would like to recognize our editor Keith Goldsmith, Amy Ryan, Tina Bennett, Bennett Ashley, Vera Grant, Joel Dreyfuss, Sheryl Salomon, Tina Brown, Arianna Huffington, Donald Yacovone, Marcus Halevi, Amy Gosdanian, Joanne Kendall; Barbara A. White, Gabrielle Foreman, Reginald Pitts, and Kathy Flynn for their discoveries that supplemented my initial research about Harriet Wilson's life and times; Hollis Robbins, Shirley Sun, the genealogists Johni Cerny and Megan Smolenyak; David Lambert, the reference librarian at the New England Genealogical Society; Jeanne Flaherty of the Mount Wollaston Cemetery, Quincy, Massachusetts; Fatin Abbas;

Karen Jackson; Art Bryan and Deborah Spratt of the Wadleigh Memorial Library, Milford, NH; Polly S. Cote and Janice Adams of Milford Historical Society; Peggy Langell, Milford town clerk; Paula Laine and Rev. Dr. Sheila Rubdi of the First Congregational Church, Milford; Bill Copley and David Smolen of the New Hampshire Historical Society; Kimberly Reynolds, Roberta Zonghi, Eugene Zepp, and William Faucon of the Boston Public Library; Mary Warnement and Pat Boulos of the Boston Athenaeum; Dominic Whitehead and the other staff at the John Rylands Research Library, Manchester, UK.

Sharon Adams and our children, Maggie and Liza, inspired my search to locate the identity of the author of this curious book in the first place, kept me in a civil, hopeful mood on those days when Harriet E. Wilson seemed to have no past at all. Angela De Leon provided great comfort and support as I continued over the past decade to pursue facts about Mrs. Wilson's life after the death of her son, and the fate of her seminal novel, which now—twenty-eight years later—is a central part of the canon of nineteenth-century American and African American literature. R. J. Ellis's enthusiasm and our shared passion for Mrs. Wilson and *Our Nig,* along with his superlative research and analytical skills, made the editing of this new edition of the novel a delight in every way.

Henry Louis Gates, Jr.
Cambridge, Massachusetts
December 10, 2010

Contents

Introduction

Henry Louis Gates, Jr., and R. J. Ellis

> I can say with much pleasure that when the Regenerator
> was first applied to my own hair it was very gray, and falling
> from my head, and my scalp was in a very unhealthy state;
> but upon a few applications I discovered a decided change,
> and soon my hair assumed its original color and health of
> youth.
>
> —Mrs. H. E. Wilson, Nashua, N.H.[1]

Harriet E. Adams Wilson's *Our Nig* (1859) is the first novel
written and published in English by an African American
woman writer. The story Wilson tells is profoundly moving
and seemingly straightforward. But this straightforwardness
is deceptive: the novel, taking as its unusual focus the fate
of a Northern mulatta, Alfrado (or Frado) Smith, explores
in unique detail the contested position of free blacks in
antebellum America, and specifically the plight of female
free blacks, at what was a highly problematic time in America's racial history.

Frado is deserted as a young girl by Mag Smith, her
white mother, following the death of her African American
father, Jim, "a kind-hearted African," and Mag's subsequent
marriage to Jim's friend, Seth Shipley. The Shipleys cannot
cope financially and decide to move away, resolving to leave

Frado behind. They deposit Frado at the home of a white New England farming family, the Bellmonts. There she becomes their farm servant, treated harshly and derogatorily nick-named "Our Nig." Two members of this family, Mrs. Bellmont and her daughter, Mary, sadistically mistreat Frado. The males of the Bellmont household and a maiden aunt, Aunt Abby, voice their support for her and sometimes even attempt to protect her but fail to assist her in any meaningful way, for lack of will and courage.

The novel depicts Frado's progress in learning to defend herself from this harsh treatment by fighting back with words and actions and finding her voice. After years of mistreat-ment, Frado completes her period of service and is allowed to leave. Wilson sketchily outlines Frado's subsequent fortunes in two closing chapters, in which she meets a young black man, Samuel, quickly marries him, and has a child. He soon deserts her, after confessing to her that he is passing himself off as a fugitive slave in order to profit from the abolition-ist lecture circuit. Left behind in New England, Frado does obtain some financial support, including public charity, but always lives in dire poverty. This destitution and her declin-ing health (precipitated by Mrs. Bellmont's sustained physical abuse) eventually force her to leave her child in foster care as she struggles to survive.

Alongside Frado's story, we learn details of the Bellmont family's own problems, generated most often by Mrs. B.'s meanness. But the novel's plot focuses principally on Frado's sufferings and her uncertain progress toward embracing Christianity. Three pseudonymous testimonials at the end of the book emphasize the Christian context of the tale and urge its authenticity, while an author's preface explains that she is publishing her story to rescue herself and her child from destitution. One of the testimonials further reveals that the author and her child have been reduced to drawing upon public relief. Published in 1859, *Our Nig* offers, through this simple story, a very rare thing indeed: a sustained representation of the life of an antebellum free black female, born and bred in New England and working as a farm servant. As Alice Walker observed in 1983 in a comment published on the dust jacket of the first Random House edition edited by Henry Louis Gates, Jr., the novel is of "enormous significance" because it represents "heretofore unexamined experience." It is one of the very first full-length books written by an African American who was not a slave; it stands as a hallmark of literary history as the first novel published by an African American woman in the United States; and it subtly combines compelling storytelling with unflinching indictments of Northern anti-black racism.

Harriet Wilson seems to have published *Our Nig* herself (though likely with some assistance from unknown patrons), which makes its composition highly unusual: very few African American writers at this time could have taken such a step, an extraordinary one for an impoverished person of any race. The book's survival was to prove precarious for more than a hundred years, since, after one apparently very limited print run,[2] it remained almost unnoticed until 1983, when Henry Louis Gates, Jr., established the identity and race of its author, recovered its history, and published the first new edition since 1859. His research revealed definitively that the book was a novel written by an African American female, thereby attracting for the first time concerted attention to Harriet E. Adams Wilson, her text, its place in literary history, and what it contributes to our understanding of the history of racism in antebellum America.[3]

This definitive new edition, a century and a half after Harriet Wilson published the first edition, carefully lays out the ways in which the author's life helps illuminate the themes and concerns of her novel. In particular, for the first time, we examine in detail Wilson's extensive commitment to and engagement with the profession of spiritualism as she struggled to make a living for herself after she published her novel. We then bring these biographical matters to bear on the composition of *Our Nig*.[4] By tracing in considerable detail just how difficult it was for her to carve out a place within Boston's spiritualist circles following the Civil War, we have established the extent of Harriet Wilson's astonishing achievements over the course of her unusual life.

Opening one of the few extant copies of the 1859 edition of *Our Nig* is a profoundly moving experience. The book was well produced, albeit with an unprepossessing board binding. Its spine contains the simplest information: the bald, disconcerting title *Our Nig* (accompanied by a colophon), but inside the title page adds a long and complex subtitle, followed by the obviously pseudonymous author's name. Nothing published before 1859 by any other black author could possibly prepare the reader for the unusual wording:

OUR NIG;

OR,

Sketches from the Life of a Free Black,

IN A TWO-STORY WHITE HOUSE, NORTH.

SHOWING THAT SLAVERY'S SHADOWS FALL EVEN

THERE.

BY "OUR NIG."

The wording "Sketches from the Life . . . by 'Our Nig'" of course reminds us of the subtitles of other narratives by African Americans, such as Frederick Douglass's 1845 slave narrative, which carries a subtitle informing us it was "Written by Himself," or Harriet Jacobs's *Incidents in the Life of a Slave Girl, Written by Herself,* published just two years after Harriet Wilson's novel appeared. But *Our Nig*'s subtitle also establishes that it is written not by a slave, but by a "Free Black" living in the North. The title page as well as the novel itself undermine all expectations that anything like a conventional slave narrative is on offer. Wilson does not usher in a story about a daring dash to freedom from the South to the North, along a road paved by literacy, as Frederick Douglass famously asserted. Instead Frado remains trapped by the hardships imposed by widespread Northern racism. In the preface the author tells us she is "forced" to write her book as an "experiment which shall aid me in supporting myself and my child" (3). What lies before us indeed turns out to be an experiment; a unified fiction informed by the genres of the sentimental novel, the gothic autobiography, the slave narrative, and realism.

Our Nig's subtitle, by announcing that it is written by a "Free Black," in itself at once establishes the book as unusual, for very few texts had been published before this time by black authors who had not formerly been slaves. Appearing in 1859, *Our Nig* is predated by only a few works of fiction by black writers, including: Frederick Douglass's novella *The Heroic Slave* (1853); William Wells Brown's novel *Clotel* (1853); Frank Webb's *The Garies and Their Friends* (1857), and Martin R. Delany's *Blake; or, The Huts of America* (the first part serialized in *The Anglo-African Magazine* in 1859 and the remainder in the *Weekly Anglo-African* newspaper between 1861 and

1862). Whereas the theme of most of these works of fiction was slavery, Frank Webb depicted the lives of free African Americans in the North, just as Wilson would two years later. (Curiously enough, another black woman writer, Maria F. dos Reis, published a novel entitled *Ursula* in Brazil, also in 1859.)

Our Nig's subtitle further surprises when it notes that, though slavery had been abolished in the North, nevertheless "Slavery's Shadows Fall Even There." Very few writers before Wilson had chosen to focus on the way that slavery could blight the lives of free African Americans in the North. The "shadows" of slavery to which Wilson refers consist, on the one hand, of anti-black racism, of which Wilson's novel is a surprisingly bold and unflinching critique. But the subtitle also refers to the shadows cast on all black people's lives by the Fugitive Slave Act. Passed in 1850 at the behest of Southern slaveholders, the act facilitated the recapture of runaway slaves in the North, although slavery had already been abolished there, state by state. The law controversially compelled Northerners, including abolitionists and free blacks, to stand by impotently as African Americans were seized by slave catchers and returned to their "owners" in the South. The act made it illegal to intervene or offer any assistance to a fugitive. It also provided Northern magistrates with a financial incentive to accept that African Americans brought before them by slave catchers were indeed escaped slaves, thus encouraging the capricious seizure of free African Americans. Such kidnappings were not rare.[5] Slavery's long shadows thus fell on all African Americans in the North, including Frado, Harriet Wilson's protagonist. At one point near her book's end she reports that Frado is "watched by kidnappers" and adds that "traps" were "slyly laid by the vicious to ensnare her" (129).

Described in the novel as "beautiful" (17), Frado would have been highly desirable prey for lascivious slave owners, since female mixed-race slaves generally commanded the highest prices in Southern slave auctions.

More important than the risk of kidnap under the Fugitive Slave Act, "slavery's shadows" also alludes to the prevalence of racism in the Northern free states, such as New Hampshire. Especially during the three decades leading up to the Civil War, Southerners, forced on the defensive by abolitionists, sought to legitimate slavery's continuation through a racist argument proposing that African Americans' color, cranium shape, facial features, and hair texture proved that they were not fully human, or instead were a different or distinct species from human beings of European descent, represented as God's chosen creation. Proslavery propaganda represented people of African descent as vastly less intelligent than white people, more prone to laziness and violence, and more likely to surrender to base impulses and appetites, especially sexual ones. The seeds of "scientific" racism sown in this way (the science was, of course, pseudo-scientific, based on prejudice and superstition, entirely unfounded in reason or fact, and drawn up to justify a profoundly exploitative economic relationship) ensured that slavery's shadows would indeed fall across the whole of the United States long after its abolition and well into the twentieth century. Even those who opposed slavery were sometimes swayed, shockingly enough, by arguments for the innate inferiority of persons of African descent. (Harriet Beecher Stowe's depiction of Miss Ophelia's reluctance to touch Topsy in *Uncle Tom's Cabin* provides one famous example among countless others.)[6]

By the time *Our Nig* was published, just two years before

the Civil War began, the abolition movement had been gaining momentum throughout the North for several decades and
had spread to popular culture. For example, the Hutchinson
Family Singers, a New Hampshire troupe closely connected
to Wilson's birthplace, Milford, toured throughout New
England winning widespread acclaim for the songs they performed, portraying their state as freedom loving and opposed
to slavery.[7] Yet, even as the antislavery cause grew, America's
leading white abolitionist, William Lloyd Garrison, was forced
to expend time and energy trying to excise individual racism
from among his followers. The New Hampshire abolitionist Nathaniel Rogers even came to believe that "laws could
never eradicate prejudice and racial domination" and that a
more fundamental, more perfect revolution than America's
War of Independence was needed.[8] What Rogers had seen in
Canaan, New Hampshire, in 1835, where an attempt to deseg-
regate Noyes Academy was greeted with violent resistance by
the local community, no doubt informed his opinion about
the deep-rooted nature of racial prejudice in American society and what it might take to eradicate it, both on an institu-
tional and a behavioral level.[9]

   Our Nig therefore has good reason to allude to racism
as "slavery's shadows" in the North, but it also establishes
the novel's central theme: exposing the many ways in which
Frado experiences anti-black racism at the hands of Northern
whites and the ways in which race and class were inextricably
intertwined in antebellum America, North and South. *Our
Nig* takes up this theme in an unusual way, since its accent falls
on abuse by white females (adapting Frederick Douglass's
dramatic observation in his 1845 slave narrative that slavery
turned many female slave owners into racists and sadists, even

those initially reared in the North). Among the Bellmonts, during Frado's period of indenture, two of its females, Mary and Mrs. Bellmont, are depicted as the physically cruel ones. After she leaves them, another Northern white woman, Mrs. Hoggs, ignoring how feeble Frado has become after her years of mistreatment, reports her as a malingerer to the town's authorities. Yet, though some of the other Bellmonts have abolitionist sympathies, they do nothing to put an end to Frado's sufferings, which continue until she leaves their house. However much James Bellmont tells her that his "mother's views were by no means general" and assures her that she is not "friendless, and utterly despised" but instead "might hope for better things in the future" (76), he does nothing to intervene, and soon she is once again being "whipped with a rawhide" (77). James's brother, Jack, provides more sympathy, but no protection either.

Indeed, the lack of effective counters to racism in the "free" North is another key theme of the book. In chapter 1, the narrator ruminates ironically on the supposedly "degraded" condition of Mag Smith, Frado's white mother, because of her decision to marry an African American: "You can philosophize, gentle reader, upon the impropriety of such unions, and preach dozens of sermons on the evils of amalgamation.... Poor Mag. She had sundered another bond which held her to her fellows. She had descended another step down the ladder of infamy" (13). Mag Smith's decision to marry a black man leads her inexorably toward a state of social death in white society, precisely because of widespread Northern prejudices against what was then, called amalgamation. Nevertheless, Wilson refrains from representing Frado's parents' liaison sentimentally. Instead, she reveals that the motivations for this marriage are, at best, deeply fraught and problematic, especially those of Frado's father, Jim, whose unrelenting desire to have a white lover she represents as perverse. Even if Jim's motivations are dubious, however, by sarcastically introducing the idea that "amalgamation," the nineteenth-century's term of choice for interracial sexual relations between whites and blacks, was "evil," Wilson challenges her readers to push back against a core argument of Southern apologists for slavery.

At the same time, Wilson—writing quite boldly about the nature of the attraction between her protagonist's father and mother—shows that sexual desire between black men and white women was inevitably informed and shaped by unequal power relations. Frado's father's determination to have sexual relations with a white woman at all costs is blind, irrational, all consuming, and indiscriminate. Jim, "the kind hearted African" whose surname we never learn (thus underscoring his allegorical status in the text) is a deeply damaged victim. Given the state of race relations in America in 1859, the year of John Brown's raid at Harpers Ferry and just two years before the start of the Civil War, Wilson is formulating a very "politically incorrect" auto-critique that would not endear her to black or white abolitionists. She is saying that if one thinks that the pernicious effects of "slavery's shadows" cause white Northerners alone to act perversely, then think again: they can also cause black men and women to act perversely. This is an astonishingly honest and frank confession for any black writer to be making in antebellum America. And this is not the novel's only politically incorrect theme; it also harbors other surprising sentiments about Northern white attitudes toward free blacks.

As *Our Nig* highlights Northern racist attitudes toward black people and the institution of slavery, it also insistently demonstrates that sanctimonious denunciations of Southerners by Northerners were hypocritical at best. But by doing this the book ran the risk of replicating in part the arguments of proslavery advocates. Northerners, proslavery advocates often claimed, treated their servants (especially their black servants) worse than slaves, coldly calculating that there was no economic advantage in keeping them healthy, since they could be easily replaced by other workers at no cost, for "free."[10] Superficially, *Our Nig* seems to support this, for Mrs. Bellmont seems to behave according to this calculation. She argues she must "beat the money out of" Frado since she "can't get her worth any other way" (90). Southerners also claimed that the very structure of the master-slave relation fostered intimate personal relations, leading in some cases to filial ties and deep affection, while Northerners, on the other hand, had no such intimacies with black people and instead often felt mere revulsion. Once again, *Our Nig* seems to support this contention. The narrator of *Our Nig* at one point exclaims, in her most impassioned outburst in the book, that even many *antislavery* Northerners were as repulsed by African Americans as the most deeply racist Southern slaveholders. Those who "didn't want slaves at the South," she cries out, didn't want "niggers in their own homes, North" either: "Faugh! to lodge one; to eat with one; to admit one through the front door; to sit next one; awful!" (129).

The vehemence of *Our Nig*'s denunciations of Northern racism and hypocrisy, combined with the use of the word "Nig" in its title, might therefore conceivably have led some readers to assume that Wilson's book was intended to function as proslavery propaganda, or that it may even have been composed by an anonymous Southern white writer, probably male. It is a bit of a stretch, but if anyone understood it in this way, *Our Nig* could have been interpreted as an inversion of the slave narratives, showing by implication that living within the institution of slavery might in some ways be preferable to being a free black person in the North.[11]

Yet to arrive at such an understanding as this would have been a poor misreading. Wilson's point is that economic exploitation exacerbates and breeds racism in the free North just as it does in the slave South. *Our Nig* portrays the lot of the Northern farm servant—a worker employed both in the farmhouse and in the fields—as exhausting and debilitating. Then it seamlessly connects the racist treatment of blacks—North and South, slave and free—as two faces of the same phenomenon. But the novel offers no support for Southern apologists' proslavery motives when attacking Northern exploitation of blacks. Instead the book squarely confronts two related, dangerously destructive problems: first, the anti-black racism upon which the enslavement and oppression of African Americans rests, and second, the intricate relation between anti-black racism and economic exploitation—even, or especially, the exploitation of the black worker who is not a slave but is ostensibly free. *Our Nig* offers, then, a Northern counternarrative, in which an attractive, lively, and intelligent girl and young woman, no matter how ground down by the behavior racism condones, resists its psychological consequences to the bitter end, gaining her voice in the process.

By now it has become apparent that, though at the start of the book Harriet Wilson insists that Frado's mistress, Mrs. Bellmont, had been "wholly imbued with *southern* principles"

(3), the book goes on to confront head-on the comfortable assumption by Northern abolitionists that being opposed to slavery is, in itself, somehow morally sufficient to free one of complicity in the existence of slavery or the oppression of free blacks in the North. *Our Nig* instead exposes how slavery depends upon racist attitudes that deny African Americans— even those who are not slaves—both their common humanity with white people and their most basic rights. Slavery's shadows, in other words, fall even on the economic exploitation of free black workers and—by extension—white workers, too. Wilson's story implicates white Northerners as either adopting or condoning the principles of Southern racism or at best being complicit in them through sins of omission (akin to the Bellmont males' general passivity). Similarly, the New England town in which Frado lives, although called Singleton, is in fact deeply divided over the issue of slavery—making it, in a heavy irony, more of a *double*-town. Just as James Bellmont assures Frado of support in terms demonstrating he is familiar with abolitionist rhetoric, while his mother is an open racist, so Singleton harbors both a schoolteacher who leaps to Frado's defense when she is bullied by young racists in the school playground and such racists as Mrs. Hoggs, prejudicially inclined to identify African Americans as idle wasters. Singleton certainly offers a "two-story." But one of Wilson's boldest moves, perhaps, is the transformation of the young black house servant, maliciously called Our Nig, overworked at will, into the narrator who confrontationally adopts as her nom de plume that very term of disparagement. By doing so, Wilson lays bare how the dehumanizing racism that obtains in the North pervades all its institutions, even its abolitionist institutions, so that she can only be identified as "Our Nig."

This message would have been very difficult for most white Northern readers to stomach.

The book's title page, in line with the title pages of slave narratives that repeatedly assert that the tale that follows is "authentic," true to the life of the slave who wrote or narrated it (as a "narrative of the life . . ."), announces that the novel contains autobiographical "sketches from the life." Yet Wilson's book is very far from being an autobiography, and to attempt to see it as this is to ignore the conventions of both genres. Wilson's obvious intention is to create a character whose life seems to have been largely based upon her own, but she is certainly not limited to or confined by it. In fact, we know so very little about the life of Harriet Wilson when she was still Harriet Adams that it is extraordinarily difficult to know how much of Frado's life reflects Wilson's experience and how much is the product of her imagination. And we shall never know. To attempt to transform this novel into an autobiography, unfortunately, is to trivialize or minimize the full import of Wilson's original contribution to African American and American literature.[12] Rather, *Our Nig* is first and foremost a fiction. It is written in the third person and its protagonist is called Alfrado Smith, not Harriet Wilson. Similarly, Wilson has chosen some of the names of her novel's characters and the name of the town they live in for their symbolic import: Mrs. Hoggs behaves like a pig, the divided town in which Frado is abused is called Singleton, and the Bellmonts, who are hardly to be looked up to, carry a name suggesting they possess "beauty" and "high" status, which is fully belied by Mrs. B.'s and Mary's vicious vindictiveness. In actuality the Bell[e]mo[u]nts are a family that stand as bellwethers of a destructive racial order that would stubbornly outlast the institution of slavery.

While Wilson's condemnation of racism and its deadly accompaniments is clear enough, what remains less clear is the identity of Wilson herself. The historical record is very thin (as is so very often the case when dealing with African American lives in the nineteenth century). For example, we remain unsure of her parents' identities, and even determining that she was a mulatta depends to a surprising degree upon the 1880 census (see appendix 3), in which she was first recorded as white, only to have this identification crossed out and the entry "Mu[latta]" substituted. This alteration suggests that Wilson was initially taken to be white by the census taker and therefore she was probably quite light skinned. But her precise skin color remains uncertain. Our point is that Wilson takes factual episodes in her own life for use as a resource upon which to construct a fictional life for her novel's protagonist, Frado, and it is all too easy for us as readers to be lured into taking as fact what she wrote as fiction beyond the point where it is reasonable to do so, simply because so little is known about her. Wilson is not Frado, and she may not even exactly correspond to the woman described in the pseudonymously written testimonials.

As our research makes clear, Our Nig, like so many first novels, builds its plot upon a hybrid mix of events, some of which we know Wilson experienced and some that she invented or changed—events that she could not possibly have experienced (such as the details of Frado's parents' courtship, to choose just one example)—switching deftly between the two. For example, she reduces the size of the family with whom she had lived when fictionalizing them as the Bellmonts. Reading *Our Nig* as a novel, as it surely should be, rather than as an autobiography, reveals how deeply indebted it is formally not only to the slave narrative but also, far more substantially, to the most popular fictional genre of the time, the sentimental novel, which commonly tells the story of a poor, abandoned child in a mode laced with gothic overtones.[13]

One subgenre of such sentimental fiction, the novel of "sorrows and trials,"[14] portrays a girl orphaned or separated from her parents falling under the control of an exploitative or abusive tormentor, usually female, and successfully escaping, sometimes by making her own way but more commonly by coming under another's protection, usually that of a sympathetic male. Obviously, the storyline of *Our Nig* closely follows this plot trajectory, but it also significantly recasts it.[15]

For example, Mag's desertion of Frado at the opening of the story is atypical of the "sorrows and trials" genre, where parental death is the most common cause of separation. (As we have seen, Mag's decision to marry two black men has led to another sort of death, a "death" defined by alienation, her own social death.) In marked contrast, Frado's mother and her second black husband resolve to desert Frado because of the couple's poverty, since they can neither afford nor want the burden of looking after two children. Frado's penury is also much starker and longer lasting than the transitory poverty typically found in sentimental novels. Furthermore, "sorrows and trials" protagonists are nowhere near so badly treated as Frado is in *Our Nig*.

Even more tellingly, *Our Nig*'s ending is completely atypical. "Sorrows and trials" novels recount their heroines' journeys toward a comparatively comfortable or even affluent station in life. This typically results from a near-magical chain of coincidences, such as a surprising inheritance or an advantageous marriage, which delivers the waif to a "land of happy endings."[16] Frado's story, by comparison, does not end happily. She may have successfully left behind Mrs. Bellmont's tyranny, but her debilitating hardships continue.

Yet the most striking contrast concerns the infliction of physical violence. Abuse is Frado's customary lot: as we have seen, she suffers great cruelty at the hands of Mrs. Bellmont and her daughter Mary.[17] Violence on this scale is quite foreign to "sorrows and trials" novels. Indeed, though drawing upon this subgenre of the sentimental novel, *Our Nig*, in these signal ways, demonstrates how black fiction, even from its beginnings, departs in both form and content from the norms of white female (or male) fiction, in order to expose a quite different kind of body politics.

The question that haunts both Frado and Wilson's readers is this: What kind of resistance can Frado offer? At a climactic moment (reminiscent of Frederick Douglass's famous confrontation with the overseer, Mr. Gore) faced with the threat of yet another unfair attack by Mrs. B., Frado picks up a stick from the woodpile and raises it: " 'Stop!' shouted Frado, 'strike me, and I'll never work a mite more for you;' and throwing down what she had gathered, stood like one who feels the stirring of free and independent thoughts. By this unexpected demonstration, her mistress, in amazement, dropped her weapon, desisting from her purpose of chastisement" (105). Later, Frado recalls this moment as her "victory at the wood-pile" (108). Frado senses that she can in a limited way shape her own future. Yet this moment is also deeply compromised, for we are almost immediately told that the whippings at the hands of Mrs. B. continue, even if they do become fewer in number, unlike the relationship that ensued after Frederick Douglass wrestled Mr. Gore to a draw.

Furthermore, Frado's resistance is not entirely her own idea but is to some extent sanctioned by Mr. Bellmont, who has just told her that she should avoid whippings. However, he then goes on to add this can only be when "she was *sure* she did not deserve" them, because she "cannot endure beating as once [she] could" (104) due to her poor health. Only after this mealy-mouthed support is offered does Frado find the resolve to stand up to Mrs. B. Yet offering any *physical* resistance, she knows, could lead to severe retribution, even more dire than her current suffering. So Frado's response is in part carefully calculated: she "stood like one who feels the stirring of free and independent thoughts." Frado at this point is not only experiencing "free and independent thoughts" but is also making manifest such thoughts, as communicated by her body language. Yet her aim is additionally to fend off the need to act, since she knows of the consequent dangers if she does.

Our Nig exhibits its greatest complexity at such moments. Up to this point Frado has often appeared in a series of tableaux, bound and gagged or with her mouth propped open. Made forcibly silent by her mistress, she is often laid out supine upon the floor, a victim of unchecked white power, as unassailable as that of any slave master's. (Frado will also be victimized by a black male as well, her husband, Thomas Wilson.) Wilson depicts Frado by the woodpile, however, in language that links her to—but does not secure her—full political resistance. The inclusiveness of the word "one" suggests how Frado's actions mark Wilson's claim for all black people, slave and free, to the Enlightenment promise of universal rights.

But these human rights turn out to be far from readily available to someone in her position: Frado's posture is one of
defiance, but she is only acting out, not taking action. She can
only stand "*like* one [with] free and independent thoughts"
and she can "feel" no more than their "stirrings." So, although
she establishes some measure of independence following her
woodpile exchange with Mrs. Bellmont, she still must also
return to the farmhouse, resume her servitude, and receive
further beatings. She recognizes her dilemma quite explicitly,
as her resolve encounters an insuperable impasse, leaving her
literally with nowhere to go: "She decided to . . . remain to do
as well as she could; to assert her rights when trampled upon,
to return once more to her meeting in the evening, which
had been prohibited. She had learned how to conquer; she
would not abuse that power. But had she not better run away?
Where?" (108).

In part, then, as was the case with Douglass, Frado's assertion of "power" generates new thoughts, especially thoughts
about running away, in language suggestive of the determined
or desperate slave, whose only recourse is to escape. (Two
years after the novel was published, Harriet Jacobs would take
up a similar theme in her characterization of herself as Linda
Brent in her slave narrative.) Yet what she in fact does is seek
the advice of Aunt Abby, herself a member of the Bellmont
family. As Frado puts it, "She had never been from the place
far enough to decide what course to take"—and the words
"far enough" refer to both literal geographical space and metaphorical mental space. Wilson depicts Frado in the process
of altering her mind while weighing consequences.

Frado's thoughts now take another, safer track, as she
determines to defy Mrs. B. by going back to the church meet-

ings that Mrs. B. had forbidden her to attend. To achieve a measure of freedom, she must put herself under another form of authority: not Aunt Abby's nor Mr. Bellmont's, but religious authority. The narrator, as well as Frado, ruminates ironically upon her state of grace—will she go to heaven?—as if Frado's progress toward becoming a good Christian follows the conventional path of a conversion narrative. This preoccupation places *Our Nig* in direct affinity with the sentimental novel, which conventionally depicted its female protagonists coming to a realization (led by their theological mentors) of what constitutes true Christian belief. But *Our Nig* again deviates decisively from any such model, since Frado remains shockingly ambivalent about what Christianity can offer. This is, quite simply, deeply unconventional.

Frado often approaches but then retreats from becoming "serious" about religion (86), as when, early on, James Bellmont explains to her that God is her Maker. This prompts her to ask who, then, made Mrs. B.? When told that God also made her mistress, Frado replies, "Well, then, I don't like him." Frado's sacrilege in this exchange is defused somewhat by the comedy invoked when she offers her reasoning for her feelings about God: "Because he made her white, and me black. Why didn't he make us both white?"(51). Nonetheless, Frado has erected a formidable barrier between herself and her Maker, between her agnosticism and true belief. Aunt Abby encourages her spiritual progress by taking her to church, where Frado enjoys singing hymns (69). However, in conversation with Aunt Abby, Frado manipulatively feigns naïveté. For example, when Frado celebrates the departure of the hated Mary Bellmont for Baltimore and Abby remonstrates, urging Frado to recall how "our good Minister told us . . . about doing good to those who hate us," Frado's saucy reply is that by helping pack Mary's bags she has done "good" (80–81).

It comes as little surprise, then, after James Bellmont's death, that we are told that any belief Frado has in a "future existence" (84) is undercut by her conclusion that heaven is "all for white people" (rather like the reserved pews and segregated sections in many "integrated" Northern churches at this time) and so she must be "unfit" to go there (84–85). Frado's chief motive for becoming more "serious" about religion seems to be, as her pastor realizes, to get nearer to the departed James. In response, Mrs. Bellmont, unhappy with this development, whatever its grounds, opposes her church attendance. So Frado again abandons her belief: "her mistress was a professor of religion; was she going to heaven? then she did not wish to go" (104). Frado's loud celebration of Mary's death underlines her disgust at the Bellmonts' racism and, by extension, her disillusionment with their kind of Christianity. Ultimately, however, and again ironically, Frado finds one redeeming aspect of Christian belief: the existence of hell, in which a person as evil as Mary Bellmont would finally receive her just deserts: "S'posen she goes to hell, she'll be black as I am. Wouldn't mistress be mad to see her a nigger!" (107). Only hell's fire could grant Frado and Mary the most ironic form of equality: eternal torment. Wilson's joke here startles readers today; we can only imagine the reaction of her contemporaries a century and a half ago. She was most certainly crossing over into sacrilege.

Soon Frado is deriving her "soul's refreshment" from schoolbooks, not the Bible (116), confirming how far she is from a conventional state of grace. Nonetheless, as the book draws to a close, having left the Bellmonts and become dependent on other people's charity, she becomes more pious once again. Indeed, a Bible is now described as "her greatest treasure" (117). Concluding her story with the conventional claim that she "repose[s] in God" (130) would have been a requirement not only if Frado wished to remain an acceptable recipient of Singleton's charity, but also for Wilson and her son to continue to receive Milford's poor relief and for Wilson to secure the "patronage" for which she appeals in the novel's preface (which, after all, is why, as she so plainly tells us, she wrote her novel in the first place).

Yet, despite this apparently devout ending, notes of prevarication linger. Very near the novel's end, for example, we are told that Frado lived with a woman who taught her "the value of useful books" and that together they read aloud "deeds historic and names renowned" while "a devout Christian *exterior* invited confidence from the . . . neighbors"—an extraordinarily unconventional reflection (124; our emphasis). The testimonials that follow a few pages later therefore seem an essential addition. Laden with Christian sentiments, they vouch for her final status as a good Christian and would seem to wish to mitigate the vein of apostasy that has gone before. And in these three principal ways—by depicting a protagonist who suffers sustained violent attacks, who does not live happily ever after, and who does not progress to become a securely moored Christian believer—Harriet Wilson, if she did not exactly create a new subgenre of the sentimental novel, at the very least introduces a stunning innovation. And this is one more crucial legacy she offers as a novelist.

One further departure from the norms of the contemporary white sentimental novel exemplifies how Wilson transforms the genre: the treatment of the relationship between Frado and her pet dog, Fido. As a mark of Jack Bellmont's sympathy, he presents Frado with a dog just after she has been cruelly whipped by Mrs. B. Yet this sympathy does not translate into any preventive action by Jack. The text marks this irony: Jack "resolved to do what he could to protect her from Mary and his mother. He bought her a dog" (37). Rather than taking on a protective role himself, he ineffectually delegates it to a pet instead. Frado herself will continue to be treated like a dog, whatever the feelings of Jack, Mr. Bellmont, or, later, James. Lest the reader miss this metaphorical connection, Frado names her dog Fido, creating a Frado/Fido allegorical leitmotif. After Mrs. B. indulges her "vixen nature" by way of "a few blows on Nig," Fido becomes the "confidant of Frado. She told him her grief as though he were human" (41–42). Frado is enduring a dog's life in the Bellmont household, yet it is the female Bellmonts who are the more carnivorous: their inhuman devouring of Frado's childhood makes them resemble a pair of vicious dogs. The Fido/Frado motif climaxes in the scene where Frado refuses to eat from a plate used by her mistress until Fido has licked it clean (71). This calculated insult, aimed at her cruel white mistress, ironically recapitulates Frado's own social situation. Instead of being offered help by her white "allies," Frado receives guilt money, tossed to her by Jack for her mistreatment and her minor act of resistance (72). By creating this association between an exploited black woman and her pet dog, Wilson economically intimates that it is less than human to regard another human as less than human.

In this last example, we can glimpse something of Wilson's strategy as a writer: how she borrows from the sentimental novel's tropes and plot structures—and from captivity and seduction narratives.[18] Her adaptation is carefully calculated and profoundly revisionist. She doesn't borrow from genres as much as transform them. Wilson has taken the conventional sentimental trope of a waif's ownership of a pet (a recurrent motif in women's novels' plotlines) and transformed it into a complex reflection on Frado's position as a dehumanized farm servant in contrast to that of a Southern slave. It has to be said in passing that Wilson has now shown herself to be very well read, and this perhaps underlines how far she was from being simply the downtrodden waif her book depicts in 1859.

Our Nig graphically establishes by way of its sweeping transformations of the sentimental novel genre that the "inalienable rights" of "liberty and the pursuit of happiness" alluded to on its title page are at best only partly realized for "free" blacks. While this was most dramatically apparent in the case of African Americans like Frado, the novel is also a fictional representation of the common practice of indenturing indigent youths, whether black or white, in New England.[19] The novel also shows how "slavery's shadows" fall on Northern labor more generally—beyond invocations of "wage slavery," a phrase concealing fundamental differences between Southern slavery and labor practices in a rapidly industrializing North. Equating wage labor and chattel slavery risks lending credence to those who supported slavery by arguing that slavery could and should constitute a salutary condition for all working people when compared to the suffering of uncared-for wage laborers.[20] However, failing to attack the idea that wage labor is unproblematically "free labor" ignores the coercive and dehumanizing abuses of an unregulated labor market.[21] Wilson's novel has to negotiate the tightrope that results. Frado's particular position, as an indigent servant who is neither slave nor free, also dramatizes the near-seamless gradations between slave labor and wage labor. Wilson's narrative is one of the earliest explorations of the lives of "free laborers" and in particular the life of farm servants and their peculiarly vulnerable position in the labor market, which all too often translated into forms of debt peonage. The sheer drudgery endured by Frado offers, quite rarely in antebellum American (and British) fiction, an insight into the hardships of rural labor.

Perhaps the sole precursor in this regard is the black female writer Nancy Prince. It seems likely Wilson was aware of Prince's work and borrowed from her (a technique commonly adopted by antislavery writers).[22] *Our Nig*'s Preface closely echoes the sentiments found in the 1853 Preface to the second edition of Prince's autobiography, *A Narrative of the Life and Travels of Mrs. Nancy Prince.*

Nancy Prince: My object is not a vain desire to appear before the public, but by [my narrative's] sale I hope to obtain the means to supply my necessities. There are many benevolent societies for the support of Widows, but I am desirous not to avail myself of them, so long as I can support myself by my own endeavors. Infirmities are come upon me, which induce me to solicit the patronage of my friends and the public, on the sale of this work. Not wishing to throw myself on them, I take this method to help myself, as health and strength are gone.[23]

Harriet E. Wilson: In offering to the public the follow-ing pages the writer confesses her inability to minister to the refined and cultivated, the pleasure supplied by abler pens. . . . Deserted by kindred, disabled by failing health, I am forced to some experiment which shall aid me in maintaining myself and child without extinguish-ing this feeble life. . . . I sincerely appeal to my colored brethren universally for patronage, hoping that they will not condemn this attempt of their sister to be erudite, but rally around me a faithful band of supporters. (3)

Prince is an apt precursor, because her short catalogue of work as a free black child servant in the North also foreshad-ows that of Frado:

Prince: I had to prepare for the wash; soap the clothes and put them into the steamer, set the kettle of water boiling, and then close in the steam, and let the pipe into the steam box. . . . At two o'clock on the [next] morning . . . the bell was rung for me to get up; but that was not all, they said I was too slow, and the washing was not done well; I had to leave the tub to tend the door and wait on the family. . . .

Hard labor and unkindness was too much for me; in three months my health and strength were gone.[24]

Wilson: Her first work was to feed the hens . . . any departure from this rule to be punished by a whipping. She was then . . . to drive the cows to pasture. . . . Upon her return she was allowed to eat her breakfast. . . . This over, she was placed on a cricket to wash the common dishes; she was to be in waiting always to bring wood and chips, to run hither and thither from room to room.

A large amount of dish-washing . . . followed dinner. Then the same after tea and going after the cows finished her first day's work. The same routine followed day after day, with slight variation; adding a little more work. (29)

Such allusions to other African American writers reinforces Wilson's claim that the "inalienable rights" of "liberty and the pursuit of happiness" are partial and relative for all African Americans—slaves and "free" blacks alike.[25] However, Wilson's vulnerable position also means she must always be circumspect: her narrative strategy necessarily entails some self-censorship, a rhetorical feature her text shares with a number of slave narratives, such as Harriet Jacobs's. In *Our Nig* she writes, "I do not pretend to divulge every transaction which the unprejudiced would declare unfavourable in comparison with the treatment of legal bondmen; I have purposely omitted that which would provoke most shame in our good anti-slavery friends" (3). She draws back from laying everything bare, lest proslavery arguments about the awfulness of "wage slavery" are granted too much legitimacy. Yet Frado's particular position, first as a kind of indentured servant who is neither a "legal bond[wo]man" nor a wage laborer, and later as a subject required to work under Milford's harsh poor laws, dramatizes how the gradations between slave labor and wage labor, far from delineating a black-and-white division ("slave" vs. "free") instead reveal that dehumanizing exploitation can emerge in many different permutations, complicated, as she insists throughout the text, by anti-black racism.

Though *Our Nig* owes complex debts to its literary forebears, in particular the sentimental tradition, when Wilson asserts, "I do not pretend to divulge every transaction," she also reminds the reader of the autobiographical elements of her book. Wilson's discussion of "her own life" in the preface (3) raises the question of how far *Our Nig* should be read as autobiographical.

First, the book's title page announces that the author and the main protagonist are one and the same: *Our Nig* by "Our Nig." The subtitle confirms this: "Sketches from the Life of a Free Black." Then there are the titles of the first three chapters: "Mag Smith, My Mother," "My Father's Death," and "A New Home for Me." These chapter headings suggest the story was originally conceived as a first-person narrative.

Furthermore, since Gates's authentication of Harriet Adams Wilson's identity as an African American woman and the author of the novel (including the recovery of her marriage license and the death certificate of her son by the researcher David A. Curtis, with the assistance of the librarian Mrs. Eugene W. Leach, Sr.), several scholars have made dramatic discoveries about Wilson's life after 1860, and about the identity of the characters Mrs. Wilson fictionalizes in her text. No doubt the most important of these were P. Gabrielle Foreman's and Reginald Pitts's recovery of Wilson's life between the Civil War and the turn of the century, especially her work as a spiritual medium, and Kathy Flynn's research on her career as an entrepreneur producing and marketing hair treatments. (Professor Foreman graciously gave Professor Gates one of the rare surviving bottles of Mrs. Wilson's hair product; see figure on page xlvi). Barbara A. White's role

was also transformative, when she established that the Bellmont family is the fictional counterpart of the Haywards, in
whose household Wilson served her period of harsh indenture. Additionally, R. J. Ellis's research presented in this
edition establishes the details of her connections with the
Congregational church in Milford, her time on Milford's pauper list, and for the first time the full extent of her fascinating
career as a spiritualist in Boston. When Gates undertook his
quest to establish Wilson's identity in the early eighties the
Internet had not been invented. Now, online searches, especially in databases of newspapers, make this sort of research
much more efficient, and Wilson scholarship has profited
enormously from this technical innovation.

The result of the work of these scholars leaves no doubt
that Harriet Wilson was a black woman, born in New Hampshire, who undertook the audacious act of writing a novel
both to testify to her particular experiences of racism in a
slave-free state in the North and to generate sufficient funds
to provide a secure living for herself and her son. Sales of her
self-published novel were never going to fulfill the author's
desire for economic self-sufficiency. Nevertheless, the text she
produced against the greatest odds stands as a testament to
the fact that, within the African American literary tradition,
the will to freedom manifested itself—for former slaves and
free Northern black people alike—as the will to write, the will
to establish one's identity through writing about one's self as
a thinking, feeling human being, even or especially if that
meant creating new forms of imaginative literature to do so.
This is another of Harriet Wilson's important legacies.

Harriet E. Wilson seems to have been born and brought
up in the historical model for *Our Nig*'s Singleton, the town
of Milford, New Hampshire, from the late 1820s onward. Her

maiden name was Adams (as clearly recorded in the 1850 U.S. census and on her first marriage certificate).[26] She probably was born or lived as a youngster in the household of Timothy Blanchard, a cooper living in Milford in the Shed[d] farmhouse (as it was generally known at the time). She seems to have been deserted in Milford by her mother around seven years of age, for she likely is the free colored female living

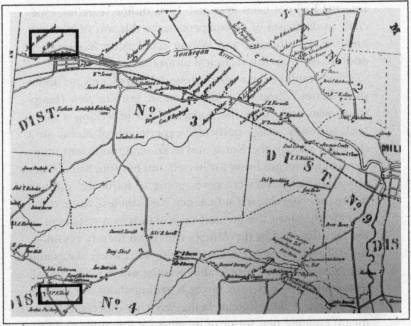

Detail from 1854 map of Milford, New Hampshire, showing the locations of Nehemiah Hayward's farmhouse where Wilson worked and the Shed[d] farmhouse close by, where she was possibly born and probably raised. (Courtesy of Milford Historical Society.)

with the Hayward family in Milford at the time of the 1840 census. The details of the Hayward family and their history mirror in most respects those of the Bellmonts. Even the farm they owned on the cliffs above the Souhegan River resembles that of their fictional counterparts. Though the Bellmont family in *Our Nig* is smaller than that of the Haywards (see the Hayward family tree, page xliv), this is one of Wilson's several fictionalizations of her lived experiences, in order to simplify the narrative. It therefore seems reasonable to conclude that Wilson lived with the Hayward family as a farm servant (one who works both in the farmhouse and the fields), under circumstances resembling those of Frado. It is likely, though not certain, that she was indentured ("bound out") to them by Milford's town council (the town's records here are incomplete).[27]

The Haywards, who were relatively prominent, had connections with the foremost abolitionists in the town, including their pastor, the Reverend Humphrey Moore, and with the Hutchinson Family Singers (to whom they became related by marriage).[28] James Bellmont's comforting of Frado in *Our Nig* echoes antislavery sentiments: "In our part of the country there were thousands upon thousands who favored the elevation of her race, disapproving of oppression in all its forms" (75). Wilson's experiences with the abolitionists in Milford are undoubtedly the source of Frado's bitterness about the hypocrisy she encounters in Singleton and within the Bellmont family. Nothing certain, however, can be gleaned about Wilson's physical treatment behind the doors of the Hayward farmhouse.

The next documentary record is her appearance in the report by Milford's overseers of the poor for the year April

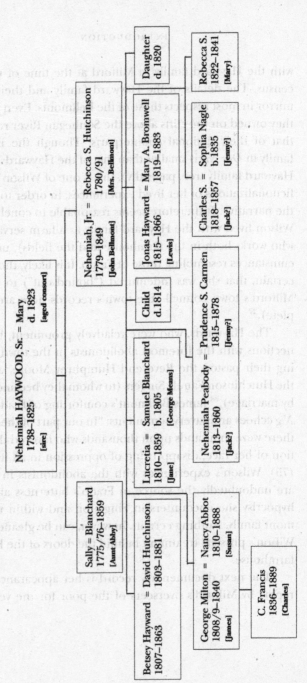

HAYWARD FAMILY TREE

(adapted from Barbara H. White)

The probable identities of the fictional characters featured in Our Nig appear in bold under their likely life-model.

Nehemiah HAYWOOD, Sr. = Mary
1738–1825   d. 1823
[sire]   **[aged consort]**

Sally = Blanchard
1775/76–1859
[Aunt Abby]

Nehemiah, Jr. = Rebecca S. Hutchinson
1779–1849   1780/91
[John Bellmont]   **[Mrs. Bellmont]**

Daughter
d. 1820

Betsey Hayward = David Hutchinson
1807–1863   1803–1881

Lucretia = Samuel Blanchard
1810–1859 b. 1805
[Jane]   **[George Means]**

Child
d.1814

Jonas Hayward = Mary A. Bromwell
1815–1866   1819–1883
[Lewis]

Charles S. = Sophia Nagle
1818–1857   b.1835
[Jack?]   **[Jenny?]**

Rebecca S.
1822–1841
[Mary]

George Milton = Nancy Abbot
1808/9–1840   1810–1888
[James]   **[Susan]**

Nehemiah Peabody = Prudence S. Carmen
1813–1860   1815–1878
[Jack?]   **[Jenny?]**

C. Francis
1836–1889
[Charles]

Note: "Jack" is probably a character compounding Nehemiah Peabody Hayward and Charles S. Hayward.

1849–March 1850, which suggests that she left the Haywards' farm sometime after 1840 and before April 1849, possibly upon reaching the age of eighteen. By 1849–50 she had been reduced to penury; she appears in the 1850 census as Harriet Adams—the same name that later appears on her marriage license—lodged with the Samuel Boyles family, and in the town's records for 1850–51 as a "pauper not on the farm." The next identifying document records her marriage to Thomas Wilson, on October 6, 1851, again as Harriet Adams.

Between being listed as a pauper for at least part of the period February 1850–February 1851 and her marriage to Thomas Wilson, Harriet probably departed from Milford and lived in a town or village (it is described as both), identified only as "W——," Massachusetts, according to the testimonial of "Allida." The identity of the town of W—— remains uncertain.[29] Frado likewise moves away from Singleton, to a town in Massachusetts where she learns to make straw bonnets (124). There Frado meets a "professed fugitive" (126) and returns to Singleton to marry him. If this was also the sequence of events in Wilson's life (and "Allida" approximately reproduces this story), it must have occurred within the space of less than a year. Wilson's life certainly matches Frado's in her novel: after her 1851 marriage, she and her husband Thomas conceive a child, born within a year, probably on the county farm, and given the name George Mason Wilson (Frado congruently reports that, after she was deserted by her husband, she was again "thrown upon the public for sustenance" and that then her child was born; "Allida" and Margaretta Thorn both support this story in their testimonials).

Harriet Wilson next surfaces in the historical record in reports by Milford's overseers of the poor for the years

1854–56. Her son was admitted briefly to the county poor farm in 1855, though appearing with her in the overseers' records for 1855–56. Then, for three successive years (spring 1856–spring 1859), Wilson's child appears on Milford's pauper lists, though she does not. During this period, it seems that Wilson remained in the New Hampshire–Massachusetts region, having learned "a valuable recipe" (129) for a product for "restoring gray hair to its former color," as "Allida" informs us (137). Foreman and Pitts demonstrated this by discovering several bottles manufactured in Manchester, New Hampshire, bearing Mrs. H. E. Wilson's name. Flynn and Foreman also located advertisements quite widely scattered in New York, New Jersey, and the New England press—one of these even appearing in the Milford *Farmer's Cabinet* in 1859.[30] Wilson sold this hair product from the mid-1850s into the early 1860s.[31]

One of the bottles carrying the information that it contained Mrs. H. E. Wilson's hair dressing produced in the early 1860s, probably in Manchester, N.H. (Gift of P. Gabrielle Foreman, from the collection of Henry Louis Gates, Jr. Photo by Marcus Halevi.)

During this period of her life, in part passed as a resident of Nashua, New Hampshire, two important incidents occur in rapid succession. *Our Nig* is copyrighted and self-published in 1859, and then George Mason Wilson, Harriet's son, dies in February 1860. Sadly, Wilson's declared intention of selling her book to support her child was overtaken by events.

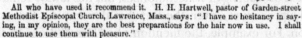
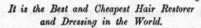
Advertisement: "Use Mrs. Wilson's Hair Regenerator and Hair Dessing," *Methodist Quarterly Review* 42, ed., D. D. Whedon (New York: Carlton and Porter, 1860, 714). The portrait is an artistic depiction of hair "regenerated" by Wilson's dressing; the person depicted may be Wilson herself. In the advertisement, "Mrs. H. E. Wilson of Nashua" endorses her hair dressing in her own words. (Photograph by R. J. Ellis.)

Constructing an account of Wilson's life involves taking these few definitive facts from the historical record and rounding them out with information and clues drawn from the text of *Our Nig* or its testimonials, but this always remains a risky procedure, given the fact that the text is a fictionalization. For example, the mention of a "Mrs. Wilson" in the report of Milford's overseers of the poor in 1863 probably refers to Harriet Wilson. Though previous records had not given Harriet this title, in her hair regenerator advertisements (if these are indeed hers) she was given the name "Mrs. Wilson." If we assume that "Mrs. Wilson" in the overseers' report is indeed Harriet, based on this evidence and the support provided by *Our Nig*'s testimonials, then we could extrapolate that the combined income from her book, sales of her hair treatment product (as described in *Our Nig*),[32] and possibly some continuing efforts at sewing still did not always provide sufficient resources, reducing her to state support again in 1863. Yet the hair treatment business "Mrs. H. E. Wilson" established in about 1857 and later developed with Henry P. Wilson seems to have been successful, according to Flynn's and Foreman's research. Possibly the explanation is that Wilson's health collapsed again, plummeting her back into indigence.

This scenario would help to explain why Wilson moved to Boston at some time in the mid-1860s (probably 1866 or 1867): simply put, she needed to find not only a more promising but also a less debilitating platform for her talents. In Boston she took up a long-lasting career in the burgeoning spiritualist community, setting herself up as a medium able to communicate with a spirit world that supposedly surrounds and oversees our lives (see appendix 1). Research initially conducted by P. Gabrielle Foreman and Reginald Pitts, now expanded very considerably by R. J. Ellis, has opened up a wealth of new information about Wilson's life as a spiritualist after she left Milford.[33] This indicates that Harriet Wilson possibly remarried in Boston in 1870 and died near the city in 1900. Though the description of Wilson as a chronic invalid in both the testimonials and the text of *Our Nig* would make it difficult to believe she survived until 1900, such recoveries were not unknown, and a career in spiritualism was not infrequently launched from a sickbed (with the medium maintaining that his or her sufferings had brought him or her into communion with the spirit world). The possibility also exists that the extent of her debility was exaggerated in her autobiographical novel.[34] Questions also remain over two central pieces of evidence discovered by Pitts and Foreman: whether a second marriage certificate from 1870 and a death record of 1900 are those of Harriet E. Wilson, due to inconsistencies in dating and the assignation of race (see marriage certificate and death certificate transcriptions in appendix 3).

Yet despite such residual doubts, our own research confirms that Wilson's life after the publication of *Our Nig* most probably did unfold in extraordinary ways. We have discovered hundreds of entries about Wilson in Boston's spiritualist press, almost all of them analyzed for the first time in this edition. These dramatically extend and deepen the initial research of Foreman and Pitts, in particular by unearthing new writing by Wilson herself concerning her spiritualist activities. These discoveries establish how her Boston career as a medium and spiritualist furnish further evidence of Wilson's extraordinary talents, even down to her daring decision in 1883, as a female and a "colored" medium, to set up her

own spiritualist Sunday school (or "lyceum") in competition
with existing spiritualist lyceums. But we have also uncovered
how this spiritualist career was troubled and troubling, posing
many challenges for Wilson as, once again, she had to wrestle
with the "shadows," both the specters and material persecu-
tions, of racism. Her later, long life in Boston sheds a fascinating, critical light on *Our Nig*.

Wilson's spiritualist career in Boston reveals her seeking to optimize her marginal position as a black female in
New England society. Just as Frado in *Our Nig* navigates the
limits imposed by white racism (picking up and brandishing
the stick at the woodpile, learning how to sew, selling a hair
treatment), so Wilson displays a similar coping ability in later
life. In becoming a "trance medium" (by her own description) she drew on the stereotype of the possessed African to
help market herself, while accepting that venturing beyond
"trance" into the more popular and lucrative terrain of "test"
mediumship (which she would have laid claim to if she had
conducted spiritualist sessions summoning up "tangible"
evidence of the spirit world's existence) would dangerously
expose her to unusually hostile scrutiny. (Even white "test"
mediums' claims were often minutely challenged.)[35] She also
drew on the popular belief that some African Americans were
skilled herbalists, harboring a deep cultural knowledge of
natural treatments (a stereotype with some truth in it), when
she offered, as part of her portfolio of spiritualist skills, "herb
packs and manipulations"[36] in the newspaper advertisements
she composed.

Though Wilson praised the spiritualist "platform" in 1868
for its commitment to "no sect, no creed, no dogma and no
caste,"[37] spiritualist circles were not free from racist stereotyp-

ing. The *Banner of Light*, a leading weekly spiritualist newspaper, can be arraigned for such stereotyping from first to last, in markedly inconsistent ways. In April 1867 an article argued that "the negro must not be pushed out of the country, as the Indian has been," but only a few weeks earlier another item advocated African colonization, so that "the race will be removed from close competition to the whites."[38] Nearly thirty years later, the *Banner* published a moving tribute to Frederick Douglass in an obituary on April 27, 1895, but it had also, earlier, carried an account of a "spirit manifestation session" during which Douglass appeared as "a kneeling slave chained to a post, with these words: 'A poor old slave.' "[39] Disturbingly dissonant examples like these are commonplace: the *Banner* also often recounted spirit communications from former slaves speaking in minstrel-style dialect.[40]

Hattie E. Wilson, as Harriet Wilson now styled herself, by consistently describing herself in the *Banner* as a "colored . . . medium," and by advancing on one occasion in 1867 "an eloquent plea for the recognition of the capacities of her race [and] the sentiment and philosophy of progress," plainly wanted to express racial pride, but also to profit from the interest and even allure her color aroused, compromised though this often was by racist overtones.[41] She needed her coping skills.[42] At a time when spiritualists claimed to be pursuing scientific validation of their abilities, she possibly felt that her skills as a medium would be met with more skepticism (and accompanying strict "tests" of her truthfulness) if she attempted to call up white spirits, so she gained a name for herself as a medium summoning up "Indian guides" (guides much favored by nineteenth-century spiritualists as communicants from the spirit world, and ones even more beset by

stereotyping than African Americans), despite the racist shad-
owings such a stereotype-infested venture carried within it.[43]
Indeed, the *Spiritual Scientist* alluded (perhaps satirically) to
this habit of Wilson's by running an article about one of her
occasional Boston receptions where she spoke "under control" as a medium under the headline, "The Red Man's New
Year."[44]

As we read of Wilson's spiritualist career, involving her
periodic switches of allegiance, we can see how she had to
thread her way carefully through professional rivalries and
financial calculations, not unrelated to the survival tactics
employed when she had been a farm servant or when kept
on the public rolls. She must have been continually aware of
the boundaries limiting what she could achieve, both in her
life with the Haywards and in her career as a spiritualist. Frado's partial rebellion against Mrs. Bellmont at the woodpile
is equivalent to Wilson's later limiting her claims to those of
a "trance medium" (eschewing any attempt to produce "test"
material manifestations) or her caution in introducing new
ideas into her lyceum classes. Her use of pseudonyms for the
Haywards and the fact that *Our Nig* is a novel, rather than an
autobiography, also speak to her awareness and acknowledg-
ment of what was allowable. She understood her limits, which
is not to say that she resided cheerfully within them.

Wilson's involvement in 1877 in a Women's Amateur
Dramatic Club production of the highly popular parlor farce
The Spirit of Seventy-Six epitomizes this fascination with cross-
ing boundaries and the care such crossings required. The
play, first published in 1868 and probably written by Ariana
Randolph Wormeley Curtis (possibly also with her husband,
Daniel Sargent Curtis), depicts a United States where the

conventional gender roles of men and women have become inverted. The play portrays how Tom Carberry struggles to come to terms with such an inversion, and its social consequences, on his return from a long trip to China. The *Banner of Light* of February 10 reports that "Mrs. Hattie Wilson, the well-known medium, appeared in her fine impersonation of 'Tom Carberry' in this production" (5). Though anti-feminist in intent, the play nevertheless makes some uncomfortable points, as Carberry complains of the injustices he must endure as a consequence of his enforced feminization. One can well imagine the cross-dressed Wilson reveling in any occasional eruptions of subversive laughter, even as she resided safely within her role.[45]

Harriet Wilson's time as a spiritualist in Boston reinforces just how circumscribed and straitened the lives of African Americans were in both antebellum and postbellum New England even in well-established black communities, such as the one in Boston, which Wilson apparently did not join. Her decision to set up a spiritualist lyceum suggests how her ambition sometimes led her to step over these limits; that her lyceum was only short-lived suggests that these constraints were very real. This in turn reminds us of how powerful *Our Nig*'s indictment of racism is, and how radical its implications are. One of the attractions of spiritualism for Wilson may have been the way that it was opposed to the established churches' conservatism. One spiritualist leader declared that "the old theologic systems" had died the moment that the modern spiritual movement was born, "at least, its death as far as the converts to spiritualism were concerned." Indeed, Wilson herself, "under control," attacked the conservatism of this "theology."[46]

Our research has revealed the source of her hostility: in her early life, Harriet Wilson had been fully exposed to the radical ups and conservative downs of New England Congregational religious life. When living in Milford and when allowed to by Mrs. Hayward, she almost certainly attended the town's Congregational church. This was the Haywards' church, as shown by church records from 1805 onward.[47] Debates about slavery gripped this church's history almost from its inception, for soon after the Reverend Humphrey Moore became its minister in 1802, he openly embraced the antislavery cause. His growing militancy in this regard may have led to his removal from his official appointment as Milford's overall town minister in 1832. He remained the minister of Milford's Congregational church, however, until 1836, and it is likely that Wilson heard him preach against slavery. Perhaps she also overheard discussions as to why he lost the town ministry. What can be said for sure is that his commitment to abolition soon led Moore into politics, and finally to election to the New Hampshire House of Representatives (in 1840) and then the state senate (in 1841). Moore's replacement as Congregational minister, the Reverend John W. Salter, likely was not a vigorous antislavery advocate; the congregation split over his appointment and he finally departed, followed by an interregnum when no minister could be agreed upon. Salter's successor, Abner B. Warner (1839–46), was strongly antislavery, though his replacement, Lycurgus P. Kimball (1847–49), probably was not—and, like Salter, he did not last long. When Ephraim N. Hidden replaced Kimball, antislavery sentiments took center stage strongly once more, and a number of antislavery motions were passed by his church.[48]

It is possible that Hidden's open commitment to abolition provides the reason why Harriet E. Adams chose him to perform her marriage to Thomas Wilson in 1851, returning to Milford (probably from Massachusetts) for the occasion. More important is that Wilson, both as a youngster and a teenager, would have listened to the changing views on slavery emanating from her church's pulpit as one minister gave way to the next. She came to realize at a tender age that whites varied widely, even wildly, in their attitudes to African Americans. This is reflected in the contrasting literary creations, on the one hand, of Mrs. Bellmont, who despite describing herself as a "professor of religion" is a vicious racist and, on the other hand, of her sons, who use abolitionist language when voicing their "disapprov[al] of oppression in all its forms" (75).

By enduring such oscillations of white opinion as well as behavior, Frado understands that she must conduct her life circumspectly. This lesson has plainly been learned by Wilson as a spiritualist in Boston. She frequently engaged in mainstream spiritualist activities, attending camp meetings, working in the lyceums, and becoming involved with new plans, such as the idea of founding a permanent "temple" devoted to spiritualism in Boston.[49] Indeed she was elected to an organization called the American Spiritual Institute (ASI), a new conservative organization of "Spiritualists who do not believe in radicalism, free love, and other so-called theories of this sect." Yet Wilson was by no means consistently conservative. In 1873 she had appeared on the same platform as the leading exponent of free love, Victoria C. Woodhull, and spoke at an 1874 meeting of the National Spiritualist Association, organized by the infamous Woodhull for "all Spiritualists, materialists, free-thinkers, free-religionists, socialists and infidels." This meeting had been vituperatively attacked and was described in the *Spiritual Scientist* as "not accurately represent[ing] the conservative and respectable Spiritualists."[50] Plainly, Wilson had to negotiate a tricky, narrow path among the Boston spiritualists, preserving her mainstream reputation (she was an energetic networker) while also always desiring to express her more radical impulses, even while recognizing that to do so might bring down opprobrium all too easily upon her head (as when the spiritualist lyceum she seems to have set up on her own initiative was inspected somewhat censoriously by members of Boston's oldest, "mother" lyceum in 1883).[51] Possibly dissatisfaction with such oppression is what lies behind the "grievances at the treatment she received from Boston Spiritualists" to which she gave vent at the 1874 meeting of the National Spiritualist Association.[52]

Wilson's career as a spiritualist faded from visibility in her old age and her end seems not to have been a wholly happy one. She passed away, after an illness of two months, in July 1900, from "inanition incident upon old age" at the home of Mrs. Catherine C. Cobb, 93 Washington Street in Quincy, Massachusetts, as indicated by her death certificate (see appendix 2). Why she was staying with Mrs. Cobb and her son, Walter, and how long she had been living there both remain unclear. Her death certificate gives her residential address as 9 Pelham Street, Boston, which had been her address since at least 1897, also during 1898, and perhaps during the early part of her terminal illness as well; certainly she was still active in Boston in 1899.[53] Her occupation is listed on her Quincy death certificate as nurse, and since Catherine Cobb's husband, Silas, had recently passed away, it has been suggested that Wilson may have nursed him. Just as possible, however, is the suggestion that Catherine Cobb took Wilson into her home as Wilson's health deteriorated. That Wilson is buried in the Cobbs' family grave lot in Mount Wollaston Cemetery certainly suggests a degree of intimacy beyond that likely to have been established by a relatively short period serving as the Cobb family's nurse, though the way her name appears on the back of the family grave's granite memorial preserves a symbolic distance. What can be said is that, either as a nurse still working though over seventy years of age (the death certificate gives her age as seventy-five) or as the subject of the Cobbs' charity, her career had not ended on a particularly successful note.[54] Cobb family lore narrates how she ended up in poverty and how Walter Cobb arranged to have her buried (see appendix 3, pages xcvii–xcix). This family lore also held her to be a Native American. It is not likely that Wilson was attempting to pass; she had consistently acknowledged herself to be colored (though sometimes taken to be white). More likely this family story was corrupted in transmission down the years and can be taken as evidence that her connection with the Cobb family stemmed from her work as a medium mostly communing with Native American spirit guides. It seems possible that one of the Cobb family, such as Catherine Cobb, was a spiritualist who used Wilson as a medium, valuing her intimacy with "Indian guides" (though this is speculative).[55] There is however an irony in the way the Cobbs' act of charity has been misremembered in a way incidentally emphasizing Wilson's complicity in processes of spiritualist stereotyping. Spiritualist "Indian guides" were almost without exception stock caricatures.

For all her endeavors, the coping, resourceful, radically inclined but cautious spiritualist Hattie Wilson that emerges in Boston could contrive no way of securing the enduring success her obvious abilities suggest she deserved. She seems to have ended up impoverished, dependent on the Cobbs' charity, and buried at their expense. They most probably inserted the notices about her death in the newspapers (see appendix 3), while the *Banner of Light* did not note her passing at all.

In *Our Nig* Wilson portrays a fictional protagonist sharing not only some of the qualities that, after she leaves the Haywards, Wilson displays in Nashua and Boston, but also the same inability to evade the inescapably punishing consequences of racism. Frado (like Wilson, later), well aware of the constraints acting upon her, represses her restlessness and rebelliousness in order to avoid further punishment. Throughout Frado restrains herself, yet throughout she cannot achieve either safety or a sufficiency through her hard work, instead finding herself beaten or reduced to poverty time and again. The marriage Frado enters into becomes yet another trap, removing her from her temporary refuge in W—— and yoking her to an unsupportive husband who exposes his family to penury.

But, above all, violence looms over Frado. Unlike abolitionist slave narratives, where violence by white men against black women, with its intimations of sexual abuse, is used to evoke a mixture of voyeurism and moral abhorrence, Frado's narrative instead displays a different kind of gothic horror: sadistic punishment at the hands of Northern white women, illuminating the disease of racism from a disturbing new perspective. Frado's chief tormentor, Mrs. B., exhibits "manifest enjoyment" after beating her (66). But it is Wilson's angle of attack that shocks. She describes Mrs. B. as "spicing the toil with 'words that burn,' and frequent blows on her head" (30). The term "spicing" piercingly highlights Mrs. B.'s brutal home economics with her servant—a recipe of abuse aimed at humiliating Frado and extracting more labor. The image of Mrs. B. "spicing" Frado's toils with blows as well as words exposes Mrs. B.'s recipe as one of cruel abuse using the key ingredients of racism and sadism.

Our Nig's realistic depiction of domestic and farm labor and their attendant racism and sexism[56] uncovers how layers of public prejudice shape, constrain, and deform private lives in the domestic sphere. Beyond this, it addresses a burning issue of its time, the vulnerable position of the growing number of free blacks in antebellum American society. But it also carries the reader much further, to the very core of the dilemmas and contradictions generated by anti-black sentiment delivering proscribed messages that, it can be argued, America is still reluctant to hear, entwined as these are with issues of class and economic exploitation: "Just think how much profit she was to us last summer. We had no work hired out; she did the work of two girls," boasts Mrs. B. "And got the whippings for two with it!" retorts her husband (90).

Our Nig offers a chilling portrait of life in the antebellum North for free blacks. It reminds the reader of racism's privations, even as Wilson uses the preface and the final three testimonials to mitigate the full horror of the novel's message. Just as in her later life Wilson blunted her protest by primarily speaking out through spirit mediums about her mistreatment by Boston spiritualists in 1874,[57] so *Our Nig* must often be oblique in its reminders of the awful, enduring consequences of discrimination on the basis of color.

This excoriating depiction prevents Wilson's text from fitting into any generic pattern within the forms of the novel available to her. *Our Nig* could not conform to the pattern of white sentimental novels, whose sugar-coated, wealth-bestrewn happy endings did not match Wilson's experience of constant struggle. Nor could the book conform to the pattern of conventional bildungsromans, which end with their protagonists' (slightly uneasy) social integration. No such integration is available to Frado. She always remains a vulnerable figure, her precarious status the consequence of pervasive racism. This is Harriet E. Wilson's key message in *Our Nig*, a pioneering novel that remains most compelling today, a novel that, since its rediscovery and publication almost thirty years ago, has rightly been welcomed into the canon of African American, American, and women's literature.

NOTES

1. "Use Mrs. Wilson's Hair Regenerator and Hair Dressing," *Methodist Quarterly Review* 42, ed. D. D. Whedon (New York: Carlton and Porter, 1860), 714.

2. See Gardner, "'This Attempt of Their Sister.'" A few further copies of *Our Nig* have been discovered since Gardner wrote his article, but these seem to confirm his hypothesis that she herself sold her book locally. See note 32.

3. See, for example, the works of Frances Smith Foster, Elizabeth J. West, Cynthia J. Davis, Julia Stern, Barbara A. White, and R. J. Ellis in the bibliography.

4. See appendix 1.

5. See, for example, the accounts collected together in William Still, *The Underground Railroad* (Philadelphia: Porter and Coates, 1872).

6. See William R. Jones, *Is God a White Racist: A Preamble to Black Theology* (Boston: Beacon Press, 1998).

7. "Song of Our Mountain Home" (1850): "Among our free hills / Are hearts true and brave, / The air of our mountains / Ne'er breathed on a slave." See Scott Gac, *Singing for Freedom: The Hutchinson Family Singers and the Nineteenth-Century Culture of Antebellum Reform* (New Haven, Conn.: Yale University Press, 2007), 15 et seq.

8. Nathaniel Rogers, quoted in Lewis Perry, *Radical Abolitionism* (Knoxville: University of Tennessee Press, 1973), 119.

9. See, for example, Ellis, *Harriet Wilson's "Our Nig,"* 53; Sterling Stuckey, "A Last Stern Struggle: Henry Highland Garnet and Liberation Theory," in *Black Leaders of the Nineteenth Century,* eds. Leon Litwack and August Meier (Urbana: University of Illinois Press, 1988), 132.

10. For the argument that slavery was advantageous to African Americans, see George Fitzhugh, *Cannibals All! Or Slaves Without Masters* (Richmond: A. Morris, 1857).

11. Examples of this sort of propaganda are known as anti–*Uncle Tom's Cabin*s. See, for example, Mary Henderson Eastman, *Aunt Phillis's Cabin; or, Southern Life as It Is* (Philadelphia: Lippincott, Grambo, 1852) and John W. Page, *Uncle Robin in His Cabin in Virginia and Uncle Tom without One in Boston* (Richmond: J. W. Randolph, 1853).

12. We here take issue with the arguments of such critics as William L. Andrews and Barbara A. White.

13. See the discussion of the "overplot" of nineteenth-century women's fiction in Nina Baym, *Women's Fiction: A Guide to the Novels by and about Women in America* (Ithaca: Cornell University Press, 1978).

14. The phrase comes from Maria Cummins, *The Lamplighter*

(New York: A. L. Burt, 1854), 47. See Ellis, *Harriet Wilson's "Our Nig,"* 70.

15. The close correlations that exist can be driven home by comparing *Our Nig* to the opening of one of the most famous of these sentimental novels, Maria Cummins's best-selling *The Lamplighter* (1854). Frado in *Our Nig* is deserted by her mother; is taken in and harshly treated by a female; sleeps in a mean attic room; is given a dog by a well-meaning, sympathetic man; resists her female tormentor by picking up a stick of wood to scare her off; and leaves to experience destitution and kindness at the hands of strangers. Very similarly, Gerty in *The Lamplighter* loses her mother; is taken in and harshly treated by a female; sleeps in a mean attic room; is given a kitten by a well-meaning, sympathetic man; resists her female tormentor by striking her with a stick of wood; and leaves to experience destitution and kindness at the hands of strangers. Such similarities must make us ever cautious about assuming that Frado's experiences in the Bellmont family are directly autobiographical.

16. Baym, *Women's Fiction*, 11.

17. See Ellis, *Harriet Wilson's "Our Nig,"* 82–83.

18. It seems most likely that any debts to seduction narrative motifs and the captivity narrative come to Wilson at secondhand from her reading of slave narratives and sentimental literature. By way of white editors' interventions within the slave narrative tradition, we would further suggest, a dialogic exchange operates between the "sorrows and trials" tradition and the slave narrative genre. Wilson takes over this dialogue for her own ends.

19. See Joan M. Jensen, *Loosening the Bonds: Women Working on the Land* (Old Westbury, N.Y.: The Feminist Press, 1986), 41–42.

20. See Herbert Aptheker's analysis in "The Negro in the Abolitionist Movement," *Science and Society* 5, no. 2 (Spring 1941): 148–72; 128.

21. See Thomas Bender, ed., *The Antislavery Debate* (Berkeley: University of California Press, 1992), x et seq.

22. See, for example, Peter A. Dorsey, "De-authorising Slavery: Realism in Stowe's *Uncle Tom's Cabin* and Brown's *Clotel*," *English Studies Quarterly* 41, no. 4 (1994): 257–88. Such practices are most probably compounded by that African tradition within which stories are owned communally. See William L. Andrews, "Preface," in *Three Classic African American Novels,* ed. William L. Andrews (New York: Mentor, 1990), 7–21.

23. Nancy Prince, *A Narrative of the Life and Travels of Mrs. Nancy Prince, Written by Herself,* 2nd ed., (Boston: Published by the Author, 1853), 3.

24. Ibid., 11.

25. Jensen, *Loosening the Bonds,* 41–42.

26. The death and marriage records for Hattie E. Wilson discovered by P. Gabrielle Foreman and Reginald H. Pitts (and discussed in their edition of *Our Nig* [New York: Penguin, 2009]) record Wilson's maiden name as Green, though all early records suggest it was Adams. No Adams and no Greens have so far been traced in the census or town records that could reasonably be taken to be Harriet Wilson's parents.

27. See George Ramsdell, *History of Milford* (Concord, N.H.: The Rumford Press, 1901), 75, and White, "'Our Nig' and the She-Devil," n. 9.

28. See White, "'Our Nig' and the She-Devil," 29, 35–37; Ellis, *Harriet Wilson's "Our Nig,"* 54–56, 88–89.

29. For competing accounts, see Ellis, *Harriet Wilson's "Our Nig,"* 28, and Wilson, *Our Nig,* ed. Foreman and Pitts, 2005, xiv–xv.

30. "Who Wants a Good Head of Hair? Mrs. Wilson's Hair Regenerator," *Farmer's Cabinet* (January 15, 1859): 4.

31. The work of P. Gabrielle Foreman and Katherine Flynn proved this. See Wilson, *Our Nig,* ed. Foreman and Pitts, 2009 ix–x, xlii.

32. The fact that inscribed copies of *Our Nig*, with one exception, bear the names of people who lived in the Milford area (see Gardner, "'This Attempt of Their Sister,'" 226–46) suggests that the book was being sold locally, and maybe even door-to-door. A copy that came to light in 2009, for example, bears the inscription "Gove," which would seem to refer to Jacob Gove, a town moderator in Milford and "earnest advocate of . . . antislavery principles, who moved there in circa 1850" (see Ramsdell, *History of Milford*, chap. 15). Our thanks to Megan Smolenyak for her research.

33. It needs to be noted that much of what Foreman and Pitts claim to have discovered about the early life of Wilson, prior to her departure to Boston, is either too speculative or simply unsupported by evidence—we would argue to a damaging degree, since on a number of occasions these speculations are not presented or are inconsistently presented as such. See the "Note on the Penguin Edition" in appendix 4. This should of course take nothing away from Flynn's and Pitts's and Foreman's many major, groundbreaking discoveries about Wilson's hair products business and her career as a Boston spiritualist.

34. See R. Laurence Moore, "The Spiritualist Medium: Female Professionalism in Victorian America," *American Quarterly* (May 1975), vol. 27: 215, 218.

35. For example, the *Spiritual Scientist,* from December 1874 through May 1875, ran a series of articles by "Diogenes," in which he visited Boston test mediums and subjected their performances to rigorous analysis, often accompanied by excoriating attacks on their authenticity. Wilson's trance medium performances did not attract his attention.

36. *Banner of Light* (hereafter cited as *BL*) XXVIII, no. 8 (November 12, 1870): 2. See also appendix 1.

37. Hattie E. Wilson, [no title], *BL* XXIV, no. 4 (October 10, 1868): 4.

38. "The Negro," *BL* XXI, no. 3 (April 6, 1867): 5; "The Messenger . . . Gabisha, a Slave," *BL* IX, no. 25 (September 14, 1861): 6. See also "African Colonization," *BL* XX, no. 25 (March 2, 1867): 4; the *Banner* had also all too happily characterized "the blacks in the North Carolina legislature" as "ignorant and superstitious" because they were prepared to expel a spiritualist named Thorpe from their legislature for his beliefs, when, in point of fact, it was not North Carolinian African Americans but "the white man's party" that had been the instrument of Thorpe's exclusion. See *BL* XXXVII, no. 3 (April 17, 1873): 3.

39. *BL* LXXVII, no. 8 (April 27, 1895): 3; Anonymous, "The Anniversary Celebration of Modern Spiritualism in Rochester, New York," *BL* XXIII, no. 6 (April 12, 1868): 2.

40. See, for example, "The Religious Test," *BL* XXXVII, no. 3 (April 17, 1873): 4; "Thorpe's Exclusion," *BL* XXXVII, no. 8 (May 22, 1875): 3; *BL* XXXII, no. 3 (September 28, 1872): 6.

41. *BL* XXI, no. 26 (September 14, 1867): 5.

42. The allusion here is to Michel de Certeau's distinction between tactics and strategy, as developed in his *The Practice of Everyday Life* (Berkeley: University of California Press, 1984), xix and passim.

43. See appendix 1. The *Banner* also felt it necessary to denounce the way that "mediums who have stood before us for years" were being subjected to testing regimes that meant they were "shamefully set upon by those claiming a faith in the verity of spirit communication" (*BL* XXXIX, no. 3, [April 15, 1876]: 8). Moore makes the point that in spiritualist circles professional jealousies constantly ran high ("The Spiritualist Medium," 201).

44. "The Red Man's New Year," *Spiritual Scientist* I, no. 19 (Janu-

ary 14, 1875): 226. It should be noted that this celebration displays Wilson at her best, creatively producing a memorable and novel event to enhance her reputation among her lyceum coworkers.

45. See Bettina Friedl, *On to Victory: Propaganda Plays of the Woman's Suffrage Movement* (Boston: Northeastern University Press, 1987), 15–18.

46. Dr. H. E. Gardner, *BL* XXXIX, no. 2 (April 8, 1876): 8; "Inauguration of the Shawmut Spiritual Lyceum, *BL* XLVII, no. 4 (April 17, 1880): 8; "The Red Man's New Year," *Spiritual Scientist* I, no. 19 (January 14, 1875): 226.

47. See White, "'Our Nig' and the She-Devil," 29; First Congregational Church, Milford Church Records: Marriages by Rev. H. Moore and Deaths.

48. See Ellis, *Harriet Wilson's "Our Nig,"* 89–91; Ramsdell, *History of Milford,* 373; White, "'Our Nig' and the She-Devil," 37.

49. It is difficult to be sure of the extent of Wilson's involvement in the struggle to establish this "temple." Certainly the *Banner* notes her election as the institute's "Educational Director" and she served on a committee that processed nominations to its "Executive Board." But anyway, the American Spiritual Institute seems to have collapsed in September 1875 without achieving anything. See "Meetings at Rochester Hall," *BL* XXXVII, no. 9 (May 29, 1875): 4. See also appendix 2.

50. "THE PROPOSED SPIRITUAL INSTITUTE," *Spiritual Scientist* II, no. 5 (April 8, 1875): 58; "American Studies Institute," *Spiritual Scientist* II, no. 14 (June 10, 1875): 166; "Concluding Session" of the "Fourth Annual Spiritualist Camp Meeting ... Plympton," *BL* XXXIII, no. 21 (August 23, 1873): 8; "National Mass Meeting of Radicals, Socialists, Infidels, Materialists, Free Religionists and Free Thinkers," *BL* XXXV, no. 26 (September 26,

1874): 8; "American Studies Institute," *Spiritual Scientist* II, no. 14 (June 10, 1875): 166.

51. See *BL* LII, no. 8 (May 12, 1883): 8.

52. Wilson never appears in the Boston journal *Facts* (1882–87), for example, which centrally featured "test" mediums' claims to have made material contact with the spirit world. Wilson's "grievances" are mentioned in "Freeloveism," *Religio-Philosophical Journal* (Chicago) XVII, no. 4 (October 10, 1874): 6.

53. The *Boston City Directory* records her as living at 9 Pelham Street in both 1897 and 1898. No entries for Wilson exist after 1898, however. This might suggest she had moved to the Cobb household at this time, since she had been annually listed in the *Boston City Directory* since 1878 and regularly since 1868. See *Boston City Directory, Embracing the City Record* (Boston: Sampson, Davenport and Co.) for 1897 (1610) and 1898 (1660). However, her Quincy death records still list her usual residence as Pelham Street, Boston, which may suggest a much shorter period spent in Quincy (for example, her health may have become too poor for her to ensure any later Boston directory listing), especially since she is listed in the *Banner* in December 1899 as an audience member at an event in Dwight Hall. See *BL* LXXXVI, no. 15 (December 20, 1899): 6.

54. See Wilson, *Our Nig*, ed. Foreman and Pitts, 2009, xlii; Commonwealth of Massachusetts Return of a Death, no. 192, Name: Hattie E. Wilson.

55. This account of Wilson's death and how she became buried in the family plot of the Cobbs in Quincy, Massachusetts, is indebted to information supplied by Russell Cobb in an e-mail to R. J. Ellis, December 13, 2010. See also our chronology of Harriet E. Wilson's life on pp. clv–clxxx.

56. For other examples, published after *Our Nig*, see Lucy Larcom, *A*

New England Girlhood, Outlined from Memory (Boston: Houghton, Mifflin & Co., 1889) and Rebecca Harding Davis, "Life in the Iron Mills; or the Korl Woman," *Atlantic Monthly*, vol. 7 (April 1861): 430–51.

57. See *BL* XXXV, no. 26 (September 26, 1874): 8.

A Note on the Text

Harriet E. Wilson published *Our Nig* herself. George C. Rand and Avery printed the 1859 edition for the author. Rand, Avery, located in 1859 at 117 Franklin Street in Boston, was a printer of some distinction; it advertised its services extensively in local business directories and newspapers, frequently in full-size advertisements. Rand, Avery, however, was not a commercial publisher, in a strict sense; we can only speculate on the terms of the agreement that Wilson struck with her printers. Nevertheless, it is this 1859 first edition that appears to have been the *only* edition of *Our Nig*, and that we have used to print this third edition.

The online WorldCat catalog, made available by OCLC Online Computer Library Center, Inc., representing 72,000 libraries worldwide, lists thirty-eight libraries holding copies of the original 1859 edition. There are no doubt other copies, held at institutions and in private collections. One of the editors of this edition possesses two copies among the titles in his private library; one of these that has been used for the printing of this edition, which is signed "Miss Mary A. Whitcomb, Hampton, N.H., February 1, 1861," and is listed as "No. 100."

This third annotated edition of *Our Nig* reprints the 1859 edition exactly. Because there appears to be extant no holograph manuscript, no corrected proofs, no subsequent editions, no external evidence of authorial revisions, no other contemporary editions, and only one impression of the text, there would seem to be no textual questions or quandaries necessary for the editors to address.

We have adopted the clear-copy method of annotation, so that Mrs. Wilson's carefully designed text, and her intentional strategies of presentation, are neither interrupted by scholarly commentary, nor revised or altered in any manner by the interests of a readership one full century removed from the novel's initial manner of publication. All notes and comments we list in a section entitled Notes to the Text. Mrs. Wilson's Appendix is composed of three letters included ostensibly to attest to the truth of the events depicted in the novel, to confirm both the character of the author and the authorship of the text, and to urge black and white readers to buy the book so that its author might be able to support herself and her son.

These notes to the text consist of several sorts. Mrs. Wilson introduces each of the twelve chapters of *Our Nig*, and its title page, with an epigraph. We have identified all but two of these, and list their identities by page number. We have, in addition, compared the biographical statements made by the three writers found in the novel's Appendix to elements in the novel's plot. We have, furthermore, included in the notes evidence gathered from public documents pertaining to Harriet, Thomas, and George Mason Wilson, and juxtaposed this with both events of the plot as well as the letters of the Appendix. To facilitate comparisons among these three, rather different, sorts of "evidence," we have compiled a "Chronology of Harriet E. Adams Wilson," in a convenient outline form. This Chronology follows the Notes to the Text.

What we know to be the case about the life of Harriet E. Wilson, although sufficient to establish her existence and her authorship, remains frustratingly sparse. The three biographical letters, appended to the novel, concern themselves essentially with the decade of Mrs. Wilson's life between 1850 and 1860; the details about Wilson's career in Boston as a spiritualist contained in the spiritualist press cover the period 1867 to 1900. Accordingly, our capacity to verify, or to qualify, the statements made in these painfully brief biographical statements is more extensive than it is for the early period in the author's life. Nevertheless, even in these decades, as is true of the preceding decades of Harriet E. Wilson's life, much of her story remains to be reassembled. We publish this edition, with its extensive notes, so that other scholars may, with some profit, pursue in ever finer detail the curiously compelling story of the life and times of Harriet E. Wilson. The editors welcome supplements and emendations to the data collected in this third Vintage edition of *Our Nig*. For, ultimately, it is to restore an author's presence to the American, the African American, and the canon of women's literature that we initially undertook this research, and accordingly share in these pages the tentative and still incomplete results of our search for Harriet E. Adams Wilson.

Following is a Facsimile of the 1859 Edition of *Our Nig*

OUR NIG;

OR,

Sketches from the Life of a Free Black,

IN A TWO-STORY WHITE HOUSE, NORTH.

SHOWING THAT SLAVERY'S SHADOWS FALL EVEN THERE.

BY "OUR NIG."

"I know
That care has iron crowns for many brows;
That Calvaries are everywhere, whereon
Virtue is crucified, and nails and spears
Draw guiltless blood; that sorrow sits and drinks
At sweetest hearts, till all their life is dry;
That gentle spirits on the rack of pain
Grow faint or fierce, and pray and curse by turns;
That hell's temptations, clad in heavenly guise
And armed with might, lie evermore in wait
Along life's path, giving assault to all." — HOLLAND.

BOSTON:
PRINTED BY GEO. C. RAND & AVERY.
1859.

PREFACE.

In offering to the public the following pages, the writer confesses her inability to minister to the refined and cultivated, the pleasure supplied by abler pens. It is not for such these crude narrations appear. Deserted by kindred, disabled by failing health, I am forced to some experiment which shall aid me in maintaining myself and child without extinguishing this feeble life. I would not from these motives even palliate slavery at the South, by disclosures of its appurtenances North. My mistress was wholly imbued with *southern* principles. I do not pretend to divulge every transaction in my own life, which the unprejudiced would declare unfavorable in comparison with treatment of legal bondmen; I have purposely omitted what would most provoke shame in our good anti-slavery friends at home.

My humble position and frank confession of errors will, I hope, shield me from severe criticism. Indeed, defects are so apparent it requires no skilful hand to expose them.

I sincerely appeal to my colored brethren universally for patronage, hoping they will not condemn this attempt of their sister to be erudite, but rally around me a faithful band of supporters and defenders.

H. E. W.

OUR NIG.

CHAPTER I.

MAG SMITH, MY MOTHER.

Oh, Grief beyond all other griefs, when fate
First leaves the young heart lone and desolate
In the wide world, without that only tie
For which it loved to live or feared to die;
Lorn as the hung-up lute, that ne'er hath spoken
Since the sad day its master-chord was broken!

MOORE.

LONELY MAG SMITH! See her as she walks with downcast eyes and heavy heart. It was not always thus. She *had* a loving, trusting heart. Early deprived of parental guardianship, far removed from relatives, she was left to guide her tiny boat over life's surges alone and inexperienced. As she merged into womanhood, unprotected, uncherished, uncared for, there fell on her ear the music of love, awakening an intensity of emotion long dormant. It whispered of an elevation before unaspired to; of ease and plenty

1*

her simple heart had never dreamed of as hers.
She knew the voice of her charmer, so ravishing,
sounded far above her. It seemed like an angel's, alluring her upward and onward. She
thought she could ascend to him and become an
equal. She surrendered to him a priceless gem,
which he proudly garnered as a trophy, with
those of other victims, and left her to her fate.
The world seemed full of hateful deceivers and
crushing arrogance. Conscious that the great
bond of union to her former companions was severed, that the disdain of others would be insup-
portable, she determined to leave the few friends
she possessed, and seek an asylum among strangers.
Her offspring came unwelcomed, and before its
nativity numbered weeks, it passed from earth,
ascending to a purer and better life.

"God be thanked," ejaculated Mag, as she saw
its breathing cease; "no one can taunt *her* with
my ruin."

Blessed release! may we all respond. How
many pure, innocent children not only inherit a
wicked heart of their own, claiming life-long
scrutiny and restraint, but are heirs also of parental disgrace and calumny, from which only

long years of patient endurance in paths of rectitude can disencumber them.

Mag's new home was soon contaminated by the publicity of her fall; she had a feeling of degradation oppressing her; but she resolved to be circumspect, and try to regain in a measure what she had lost. Then some foul tongue would jest of her shame, and averted looks and cold greetings disheartened her. She saw she could not bury in forgetfulness her misdeed, so she resolved to leave her home and seek another in the place she at first fled from.

Alas, how fearful are we to be first in extending a helping hand to those who stagger in the mires of infamy; to speak the first words of hope and warning to those emerging into the sunlight of morality! Who can tell what numbers, advancing just far enough to hear a cold welcome and join in the reserved converse of professed reformers, disappointed, disheartened, have chosen to dwell in unclean places, rather than encounter these "holier-than-thou" of the great brotherhood of man!

Such was Mag's experience; and disdaining to ask favor or friendship from a sneering world,

she resolved to shut herself up in a hovel she
had often passed in better days, and which she
knew to be untenanted. She vowed to ask no
favors of familiar faces; to die neglected and forgotten before she would be dependent on any.
Removed from the village, she was seldom seen
except as upon your introduction, gentle reader,
with downcast visage, returning her work to her
employer, and thus providing herself with the
means of subsistence. In two years many hands
craved the same avocation; foreigners who
cheapened toil and clamored for a livelihood,
competed with her, and she could not thus sustain herself. She was now above no drudgery.
Occasionally old acquaintances called to be favored with help of some kind, which she was glad
to bestow for the sake of the money it would
bring her; but the association with them was
such a painful reminder of by-gones, she returned to her hut morose and revengeful, re-
fusing all offers of a better home than she possessed. Thus she lived for years, hugging her
wrongs, but making no effort to escape. She
had never known plenty, scarcely competency;
but the present was beyond comparison with

those innocent years when the coronet of virtue was hers.

Every year her melancholy increased, her means diminished. At last no one seemed to notice her, save a kind-hearted African, who often called to inquire after her health and to see if she needed any fuel, he having the responsibility of furnishing that article, and she in return mending or making garments.

"How much you earn dis week, Mag?" asked he one Saturday evening.

"Little enough, Jim. Two or three days without any dinner. I washed for the Reeds, and did a small job for Mrs. Bellmont; that's all. I shall starve soon, unless I can get more to do. Folks seem as afraid to come here as if they expected to get some awful disease. I do n't believe there is a person in the world but would be glad to have me dead and out of the way."

"No, no, Mag! do n't talk so. You shan't starve so long as I have barrels to hoop. Peter Greene boards me cheap. I'll help you, if nobody else will."

A tear stood in Mag's faded eye. "I'm glad," she said, with a softer tone than before, "if there

is *one* who is n't glad to see me suffer. I b'lieve
all Singleton wants to see me punished, and feel
as if they could tell when I 've been punished
long enough. It 's a long day ahead they 'll set
it, I reckon."

After the usual supply of fuel was prepared,
Jim returned home. Full of pity for Mag, he set
about devising measures for her relief. "By
golly!" said he to himself one day — for he had
become so absorbed in Mag's interest that he had
fallen into a habit of musing aloud — "By golly!
I wish she 'd *marry* me."

"Who?" shouted Pete Greene, suddenly starting from an unobserved corner of the rude shop.

"Where you come from, you sly nigger!" exclaimed Jim.

"Come, tell me, who is 't?" said Pete; "Mag
Smith, you want to marry?"

"Git out, Pete! and when you come in dis shop
again, let a nigger know it. Do n't steal in like
a thief."

Pity and love know little severance. One
attends the other. Jim acknowledged the presence of the former, and his efforts in Mag's behalf
told also of a finer principle.

This sudden expedient which he had uninten
tionally disclosed, roused his thinking and invent-
ive powers to study upon the best method of
introducing the subject to Mag.

He belted his barrels, with many a scheme revolving in his mind, none of which quite satisfied
him, or seemed, on the whole, expedient. He
thought of the pleasing contrast between her fair
face and his own dark skin; the smooth, straight
hair, which he had once, in expression of pity,
kindly stroked on her now wrinkled but once
fair brow. There was a tempest gathering in his
heart, and at last, to ease his pent-up passion, he
exclaimed aloud, "By golly!" Recollecting his
former exposure, he glanced around to see if
Pete was in hearing again. Satisfied on this
point, he continued: "She'd be as much of a prize
to me as she'd fall short of coming up to the
mark with white folks. I do n't care for past
things. I've done things 'fore now I's 'shamed
of. She's good enough for me, any how."

One more glance about the premises to be sure
Pete was away.

The next Saturday night brought Jim to the
hovel again. The cold was fast coming to tarry

its apportioned time. Mag was nearly despairing of meeting its rigor.

"How's the wood, Mag?" asked Jim.

"All gone; and no more to cut, any how," was the reply.

"Too bad!" Jim said. His truthful reply would have been, I'm glad.

"Anything to eat in the house?" continued he.

"No," replied Mag.

"Too bad!" again, orally, with the same *inward* gratulation as before.

"Well, Mag," said Jim, after a short pause, "you's down low enough. I do n't see but I 've got to take care of ye. 'Sposin' we marry!"

Mag raised her eyes, full of amazement, and uttered a sonorous "What?"

Jim felt abashed for a moment. He knew well what were her objections.

"You's had trial of white folks, any how. They run off and left ye, and now none of 'em come near ye to see if you's dead or alive. I's black outside, I know, but I's got a white heart inside. Which you rather have, a black heart in a white skin, or a white heart in a black one?"

"Oh, dear!" sighed Mag; "Nobody on earth cares for *me* — "

"I do," interrupted Jim.

"I can do but two things," said she, "beg my living, or get it from you."

"Take me, Mag. I can give you a better home than this, and not let you suffer so."

He prevailed; they married. You can philosophize, gentle reader, upon the impropriety of such unions, and preach dozens of sermons on the evils of amalgamation. Want is a more powerful philosopher and preacher. Poor Mag. She has sundered another bond which held her to her fellows. She has descended another step down the ladder of infamy.

2

CHAPTER II.

MY FATHER'S DEATH.

Misery! we have known each other,
Like a sister and a brother,
Living in the same lone home
Many years — we must live some
Hours or ages yet to come.

SHELLEY.

JIM, proud of his treasure, — a white wife, — tried hard to fulfil his promises; and furnished her with a more comfortable dwelling, diet, and apparel. It was comparatively a comfortable winter she passed after her marriage. When Jim could work, all went on well. Industrious, and fond of Mag, he was determined she should not regret her union to him. Time levied an additional charge upon him, in the form of two pretty mulattos, whose infantile pranks amply repaid the additional toil. A few years, and a severe cough and pain in his side compelled him to be an idler for weeks together, and Mag had thus a reminder of by-gones. She cared for him only as a means to subserve her own comfort; yet she nursed him faithfully and true to marriage vows till death released her. He became the victim of consumption. He loved Mag to the last. So long as life continued, he stifled his sensibility to pain, and toiled for her sustenance long after he was able to do so.

A few expressive wishes for her welfare; a hope of better days for her; an anxiety lest they should not all go to the "good place;" brief advice about their children; a hope expressed that Mag would not be neglected as she used to be; the manifestation of Christian patience; these were *all* the legacy of miserable Mag. A feeling of cold desolation came over her, as she turned from the grave of one who had been truly faithful to her.

She was now expelled from companionship with white people; this last step — her union with a black — was the climax of repulsion.

Seth Shipley, a partner in Jim's business, wished her to remain in her present home; but she declined, and returned to her hovel again, with obstacles threefold more iusurmountable

than before. Seth accompanied her, giving her
a weekly allowance which furnished most of the
food necessary for the four inmates. After a
time, work failed ; their means were reduced.

How Mag toiled and suffered, yielding to fits
of desperation, bursts of anger, and uttering
curses too fearful to repeat. When both were
supplied with work, they prospered; if idle, they
were hungry together. In this way their interests became united ; they planned for the future
together. Mag had lived an outcast for years.
She had ceased to feel the gushings of peni-
tence ; she had crushed the sharp agonies of an
awakened conscience. She had no longings for
a purer heart, a better life. Far easier to
descend lower. She entered the darkness of
perpetual infamy. She asked not the rite of
civilization or Christianity. Her will made her
the wife of Seth. Soon followed scenes familiar
and trying.

"It's no use," said Seth one day ; "we must
give the children away, and try to get work in
some other place."

"Who 'll take the black devils?" snarled Mag.

"They're none of mine," said Seth; "what you growling about?"

"Nobody will want any thing of mine, or yours either," she replied.

"We'll make 'em, p'r'aps," he said. "There's Frado's six years old, and pretty, if she is yours, and white folks 'll say so. She'd be a prize somewhere," he continued, tipping his chair back against the wall, and placing his feet upon the rounds, as if he had much more to say when in the right position.

Frado, as they called one of Mag's children, was a beautiful mulatto, with long, curly black hair, and handsome, roguish eyes, sparkling with an exuberance of spirit almost beyond restraint.

Hearing her name mentioned, she looked up from her play, to see what Seth had to say of her.

"Would n't the Bellmonts take her?" asked Seth.

"Bellmonts?" shouted Mag. "His wife is a right she-devil! and if—"

"Had n't they better be all together?" inter-

2*

rupted Seth, reminding her of a like epithet used in reference to her little ones.

Without seeming to notice him, she continued, "She can't keep a girl in the house over a week; and Mr. Bellmont wants to hire a boy to work for him, but he can't find one that will live in the house with her; she's so ugly, they can't."

"Well, we've got to make a move soon," answered Seth; "if you go with me, we shall go right off. Had you rather spare the other one?" asked Seth, after a short pause.

"One's as bad as t' other," replied Mag. "Frado is such a wild, frolicky thing, and means to do jest as she's a mind to; she wo n't go if she do n't want to. I do n't want to tell her she is to be given away."

"I will," said Seth. "Come here, Frado?"

The child seemed to have some dim foreshadowing of evil, and declined.

"Come here," he continued; "I want to tell you something."

She came reluctantly. He took her hand and said: "We're going to move, by-'m-bye; will you go?"

"No!" screamed she; and giving a sudden jerk which destroyed Seth's equilibrium, left him sprawling on the floor, while she escaped through the open door.

"She's a hard one," said Seth, brushing his patched coat sleeve. "I'd risk her at Bellmont's."

They discussed the expediency of a speedy departure. Seth would first seek employment, and then return for Mag. They would take with them what they could carry, and leave the rest with Pete Greene, and come for them when they were wanted. They were long in arranging affairs satisfactorily, and were not a little startled at the close of their conference to find Frado missing. They thought approaching night would bring her. Twilight passed into darkness, and she did not come. They thought she had understood their plans, and had, perhaps, permanently withdrawn. They could not rest without making some effort to ascertain her retreat. Seth went in pursuit, and returned without her. They rallied others when they discovered that another little colored girl was missing, a favorite playmate of Frado's. All effort

proved unavailing. Mag felt sure her fears
were realized, and that she might never see her
again. Before her anxieties became realities,
both were safely returned, and from them and
their attendant they learned that they went to
walk, and not minding the direction soon found
themselves lost. They had climbed fences and
walls, passed through thickets and marshes, and
when night approached selected a thick cluster
of shrubbery as a covert for the night. They
were discovered by the person who now restored
them, chatting of their prospects, Frado attempting to banish the childish fears of her companion. As they were some miles from home,
they were kindly cared for until morning. Mag
was relieved to know her child was not driven
to desperation by their intentions to relieve
themselves of her, and she was inclined to think
severe restraint would be healthful.

The removal was all arranged; the few days
necessary for such migrations passed quickly,
and one bright summer morning they bade farewell to their Singleton hovel, and with budgets
and bundles commenced their weary march.
As they neared the village, they heard the

merry shouts of children gathered around the
schoolroom, awaiting the coming of their teacher.

"Halloo!" screamed one, "Black, white and
yeller!" "Black, white and yeller," echoed a
dozen voices.

It did not grate so harshly on poor Mag as
once it would. She did not even turn her head
to look at them. She had passed into an insen-
sibility no childish taunt could penetrate, else
she would have reproached herself as she passed
familiar scenes, for extending the separation
once so easily annihilated by steadfast integrity.
Two miles beyond lived the Bellmonts, in a
large, old fashioned, two-story white house, environed by fruitful acres, and embellished by
shrubbery and shade trees. Years ago a youthful couple consecrated it as home; and after
many little feet had worn paths to favorite fruit
trees, and over its green hills, and mingled at
last with brother man in the race which belongs
neither to the swift or strong, the sire became
grey-haired and decrepid, and went to his last
repose. His aged consort soon followed him.
The old homestead thus passed into the hands
of a son, to whose wife Mag had applied the

epithet "she-devil," as may be remembered.
John, the son, had not in his family arrangements departed from the example of the father.
The pastimes of his boyhood were ever freshly
revived by witnessing the games of his own sons
as they rallied about the same goal his youthful
feet had often won; as well as by the amuse-
ments of his daughters in their imitations of
maternal duties.

At the time we introduce them, however,
John is wearing the badge of age. Most of his
children were from home; some seeking employment; some were already settled in homes
of their own. A maiden sister shared with him
the estate on which he resided, and occupied a
portion of the house.

Within sight of the house, Seth seated himself
with his bundles and the child he had been leading, while Mag walked onward to the house
leading Frado. A knock at the door brought
Mrs. Bellmont, and Mag asked if she would be
willing to let that child stop there while she
went to the Reed's house to wash, and when she
came back she would call and get her. It
seemed a novel request, but she consented.

Why the impetuous child entered the house, we cannot tell; the door closed, and Mag hastily departed. Frado waited for the close of day, which was to bring back her mother. Alas! it never came. It was the last time she ever saw or heard of her mother.

CHAPTER III.

A NEW HOME FOR ME.

Oh! did we but know of the shadows so nigh,
  The world would indeed be a prison of gloom;
All light would be quenched in youth's eloquent eye,
  And the prayer-lisping infant would ask for the tomb.

For if Hope be a star that may lead us astray,
  And " deceiveth the heart," as the aged ones preach;
Yet 'twas Mercy that gave it, to beacon our way,
  Though its halo illumes where it never can reach.

ELIZA COOK.

As the day closed and Mag did not appear,
surmises were expressed by the family that she
never intended to return. Mr. Bellmont was a
kind, humane man, who would not grudge hospitality to the poorest wanderer, nor fail to sympathize with any sufferer, however humble.
The child's desertion by her mother appealed to
his symathy, and he felt inclined to succor her.
To do this in opposition to Mrs. Bellmont's
wishes, would be like encountering a whirlwind

charged with fire, daggers and spikes. She was not as susceptible of fine emotions as her spouse. Mag's opinion of her was not without foundation. She was self-willed, haughty, undisciplined, arbitrary and severe. In common parlance, she was a *scold*, a thorough one. Mr. B. remained silent during the consultation which follows, engaged in by mother, Mary and John, or Jack, as he was familiarly called.

"Send her to the County House," said Mary, in reply to the query what should be done with her, in a tone which indicated self-importance in the speaker. She was indeed the idol of her mother, and more nearly resembled her in disposition and manners than the others.

Jane, an invalid daughter, the eldest of those at home, was reclining on a sofa apparently uninterested.

"Keep her," said Jack. "She's real handsome and bright, and not very black, either."

"Yes," rejoined Mary; "that's just like you, Jack. She'll be of no use at all these three years, right under foot all the time."

"Poh! Miss Mary; if she should stay, it would n't be two days before you would be tell-

3

ing the girls about *our* nig, *our* nig!" retorted
Jack.

"I do n't want a nigger 'round *me*, do you,
mother?" asked Mary.

"I do n't mind the nigger in the child. I
should like a dozen better than one," replied her
mother. "If I could make her do my work in
a few years, I would keep her. I have so much
trouble with girls I hire, I am almost persuaded
if I have one to train up in my way from a
child, I shall be able to keep them awhile. I
am tired of changing every few months."

"Where could she sleep?" asked Mary. "I
do n't want her near me."

"In the L chamber," answered the mother.

"How 'll she get there?" asked Jack. "She'll
be afraid to go through that dark passage,
and she can't climb the ladder safely."

"She 'll have to go there; it 's good enough
for a nigger," was the reply.

Jack was sent on horseback to ascertain if
Mag was at her home. He returned with the
testimony of Pete Greene that they were fairly
departed, and that the child was intentionally
thrust upon their family.

The imposition was not at all relished by Mrs. B., or the pert, haughty Mary, who had just glided into her teens.

"Show the child to bed, Jack," said his mother. "You seem most pleased with the little nigger, so you may introduce her to her room."

He went to the kitchen, and, taking Frado gently by the hand, told her he would put her in bed now; perhaps her mother would come the next night after her.

It was not yet quite dark, so they ascended the stairs without any light, passing through nicely furnished rooms, which were a source of great amazement to the child. He opened the door which connected with her room by a dark, unfinished passage-way. "Don't bump your head," said Jack, and stepped before to open the door leading into her apartment,— an unfinished chamber over the kitchen, the roof slanting nearly to the floor, so that the bed could stand only in the middle of the room. A small half window furnished light and air. Jack returned to the sitting room with the remark that the child would soon outgrow those quarters.

"When she *does,* she'll outgrow the house,"
remarked the mother.

"What can she do to help you?" asked Mary.
"She came just in the right time, did n't she?
Just the very day after Bridget left," continued
she.

"I'll see what she can do in the morning,"
was the answer.

While this conversation was passing below,
Frado lay, revolving in her little mind whether
she would remain or not until her mother's
return. She was of wilful, determined nature,
a stranger to fear, and would not hesitate to
wander away should she decide to. She remembered the conversation of her mother with Seth,
the words " given away " which she heard used
in reference to herself; and though she did not
know their full import, she thought she should,
by remaining, be in some relation to white
people she was never favored with before. So
she resolved to tarry, with the hope that mother
would come and get her some time. The hot
sun had penetrated her room, and it was long
before a cooling breeze reduced the temperature
so that she could sleep.

Frado was called early in the morning by her new mistress. Her first work was to feed the hens. She was shown how it was *always* to be done, and in no other way; any departure from this rule to be punished by a whipping. She was then accompanied by Jack to drive the cows to pasture, so she might learn the way. Upon her return she was allowed to eat her breakfast, consisting of a bowl of skimmed milk, with brown bread crusts, which she was told to eat, standing, by the kitchen table, and must not be over ten minutes about it. Meanwhile the family were taking their morning meal in the dining-room. This over, she was placed on a cricket to wash the common dishes; she was to be in waiting always to bring wood and chips, to run hither and thither from room to room.

A large amount of dish-washing for small hands followed dinner. Then the same after tea and going after the cows finished her first day's work. It was a new discipline to the child. She found some attractions about the place, and she retired to rest at night more willing to remain. The same routine followed day after day, with slight variation; adding a little more work, and

3*

spicing the toil with "words that burn," and frequent blows on her head. These were great
annoyances to Frado, and had she known where
her mother was, she would have gone at once to
her. She was often greatly wearied, and silently
wept over her sad fate. At first she wept aloud,
which Mrs. Bellmont noticed by applying a raw-
hide, always at hand in the kitchen. It was a
symptom of discontent and complaining which
must be "nipped in the bud," she said.

Thus passed a year. No intelligence of Mag.
It was now certain Frado was to become a permanent member of the family. Her labors were
multiplied; she was quite indispensable, although
but seven years old. She had never learned to
read, never heard of a school until her residence
in the family.

Mrs. Bellmont was in doubt about the utility
of attempting to educate people of color, who
were incapable of elevation. This subject occa-
sioned a lengthy discussion in the family. Mr.
Bellmont, Jane and Jack arguing for Frado's
education; Mary and her mother objecting. At
last Mr. Bellmont declared decisively that she
should go to school. He was a man who seldom

decided controversies at home. The word once spoken admitted of no appeal; so, notwithstanding Mary's objection that she would have to attend the same school she did, the word became law.

It was to be a new scene to Frado, and Jack had many queries and conjectures to answer. He was himself too far advanced to attend the summer school, which Frado regretted, having had too many opportunities of witnessing Miss Mary's temper to feel safe in her company alone.

The opening day of school came. Frado sauntered on far in the rear of Mary, who was ashamed to be seen "walking with a nigger." As soon as she appeared, with scanty clothing and bared feet, the children assembled, noisily published her approach: "See that nigger," shouted one. "Look! look!" cried another. "I won't play with her," said one little girl. "Nor I neither," replied another.

Mary evidently relished these sharp attacks, and saw a fair prospect of lowering Nig where, according to her views, she belonged. Poor Frado, chagrined and grieved, felt that her anticipations of pleasure at such a place were far

from being realized. She was just deciding
to return home, and never come there again,
when the teacher appeared, and observing the
downcast looks of the child, took her by the
hand, and led her into the school-room. All followed, and, after the bustle of securing seats
was over, Miss Marsh inquired if the children
knew "any cause for the sorrow of that little
girl?" pointing to Frado. It was soon all told.
She then reminded them of their duties to the
poor and friendless; their cowardice in attacking a young innocent child; referred them to
one who looks not on outward appearances, but
on the heart. "She looks like a good girl; I
think *I* shall love her, so lay aside all prejudice,
and vie with each other in shewing kindness
and good-will to one who seems different from
you," were the closing remarks of the kind lady.
Those kind words! The most agreeable sound
which ever meets the ear of sorrowing, grieving childhood.

Example rendered her words efficacious. Day
by day there was a manifest change of de-
portment towards "Nig." Her speeches often
drew merriment from the children; no one

could do more to enliven their favorite pastimes than Frado. Mary could not endure to see her thus noticed, yet knew not how to prevent it. She could not influence her schoolmates as she wished. She had not gained their affections by winning ways and yielding points of controversy. On the contrary, she was self-willed, domineering; every day reported "mad" by some of her companions. She availed herself of the only alternative, abuse and taunts, as they returned from school. This was not satisfactory; she wanted to use physical force "to subdue her," to "keep her down."

There was, on their way home, a field intersected by a stream over which a single plank was placed for a crossing. It occurred to Mary that it would be a punishment to Nig to compel her to cross over; so she dragged her to the edge, and told her authoritatively to go over. Nig hesitated, resisted. Mary placed herself behind the child, and, in the struggle to force her over, lost her footing and plunged into the stream. Some of the larger scholars being in sight, ran, and thus prevented Mary from drowning and Frado from falling. Nig scampered home fast as possible, and Mary went to the nearest house, dripping, to procure a change of garments. She came loitering home, half crying, exclaiming, "Nig pushed me into the stream!" She then related the particulars. Nig was called from the kitchen. Mary stood with anger flashing in her eyes. Mr. Bellmont sat quietly reading his paper. He had witnessed too many of Miss Mary's outbreaks to be startled. Mrs. Bellmont interrogated Nig.

"I didn't do it! I didn't do it!" answered Nig, passionately, and then related the occurrence truthfully.

The discrepancy greatly enraged Mrs. Bellmont. With loud accusations and angry gestures she approached the child. Turning to her husband, she asked,

"Will you sit still, there, and hear that black nigger call Mary a liar?"

"How do we know but she has told the truth? I shall not punish her," he replied, and left the house, as he usually did when a tempest threatened to envelop him. No sooner was he out of sight than Mrs. B. and Mary commenced beating her inhumanly;

then propping her mouth open with a piece
of wood, shut her up in a dark room, without any supper. For employment, while the
tempest raged within, Mr. Bellmont went for
the cows, a task belonging to Frado, and thus
unintentionally prolonged her pain. At dark
Jack came in, and seeing Mary, accosted her
with, "So you thought you'd vent your spite
on Nig, did you? Why can't you let her
alone? It was good enough for you to get
a ducking, only you did not stay in half long
enough."

"Stop!" said his mother. "You shall never
talk so before me. You would have that little
nigger trample on Mary, would you? She
came home with a lie; it made Mary's story
false."

"What was Mary's story?" asked Jack.

It was related.

"Now," said Jack, sallying into a chair, "the
school-children happened to see it all, and they
tell the same story Nig does. Which is most
likely to be true, what a dozen agree they
saw, or the contrary?"

"It is very strange you will believe what

others say against your sister," retorted his
mother, with flashing eye. "I think it is time
your father subdued you."

"Father is a sensible man," argued Jack.
"He would not wrong a dog. Where *is* Frado?" he continued.

"Mother gave her a good whipping and
shut her up," replied Mary.

Just then Mr. Bellmont entered, and asked if
Frado was "shut up yet."

The knowledge of her innocence, the perfidy
of his sister, worked fearfully on Jack. He
bounded from his chair, searched every room
till he found the child; her mouth wedged
apart, her face swollen, and full of pain.

How Jack pitied her! He relieved her jaws,
brought her some supper, took her to her room,
comforted her as well as he knew how, sat by her
till she fell asleep, and then left for the sitting
room. As he passed his mother, he remarked,
"If that was the way Frado was to be treated, he
hoped she would never wake again!" He then
imparted her situation to his father, who seemed
untouched, till a glance at Jack exposed a tearful eye. Jack went early to her next morning.

She awoke sad, but refreshed. After breakfast
Jack took her with him to the field, and kept
her through the day. But it could not be so
generally. She must return to school, to her
household duties. He resolved to do what he
could to protect her from Mary and his mother.
He bought her a dog, which became a great
favorite with both. The invalid, Jane, would
gladly befriend her ; but she had not the
strength to brave the iron will of her mother.
Kind words and affectionate glances were the
only expressions of sympathy she could safely
indulge in. The men employed on the farm
were always glad to hear her prattle ; she was
a great favorite with them. Mrs. Bellmont allowed them the privilege of talking with her in
the kitchen. She did not fear but she should
have ample opportunity of subduing her when
they were away. Three months of schooling,
summer and winter, she enjoyed for three years.
Her winter over-dress was a cast-off overcoat,
once worn by Jack, and a sun-bonnet. It was a
source of great merriment to the scholars, but
Nig's retorts were so mirthful, and their satisfaction so evident in attributing the selection to

4

"Old Granny Bellmont," that it was not painful
to Nig or pleasurable to Mary. Her jollity was
not to be quenched by whipping or scolding.
In Mrs. Bellmont's presence she was under restraint; but in the kitchen, and among her
schoolmates, the pent up fires burst forth. She
was ever at some sly prank when unseen by her
teacher, in school hours; not unfrequently some
outburst of merriment, of which she was the
original, was charged upon some innocent mate,
and punishment inflicted which she merited.
They enjoyed her antics so fully that any of
them would suffer wrongfully to keep open the
avenues of mirth. She would venture far beyond propriety, thus shielded and countenanced.

The teacher's desk was supplied with drawers,
in which were stored his books and other *et
ceteras* of the profession. The children observed
Nig very busy there one morning before school,
as they flitted in occasionally from their play
outside. The master came; called the children
to order; opened a drawer to take the book the
occasion required; when out poured a volume of
smoke. "Fire! fire!" screamed he, at the top of
his voice. By this time he had become suf-

ficiently acquainted with the peculiar odor, to know he was imposed upon. The scholars shouted with laughter to see the terror of the dupe, who, feeling abashed at the needless fright, made no very strict investigation, and Nig once more escaped punishment. She had provided herself with cigars, and puffing, puffing away at the crack of the drawer, had filled it with smoke, and then closed it tightly to deceive the teacher, and amuse the scholars. The interim of terms was filled up with a variety of duties new and peculiar. At home, no matter how powerful the heat when sent to rake hay or guard the grazing herd, she was never permitted to shield her skin from the sun. She was not many shades darker than Mary now; what a calamity it would be ever to hear the contrast spoken of. Mrs. Bellmont was determined the sun should have full power to darken the shade which nature had first bestowed upon her as best befitting.

CHAPTER IV.

A FRIEND FOR NIG.

"Hours of my youth! when nurtured in my breast,
To love a stranger, friendship made me blest; —
Friendship, the dear peculiar bond of youth,
When every artless bosom throbs with truth;
Untaught by worldly wisdom how to feign;
And check each impulse with prudential reign;
When all we feel our honest souls disclose —
In love to friends, in open hate to foes;
No varnished tales the lips of youth repeat,
No dear-bought knowledge purchased by deceit."

BYRON.

WITH what differing emotions have the denizens of earth awaited the approach of to-day. Some sufferer has counted the vibrations of the pendulum impatient for its dawn, who, now that it has arrived, is anxious for its close. The votary of pleasure, conscious of yesterday's void, wishes for power to arrest time's haste till a few more hours of mirth shall be enjoyed. The unfortunate are yet gazing in vain for golden-edged clouds they fancied would appear in their horizon. The good man feels that he has accom-

plished too little for the Master, and sighs that
another day must so soon close. Innocent childhood, weary of its stay, longs for another morrow; busy manhood cries, hold! hold! and pur-
sues it to another's dawn. All are dissatisfied.
All crave some good not yet possessed, which
time is expected to bring with all its morrows.

Was it strange that, to a disconsolate child,
three years should seem a long, long time?
During school time she had rest from Mrs. Bellmont's tyranny. She was now nine years old;
time, her mistress said, such privileges should
cease.

She could now read and spell, and knew the
elementary steps in grammar, arithmetic, and
writing. Her education completed, as *she* said, Mrs.
Bellmont felt that her time and person belonged
solely to her. She was under her in every sense
of the word. What an opportunity to indulge
her vixen nature! No matter what occurred to
ruffle her, or from what source provocation came,
real or fancied, a few blows on Nig seemed to
relieve her of a portion of ill-will.

These were days when Fido was the entire
confidant of Frado. She told him her griefs as

4*

though he were human; and he sat so still, and listened so attentively, she really believed he knew her sorrows. All the leisure moments she could gain were used in teaching him some feat of dog-agility, so that Jack pronounced him very knowing, and was truly gratified to know he had furnished her with a gift answering his intentions.

Fido was the constant attendant of Frado, when sent from the house on errands, going and returning with the cows, out in the fields, to the village. If ever she forgot her hardships it was in his company.

Spring was now retiring. James, one of the absent sons, was expected home on a visit. He had never seen the last acquisition to the family. Jack had written faithfully of all the merits of his colored *protegé*, and hinted plainly that mother did not always treat her just right. Many were the preparations to make the visit pleasant, and as the day approached when he was to arrive, great exertions were made to cook the favorite viands, to prepare the choicest table-fare.

The morning of the arrival day was a busy

one. Frado knew not who would be of so much importance; her feet were speeding hither and thither so unsparingly. Mrs. Bellmont seemed a trifle fatigued, and her shoes which had, early in the morning, a methodic squeak, altered to an irregular, peevish snap.

"Get some little wood to make the fire burn," said Mrs. Bellmont, in a sharp tone. Frado obeyed, bringing the smallest she could find.

Mrs. Bellmont approached her, and, giving her a box on her ear, reiterated the command.

The first the child brought was the smallest to be found; of course, the second must be a trifle larger. She well knew it was, as she threw it into a box on the hearth. To Mrs. Bellmont it was a greater affront, as well as larger wood, so she "taught her" with the raw-hide, and sent her the third time for "little wood."

Nig, weeping, knew not what to do. She had carried the smallest; none left would suit her mistress; of course further punishment await-ed her; so she gathered up whatever came first, and threw it down on the hearth. As she ex-pected, Mrs. Bellmont, enraged, approached her, and kicked her so forcibly as to throw her upon

the floor. Before she could rise, another foiled
the attempt, and then followed kick after kick in
quick succession and power, till she reached the
door. Mr. Bellmont and Anut Abby, hearing the
noise, rushed in, just in time to see the last of
the performance. Nig jumped up, and rushed
from the house, out of sight.

Aunt Abby returned to her apartment, followed by John, who was muttering to himself.

"What were you saying?" asked Aunt Abby.

"I said I hoped the child never would come
into the house again."

"What would become of her? You cannot
mean *that*," continued his sister.

"I do mean it. The child does as much work
as a woman ought to; and just see how she is
kicked about!"

"Why do you have it so, John?" asked his
sister.

"How am I to help it? Women rule the
earth, and all in it."

"I think I should rule my own house, John,"—

"And live in hell meantime," added Mr.
Bellmont.

John now sauntered out to the barn to await the quieting of the storm.

Aunt Abby had a glimpse of Nig as she passed out of the yard; but to arrest her, or shew her that *she* would shelter her, in Mrs. Bellmont's presence, would only bring reserved wrath on her defenceless head. Her sister-in-law had great prejudices against her. One cause of the alienation was that she did not give her right in the homestead to John, and leave it forever; another was that she was a professor of religion, (so was Mrs. Bellmont;) but Nab, as she called her, did not live according to her profession; another, that she *would* sometimes give Nig cake and pie, which she was never allowed to have at home. Mary had often noticed and spoken of her inconsistencies.

The dinner hour passed. Frado had not appeared. Mrs. B. made no inquiry or search. Aunt Abby looked long, and found her concealed in an outbuilding. "Come into the house with me," implored Aunt Abby.

"I ain't going in any more," sobbed the child.

"What will you do?" asked Aunt Abby.

"I've got to stay out here and die. I ha'n't got no mother, no home. I wish I was dead."

"Poor thing," muttered Aunt Abby; and slyly providing her with some dinner, left her to her grief.

Jane went to confer with her Aunt about the affair; and learned from her the retreat. She would gladly have concealed her in her own chamber, and ministered to her wants; but she was dependent on Mary and her mother for care, and any displeasure caused by attention to Nig, was seriously felt.

Toward night the coach brought James. A time of general greeting, inquiries for absent members of the family, a visit to Aunt Abby's room, undoing a few delicacies for Jane, brought them to the tea hour.

"Where's Frado?" asked Mr. Bellmont, observing she was not in her usual place, behind her mistress' chair.

"I don't know, and I don't care. If she makes her appearance again, I'll take the skin from her body," replied his wife.

James, a fine looking young man, with a pleasant countenance, placid, and yet decidedly serious, yet not stern, looked up confounded. He was no stranger to his mother's nature; but years of absence had erased the occurrences once so familiar, and he asked, "Is this that pretty little Nig, Jack writes to me about, that you are so severe upon, mother?"

"I'll not leave much of her beauty to be seen, if she comes in sight; and now, John," said Mrs. B., turning to her husband, "you need not think you are going to learn her to treat me in this way; just see how saucy she was this morning. She shall learn her place."

Mr. Bellmont raised his calm, determined eye full upon her, and said, in a decisive manner: "You shall not strike, or scald, or skin her, as you call it, if she comes back again. Remember!" and he brought his hand down upon the table. "I have searched an hour for her now, and she is not to be found on the premises. Do *you* know where she is? Is she *your* prisoner?"

"No! I have just told you I did not know where she was. Nab has her hid somewhere, I suppose. Oh, dear! I did not think it would come to this; that my own husband would treat me so." Then came fast flowing tears, which no

one but Mary seemed to notice. Jane crept
into Aunt Abby's room; Mr. Bellmont and
James went out of doors, and Mary remained to
condole with her parent.

"Do you know where Frado is?" asked Jane
of her aunt.

"No," she replied. "I have hunted everywhere. She has left her first hiding-place. I
cannot think what has become of her. There
comes Jack and Fido; perhaps he knows;" and
she walked to a window near, where James and
his father were conversing together.

The two brothers exchanged a hearty greeting, and then Mr. Bellmont told Jack to eat his
supper; afterward he wished to send him away.
He immediately went in. Accustomed to all
the phases of indoor storms, from a whine to
thunder and lightning, he saw at a glance marks
of disturbance. He had been absent through
the day, with the hired men.

"What's the fuss?" asked he, rushing into
Aunt Abby's.

"Eat your supper," said Jane; "go home,
Jack."

Back again through the dining-room, and out
to his father.

"What's the fuss?" again inquired he of his
father.

"Eat your supper, Jack, and see if you can
find Frado. She's not been seen since morning,
and then she was kicked out of the house."

"I shan't eat my supper till I find her," said
Jack, indignantly. "Come, James, and see the
little creature mother treats so."

They started, calling, searching, coaxing, all
their way along. No Frado. They returned to
the house to consult. James and Jack declared
they would not sleep till she was found.

Mrs. Bellmont attempted to dissuade them
from the search. "It was a shame a little *nigger*
should make so much trouble."

Just then Fido came running up, and Jack
exclaimed, "Fido knows where she is, I'll bet."

"So I believe," said his father; "but we shall
not be wiser unless we can outwit him. He will
not do what his mistress forbids him."

"I know how to fix him," said Jack. Taking
a plate from the table, which was still waiting,
he called, "Fido! Fido! Frado wants some sup-

5

per. Come!" Jack started, the dog followed,
and soon capered on before, far, far into the
fields, over walls and through fences, into a
piece of swampy land. Jack followed close, and
soon appeared to James, who was quite in the
rear, coaxing and forcing Frado along with him.

A frail child, driven from shelter by the cruelty of his mother, was an object of interest to
James. They persuaded her to go home with
them, warmed her by the kitchen fire, gave her
a good supper, and took her with them into the
sitting-room.

"Take that nigger out of my sight," was Mrs.
Bellmont's command, before they could be
seated.

James led her into Aunt Abby's, where he
knew they were welcome. They chatted awhile
until Frado seemed cheerful; then James led
her to her room, and waited until she retired.

"Are you glad I've come home?" asked
James.

"Yes; if you won't let me be whipped to-
morrow."

"You won't be whipped. You must try to
be a good girl," counselled James.

"If I do, I get whipped;" sobbed the child.
"They won't believe what I say. Oh, I wish I
had my mother back; then I should not be
kicked and whipped so. Who made me so?"

"God;" answered James.

"Did God make you?"

"Yes."

"Who made Aunt Abby?"

"God."

"Who made your mother?"

"God."

"Did the same God that made her make
me?"

"Yes."

"Well, then, I don't like him."

"Why not?"

"Because he made her white, and me black.
Why didn't he make us *both* white?"

"I don't know; try to go to sleep, and you
will feel better in the morning," was all the reply he could make to her knotty queries. It
was a long time before she fell asleep; and a
number of days before James felt in a mood to
visit and entertain old associates and friends.

CHAPTER V.

DEPARTURES.

Life is a strange avenue of various trees and flowers;
Lightsome at commencement, but darkening to its end in a distant,
    massy portal.
It beginneth as a little path, edged with the violet and primrose,
A little path of lawny grass and soft to tiny feet.
Soon, spring thistles in the way.

TUPPER.

JAMES' visit concluded. Frado had become greatly attached to him, and with sorrow she listened and joined in the farewells which preceded his exit. The remembrance of his kindness cheered her through many a weary month, and an occasional word to her in letters to Jack, were like "cold waters to a thirsty soul." Intelligence came that James would soon marry; Frado hoped he would, and remove her from such severe treatment as she was subject to. There had been additional burdens laid on her since his return. She must now *milk* the cows, she had then only to drive. Flocks of sheep had been added to the farm, which daily claimed

a portion of her time. In the absence of the
men, she must harness the horse for Mary and
her mother to ride, go to mill, in short, do the
work of a boy, could one be procured to endure
the tirades of Mrs. Bellmont. She was first up
in the morning, doing what she could towards
breakfast. Occasionally, she would utter some
funny thing for Jack's benefit, while she was
waiting on the table, provoking a sharp look
from his mother, or expulsion from the room.

On one such occasion, they found her on the
roof of the barn. Some repairs having been
necessary, a staging had been erected, and was
not wholly removed. Availing herself of lad-
ders, she was mounted in high glee on the top-
most board. Mr. Bellmont called sternly for her
to come down; poor Jane nearly fainted from
fear. Mrs. B. and Mary did not care if she
"broke her neck," while Jack and the men
laughed at her fearlessness. Strange, one spark
of playfulness could remain amid such constant
toil; but her natural temperament was in a
high degree mirthful, and the encouragement
she received from Jack and the hired men, constantly nurtured the inclination. When she had

5*

none of the family around to be merry with,
she would amuse herself with the animals.
Among the sheep was a willful leader, who always persisted in being first served, and many
times in his fury he had thrown down Nig, till,
provoked, she resolved to punish him.   The pasture in which the sheep grazed was bounded on
three sides by a wide stream, which flowed on
one side at the base of precipitous banks.   The
first spare moments at her command, she ran to
the pasture with a dish in her hand, and mount-
ing the highest point of land nearest the stream,
called the flock to their mock repast.   Mr Bellmont, with his laborers, were in sight, though
unseen by Frado.   They paused to see what she
was about to do.   Should she by any mishap
lose her footing, she must roll into the stream,
and, without aid, must drown.   They thought of
shouting ; but they feared an unexpected salute
might startle her, and thus ensure what they
were anxious to prevent.   They watched in
breathless silence.   The willful sheep came furi-
ously leaping and bounding far in advance of
the flock.   Just as he leaped for the dish, she
suddenly jumped one side, when down he rolled

into the river, and swimming across, remained
alone till night. The men lay down, convulsed
with laughter at the trick, and guessed at once
its object. Mr. Bellmont talked seriously to the
child for exposing herself to such danger; but
she hopped about on her toes, and with laugha-
ble grimaces replied, she knew she was quick
enough to "give him a slide."

But to return. James married a Baltimorean
lady of wealthy parentage, an indispensable
requisite, his mother had always taught him.
He did not marry her wealth, though; he loved
her, sincerely. She was not unlike his sister
Jane, who had a social, gentle, loving nature,
rather *too* yielding, her brother thought. His
Susan had a firmness which Jane needed to
complete her character, but which her ill health
may in a measure have failed to produce. Although an invalid, she was not excluded from
society. Was it strange *she* should seem a desirable companion, a treasure as a wife?

Two young men seemed desirous of possessing her. One was a neighbor, Henry Reed, a
tall, spare young man, with sandy hair, and blue,
sinister eyes. He seemed to appreciate her

wants, and watch with interest her improvement
or decay. His kindness she received, and by it
was almost won. Her mother wished her to en-
courage his attentions. She had counted the
acres which were to be transmitted to an only
son; she knew there was silver in the purse;
she would not have Jane too sentimental.

The eagerness with which he amassed wealth,
was repulsive to Jane; he did not spare his person or beasts in its pursuit. She felt that to
such a man she should be considered an incum-
brance; she doubted if he would desire her, if
he did not know she would bring a handsome
patrimony. Her mother, full in favor with the
parents of Henry, commanded her to accept
him. She engaged herself, yielding to her
mother's wishes, because she had not strength to
oppose them; and sometimes, when witness of
her mother's and Mary's tyranny, she felt any
change would be preferable, even such a one as
this. She knew her husband should be the man
of her own selecting, one she was conscious of
preferring before all others. She could not say
this of Henry.

In this dilemma, a visitor came to Aunt

Abby's; one of her boy-favorites, George Means, from an adjoining State. Sensible, plain looking, agreeable, talented, he could not long be a stranger to any one who wished to know him. Jane was accustomed to sit much with Aunt Abby always; her presence now seemed necessary to assist in entertaining this youthful friend. Jane was more pleased with him each day, and silently wished Henry possessed more refinement, and the polished manners of George. She felt dissatisfied with her relation to him. His calls while George was there, brought their opposing qualities vividly before her, and she found it disagreeable to force herself into those attentions belonging to him. She received him apparently only as a neighbor.

George returned home, and Jane endeavored to stifle the risings of dissatisfaction, and had nearly succeeded, when a letter came which needed but one glance to assure her of its birthplace; and she retired for its perusal. Well was it for her that her mother's suspicion was not aroused, or her curiosity startled to inquire who it came from. After reading it, she glided into Aunt Abby's, and placed it in her hands, who was no stranger to Jane's trials.

George could not rest after his return, he wrote, until he had communicated to Jane the emotions her presence awakened, and his desire to love and possess her as his own. He begged to know if his affections were reciprocated, or could be; if she would permit him to write to her; if she was free from all obligation to another.

"What would mother say?" queried Jane, as she received the letter from her aunt.

"Not much to comfort you."

"Now, aunt, George is just such a man as I could really love, I think, from all I have seen of him; you know I never could say that of Henry" —

"Then don't marry him," interrupted Aunt Abby.

"Mother will make me."

"Your father wo n't."

"Well, aunt, what can I do? Would you answer the letter, or not?"

"Yes, answer it. Tell him your situation."

"I shall not tell him all my feelings."

Jane answered that she had enjoyed his company much; she had seen nothing offensive in his manner or appearance; that she was under no obligations which forbade her receiving letters from him as a friend and acquaintance. George was puzzled by the reply. He wrote to Aunt Abby, and from her learned all. He could not see Jane thus sacrificed, without making an effort to rescue her. Another visit followed. George heard Jane say she preferred *him*. He then conferred with Henry at his home. It was not a pleasant subject to talk upon. To be thus supplanted, was not to be thought of. He would sacrifice everything but his inheritance to secure his betrothed.

"And so you are the cause of her late coldness towards me. Leave! I will talk no more about it; the business is settled between us; there it will remain," said Henry.

"Have you no wish to know the real state of Jane's affections towards you?" asked George.

"No! Go, I say! go!" and Henry opened the door for him to pass out.

He retired to Aunt Abby's. Henry soon followed, and presented his cause to Mrs. Bellmont.

Provoked, surprised, indignant, she summoned Jane to her presence, and after a lengthy tirade

upon Nab, and her satanic influence, told her
she could not break the bonds which held her
to Henry; she should not. George Means was
rightly named; he was, truly, mean enough;
she knew his family of old; his father had four
wives, and five times as many children.

  " Go to your room, Miss Jane," she continued.
" Do n't let me know of your being in Nab's for
one while."

  The storm was now visible to all beholders.
Mr. Bellmont sought Jane. She told him her objections to Henry; showed him George's letter;
told her answer, the occasion of his visit. He
bade her not make herself sick; he would see
that she was not compelled to violate her free
choice in so important a transaction. He then
sought the two young men; told them he could
not as a father see his child compelled to an un-
congenial union; a free, voluntary choice was of
such importance to one of her health. She must
be left free to her own choice.

  Jane sent Henry a letter of dismission; he her
one of a legal bearing, in which he balanced his
disappointment by a few hundreds.

  To brave her mother's fury, nearly overcame

her, but the consolations of a kind father and
aunt cheered her on. After a suitable interval
she was married to George, and removed to his
home in Vermont. Thus another light disappeared from Nig's horizon. Another was soon to
follow. Jack was anxious to try his skill in providing for his own support; so a situation as
clerk in a store was procured in a Western city,
and six months after Jane's departure, was Nig
abandoned to the tender mercies of Mary and
her mother. As if to remove the last vestige of
earthly joy, Mrs. Bellmont sold the companion and
pet of Frado, the dog Fido.

6

CHAPTER VI.

VARIETIES.

" Hard are life's early steps; and but that youth is buoyant, confident, and strong in hope, men would behold its threshold and despair."

THE sorrow of Frado was very great for her pet, and Mr. Bellmont by great exertion obtained it again, much to the relief of the child. To be thus deprived of all her sources of pleasure was a sure way to exalt their worth, and Fido became, in her estimation, a more valuable presence than the human beings who surrounded her.

James had now been married a number of years, and frequent requests for a visit from the family were at last accepted, and Mrs. Bellmont made great preparations for a fall sojourn in Baltimore. Mary was installed housekeper — in name merely, for Nig was the only moving power in the house. Although suffering from their joint severity, she felt safer than to be thrown wholly upon an ardent, passionate, unrestrained young lady, whom she always hated and felt it hard to be obliged to obey. The trial she must meet. Were Jack or Jane at home she would have some refuge; one only remained; good Aunt Abby was still in the house.

She saw the fast receding coach which conveyed her master and mistress with regret, and begged for one favor only, that James would send for her when they returned, a hope she had confidently cherished all these five years.

She was now able to do all the washing, ironing, baking, and the common *et cetera* of household duties, though but fourteen. Mary left all for her to do, though she affected great responsibility. She would show herself in the kitchen long enough to relieve herself of some command, better withheld; or insist upon some compliance to her wishes in some department which she was very imperfectly acquainted with, very much less than the person she was addressing; and so impetuous till her orders were obeyed, that to escape the turmoil, Nig would often go contrary to her own knowledge to gain a respite.

Nig was taken sick! What could be done

The *work*, certainly, but not by Miss Mary. So
Nig would work while she could remain erect,
then sink down upon the floor, or a chair,
till she could rally for a fresh effort. Mary would
look in upon her, chide her for her laziness,
threaten to tell mother when she came home,
and so forth.

"Nig!" screamed Mary, one of her sickest
days, "come here, and sweep these threads from
the carpet." She attempted to drag her weary
limbs along, using the broom as support. Impatient of delay, she called again, but with a different request. "Bring me some wood, you lazy
jade, quick." Nig rested the broom against the
wall, and started on the fresh behest.

Too long gone. Flushed with anger, she rose
and greeted her with, "What are you gone so
long, for? Bring it in quick, I say."

"I am coming as quick as I can," she replied,
entering the door.

"Saucy, impudent nigger, you! is this the way
you answer me?" and taking a large carving
knife from the table, she hurled it, in her rage,
at the defenceless girl.

Dodging quickly, it fastened in the ceiling a

few inches from where she stood. There rushed
on Mary's mental vision a picture of bloodshed,
in which she was the perpetrator, and the sad
consequences of what was so nearly an actual
occurrence.

"Tell anybody of this, if you dare. If you tell
Aunt Abby, I'll certainly kill you," said she,
terrified. She returned to her room, brushed
her threads herself; was for a day or two more
guarded, and so escaped deserved and merited
penalty.

Oh, how long the weeks seemed which held
Nig in subjection to Mary; but they passed like
all earth's sorrows and joys. Mr. and Mrs. B.
returned delighted with their visit, and laden
with rich presents for Mary. No word of hope
for Nig. James was quite unwell, and would
come home the next spring for a visit.

This, thought Nig, will be my time of release.
I shall go back with him.

From early dawn until after all were retired,
was she toiling, overworked, disheartened, longing for relief.

Exposure from heat to cold, or the reverse,
often destroyed her health for short intervals.

6*

She wore no shoes until after frost, and snow even, appeared; and bared her feet again before the last vestige of winter disappeared. These sudden changes she was so illy guarded against, nearly conquered her physical system. Any word of complaint was severely repulsed or cruelly punished.

She was told she had much more than she deserved. So that manual labor was not in reality her only burden; but such an incessant torrent of scolding and boxing and threatening, was enough to deter one of maturer years from remaining within sound of the strife.

It is impossible to give an impression of the manifest enjoyment of Mrs. B. in these kitchen scenes. It was her favorite exercise to enter the appartment noisily, vociferate orders, give a few sudden blows to quicken Nig's pace, then return to the sitting room with *such* a satisfied expression, congratulating herself upon her thorough house-keeping qualities.

She usually rose in the morning at the ringing of the bell for breakfast; if she were heard stirring before that time, Nig knew well there was an extra amount of scolding to be borne.

No one now stood between herself and Frado, but Aunt Abby. And if *she* dared to interfere in the least, she was ordered back to her "own quarters." Nig would creep slyly into her room, learn what she could of her regarding the absent, and thus gain some light in the thick gloom of care and toil and sorrow in which she was immersed.

The first of spring a letter came from James, announcing declining health. He must try northern air as a restorative; so Frado joyfully prepared for this agreeable increase of the family, this addition to her cares.

He arrived feeble, lame, from his disease, so changed Frado wept at his appearance, fearing he would be removed from her forever. He kindly greeted her, took her to the parlor to see his wife and child, and said many things to kindle smiles on her sad face.

Frado felt so happy in his presence, so safe from maltreatment! He was to her a shelter. He observed, silently, the ways of the house a few days; Nig still took her meals in the same manner as formerly, having the same allowance

of food. He, one day, bade her not remove the
food, but sit down to the table and eat.

"She *will*, mother," said he, calmly, but imperatively; I'm determined; she works hard; I've
watched her. Now, while I stay, she is going to
sit down *here*, and eat such food as we eat."

A few sparks from the mother's black eyes
were the only reply; she feared to oppose where
she knew she could not prevail. So Nig's standing attitude, and selected diet vanished.

Her clothing was yet poor and scanty; she was
not blessed with a Sunday attire; for she was
never permitted to attend church with her mistress. "Religion was not meant for niggers," *she*
said; when the husband and brothers were
absent, she would drive Mrs. B. and Mary there,
then return, and go for them at the close of the
service, but never remain. Aunt Abby would
take her to evening meetings, held in the neigh-
borhood, which Mrs. B. never attended; and im-
part to her lessons of truth and grace as they
walked to the place of prayer.

Many of less piety would scorn to present so
doleful a figure; Mrs. B. had shaved her glossy
ringlets; and, in her coarse cloth gown and an-

cient bonnet, she was anything but an enticing object. But Aunt Abby looked within. She saw a soul to save, an immortality of happiness to secure.

These evenings were eagerly anticipated by Nig; it was such a pleasant release from labor.

Such perfect contrast in the melody and prayers of these good people to the harsh tones which fell on her ears during the day.

Soon she had all their sacred songs at command, and enlivened her toil by accompanying it with this melody.

James encouraged his aunt in her efforts. He had found the *Saviour*, he wished to have Frado's desolate heart gladdened, quieted, sustained, by *His* presence. He felt sure there were elements in her heart which, transformed and purified by the gospel, would make her worthy the esteem and friendship of the world. A kind, affectionate heart, native wit, and common sense, and the pertness she sometimes exhibited, he felt if restrained properly, might become useful in originating a self-reliance which would be of service to her in after years.

Yet it was not possible to compass all this, while she remained where she was. He wished to be cautious about pressing too closely her claims on his mother, as it would increase the burdened one he so anxiously wished to relieve. He cheered her on with the hope of returning with his family, when he recovered sufficiently.

Nig seemed awakened to new hopes and aspirations, and realized a longing for the future, hitherto unknown.

To complete Nig's enjoyment, Jack arrived unexpectedly. His greeting was as hearty to herself as to any of the family.

"Where are your curls, Fra?" asked Jack, after the usual salutation.

"Your mother cut them off."

"Thought you were getting handsome, did she? Same old story, is it; knocks and bumps? Better times coming; never fear, Nig."

How different this appellative sounded from him; he said it in such a tone, with such a rogueish look!

She laughed, and replied that he had better take her West for a housekeeper.

Jack was pleased with James's innovations of

table discipline, and would often tarry in the dining-room, to see Nig in her new place at the family table. As he was thus sitting one day, after the family had finished dinner, Frado seated herself in her mistress' chair, and was just reaching for a clean dessert plate which was on the table, when her mistress entered.

"Put that plate down; you shall not have a clean one; eat from mine," continued she. Nig hesitated. To eat after James, his wife or Jack, would have been pleasant; but to be commanded to do what was disagreeable by her mistress, *because* it was disagreeable, was trying. Quickly looking about, she took the plate, called Fido to wash it, which he did to the best of his ability; then, wiping her knife and fork on the cloth, she proceeded to eat her dinner.

Nig never looked toward her mistress during the process. She had Jack near; she did not fear her now.

Insulted, full of rage, Mrs. Bellmont rushed to her husband, and commanded him to notice this insult; to whip that child; if he would not do it, James ought.

James came to hear the kitchen version of the

affair. Jack was boiling over with laughter. He related all the circumstances to James, and pulling a bright, silver half-dollar from his pocket, he threw it at Nig, saying, "There, take that; 't was worth paying for."

James sought his mother; told her he "would not excuse or palliate Nig's impudence; but she should not be whipped or be punished at all. You have not treated her, mother, so as to gain her love; she is only exhibiting your remissness in this matter."

She only smothered her resentment until a convenient opportunity offered. The first time she was left alone with Nig, she gave her a thorough beating, to bring up arrearages; and threatened, if she ever exposed her to James, she would "cut her tongue out."

James found her, upon his return, sobbing; but fearful of revenge, she dared not answer his queries. He guessed their cause, and longed for returning health to take her under his protection.

CHAPTER VII.

SPIRITUAL CONDITION OF NIG.

"What are our joys but dreams? and what our hopes
But goodly shadows in the summer cloud?"

H. K. W.

JAMES did not improve as was hoped. Month after month passed away, and brought no prospect of returning health. He could not walk far from the house for want of strength; but he loved to sit with Aunt Abby in her quiet room, talking of unseen glories, and heart-experiences, while planning for the spiritual benefit of those around them. In these confidential interviews, Frado was never omitted. They would discuss the prevalent opinion of the public, that people of color are really inferior; incapable of cultivation and refinement. They would glance at the qualities of Nig, which promised so much if rightly directed. "I wish you would take her, James, when you are well, home with *you*," said Aunt Abby, in one of these seasons.

7

"Just what I am longing to do, Aunt Abby. Susan is just of my mind, and we intend to take her; I have been wishing to do so for years."

"She seems much affected by what she hears at the evening meetings, and asks me many questions on serious things; seems to love to read the Bible; I feel hopes of her."

"I hope she *is* thoughtful; no one has a kinder heart, one capable of loving more devotedly. But to think how prejudiced the world are towards her people; that she must be reared in such ignorance as to drown all the finer feelings. When I think of what she might be, of what she will be, I feel like grasping time till opinions change, and thousands like her rise into a noble freedom. I have seen Frado's grief, because she is black, amount to agony. It makes me sick to recall these scenes. Mother pretends to think she don't know enough to sorrow for anything; but if she could see her as I have, when she supposed herself entirely alone, except her little dog Fido, lamenting her loneliness and complexion, I think, if she is not past feeling, she would retract. In the summer I was walking near the barn, and as I stood I heard sobs. 'Oh! oh!' I heard,

'why was I made? why can't I die? Oh, what
have I to live for? No one cares for me only to
get my work. And I feel sick; who cares for
that? Work as long as I can stand, and then
fall down and lay there till I can get up. No
mother, father, brother or sister to care for me,
and then it is, You lazy nigger, lazy nigger — all
because I am black! Oh, if I could die!'

"I stepped into the barn, where I could see
her. She was crouched down by the hay with
her faithful friend Fido, and as she ceased speaking, buried her face in her hands, and cried bitterly; then, patting Fido, she kissed him, saying,
'You love me, Fido, don't you? but we must go
work in the field.' She started on her mission;
I called her to me, and told her she need not go,
the hay was doing well.

"She has such confidence in me that she will
do just as I tell her; so we found a seat under
a shady tree, and there I took the opportunity to
combat the notions she seemed to entertain
respecting the loneliness of her condition and
want of sympathizing friends. I assured her that
mother's views were by no means general; that
in our part of the country there were thousands

upon thousands who favored the elevation of her race, disapproving of oppression in all its forms; that she was not unpitied, friendless, and utterly despised; that she might hope for better things in the future. Having spoken these words of comfort, I rose with the resolution that if I recovered my health I would take her home with me, whether mother was willing or not."

"I don't know what your mother would do without her; still, I wish she was away."

Susan now came for her long absent husband, and they returned home to their room.

The month of November was one of great anxiety on James's account. He was rapidly wasting away.

A celebrated physician was called, and performed a surgical operation, as a last means. Should this fail, there was no hope. Of course he was confined wholly to his room, mostly to his bed. With all his bodily suffering, all his anxiety for his family, whom he might not live to protect, he did not forget Frado. He shielded her from many beatings, and every day imparted religious instructions. No one, but his wife, could move him so easily as Frado; so that in addition to her daily toil she was often deprived of her rest at night.

Yet she insisted on being called; she wished to show her love for one who had been such a friend to her. Her anxiety and grief increased as the probabilities of his recovery became doubtful.

Mrs. Bellmont found her weeping on his account, shut her up, and whipped her with the raw-hide, adding an injunction never to be seen snivelling again because she had a little work to do. She was very careful never to shed tears on his account, in her presence, afterwards.

7*

CHAPTER VIII.

VISITOR AND DEPARTURE.

— " Other cares engross me, and my tired soul with emulative haste,
Looks to its God."

THE brother associated with James in business, in Baltimore, was sent for to confer with one who might never be able to see him there.

James began to speak of life as closing; of heaven, as of a place in immediate prospect; of aspirations, which waited for fruition in glory. His brother, Lewis by name, was an especial favorite of sister Mary; more like her, in disposition and preferences than James or Jack.

He arrived as soon as possible after the request, and saw with regret the sure indications of fatality in his sick brother, and listened to his admonitions — admonitions to a Christian life — with tears, and uttered some promises of attention to the subject so dear to the heart of James.

How gladly he would have extended healing

aid. But, alas! it was not in his power; so, after listening to his wishes and arrangements for his family and business, he decided to return home.

Anxious for company home, he persuaded his father and mother to permit Mary to attend him. She was not at all needed in the sick room; she did not choose to be useful in the kitchen, and then she was fully determined to go.

So all the trunks were assembled and crammed with the best selections from the wardrobe of herself and mother, where the last-mentioned articles could be appropriated.

"Nig was never so helpful before," Mary remarked, and wondered what had induced such a change in place of former sullenness.

Nig was looking further than the present, and congratulating herself upon some days of peace, for Mary never lost opportunity of informing her mother of Nig's delinquincies, were she otherwise ignorant.

Was it strange if she were officious, with such relief in prospect?

The parting from the sick brother was tearful and sad. James prayed in their presence for their renewal in holiness; and urged their immediate attention to eternal realities, and gained a promise that Susan and Charlie should share their kindest regards.

No sooner were they on their way, than Nig slyly crept round to Aunt Abby's room, and tiptoeing and twisting herself into all shapes, she exclaimed, —

"She's gone, Aunt Abby, she's gone, fairly gone;" and jumped up and down, till Aunt Abby feared she would attract the notice of her mistress by such demonstrations.

"Well, she's gone, gone, Aunt Abby. I hope she'll never come back again."

"No! no! Frado, that's wrong! you would be wishing her dead; that won't do."

"Well, I'll bet she'll never come back again; somehow, I feel as though she wouldn't."

"She is James's sister," remonstrated Aunt Abby.

"So is our cross sheep just as much, that I ducked in the river; I'd like to try my hand at curing her too."

"But you forget what our good minister told us last week, about doing good to those that hate us."

"Did n't I do good, Aunt Abby, when I washed and ironed and packed her old duds to get rid of her, and helped her pack her trunks, and run here and there for her?"

"Well, well, Frado; you must go finish your work, or your mistress will be after you, and remind you severely of Miss Mary, and some others beside."

Nig went as she was told, and her clear voice was heard as she went, singing in joyous notes the relief she felt at the removal of one of her tormentors.

Day by day the quiet of the sick man's room was increased. He was helpless and nervous; and often wished change of position, thereby hoping to gain momentary relief. The calls upon Frado were consequently more frequent, her nights less tranquil. Her health was impaired by lifting the sick man, and by drudgery in the kitchen. Her ill health she endeavored to conceal from James, fearing he might have less repose if there should be a change of attendants; and Mrs. Bellmont, she well knew, would have no sympathy for her. She was at last so much reduced as to be unable to stand erect for any great length of time. She would *sit* at the table to wash her dishes; if she heard the well-known step of her mistress, she would rise till she returned to her room, and then sink down for further rest. Of course she was longer than usual in completing the services assigned her. This was a subject of complaint to Mrs. Bellmont; and Frado endeavored to throw off all appearance of sickness in her presence.

But it was increasing upon her, and she could no longer hide her indisposition. Her mistress entered one day, and finding her seated, commanded her to go to work. "I am sick," replied Frado, rising and walking slowly to her unfinished task, "and cannot stand long, I feel so bad."

Angry that she should venture a reply to her command, she suddenly inflicted a blow which lay the tottering girl prostrate on the floor. Excited by so much indulgence of a dangerous passion, she seemed left to unrestrained malice; and snatching a towel, stuffed the mouth of the sufferer, and beat her cruelly.

Frado hoped she would end her misery by whipping her to death. She bore it with the

hope of a martyr, that her misery would soon
close. Though her mouth was muffled, and the
sounds much stifled, there was a sensible commotion, which James' quick ear detected.

"Call Frado to come here," he said faintly, "I
have not seen her to-day."

Susan retired with the request to the kitchen,
where it was evident some brutal scene had just
been enacted.

Mrs. Bellmont replied that she had "some
work to do just now ; when that was done, she
might come."

Susan's appearance confirmed her husband's
fears, and he requested his father, who sat by
the bedside, to go for her. This was a messenger, as James well knew, who could not be de-
nied ; and the girl entered the room, sobbing
and faint with anguish.

James called her to him, and inquired the
cause of her sorrow. She was afraid to expose
the cruel author of her misery, lest she should
provoke new attacks. But after much entreaty,
she told him all, much which had escaped his
watchful ear. Poor James shut his eyes in
silence, as if pained to forgetfulness by the re-

cital. Then turning to Susan, he asked her to
take Charlie, and walk out; "she needed the
fresh air," he said. "And say to mother I wish
Frado to sit by me till you return. I think you
are fading, from staying so long in this sick
room." Mr. B. also left, and Frado was thus left
alone with her friend. Aunt Abby came in to
make her daily visit, and seeing the sick countenance of the attendant, took her home with
her to administer some cordial. She soon returned, however, and James kept her with him
the rest of the day; and a comfortable night's
repose following, she was enabled to continue, as
usual, her labors. James insisted on her attending religious meetings in the vicinity with Aunt
Abby.

Frado, under the instructions of Aunt Abby
and the minister, became a believer in a future
existence — one of happiness or misery. Her
doubt was, *is* there a heaven for the black? She
knew there was one for James, and Aunt Abby,
and all good white people; but was there any
for blacks? She had listened attentively to all
the minister said, and all Aunt Abby had told
her; but then it was all for white people.

As James approached that blessed world, she
felt a strong desire to follow, and be with one
who was such a dear, kind friend to her.

While she was exercised with these desires
and aspirations, she attended an evening meeting with Aunt Abby, and the good man urged
all, young or old, to accept the offers of mercy,
to receive a compassionate Jesus as their Saviour. " Come to Christ," he urged, " all, young
or old, white or black, bond or free, come all to
Christ for pardon; repent, believe."

This was the message she longed to hear; it
seemed to be spoken for her. But he had told
them to repent; " what was that ?" she asked.
She knew she was unfit for any heaven, made
for whites or blacks. She would gladly repent,
or do anything which would admit her to share
the abode of James.

Her anxiety increased; her countenance bore
marks of solicitude unseen before; and though
she said nothing of her inward contest, they all
observed a change.

James and Aunt Abby hoped it was the
springing of good seed sown by the Spirit of
God. Her tearful attention at the last meeting

8

encouraged his aunt to hope that her mind was awakened, her conscience aroused. Aunt Abby noticed that she was particularly engaged in reading the Bible; and this strengthened her conviction that a heavenly Messenger was striving with her. The neighbors dropped in to inquire after the sick, and also if Frado was " *serious ?* " They noticed she seemed very thoughtful and tearful at the meetings. Mrs. Reed was very inquisitive; but Mrs. Bellmont saw no appearance of change for the better. She did not feel responsible for her spiritual culture, and hardly believed she had a soul.

Nig was in truth suffering much; her feelings were very intense on any subject, when once aroused. She read her Bible carefully, and as often as an opportunity presented, which was when entirely secluded in her own apartment, or by Aunt Abby's side, who kindly directed her to Christ, and instructed her in the way of salvation.

Mrs. Bellmont found her one day quietly reading her Bible. Amazed and half crediting the reports of officious neighbors, she felt it was time to interfere. Here she was, reading and shedding tears over the Bible. She ordered her to put up the book, and go to work, and not be snivelling about the house, or stop to read again.

But there was one little spot seldom penetrated by her mistress' watchful eye : this was her room, uninviting and comfortless; but to herself a safe retreat. Here she would listen to the pleadings of a Saviour, and try to penetrate the veil of doubt and sin which clouded her soul, and long to cast off the fetters of sin, and rise to the communion of saints.

Mrs. Bellmont, as we before said, did not trouble herself about the future destiny of her servant. If she did what she desired for *her* benefit, it was all the responsibility she acknowledged. But she seemed to have great aversion to the notice Nig would attract should she become pious. How could she meet this case? She resolved to make her complaint to John. Strange, when she was always foiled in this direction, she should resort to him. It was time something was done; she had begun to read the Bible openly.

The night of this discovery, as they were

retiring, Mrs. Bellmont introduced the conversation, by saying:

"I want your attention to what I am going to say. I have let Nig go out to evening meetings a few times, and, if you will believe it, I found her reading the Bible to-day, just as though she expected to turn pious nigger, and preach to white folks. So now you see what good comes of sending her to school. If she should get converted she would have to go to meeting: at least, as long as James lives. I wish he had not such queer notions about her. It seems to trouble him to know he must die and leave her. He says if he should get well he would take her home with him, or educate her here. Oh, how awful! What can the child mean? So careful, too, of her! He says we shall ruin her health making her work so hard, and sleep in such a place. O, John! do you think he is in his right mind?"

"Yes, yes; she is slender."

"Yes, *yes!*" she repeated sarcastically, "you know these niggers are just like black snakes; you *can't* kill them. If she wasn't tough she

would have been killed long ago. There was
never one of my girls could do half the work."

"Did they ever try?" interposed her husband.
"I think she can do more than all of them
together."

"What a man!" said she, peevishly. "But I
want to know what is going to be done with her
about getting pious?"

"Let her do just as she has a mind to. If it
is a comfort to her, let her enjoy the privilege of
being good. I see no objection."

"I should think *you* were crazy, sure. Don't
you know that every night she will want to go
toting off to meeting? and Sundays, too? and
you know we have a great deal of company
Sundays, and she can't be spared."

"I thought you Christians held to going to
church," remarked Mr. B.

"Yes, but who ever thought of having a nigger go, except to drive others there? Why,
according to you and James, we should very
soon have her in the parlor, as smart as our
own girls. It's of no use talking to you or
James. If you should go on as you would like,
it would not be six months before she would be

8*

leaving me; and that won't do. Just think how
much profit she was to us last summer. We
had no work hired out; she did the work of two
girls —"

"And got the whippings for two with it!"
remarked Mr. Bellmont.

"I'll beat the money out of her, if I can't get
her worth any other way," retorted Mrs. B.
sharply. While this scene was passing, Frado
was trying to utter the prayer of the publican,
"God be merciful to me a sinner."

CHAPTER IX.

DEATH.

We have now
But a small portion of what men call time,
To hold communion.

SPRING opened, and James, instead of rallying, as was hoped, grew worse daily. Aunt Abby and Frado were the constant allies of Susan. Mrs. Bellmont dared not lift him. She was not "strong enough," she said.

It was very offensive to Mrs. B. to have Nab about James so much. She had thrown out many a hint to detain her from so often visiting the sick-room; but Aunt Abby was too well accustomed to her ways to mind them. After various unsuccessful efforts, she resorted to the following expedient. As she heard her cross the entry below, to ascend the stairs, she slipped out and held the latch of the door which led into the upper entry.

"James does not want to see you, or any one else," she said.

Aunt Abby hesitated, and returned slowly to her own room; wondering if it were really James' wish not to see her. She did not venture again that day, but still felt disturbed and anxious about him. She inquired of Frado, and learned that he was no worse. She asked her if James did not wish her to come and see him; what could it mean?

Quite late next morning, Susan came to see what had become of her aunt.

"Your mother said James did not wish to see me, and I was afraid I tired him."

Why, aunt, that is a mistake, I *know*. W at could mother mean?" asked Susan.

The next time she went to the sitting-room she asked her mother, —

"Why does not Aunt Abby visit James as she has done? Where is she?"

"At home. I hope that she will stay there," was the answer.

"I should think she would come in and see James," continued Susan.

"I told her he did want to see her, and to stay out. You need make no stir about it; remember:" she added, with one of her fiery glances.

Susan kept silence. It was a day or two before James spoke of her absence. The family were at dinner, and Frado was watching beside him. He inquired the cause of her absence, and *she* told him all. After the family returned he sent his wife for her. When she entered, he took her hand, and said, " Come to me often, Aunt. Come any time, — I am always glad to see you. I have but a little longer to be with you, — come often, Aunt. Now please help lift me up, and see if I can rest a little."

Frado was called in, and Susan and Mrs. B. all attempted; Mrs. B. was too weak; she did not feel able to lift so much. So the three succeeded in relieving the sufferer.

Frado returned to her work. Mrs. B. followed. Seizing Frado, she said she would " cure her of tale-bearing," and, placing the wedge of wood between her teeth, she beat her cruelly with the raw-hide. Aunt Abby heard the blows, and came to see if she could hinder them.

Surprised at her sudden appearance, Mrs. B. suddenly stopped, but forbade her removing the wood till she gave her permission, and commanded Nab to go home.

She was thus tortured when Mr. Bellmont
came in, and, making inquiries which she did
not, because she could not, answer, approached
her; and seeing her situation, quickly removed
the instrument of torture, and sought his wife.
Their conversation we will omit; suffice it to
say, a storm raged which required many days to
exhaust its strength.

Frado was becoming seriously ill. She had
no relish for food, and was constantly overworked, and then she had such solicitude about
the future. She wished to pray for pardon.
She did try to pray. Her mistress had told her
it would "do no good for her to attempt prayer;
prayer was for whites, not for blacks. If she
minded her mistress, and did what she commanded, it was all that was required of her."

This did not satisfy her, or appease her longings. She knew her instructions did not har-
monize with those of the man of God or Aunt
Abby's. She resolved to persevere. She said
nothing on the subject, unless asked. It was
evident to all her mind was deeply exercised.
James longed to speak with her alone on the
subject. An opportunity presented soon, while

the family were at tea It was usual to summon Aunt Abby to keep company with her, as his death was expected hourly.

As she took her accustomed seat, he asked, "Are you afraid to stay with me alone, Frado?"

"No," she replied, and stepped to the window to conceal her emotion.

"Come here, and sit by me; I wish to talk with you."

She approached him, and, taking her hand, he remarked:

"How poor you are, Frado! I want to tell you that I fear I shall never be able to talk with you again. It is the last time, perhaps, I shall *ever* talk with you. You are old enough to remember my dying words and profit by them. I have been sick a long time; I shall die pretty soon. My Heavenly Father is calling me home. Had it been his will to let me live I should take you to live with me; but, as it is, I shall go and leave you. But, Frado, if you will be a good girl, and love and serve God, it will be but a short time before we are in a *heavenly* home together. There will never be any sickness or sorrow there."

Frado, overcome with grief, sobbed, and buried her face in his pillow. She expected he would die; but to hear him speak of his departure himself was unexpected.

"Bid me good bye, Frado."

She kissed him, and sank on her knees by his bedside; his hand rested on her head; his eyes were closed; his lips moved in prayer for this disconsolate child.

His wife entered, and interpreting the scene, gave him some restoratives, and withdrew for a short time.

It was a great effort for Frado to cease sobbing; but she dared not be seen below in tears; so she choked her grief, and descended to her usual toil. Susan perceived a change in her husband. She felt that death was near.

He tenderly looked on her, and said, "Susan, my wife, our farewells are all spoken. I feel prepared to go. I shall meet you in heaven. Death is indeed creeping fast upon me. Let me see them all once more. Teach Charlie the way to heaven; lead him up as you come."

The family all assembled. He could not talk as he wished to them. He seemed to

sink into unconsciousness. They watched him
for hours. He had labored hard for breath
some time, when he seemed to awake suddenly, and exclaimed, "Hark! do you hear
it?"

"Hear what, my son?" asked the father.

"Their call. Look, look, at the shining
ones! Oh, let me go and be at rest!"

As if waiting for this petition, the Angel of
Death severed the golden thread, and he was
in heaven. At midnight the messenger came.

They called Frado to see his last struggle.
Sinking on her knees at the foot of his bed,
she buried her face in the clothes, and wept
like one inconsolable. They led her from the
room. She seemed to be too much absorbed
to know it was necessary for her to leave.
Next day she would steal into the chamber
as often as she could, to weep over his remains,
and ponder his last words to her. She moved
about the house like an automaton. Every
duty performed—but an abstraction from all,
which shewed her thoughts were busied elsewhere. Susan wished her to attend his burial
as one of the family. Lewis and Mary and

9

Jack it was not thought best to send for, as the season would not allow them time for the journey. Susan provided her with a dress for the occasion, which was her first intimation that she would be allowed to mingle her grief with others.

The day of the burial she was attired in her mourning dress; but Susan, in her grief, had forgotten a bonnet.

She hastily ransacked the closets, and found one of Mary's, trimmed with bright pink ribbon. It was too late to change the ribbon, and she was unwilling to leave Frado at home; she knew it would be the wish of James she should go with her. So tying it on, she said, "Never mind, Frado, you shall see where our dear James is buried." As she passed out, she heard the whispers of the by-standers, "Look there! see there! how that looks,— a black dress and a pink ribbon!"

Another time, such remarks would have wounded Frado. She had now a sorrow with which such were small in comparison.

As she saw his body lowered in the grave she wished to share it; but she was not fit to

die. She could not go where he was if she
did. She did not love God; she did not serve
him or know how to.

She retired at night to mourn over her
unfitness for heaven, and gaze out upon the
stars, which, she felt, studded the entrance of
heaven, above which James reposed in the
bosom of Jesus, to which her desires were has-
tening. She wished she could see God, and
ask him for eternal life. Aunt Abby had taught
her that He was ever looking upon her. Oh,
if she could see him, or hear him speak words
of forgiveness. Her anxiety increased; her
health seemed impaired, and she felt constrained
to go to aunt Abby and tell her all about her
conflicts.

She received her like a returning wanderer;
seriously urged her to accept of Christ; explained the way; read to her from the Bible,
and remarked upon such passages as applied
to her state. She warned her against stifling
that voice which was calling her to heaven;
echoed the farewell words of James, and told
her to come to her with her difficulties, and

not to delay a duty so important as attention
to the truths of religion, and her soul's interests.

Mrs. Bellmont would occasionally give in-
struction, though far different. She would tell
her she could not go where James was; she
need not try. If she should get to heaven at
all, she would never be as high up as he.

He was the attraction. Should she "want
to go there if she could not see him?"

Mrs. B. seldom mentioned her bereavement,
unless in such allusion to Frado. She donned
her weeds from custom; kept close her crape
veil for so many Sabbaths, and abated nothing
of her characteristic harshness.

The clergyman called to minister consolation
to the afflicted widow and mother. Aunt Abby
seeing him approach the dwelling, knew at once
the object of his visit, and followed him to the
parlor, unasked by Mrs. B! What a daring
affront! The good man dispensed the consolations, of which he was steward, to the apparently grief-smitten mother, who talked like one
schooled in a heavenly atmosphere. Such resignation expressed, as might have graced the trial
of the holiest. Susan, like a mute sufferer,

bared her soul to his sympathy and godly
counsel, but only replied to his questions in
short syllables. When he offered prayer, Frado
stole to the door that she might hear of the
heavenly bliss of one who was her friend on
earth. The prayer caused profuse weeping, as
any tender reminder of the heaven-born was
sure to. When the good man's voice ceased,
she returned to her toil, carefully removing all
trace of sorrow. Her mistress soon followed,
irritated by Nab's impudence in presenting herself unasked in the parlor, and upraided her
with indolence, and bade her apply herself more
diligently. Stung by unmerited rebuke, weak
from sorrow and anxiety, the tears rolled down
her dark face, soon followed by sobs, and then
losing all control of herself, she wept aloud.
This was an act of disobedience. Her mistress
grasping her raw-hide, caused a longer flow of
tears, and wounded a spirit that was craving
healing mercies.

CHAPTER X.

PERPLEXITIES.—ANOTHER DEATH.

Neath the billows of the ocean,
Hidden treasures wait the hand,
That again to light shall raise them
With the diver's magic wand.

G. W. Cook.

THE family, gathered by James' decease, returned to their homes. Susan and Charles returned to Baltimore. Letters were received from the absent, expressing their sympathy and grief. The father bowed like a "bruised reed," under the loss of his beloved son. He felt desirous to die the death of the righteous; also, conscious that he was unprepared, he resolved to start on the narrow way, and some time solicit entrance through the gate which leads to the celestial city. He acknowledged his too ready acquiescence with Mrs. B., in permitting Frado to be deprived of her only religious privileges for weeks together. He accordingly asked his sister to take her to meeting once more, which she was ready at once to do.

The first opportunity they once more attended meeting together. The minister conversed faithfully with every person present. He was surprised to find the little colored girl so solicitous, and kindly directed her to the flowing fountain where she might wash and be clean. He inquired of the origin of her anxiety, of her progress up to this time, and endeavored to make Christ, instead of James, the attraction of Heaven. He invited her to come to his house, to speak freely her mind to him, to pray much, to read her Bible often.

The neighbors, who were at meeting,—among them Mrs. Reed,—discussed the opinions Mrs. Bellmont would express on the subject. Mrs. Reed called and informed Mrs. B. that her colored girl "related her experience the other night at the meeting."

"What experience?" asked she, quickly, as if she expected to hear the number of times she had whipped Frado, and the number of lashes set forth in plain Arabic numbers.

"Why, you know she is serious, don't you? She told the minister about it."

Mrs. B. made no reply, but changed the subject adroitly. Next morning she told Frado she "should not go out of the house for one while, except on errands; and if she did not stop trying to be religious, she would whip her to death."

Frado pondered; her mistress was a professor of religion; was *she* going to heaven? then she did not wish to go. If she should be near James, even, she could not be happy with those fiery eyes watching her ascending path. She resolved to give over all thought of the future world, and strove daily to put her anxiety far from her.

Mr. Bellmont found himself unable to do what James or Jack could accomplish for her. He talked with her seriously, told her he had seen her many times punished undeservedly; he did not wish to have her saucy or disrespectful, but when she was *sure* she did not deserve a whipping, to avoid it if she could. "You are looking sick," he added, "you cannot endure beating as you once could."

It was not long before an opportunity offered of profiting by his advice. She was sent for wood, and not returning as soon as Mrs. B. calculated, she followed her, and, snatching from the pile a stick, raised it over her.

"Stop!" shouted Frado, "strike me, and I'll never work a mite more for you;" and throwing down what she had gathered, stood like one who feels the stirring of free and independent thoughts.

By this unexpected demonstration, her mistress, in amazement, dropped her weapon, desisting from her purpose of chastisement. Frado walked towards the house, her mistress following with the wood she herself was sent after. She did not know, before, that she had a power to ward off assaults. Her triumph in seeing her enter the door with *her* burden, repaid her for much of her former suffering.

It was characteristic of Mrs. B. never to rise in her majesty, unless she was sure she should be victorious.

This affair never met with an "after clap," like many others.

Thus passed a year. The usual amount of

scolding, but fewer whippings. Mrs. B. longed
once more for Mary's return, who had been
absent over a year; and she wrote imperatively
for her to come quickly to her. A letter came
in reply, announcing that she would comply as
soon as she was sufficiently recovered from an
illness which detained her.

No serious apprehensions were cherished by
either parent, who constantly looked for notice
of her arrival, by mail. Another letter brought
tidings that Mary was seriously ill; her mother's
presence was solicited.

She started without delay. Before she reached
her destination, a letter came to the parents
announcing her death.

No sooner was the astounding news received,
than Frado rushed into Aunt Abby's, exclaiming: —

"She's dead, Aunt Abby!"

"Who?" she asked, terrified by the unpre-
faced announcement.

"Mary; they've just had a letter."

As Mrs. B. was away, the brother and sister
could freely sympathize, and she sought him in
this fresh sorrow, to communicate such solace as

she could, and to learn particulars of Mary's untimely death, and assist him in his journey thither.

It seemed a thanksgiving to Frado. Every hour or two she would pop in into Aunt Abby's room with some strange query:

"She got into the *river* again, Aunt Abby, did n't she; the Jordan is a big one to tumble into, any how. S'posen she goes to hell, she 'll be as black as I am. Would n't mistress be mad to see her a nigger!" and others of a similar stamp, not at all acceptable to the pious, sympathetic dame; but she could not evade them.

The family returned from their sorrowful journey, leaving the dead behind. Nig looked for a change in her tyrant; what could subdue her, if the loss of her idol could not?

Never was Mrs. B. known to shed tears so profusely, as when she reiterated to one and another the sad particulars of her darling's sickness and death. There was, indeed, a season of quiet grief; it was the lull of the fiery elements. A few weeks revived the former tempests, and so at variance did they seem with chastisement sanctified, that Frado felt them to be unbear-

able. She determined to flee. But where?
Who would take her? Mrs. B. had always represented her ugly. Perhaps every one thought
her so. Then no one would take her. She was
black, no one would love her. She might have
to return, and then she would be more in her
mistress' power than ever.

She remembered her victory at the wood-pile.
She decided to remain to do as well as she could;
to assert her rights when they were trampled
on; to return once more to her meeting in
the evening, which had been prohibited. She
had learned how to conquer; she would not
abuse the power while Mr. Bellmont was at
home.

But had she not better run away? Where?
She had never been from the place far enough
to decide what course to take. She resolved to
speak to Aunt Abby. *She* mapped the dangers
of her course, her liability to fail in finding so
good friends as John and herself. Frado's mind
was busy for days and nights. She contem-
plated administering poison to her mistress, to
rid herself and the house of so detestable a
plague.

But she was restrained by an overruling Providence; and finally decided to stay contentedly through her period of service, which would expire when she was eighteen years of age.

In a few months Jane returned home with her family, to relieve her parents, upon whom years and affliction had left the marks of age. The years intervening since she had left her home, had, in some degree, softened the opposition to her unsanctioned marriage with George. The more Mrs. B. had about her, the more energetic seemed her directing capabilities, and her fault-finding propensities. Her own, she had full power over; and Jane after vain endeavors, became disgusted, weary, and perplexed, and decided that, though her mother might suffer, she could not endure her home. They followed Jack to the West. Thus vanished all hopes of sympathy or relief from this source to Frado. There seemed no one capable of enduring the oppressions of the house but her. She turned to the darkness of the future with the determination previously formed, to remain until she should be eighteen. Jane begged her to follow her so

10

soon as she should be released; but so wearied out was she by her mistress, she felt disposed to flee from any and every one having her similitude of name or feature.

CHAPTER XI.

MARRIAGE AGAIN.

Crucified the hopes that cheered me,
All that to the earth endeared me ;
Love of wealth and fame and power,
Love, — all have been crucified.

C. E.

DARKNESS before day. Jane left, but Jack was now to come again. After Mary's death he visited home, leaving a wife behind. An orphan whose home was with a relative, gentle, loving, the true mate of kind, generous Jack. His mother was a stranger to her, of course, and had perfect right to interrogate :

"Is she good looking, Jack ?" asked his mother.

"Looks well to me," was the laconic reply.

"Was her *father* rich ?"

"Not worth a copper, as I know of; I never asked him," answered Jack.

"Hadn't she any property ? What did you marry her for," asked his mother.

"Oh, she's *worth a million* dollars, mother, though not a cent of it is in money."

"Jack! what do you want to bring such a poor being into the family, for? You'd better stay here, at home, and let your wife go. Why could n't you try to do better, and not disgrace your parents?"

"Don't judge, till you see her," was Jack's reply, and immediately changed the subject. It was no recommendation to his mother, and she did not feel prepared to welcome her cordially now he was to come with his wife. He was indignant at his mother's advice to desert her. It rankled bitterly in his soul, the bare suggestion. He had more to bring. He now came with a child also. He decided to leave the West, but not his family.

Upon their arrival, Mrs. B. extended a cold welcome to her new daughter, eyeing her dress with closest scrutiny. Poverty was to her a disgrace, and she could not associate with any thus dishonored. This coldness was felt by Jack's worthy wife, who only strove the harder to recommend herself by her obliging, winning ways.

Mrs. B. could never let Jack be with her alone without complaining of this or that deficiency in his wife.

He cared not so long as the complaints were piercing his own ears. He would not have Jenny disquieted. He passed his time in seeking employment.

A letter came from his brother Lewis, then at the South, soliciting his services. Leaving his wife, he repaired thither.

Mrs. B. felt that great restraint was removed, that Jenny was more in her own power. She wished to make her feel her inferiority; to relieve Jack of his burden if he would not do it himself. She watched her incessantly, to catch at some act of Jenny's which might be construed into conjugal unfaithfulness.

Near by were a family of cousins, one a young man of Jack's age, who, from love to his cousin, proffered all needful courtesy to his stranger relative. Soon news reached Jack that Jenny was deserting her covenant vows, and had formed an illegal intimacy with his cousin. Meantime Jenny was told by her mother-in-law that Jack did not marry her untrammelled.

10*

He had another love whom he would be glad, even now, if he could, to marry. It was very doubtful if he ever came for her.

Jenny would feel pained by her unwelcome gossip, and, glancing at her child, she decided, however true it might be, she had a pledge which would enchain him yet. Ere long, the mother's inveterate hate crept out into some neighbor's enclosure, and, caught up hastily, they passed the secret round till it became none, and Lewis was sent for, the brother by whom Jack was employed. The neighbors saw her fade in health and spirits; they found letters never reached their destination when sent by either. Lewis arrived with the joyful news that he had come to take Jenny home with him.

What a relief to her to be freed from the gnawing taunts of her adversary.

Jenny retired to prepare for the journey, and Mrs. B. and Henry had a long interview. Next morning he informed Jenny that new clothes would be necessary, in order to make her presentable to Baltimore society, and he should return without her, and she must stay till she was suitably attired.

Disheartened, she rushed to her room, and, after relief from weeping, wrote to Jack to come; to have pity on her, and take her to him. No answer came. Mrs. Smith, a neighbor, watchful and friendly, suggested that she write away from home, and employ some one to carry it to the office who would elude Mrs. B., who, they very well knew, had intercepted Jenny's letter, and influenced Lewis to leave her behind. She accepted the offer, and Frado succeeded in managing the affair so that Jack soon came to the rescue, angry, wounded, and forever after alienated from his early home and his mother. Many times would Frado steal up into Jenny's room, when she knew she was tortured by her mistress' malignity, and tell some of her own encounters with her, and tell her she might "be sure it would n't kill her, for she should have died long before at the same treatment."

Susan and her child succeeded Jenny as visitors. Frado had merged into womanhood, and, retaining what she had learned, in spite of the few privileges enjoyed formerly, was striving to enrich her mind. Her school-books were her constant companions, and every leisure moment

was applied to them. Susan was delighted to
witness her progress, and some little book from
her was a reward sufficient for any task imposed, however difficult. She had her book
always fastened open near her, where she could
glance from toil to soul refreshment. The
approaching spring would close the term of
years which Mrs. B. claimed as the period of
her servitude. Often as she passed the way-
marks of former years did she pause to ponder
on her situation, and wonder if she *could* succeed
in providing for her own wants. Her health
was delicate, yet she resolved to try.

Soon she counted the time by days which
should release her. Mrs. B. felt that she could
not well spare one who could so well adapt herself to all departments — man, boy, housekeeper,
domestic, etc. She begged Mrs. Smith to talk
with her, to show her how ungrateful it would
appear to leave a home of such comfort — how
wicked it was to be ungrateful! But Frado
replied that she had had enough of such comforts; she wanted some new ones; and as it was
so wicked to be ungrateful, she would go from
temptation; Aunt Abby said "we must n't put
ourselves in the way of temptation."

Poor little Fido! She shed more tears over him than over all beside.

The morning for departure dawned. Frado engaged to work for a family a mile distant. Mrs. Bellmont dismissed her with the assurance that she would soon wish herself back again, and a present of a silver half dollar.

Her wardrobe consisted of one decent dress, without any superfluous accompaniments. A Bible from Susan she felt was her greatest treasure.

Now was she alone in the world. The past year had been one of suffering resulting from a fall, which had left her lame.

The first summer passed pleasantly, and the wages earned were expended in garments necessary for health and cleanliness. Though feeble, she was well satisfied with her progress. Shut up in her room, after her toil was finished, she studied what poor samples of apparel she had, and, for the first time, prepared her own garments.

Mrs. Moore, who employed her, was a kind friend to her, and attempted to heal her wounded spirit by sympathy and advice, bury-

ing the past in the prospects of the future.
But her failing health was a cloud no kindly
human hand could dissipate. A little light
work was all she could accomplish. A clergyman, whose family was small, sought her, and
she was removed there. Her engagement with
Mrs. Moore finished in the fall. Frado was
anxious to keep up her reputation for efficiency,
and often pressed far beyond prudence. In the
winter she entirely gave up work, and confessed
herself thoroughly sick. Mrs. Hale, soon overcome by additional cares, was taken sick also,
and now it became necessary to adopt some
measures for Frado's comfort, as well as to
relieve Mrs. Hale. Such dark forebodings as
visited her as she lay, solitary and sad, no moans
or sighs could relieve.

The family physician pronounced her case
one of doubtful issue. Frado hoped it was final.
She could not feel relentings that her former
home was abandoned, and yet, should she be in
need of succor could she obtain it from one who
would now so grudgingly bestow it? The
family were applied to, and it was decided to
take her there. She was removed to a room

built out from the main building, used formerly
as a workshop, where cold and rain found unob-
structed access, and here she fought with bitter
reminiscences and future prospects till she became reckless of her faith and hopes and person,
and half wished to end what nature seemed so
tardily to take.

Aunt Abby made her frequent visits, and at
last had her removed to her own apartment,
where she might supply her wants, and minister
to her once more in heavenly things.

Then came the family consultation.

"What is to be done with her," asked Mrs. B.,
"after she is moved there with Nab?"

"Send for the Dr., your brother," Mr. B. replied.

"When?"

"To-night."

"To-night! and for her! Wait till morning,"
she continued.

"She has waited too long now; I think something should be done soon."

"I doubt if she is much sick," sharply interrupted Mrs. B.

"Well, we'll see what our brother thinks."

His coming was longed for by Frado, who had known him well during her long sojourn in the family; and his praise of her nice butter and cheese, from which his table was supplied, she knew he felt as well as spoke.

"You're sick, very sick," he said, quickly, after a moment's pause. "Take good care of her, Abby, or she'll never get well. All broken down."

"Yes, it was at Mrs. Moore's," said Mrs. B., "all this was done. She did but little the latter part of the time she was here."

"It was commenced longer ago than last summer. Take good care of her; she may never get well," remarked the Dr.

"We sha'n't pay you for doctoring her; you may look to the town for that, sir," said Mrs. B., and abruptly left the room.

"Oh dear! oh dear!" exclaimed Frado, and buried her face in the pillow.

A few kind words of consolation, and she was once more alone in the darkness which enveloped her previous days. Yet she felt sure they owed her a shelter and attention, when disabled, and she resolved to feel patient, and remain till she could help herself. Mrs. B. would not attend her, nor permit her domestic to stay with her at all. Aunt Abby was her sole comforter. Aunt Abby's nursing had the desired effect, and she slowly improved. As soon as she was able to be moved, the kind Mrs. Moore took her to her home again, and completed what Aunt Abby had so well commenced. Not that she was well, or ever would be; but she had recovered so far as rendered it hopeful she might provide for her own wants. The clergyman at whose house she was taken sick, was now seeking some one to watch his sick children, and as soon as he heard of her recovery, again asked for her services.

What seemed so light and easy to others, was too much for Frado; and it became necessary to ask once more where the sick should find an asylum.

All felt that the place where her declining health began, should be the place of relief; so they applied once more for a shelter.

"No," exclaimed the indignant Mrs. B.; "she she shall never come under this roof again; never! never!" she repeated, as if each repetition were a bolt to prevent admission.

11

One only resource; the public must pay the expense. So she was removed to the home of two maidens, (old,) who had principle enough to be willing to earn the money a charitable public disburses.

Three years of weary sickness wasted her, without extinguishing a life apparently so feeble. Two years had these maidens watched and cared for her, and they began to weary, and finally to request the authorities to remove her.

Mrs. Hoggs was a lover of gold and silver, and she asked the favor of filling her coffers by caring for the sick. The removal caused severe sickness.

By being bolstered in the bed, after a time she could use her hands, and often would ask for sewing to beguile the tedium. She had become very expert with her needle the first year of her release from Mrs. B., and she had forgotten none of her skill. Mrs. H. praised her, and as she improved in health, was anxious to employ her. She told her she could in this way replace her clothes, and as her board would be paid for, she would thus gain something.

Many times her hands wrought when her

body was in pain ; but the hope that she might yet help herself, impelled her on.

Thus she reckoned her store of means by a few dollars, and was hoping soon to come in possession, when she was startled by the announcement that Mrs. Hoggs had reported her to the physician and town officers as an impostor. That she was, in truth, able to get up and go to work.

This brought on a severe sickness of two weeks, when Mrs. Moore again sought her, and took her to her home. She had formerly had wealth at her command, but misfortune had deprived her of it, and unlocked her heart to sympathies and favors she had never known while it lasted. Her husband, defrauded of his last means by a branch of the Bellmont family, had supported them by manual labor, gone to the West, and left his wife and four young children. But she felt humanity required her to give a shelter to one she knew to be worthy of a hospitable reception. Mrs. Moore's physician was called, and pronounced her a very sick girl, and encouraged Mrs. M. to keep her and care for her, and he would see that the authorities were informed of Frado's helplessness, and pledged assistance.

Here she remained till sufficiently restored to sew again. Then came the old resolution to take care of herself, to cast off the unpleasant charities of the public.

She learned that in some towns in Massachusetts, girls make straw bonnets — that it was easy and profitable. But how should *she*, black, feeble and poor, find any one to teach her. But God prepares the way, when human agencies see no path. Here was found a plain, poor, simple woman, who could see merit beneath a dark skin ; and when the invalid mulatto told her sorrows, she opened her door and her heart, and took the stranger in. Expert with the needle, Frado soon equalled her instructress ; and she sought also to teach her the value of useful books ; and while one read aloud to the other of deeds historic and names renowned, Frado experienced a new impulse. She felt herself capable of elevation ; she felt that this book information supplied an undefined dissatisfaction she had long felt, but could not express. Every leisure moment was carefully applied to self-improvement, and a devout and Christian exterior invited confidence from the villagers. Thus she passed months of quiet, growing in the confidence of her neighbors and new found friends.

11*

CHAPTER XII.

THE WINDING UP OF THE MATTER.

Nothing new under the sun.
SOLOMON.

A FEW years ago, within the compass of my narrative, there appeared often in some of our New England villages, professed fugitives from slavery, who recounted their personal experience in homely phrase, and awakened the indignation of non-slaveholders against brother Pro. Such a one appeared in the new home of Frado; and as people of color were rare there, was it strange she should attract her dark brother; that he should inquire her out; succeed in seeing her; feel a strange sensation in his heart towards her; that he should toy with her shining curls, feel proud to provoke her to smile and expose the ivory concealed by thin, ruby lips; that her sparkling eyes should fascinate; that he should propose; that they should marry? A short acquaintance was indeed an objection, but she saw him often, and thought she knew him. He never spoke of his enslavement to her when alone, but she felt that, like her own oppression, it was painful to disturb oftener than was needful.

He was a fine, straight negro, whose back showed no marks of the lash, erect as if it never crouched beneath a burden. There was a silent sympathy which Frado felt attracted her, and she opened her heart to the presence of love — that arbitrary and inexorable tyrant.

She removed to Singleton, her former residence, and there was married. Here were Frado's first feelings of trust and repose on human arm. She realized, for the first time, the relief of looking to another for comfortable support. Occasionally he would leave her to " lecture."

Those tours were prolonged often to weeks. Of course he had little spare money. Frado was again feeling her self-dependence, and was at last compelled to resort alone to that. Samuel was kind to her when at home, but made no provision for his absence, which was at last unprecedented.

He left her to her fate — embarked at sea,

with the disclosure that he had never seen the
South, and that his illiterate harangues were
humbugs for hungry abolitionists. Once more
alone! Yet not alone. A still newer companionship would soon force itself upon her. No
one wanted her with such prospects. Herself
was burden enough; who would have an additional
one?

The horrors of her condition nearly prostrated
her, and she was again thrown upon the public
for sustenance. Then followed the birth of her
child. The long absent Samuel unexpectedly
returned, and rescued her from charity. Recov-
ering from her expected illness, she once more
commenced toil for herself and child, in a room
obtained of a poor woman, but with better for-
tune. One so well known would not be wholly
neglected. Kind friends watched her when Samuel was from home, prevented her from suffering,
and when the cold weather pinched the warmly
clad, a kind friend took them in, and thus pre-
served them. At last Samuel's business became
very engrossing, and after long desertion, news
reached his family that he had become a victim
of yellow fever, in New Orleans.

So much toil as was necessary to sustain Frado, was more than she could endure. As soon as her babe could be nourished without his mother, she left him in charge of a Mrs. Capon, and procured an agency, hoping to recruit her health, and gain an easier livelihood for herself and child. This afforded her better maintenance than she had yet found. She passed into the various towns of the State she lived in, then into Massachusetts. Strange were some of her adventures. Watched by kidnappers, maltreated by professed abolitionists, who did n't want slaves at the South, nor niggers in their own houses, North. Faugh! to lodge one; to eat with one; to admit one through the front door; to sit next one; awful!

Traps slyly laid by the vicious to ensnare her, she resolutely avoided. In one of her tours, Providence favored her with a friend who, pitying her cheerless lot, kindly provided her with a valuable recipe, from which she might herself manufacture a useful article for her maintenance. This proved a more agreeable, and an easier way of sustenance.

And thus, to the present time, may you see

her busily employed in preparing her merchandise; then sallying forth to encounter many frowns, but some kind friends and purchasers. Nothing turns her from her steadfast purpose of elevating herself. Reposing on God, she has thus far journeyed securely. Still an invalid, she asks your symyathy, gentle reader. Refuse not, because some part of her history is unknown, save by the Omniscient God. Enough has been unrolled to demand your sympathy and aid.

Do you ask the destiny of those connected with her *early* history? A few years only have elapsed since Mr. and Mrs. B. passed into another world. As age increased, Mrs. B. became more irritable, so that no one, even her own children, could remain with her; and she was accompanied by her husband to the home of Lewis, where, after an agony in death unspeakable, she passed away. Only a few months since, Aunt Abby entered heaven. Jack and his wife rest in heaven, disturbed by no intruders; and Susan and her child are yet with the living. Jane has silver locks in place of auburn tresses, but she has the early love of Henry still, and has never regretted her exchange of lovers. Frado has passed from their memories, as Joseph from the butler's, but she will never cease to track them till beyond mortal vision.

APPENDIX.

"Truth is stranger than fiction;" and whoever reads the narrative of Alfrado, will find the assertion verified.

About eight years ago I became acquainted with the author of this book, and I feel it a privilege to speak a few words in her behalf. Through the instrumentality of an itinerant colored lecturer, she was brought to W——, Mass. This is an ancient town, where the mothers and daughters seek, not "wool and flax," but *straw*, — working willingly with their hands! Here she was introduced to the family of Mrs. Walker, who kindly consented to receive her as an inmate of her household, and immediately succeeded in procuring work for her as a "straw sewer." Being very ingenious, she soon acquired the art of making hats; but on account of former hard treatment, her constitution was greatly impaired, and she was subject to seasons of sickness. On this account Mrs. W. gave her a room joining her own chamber, where she could hear her faintest call. Never shall I forget the expression of her "black, but comely" face, as she came to me one day, exclaiming, "O, aunt J——, I have at last found a *home*, — and not only a home, but a *mother*. My cup runneth over. What shall I render to the Lord for all his benefits?"

Months passed on, and she was *happy* — truly happy. Her health began to improve under the genial sunshine in which she lived, and she even looked forward with *hope* — joyful hope to the future. But, alas, "it is not in man that walketh to direct his steps." One beautiful morning in the early spring of 1842, as she was taking her usual walk, she chanced to meet her old friend, the "lecturer," who brought her to W——, and with him was a fugitive slave. Young, well-formed and very handsome, he said he had been a *house-servant*, which seemed to account in some measure for his gentlemanly manners and pleasing address. The meeting was entirely accidental; but it was a sad occurrence for poor Alfrado, as her own sequel tells. Suffice it to say, an acquaintance and attachment was formed, which, in due time, resulted in marriage. In a few days she left W——, and *all* her home comforts, and took up her abode in New Hampshire. For a while everything went on well, and she dreamed not of danger; but in an evil hour he left his young and trusting wife, and embarked for sea. She knew nothing of all this, and waited for his return. But she waited in vain. Days passed, weeks passed, and he came not; then her heart failed her. She felt herself deserted at a time, when, of all others, she most needed the care and soothing attentions of a devoted husband. For a time she tried to sustain *herself*, but this was impossible. She had friends, but they were mostly of that class who are poor in the things of earth, but "rich in faith." The charity on which she depended failed at last, and there was nothing to save her from the "County House;" *go she must*. But her feelings on her way thither, and after her arrival, can be given better in her own language; and I trust it will be no breach of confidence if I here insert part of a letter she wrote her mother Walker, concerning the matter.

* * * "The evening before I left for my dreaded journey to the 'house' which was to be my abode, I packed my trunk, carefully placing in it every little memento of affection received from *you* and my friends in W——, among which was the portable inkstand, pens and paper. My beautiful

little Bible was laid aside, as a place nearer my heart was reserved for that. I need not tell you I slept not a moment that night. My home, my peaceful, quiet home with you, was before me. I could see my dear little room, with its pleasant eastern window opening to the morning; but more than all, I beheld *you*, my mother, gliding softly in and kneeling by my bed to read, as no one but you *can* read, ' The Lord is my shepherd, — I shall not want ' But I cannot go on, for tears blind me. For a description of the morning, and of the scant breakfast, I must wait until another time.

"We started. The man who came for me was kind as he could be, — helped me carefully into the wagon, (for I had no strength,) and drove on. For miles I spoke not a word. Then the silence would be broken by the driver uttering some sort of word the horse seemed to understand; for he invariably quickened his pace. And so, just before nightfall, we halted at the institution, prepared for the *homeless*. With cold civility the matron received me, and bade one of the inmates shew me my room. She did so; and I followed up two flights of stairs. I crept as I was able; and when she said, 'Go in there,' I obeyed, asking for my trunk, which was soon placed by me. My room was furnished some like the 'prophet's chamber,' except there was no ' candlestick;' so when I could creep down I begged for a light, and it was granted. Then I flung myself on the bed and cried, until I could cry no longer. I rose up and tried to pray; the Saviour seemed near. I opened my precious little Bible, and the first verse that caught my eye was— 'I am poor and needy, yet the Lord thinketh upon me.' O, my mother, could I tell you the comfort this was to me. I sat down, calm, almost happy, took my pen and wrote on the inspiration of the moment —

"O, holy Father, by thy power,
   Thus far in life I'm brought;
And now in this dark, trying hour,
   O God, forsake me not.

" Dids't thou not nourish and sustain
    My infancy and youth ?
Have I not testimonials plain,
    Of thy unchanging truth ?

" Though I've no home to call my own,
    My heart shall not repine ;
The saint may live on earth unknown,
    And yet in glory shine.

" When my Redeemer dwelt below,
    He chose a lowly lot ;
He came unto his own, but lo !
    His own received him not.

" Oft was the mountain his abode,
    The cold, cold earth his bed ;
The midnight moon shone softly down
    On his unsheltered head.

" But *my* head *was sheltered*, and I tried to feel thankful."

* * * * * * *

Two or three letters were received after this by her friends in
W——, and then all was silent. No one of us knew whether
she still lived or had gone to her home on high. But it seems
she remained in this house until after the birth of her babe ;
then her faithless husband returned, and took her to some town
in New Hampshire, where, for a time, he supported her and his
little son decently well. But again he left her as before — suddenly and unexpectedly, and she saw him no more. Her efforts
were again successful in a measure in securing a meagre maintenance for a time ; but her struggles with poverty and sickness
were severe. At length, a door of hope was opened. A kind
gentleman and lady took her little boy into their own family,
and provided everything necessary for his good ; and all this without the hope of remuneration. But let them know, they shall

be " recompensed at the resurrection of the just." God is not unmindful of this work, — this labor of love. As for the afflicted mother, she too has been remembered. The heart of a stranger was moved with compassion, and bestowed a recipe upon her for restoring gray hair to its former color. She availed herself of this great help, and has been quite successful; but her health is again falling, and she has felt herself obliged to resort to another method of procuring her bread — that of writing an Autobiography.

I trust she will find a ready sale for her interesting work ; and let all the friends who purchase a volume, remember they are doing good to one of the most worthy, and I had almost said most unfortunate, of the human family. I will only add in conclusion, a few lines, calculated to comfort and strengthen this sorrowful, homeless one. " I will help thee, saith the Lord."

> " I will help thee," promise kind,
>   Made by our High Priest above ;
> Soothing to the troubled mind,
>   Full of tenderness and love.
>
> " I will help thee " when the storm
>   Gathers dark on every side ;
> Safely from impending harm,
>   In my sheltering bosom hide.
>
> " I will help thee," weary saint,
>   Cast thy burdens *all on me ;*
> Oh, how cans't thou tire or faint,
>   While my arm encircles thee.
>
> I have pitied every tear,
>   Heard and *counted* every sigh ;
> Ever lend a gracious ear
>   To thy supplicating cry.

What though thy wounded bosom bleed,
　　Pierced by affliction's dart ;
Do I not all thy sorrows heed,
　　And bear thee on my heart?

Soon will the lowly grave become
　　Thy quiet resting place ;
Thy spirit find a peaceful home
　　In mansions *near my face*.

There are thy robes and glittering crown,
　　Outshining yonder sun ;
Soon shalt thou lay the body down,
　　And put those glories on.

Long has thy golden lyre been strung,
　　Which angels cannot move ;
No song to this is ever sung,
　　But bleeding, dying Love.

　　　　　　　　　　　　ALLIDA.

To THE FRIENDS OF OUR DARK-COMPLEXIONED BRETHREN AND
SISTERS, THIS NOTE IS INTENDED.

Having known the writer of this book for a number of years,
and knowing the many privations and mortifications she has had
to pass through, I the more willingly add my testimony to the
truth of her assertions. She is one of that class, who by some
are considered not only as little lower than the angels, but far
beneath them ; but I have long since learned that we are not
to look at the color of the hair, the eyes, or the skin, for the
man or woman ; their life is the criterion we are to judge by.
The writer of this book has seemed to be a child of misfortune.

Early in life she was deprived of her parents, and all those
endearing associations to which childhood clings. Indeed, she

may be said not to have had that happy period; for, being taken from home so young, and placed where she had nothing to love or cling to, I often wonder she had not grown up a *monster;* and those very people calling themselves Christians, (the good Lord deliver me from such,) and they likewise ruined her health by hard work, both in the field and house. She was indeed a slave, in every sense of the word; and a lonely one, too.

But she has found some friends in this degraded world, that were willing to do by others as they would have others do by them; that were willing she should live, and have an existence on the earth with them. She has never enjoyed any degree of comfortable health since she was eighteen years of age, and a great deal of the time has been confined to her room and bed. She is now trying to write a book; and I hope the public will look favorably on it, and patronize the same, for she is a worthy woman.

Her own health being poor, and having a child to care for, (for, by the way, she has been married,) and she wishes to educate him; in her sickness he has been taken from her, and sent to the county farm, because she could not pay his board every week; but as soon as she was able, she took him from that *place,* and now he has a home where he is contented and happy, and where he is considered as good as those he is with. He is an intelligent, smart boy, and no doubt will make a smart man, if he is rightly managed. He is beloved by his playmates, and by all the friends of the family; for the family do not recognize those as friends who do not include him in their family, or as one of them, and his mother as a daughter — for they treat her as such; and she certainly deserves all the affection and kindness that is bestowed upon her, and they are always happy to have her visit them whenever she will. They are not wealthy, but the latch-string is always out when suffering humanity needs a shelter; the last loaf they are willing to divide with those more needy than themselves, remembering these words, Do good as we have opportunity; and we can always find opportunity, if we have the disposition.

And now I would say, I hope those who call themselves friends of our dark-skinned brethren, will lend a helping hand, and assist our sister, not in giving, but in buying a book; the expense is trifling, and the reward of doing good is great. Our duty is to our fellow-beings, and when we let an opportunity pass, we know not what we lose. Therefore we should do with all our might what our hands find to do; and remember the words of Him who went about doing good, that inasmuch as ye have done a good deed to one of the least of these my brethren, ye have done it to me; and even a cup of water is not forgotten. Therefore, let us work while the day lasts, and we shall in no wise lose our reward.

MARGARETTA THORN.

MILFORD, JULY 20th, 1859.

Feeling a deep interest in the welfare of the writer of this book, and hoping that its circulation will be extensive, I wish to say a few words in her behalf. I have been acquainted with her for several years, and have always found her worthy the esteem of all friends of humanity; one whose soul is alive to the work to which she puts her hand. . Although her complexion is a little darker than my own, I esteem it a privilege to associate with her, and assist her whenever an opportunity presents itself. It is with this motive that I write these few lines, knowing this book must be interesting to all who have any knowledge of the writer's character, or wish to have. I hope no one will refuse to aid her in her work, as she is worthy the sympathy of all Christians, and those who have a spark of humanity in their breasts.

Thinking it unnecessary for me to write a long epistle, I will close by bidding her God speed.   C. D. S.

The End of the Facsimile Edition

APPENDIX 1:

Harriet Wilson's Career as a Spiritualist

This appendix traces Harriet Wilson's career in spiritualism in Boston after 1867 and explores how it might shed light on her earlier life and the sources of her literary creativity.

We know that Harriet Wilson arrived in Boston in early 1867. In May the important Boston spiritualist weekly newspaper, the *Banner of Light*, began to make multiple references to her, the first of these noting a speaking appointment in Chelsea, Massachusetts, on May 18, 1867. Not long afterward, in June, the *Banner* recounted her contribution to a spiritualist convention. Describing her as "the earnest and eloquent colored trance medium," it detailed how "The President [of the Convention], on taking the Chair, called upon Mrs Wilson, the colored speaker, to occupy the platform. . . . She improved the opportunity, or rather the intelligence controlling her, by delivering a fluent speech in favour of labor reform and the education of children in the doctrines of spiritualism."[1] In this account, the spirit that speaks through Wilson advocates both labor reform and educating children in spiritualist precepts—the first being a cause dear to Wilson, after her experiences with the Haywards, the second even dearer to her spiritualist audience's hearts.[2] Wilson in her various careers always had to keep one eye on what her market wanted.

The *Banner of Light* is an important source for understanding Wilson's spiritualist career over several decades. She is listed in the

June 29, 1867, issue as living in "East Cambridge, Mass., for the present" (she soon moved to Boston). At the end of August, she was "excit[ing] thrilling interest" at a "Great Spiritualist Camp Meeting at Pierpont Grove" by making an "eloquent appeal for the recognition of the capacities of her race, the sentiment and philosophy of progress, under the figure of a moving camp tenting each night 'a day's march nearer home.'" By October 19, the *Banner* provides a quite long list of lecturing appointments that Wilson holds: "Mrs. Hattie E. Wilson (colored), trance speaker, will lecture in Lynn, Mass. . . . Hartford, Conn. . . . Stoneham, Mass. . . . [and] Stoughton."[3]

That this list includes Lynn, Massachusetts, for a long time the seat of the Hutchinson Family Singers, suggests the family may possibly have been sponsors of Wilson's move to Cambridge. (The Hutchinsons were related by marriage to the Haywards, for whom Wilson had been a servant in Milford.) It is, however, perhaps more important to note that on numerous occasions in these early days Wilson's name was accompanied by that of the prominent spiritualist C. Fannie Allyn, which suggests a close association between the two, making her Wilson's most likely sponsor. Allyn had spoken in both Milford and Worcester in the mid-1860s. Also, the *Banner*'s first record of Wilson notes that she had arranged to speak in Chelsea at a "Spiritualist Meeting" on three dates, "June 2, June 9 and June 26," 1867, and in "Charlestown, May 19 and 26," when, only a few weeks previously, it had also noted that "Mrs. C. Fannie Allyn" would be speaking in Chelsea (on March 17, 24, and 31) and in Charlestown "during April." Soon after that, when reannouncing Wilson's engagement to speak in Chelsea, the *Banner* also notes that Allyn is returning there: "Meeting and Lyceums . . . Chelsea . . . Mrs H. E. Wilson speaks for us the first three Sundays in June and Mrs. C. Fannie Allyn the last two."[4] Similarly, when Wilson made her address at Pierpont

Grove in August 1867, Allyn was also a speaker. All this suggests that Allyn may have been recommending Wilson to her patrons.

Certainly, during the late 1860s, Wilson begins to be regularly listed in the *Banner*'s directory of spiritualist speakers (often with details of speaking engagements) and also (less often) in the "Movements of Lecturers and Mediums." Her rising profile in spiritualist circles was confirmed in January 1868 by her election at the "Third Annual Convention of the Massachusetts Spiritual Association" to the MSA's "Finance Committee" to look after "the monetary matters of the Convention."[5] This report also identifies her as volunteering to lecture "gratuitously" for the association. On May 30, 1868, the *Banner* lists her attendance at an executive committee meeting of the MSA. The MSA was by its own description a "liberal Christian" organization.[6] Its espousal of the abolition of slavery worldwide, successful reconstruction in the South, women's rights, temperance, and abstinence from tobacco would certainly have appealed to Wilson, while reminding us how constructive and socially engaged the spiritualist movement could be at its best.[7]

In August 1868 she attended a "Spiritual Camp Meeting at Cape Cod," undoubtedly one of the pinnacles in her career as a spiritualist platform speaker. At this camp meeting she spoke three times. First she addressed the theme "Who and what is God, and in whom and how are His powers and goodness most manifest?" The *Banner* describes this lecture as "spirited and contain[ing] many good points" and as being delivered "through" her while in a trance. The second, addressed to an audience of "twenty-five hundred," considered the "practical uses of spiritualism," while the last, a "short and pithy" speech, took as its subject "the general theme of spiritualism, its teachings and lessons, and especially . . . the power of love to conquer and subdue all the evil passions of the world."[8] During this Cape

Cod gathering, Wilson shared the stage with such prominent Boston spiritualists as Dr. H. B. Storer and (again, significantly) C. Fannie Allyn. She then traveled on to Maine to keep speaking appointments there, and from Maine sent a letter to the *Banner*, published on October 10, 1868, offering a glowing tribute to the spiritualist enterprise and praising in particular the Cape Cod meeting: "Mrs. Hattie Wilson, writing from Garland, Maine . . . says: 'I have been a labourer in the spiritual ranks for seven years, and if their platform is known to me, it is no bond, no sect, no creed, no dogma and no caste. Never have I seen it so practically illustrated, either in public or private, as at the Cape Cod Meeting. May the Gods of Knowledge and Wisdom protect that spirit gained until another year, when the principles that inspired us may have become eighteen carats more refined, spiritually.'"[9]

Wilson's sentiments again shed light—in her own words—on why spiritualism was such a powerful progressive and liberal influence. In particular it provided some African Americans and a substantial number of women with a platform, making this movement an important sociocultural phenomenon, disturbing conventional gender and ethnic hierarchies.[10] Notice how Wilson slips in an oblique reminder about the shortcomings of the Christianity she had encountered in Milford, by way of her reference to "the *Gods* of Knowledge and Wisdom" (our italics)—hearkening back, as this does, to the way that "a devout Christian *exterior*" masked the unsteadiness of Frado's embrace of institutionalized religion and her preference for "the value of useful books," apparently rather than the Bible, in *Our Nig* (124). By making such an open remark, pluralizing the word "Gods," Wilson is also showing confidence that the *Banner* will not object to such an unconventional sentiment. She also suggests that the Cape Cod spiritualist camp offered her much greater tolerance than that which she had previously encountered.

In these ways spiritualist circles indeed offered her "no sect, no creed, no dogma and no caste." Spiritualists also proudly pointed to their movement's nonelite origins, depicting it as popular, even populist: "Modern Spiritualism began its rich unfolding amongst the common people instead of starting among the leaders of the Orthodox Churches."[11] Even if this claim is not entirely accurate—spiritualism being largely a white middle-class preserve—such sentiments must have appealed to Wilson.

Wilson's embrace of spiritualism was wholehearted enough for the *Banner* to praise her as a "valued friend" when promoting her forthcoming tour: "We learn that our valued friend, Mrs. Hattie E. Wilson, the colored medium, will probably visit Maine and the West during the Summer. She has been constantly and successfully engaged the past year in the vicinity as a healing medium and trance speaker and now has a host of friends. We cordially commend her to the hospitality of the spiritual brotherhood everywhere."[12] Wilson, however, does not seem to have traveled on west; instead, from October 1868 through the end of the year, Maine remained the location given for her in the *Banner* until she reappears in Boston.

After her return to Boston, Wilson continued for a short while to be in some demand, speaking, for example, to the Boston Christian Spiritualists on March 7 and 14, 1869. The source of her success was, as one *Banner* correspondent noted, her ability to give "utterance to many great truths of Spiritualism in a manner that reached the comprehension at once . . . her lecture was superior to the efforts of the reverend-divines in that place."[13] Wilson's facility with language, as displayed in *Our Nig*, helped her greatly in her spiritualist activities, and she flourished because of her much praised oratorical skills.

The following year Wilson addressed the "Massachusetts Spiritual Convention at Haverhill . . . October 22 and 23." Others appearing on this stage included the well-known Massachusetts spiritualists

Dr. H. B. Storer and Isaiah C. Ray. At this event, Wilson again spoke three times. On the first occasion she merely became "entranced" and "spoke briefly." The next two contributions, however, were more substantial. Her second was, according to the *Banner,* a "deeply affecting" address, winning "implicit confidence in its truth, by the simple natural manner in which all its details were presented." The third and final contribution demonstrates another sign of her growing prominence by the way it was reported in the *Banner of Light*—a report that (in typical *Banner* fashion) slides into direct paraphrase:

> Mrs. Hattie Robinson [Wilson] followed in deeply interesting remarks, based upon her experience as a medium, affirming the prominence of the relations between parents and children, although death might apparently divide them. Invisible to you, fathers and mothers, are the children, given to you to educate, and your influence affects them spiritually, after they have gone out of your sight, as truly as though they had remained upon the earth. You may be angels to them as well as they to you. If your spiritualist eyes could be opened, as mine frequently are, you would *know* this to be true. In our homes and in our midst are our children, our parents, our friends, and we mutually act upon each other.[14]

These are, on the one hand, conventional enough sentiments, rooted in mainstream spiritualist tenets. However, in Wilson's words perhaps also reside traces of the sadness she felt about the loss of her father (accepting *Our Nig*'s account of Frado's father's death as autobiographically accurate) and, perhaps more emphatically, regret about the fate of her child, who was abandoned for so many years by necessity in Milford before dying prematurely. This is one way of understanding how she became engaged with spiritualism. In

1868 she claimed to have been "a labourer in the spiritual ranks for seven years"[15] (*Banner of Light*, XXIV, no. 4 [October 10, 1868]: 4), which dates her initial involvement to circa 1861—some time after *Our Nig*'s publication but not that long after her son's death. It also underlines how spiritualism offered consolation to the bereaved and why it proved so popular in postbellum America. Spiritualism's swift spread to all quarters of New England at this time can be seen as offering solace to the many soldiers' families in mourning for their dead, many of whose bodies were never recovered from the battlefields.[16]

After this Haverhill event, Wilson faded from prominence as a platform speaker. Her career, however, can still be traced in the *Banner*, for she instead gradually developed a significant role in the Boston spiritualist "lyceums" (as the Sunday schools intended for the children of spiritualists and fellow travelers were called). This reorientation may have started as early as July 1870, with an address at the Boston Mercantile Hall Lyceum. The transition from touring speaker to Boston lyceum stalwart then continues by way of a relatively long-lasting involvement with the spiritualist Boylston Street Association at Temple Hall (her first sustained involvement fixed with just one spiritualist organization). At first, she "occupie[s] the platform" in September 1871, presumably as just another touring speaker, to the "general acceptance of those attending." Shortly after this, however, following the departure of the regular, resident Temple Hall trance speaker, Mrs. Bowditch, Wilson becomes something like her replacement, and for the next twelve months or so she is mentioned as addressing the Temple Hall meetings with some regularity:[17] "The meetings at Temple Hall still continue with unabated interest. . . . Mrs. Hattie Wilson gives general satisfaction."[18] However, within eighteen months Wilson is clearly no longer the resident medium, being only one among several speakers, and the following

week she is instead listed as elected to be one of the "Leaders" to
a group of pupils attending the Temple Hall Association's "Independent Children's Progressive Lyceum." An important transition
has been completed. Wilson has switched from being a touring
platform speaker to displaying a commitment to Boston spiritualist children's education. Tellingly, in this same issue of the *Banner*
she is also mentioned as speaking at the wedding of the Children's
Lyceum "conductor" (as lyceum heads were called) at Boston's Eliot
Hall;[19] henceforth the *Banner*'s mentions of Wilson revolve almost
exclusively around her involvement in the Boston children's lyceum
movement.

Wilson remained with the Temple Hall lyceum only for a short
time, soon transferring her labors instead to the "Children's Progressive Lyceum and Library Association No. 1," to which she was elected
as a "Supplementary Leader" at a meeting on September 2, 1873.[20]
It is not clear why she made this move from Temple Hall. However,
it worked out well for her because this lyceum was poised to become
the most energetic and prominent of the spiritualist lyceums in Boston. Perhaps Wilson saw how things were developing; perhaps, less
voluntarily, she had exhausted her opportunities at Temple Hall,
after losing her place as its leading trance medium.[21]

Wilson in the Spiritualist Lyceum Movement

The "Children's Progressive Lyceum No. 1," as it was commonly
called, had been formed "seven or eight years" earlier (in Boston's
Mercantile Hall, circa 1865), making it one of the earliest "progressive lyceums" to be founded after the movement began in 1864.[22] It
was generally regarded as Boston's "Mother Lyceum."[23] Wilson was
for some time after September 1873 regularly named in the *Banner*
as one of this lyceum's "group leaders." For example, the Septem-

ber 12, 1874, issue noted how "Mrs. Hattie Wilson" was elected as the leader of the "Lake" group in the lyceum. Group leaders were seen as crucial to a lyceum's success: "The most important position in this school is that of the Leaders of the Groups. . . . The leaders must interest the children, and the children should work in unison with them."[24] Wilson's election as a leader is a sure sign of her integration into the Children's Progressive Lyceum No. 1. She had networked hard to secure this position: for example, on February 13, 1874, she held a gathering that included her new lyceum's officers in her residence at 46 Carver Street, "in honor of her spirit father . . . after which the company adjourned to John A. Andrew Hall," where Dr. H. B. Storer and others "offered" some "remarks appropriate to the occasion," with "the hostess (entranced) making due reply." She participated in a series of such gatherings, the like of which were mentioned with some frequency in the *Banner* in the coming years.[25] Luther Colby, the *Banner of Light*'s editor, was deeply committed to the lyceum movement and, being familiar with Wilson's work, was in a position to advance her lyceum career and monitor its progress in the pages of the *Banner*.

By 1873 the Children's Progressive Lyceum No. 1's importance had grown so much that it organized Boston's most significant anniversary celebrations for the "Advent Day of Modern Spiritualism," commemorating the 1848 "Rochester rappings," as they are commonly called, heard through the "mediumship" of two sisters, Kate and Margaret Fox, at Hydesville, New York.[26] The *Banner* covered the "Twenty-Sixth Anniversary" events held at the John A. Andrew Hall and "at New Fraternity and the Parker Memorial," which included not only speeches by prominent Boston spiritualists, including Lizzie Doten, I. P. Greenleaf, and Dr. H. B. Storer, but also, during the second, children's day, a "speech . . . to the children" by Hattie E. Wilson (among others). Wilson at this time spoke in some other

Boston venues as well, including Nassau Hall on July 19, 1874, and she made a "vigorous and entertaining" contribution, "under direct spirit control," at a camp meeting at Silver Lake sponsored by the Lyceum No. 1.[27]

This second, lyceum-based rise to prominence by Wilson, if on a rather more localized Boston basis, was accompanied by one other, more daring foray. This occurred when Wilson attended a meeting called by Victoria Woodhull, the radical spiritualist reformer and free love proponent, in September 1874—a "National Mass Meeting of Radicals, Socialists, Infidels, Materialists, Free Religionists and Free Thinkers." Woodhull could not attend, but her involvement meant the event attracted much controversy. Those who went were largely branded as "that clique who follow Victoria Woodhull in her efforts to attain notoriety by the enunciation of the most radical free love doctrine," while the meeting itself was described as "the quintessence of nastiness."[28] Spiritualism, not free love, however, dominated the debates, as when a resolution was passed arguing that "the instincts of true womanhood are against bearing children for the State, and handing them over to its cares, whilst so stupidly ignoring the best modes of moral and spiritual culture"—a reference to a widespread feeling among the movement's more radical members that a spiritualist lyceum education would be better than any education provided by the state. Wilson added her voice to these sentiments at the meeting, "express[ing] dissent from the doctrine of handing children over to the State, speaking from her own personal experience as one who/NEVER HAD A FATHER/never had a mother." She also, in "an address of great vigor and enthusiasm" commented upon "the conduct of Spiritualists to each other," speaking of her "grievances at the treatment she received from Boston Spiritualists."[29] It is difficult to be sure what these grievances were, though commonly at this time mediums were subjecting one another to accusations of chicanery in their performances. Possibly Wilson had been recently challenged at Temple Hall. However, she may have been complaining about a strain of racism in the spiritualist movement (a suggestion perhaps supported by the "eloquence" that she brought to her "plea for the recognition of her race [and] . . . philosophy of universal brotherhood" advanced at the Melrose meeting in September 1867).[30] It is, however, in itself significant that she should turn up at and address such a radical and controversial event. Although she performed her lyceum functions, it seems she did not rest happily in mainstream spiritualism's embrace, which may be why she is constantly shifting her location within the movement.

For the time being, Wilson's substantial contributions to the Children's Progressive Lyceum No. 1 continued and were further recognized when some Boston spiritualists launched an ambitious though unsuccessful attempt to expand their activities by reconfiguring the Boston Spiritualists' Union as the "American Spiritual Institute" and appointed her as its "Director—Educational Department." Reports in the *Spiritual Scientist* make it clear that this new body never took off, and that Wilson's involvement was probably not substantial,[31] but Wilson's initial appointment does signal her good standing in the movement. More recognition followed, including a gathering at her residence to celebrate her birthday in 1875, graced by the presence of such prominent Boston spiritualists as Dr. A. H. Richardson and Dr. John H. Currier. She also addressed "the Twenty-Eighth Anniversary of the Advent of Modern Spiritualism; Commemorative Exercises at Paine Hall, Boston; . . . The 31st March, 1876."

> Dr. Richardson next called upon Hattie Wilson to address the audience. The intelligence controlling her said it was the duty of the adherents of Spiritualism to endeavour so to live that on the passage of each year they might perceive with their

spiritual senses that they had ascended another round in the ladder which led upward to the heavenly heights—that they occupied a position in advance of what they previously held; but it really seemed to the speaker that too many of the Spiritualists were halting just where they were twenty-eight years ago—they were "halting on the old camp ground," where they had established themselves when the knowledge of the possibility of spirit communion first reached them. . . . The process of decease was but the gaining of a new tent in the camp ground of the Infinite, and the character of that tent and its location as to desirability or otherwise depended on the efforts made in this sphere of life to gain knowledge of higher things and to clothe it with deeds done for the good of humanity. The spirit controlling prophesied that great as had been the trials of the spiritual media in the past, there were still more serious ones in store for them and the cause they represented.

Isaiah C. Ray of New Bedford referred in a highly complimentary manner to the work accomplished by the previous speaker [Wilson].[32]

The sentiments expressed by Wilson were commonplace. Spiritualists were often questioning the movement's ability to sustain its momentum at this time. Wilson also delivered her lecture through the "spirit controlling her," and thus adhered to a wholly conventional, and for her typical, trance medium presentation. Even so, the high praise by the prominent speaker following her at such an important occasion would have added to Wilson's reputation.

But this second emergence into minor celebrity was again followed by a steady falling away, though this time the decline was slower. In 1876 Wilson is still to be found speaking at another event organized by the Children's Progressive Lyceum No. 1, a "Gathering at Highland Lake Grove," that was "a great success." There she delivered a "trance address mainly upon freedom of thought, showing how this had been upheld or violated in the events of American history, since the landing of the pilgrim fathers."[33] This must have drawn distantly on her reading of "deeds historic and names renowned" (124) back in New Hampshire, and shows her continuing sense of how important it was to resist erosions of freedom. But after this speech, references to Wilson thin out to almost nothing until 1879, when the *Banner* names her as one of those involved in setting up a new lyceum, planned by J. B. Hatch, C. F. Rand, and others, including Mrs. Maggie Folsom and Mrs. C. Fannie Allyn—who had both long been closely associated with Wilson.

This new lyceum decided to call itself the "Children's Progressive Lyceum No. 2 Charlestown District, Boston"—a name disconcertingly similar to that of the movement's preeminent lyceum in Boston, the Children's Progressive Lyceum No. 1. Wilson, from the beginning, performed a prominent role, and her involvement saw her third, rather lesser rise to prominence. In the inaugural announcement of the lyceum in the *Banner,* April 26, 1879, "Mrs. Hattie E. Wilson" is named as the organizer of a "course of Sunday evening lectures and concerts" and the following week is identified as a member of the Lyceum's "Standing Committee." Soon the Children's Progressive Lyceum No. 2 was claiming success, stating on May 10 that "over 200 children" attended its "May Day Party" and the following week asserting that "two lyceums dedicated to the service of the angel-world . . . have become an absolute fact in Boston." The following week (May 15), details were provided about "exercises" organized by Wilson and under her "direction," specifically two "farces," *"Love of a Bonnet"* and *"Courtship under Difficulties,"* in which Wilson also participated. At the end of the evening, "the exercises were closed with dancing." By December, after the election of officers, she appears on the "roster" as the lyceum's "Treasurer."[34]

This brash new lyceum, led by J. B. Hatch, the former conductor of Children's Progressive Lyceum No. 1, who possibly recruited Wilson to the new lyceum,[35] invited members of the Children's Progressive Lyceum No. 1 to come to its "Decoration Sunday" event on June 8, 1879. Their polite refusal perhaps hints at a rivalry, which would have been exacerbated when Children's Progressive Lyceum No. 2 moved in the autumn from Charlestown to the center of Boston—to Amory Hall, which had only recently been vacated by the Children's Progressive Lyceum No. 1 (which had just moved to Paine Memorial Hall).[36] Soon, Lyceum No. 2's ambitions overreached those of its senior sibling: it forged relationships with the main spiritualist lyceums in Brooklyn and New York City and organized exchange visits, which were covered in the *Banner*. Wilson played a role on the organizing committee and probably visited New York.

As it entered its second year of existence in April 1880, the Children's Progressive Lyceum No. 2 renamed itself (perhaps in an effort to ease rising tensions) the Shawmut Spiritual Lyceum—a name "handed down . . . from the spirit world, in commemoration of the coming of the Indian bands, who return to you from the upper hunting ground."[37] The Shawmut Spiritual Lyceum then took the lead in organizing the "Thirty Third Anniversary in Boston" of the advent of modern spiritualism—an anniversary celebration long overseen by Boston's Children's Progressive Lyceum No. 1, so No. 2's intervention into the annual event can only have caused further irritation. In the March 26, 1881, issue of the *Banner*, the Shawmut Lyceum announced that it had established a committee, including J. B. Hatch, C. Frank Rand, J. B. Hatch, Jr., and Hattie Wilson, to organize the celebration. The Children's Progressive Lyceum No. 1

persisted in organizing its own celebration, so the two ran (and were reported in the *Banner*) in parallel, but it was the Shawmut event that made the *Banner*'s front page, not least because it secured the services of the internationally prominent mediums W. J. Colville and J. Frank Baxter.[38] The rivalry never surfaced openly in the *Banner*'s pages but can be inferred from the abrupt conclusion to a report by the Children's Progressive Lyceum No. 1 in May 1881: "We noticed with pleasure the face of the Conductor of Shawmut Lyceum among the visitors; also a number of his co-workers. *This is as it should be.*"[39] By the summer of 1881, the Shawmut was so confident of its primacy that it hired Boston's large Music Hall for its "Floral Sunday" celebrations of June 5, which, as reported in the *Banner*, opened with a "Banner March" of 140 people. Wilson was involved, as indicated in the August 20, 1881, issue of the *Banner*, which noted that "as [is] customary upon the opening Sunday [after the summer break], remarks were made by Conductor Hatch, Assistant Rand, Mrs. H. E. Wilson, [and] Mrs. Maggie Folsom."[40]

The Shawmut Lyceum seems to have been the more radical of these two big Boston lyceums. In particular, it proposed the controversial step, advocated by a "Mrs Carlisle Ireland" in October 1880, of "hold[ing] seances whereat the children can be present and can hold converse with the spirit world." Since the spirits (according to spiritualist lore) controlled such events, not the mediums, they could become unpredictably rambunctious and even disruptive, so the Boston lyceums' youngsters were almost never exposed to them.[41] Wilson, however, as the *Banner* report noted, supported this change, along with Conductor Hatch. After a cautious delay, this step was enacted two years later by the Shawmut, as the *Banner* reported in January 1882: "The Spirit 'LULU' . . . addressed the children through the mediumship of Mrs. Brown." Once the precedent had been set, it continued, mostly revolving around the work of the well-established medium Mrs. Maud E. Lord, who aimed her trance addresses chiefly at the general audience, though sometimes at the children.[42]

By this time, however, it seems that Wilson's role at the Shawmut Lyceum had begun to fade, coinciding with the emergence of dissension within the lyceum, marked by "earnest pleas" by its conductor, J. L. Hatch, "for harmony."[43] Wilson still appeared on occasion, for example when she was featured as the medium through which "Spirit Dr. Hammond [gave] one of his old-fashioned healing and developing circles" for the "Shawmut Sewing Circle" in January 1882. Attendees were charged ten cents—a detail that suggests that Wilson's involvement with the lyceum system had a financial motive (though she certainly was also holding regular private sessions for clients in her chambers for which she would have charged). Generally, however, she became less evident in the Shawmut.[44] Her occasional appearances were now minor, as when on May 6, 1882, she, along with Maggie Folsom, "made some impressive remarks" about the death of two of their lyceum co-workers, suggesting that "the noble work they had done on earth" was "small as in comparison with what they will do now that they have passed to the higher life."[45]

Once again Wilson's presence fades away soon after achieving notable success in Boston's spiritualist circles. We suspect that Wilson's repeated failure to sustain her position may have had something to do with issues of race. For example, when the *Banner* carried a report in 1882 of a gathering "on the evening of Monday Jan. 2d." of "a large delegation of the friends of Mr. and Mrs. J. A. Hatch— including among others representatives of the board of officers and the members of the Shawmut . . . at their residence . . . to observe the birthday of Mrs. Hatch," "Hattie Wilson" was very noticeably the only individual not given a title before her name, even though she was one of those offering "brief remarks."[46] This omission is one of the repeated minor signs that she never fitted in very comfortably.

Wilson's Own Spiritual School

Within the year another quite extraordinary development in Wilson's spiritualist career occurs: Wilson now opens her own lyceum, or, as she called it, her school. It might be identified as her next rise in, and the high point of, her local Bostonian prominence, were it not for an underlying sense that it marks a deep-rooted departure from the spiritualist mainstream and a consequent marginalization. It seems to be a bold and quite sudden change from her past involvements—one announced in the *Banner* in February 1883, with no advance publicity:

Notice. The first meeting of a Progressive School for children which is being formed in the *Ladies' Aid Parlors,* met Sunday morning, February 4th, and will continue to meet there every Sunday morning. The children's friend, Mrs. Hattie E. Wilson, with a few others, have undertaken to form a school that will aim to be both pleasing and instructive to the children, and hope to have the assistance of all liberal minded people to help them carry on the work. Children and friends of the children are cordially invited to meet with us next Sunday morning, and those who would like to take an active part or feel an interest in the undertaking, are invited to meet at the residence of Mrs. H. E. Wilson No. 15 Village street, next Friday evening, to offer any suggestions they may have to offer or express their views as regards the best mode of instructing the children that may favour us with their attendance. MRS. HATTIE E. WILSON[47]

Wilson's "liberal" school met in the parlors of the Ladies' Aid Society, whose activities centered on spiritualist events. A typical "Ladies' Aid" evening would involve a "conference on matters spiritual and progressive" during one of which, for example, "the subject was 'Experiences,' and some new people appeared interestingly in the *rôle* of speakers . . . changing 'mute inglorious Miltons into active ones.'"[48] Wilson's school, however, does not seem to have been directly linked with these other activities, which it now ran alongside.

For a short while Harriet Wilson wrote the reports of the meetings of the school she had established, known variously as the "First Spiritual Progressive School," the "Spiritual Progressive School," and the "Progressive School." As these notices constitute almost all the writing known to be by Wilson outside the pages of *Our Nig* we quote them in full:

LADIES' AID PARLORS—The "First Spiritual Progressive School" met in this hall this morning and not withstanding the inclemency of the weather, we had quite an interesting meeting. We are not fully organized, but hope to be able next Sunday to begin our work in good earnest. The exercises this morning consisted of local and instrumental music, remarks by Mrs. H. E. Wilson and Mr. Street, and readings by the children. We shall endeavor to have a teacher of elocution, also one of music. After the readings of the children, remarks were made by Mrs. M. J. Folsom, which were heartily responded to by the audience. Mrs. Maud E. Lord favored us with some very pleasing remarks, which were enthusiastically received. In conclusion Mr. Cherrington gave us some very flattering predictions for our school, which we all hope will prove true.

This week we shall issue the first number of a little paper, or lesson sheet called "The Temple Within," to appear once a month. It is to be the property of the school, and no doubt will prove a benefit to it.

In closing, the thanks of the school are tendered to those who favored us with their services on this occasion. Our sessions will be held every Sunday morning. Let our work show that we merit the confidence and good will of our many friends. MRS. HATTIE E. WILSON.

LADIES' AID PARLORS—The First Spiritualist Progressive School met Sunday morning, Feb. 18th as usual. The first number of our newspaper, "*The Temple Within,*" made its appearance and met with a hearty welcome. It needs no recommendation from me; its golden lessons and bright thoughts will make friends for it wherever it goes. Besides our exercises for the children this morning we were favored with short speeches from Mr. J. C. Street, Mrs. A. M. H. Tyler, Mr. David Brown and Mrs. [M.] J. Folsom, after which a generous contribution was made to our funds by the audience, for which the donors will please accept our thanks. We shall always be pleased to meet the children's friends and hear a kind word for them. MRS. HATTIE E. WILSON

LADIES' AID PARLORS—At the Spiritual Progressive School we are pleased to see many additions to our ranks. The time was occupied with lessons from "*The Temple Within,*" music lessons and a march. Our school aims to teach the children those spiritual truths that will be of lasting benefit to them, and we cordially invite all to pay us a visit, and lend us a helping hand in the work we have undertaken. We expect uphill work at first, as others have had before us; but if we are not successful it shall not be our fault. On this occasion we listened with pleasure to kind words from Mr. J. C. Street and Dr. Wyman, and hope to hear from them and many more of our friends often. MRS HATTIE WILSON Boston, Feb. 25th, 1883

The announcements concerning the school continued in this vein:

LADIES' AID PARLORS—The Spiritualist Progressive School was attended on Sunday last by a goodly number of children, all of whom took an active interest in the lessons, as well as what was said to them. Mr. Street's talk about their Lesson Sheet or Paper formed a pleasing feature and held the attention of the pupils to the subject. Dr. Richardson favored us with an interesting speech, and was followed by Mrs. M. J. Folsom and Mrs. H. E. Wilson. All who have the interest of the school at heart, and wish to become charter members, will please meet at the residence of Mrs. Wilson, 15 Village street, next Friday evening at 8 o'clock. We hope to hear from many old workers who have expressed a wish to help us. MRS HATTIE E. WILSON

LADIES' AID PARLORS—The Progressive school held a very interesting session last Sunday. All expressed themselves much pleased with the exercises, which consisted of singing, a short march, and a lesson from our paper. The question, "What does Spiritualism Teach?" was responded to by nearly every scholar. A lesson in vocal music and one on elocution were given, with which all were very much pleased. After a few recitations from the children, we listened to a few able remarks from Father Locke. The school will hold an Easter Festival this afternoon and evening of the 24th, and we hope our friends will help us to make it a success. Next Sunday the particulars will be given and tickets for sale. HATTIE E. WILSON

LADIES' AID PARLORS—The Progressive School is fast increasing in numbers. Last Sunday the lessons, in which all were deeply interested, occupied all the time, giving no opportunity for recitations or speeches. This week the second issue of *The Temple Within* will appear. Next Saturday the children will hold an Easter Festival in this place. The children meet in the afternoon for social recreation and supper. In the evening a public entertainment will be given. Admission: adults, ten cents; children not belonging to the school, five cents. All interested in the school, and wishing to become members of the association, are invited to meet in the residence of Miss Hartwell, no. 24 Dover street, Friday evening, March 23d, at eight o'clock.

MRS. HATTIE E. WILSON Boston, March 18th, 1883.[49]

This was the last entry in the *Banner* to be penned by Wilson. The next, which announced the success of the Easter festival and called another meeting at the "room" of Mrs. Maggie J. Folsom, No. 2 Hamilton Place, room 6, was signed by "Albert A. Lord, *Secretary.*" Lord was to write such notices from then on until November 1883.[50]

What occurred to usher in this change of authorship is not clear. The most obvious explanation is that, as the school grew, Wilson was kept busy by the demands of overseeing its success and so delegated the task of submitting copy to the *Banner* to the secretary of the "Association" that the *Banner* noted had been established to run the school in March 1883.[51] However, the position of Wilson in this association was never defined, and as the school's history unfolds in the *Banner,* it becomes clear that Wilson's role was less central than might be expected, given the part she played in the school's founding. This sidelining may again be connected to her racial identity, which may have created a problem if she proposed to run a school for children in a predominantly white social movement (though her gender certainly played a role, too). By September 1883 the "President" of the school was named as J. C. Street, and in October 1883 he became its "conductor." His resignation from this position, however, followed soon after, occurring at a "regular business meeting" described in the *Banner* on November 10. Since Albert A. Lord never wrote another notice about the school, he seems to have left at about the same time.

Within two months, reports about the school's activities stopped appearing in the *Banner.*[52] The last mention of the Progressive School in its pages was in April 1884, when, at a "Lyceum Union Anniversary" in Paine Hall, where one of her former havens, the Progressive Lyceum No. 1, met each week, Hattie Wilson, "aided by her good controls," ended her address as follows: "May harmony ever exist between the two schools represented here today. Allow me to thank you, on behalf of the officers and members of the Progressive School, for your cordial invitation and warm reception."[53] These words seem to be an effort at bridge building, possibly hinting at a more general desire within the movement at that time to unify the Boston lyceums, as the meeting's very name (a "Lyceum Union") implies. Wilson's school, nevertheless, seems to have ceased to operate soon after this. Possibly the meeting indicated that, in a contracting market (by 1884, Civil War memories were fading), the spiritualist lyceums recognized that some retrenchment was essential.

In total, Wilson wrote slightly more than one thousand words about her school in the *Banner*—that is to say, about 2 percent of the total number of words that have been identified as written by her.[54] The specific entries are as much advertisements as they are school reports. However, they can serve as a reminder that Frado's school attendance in Singleton was one of the few positive experiences depicted in *Our Nig*. Wilson's commitment to teaching at spiritualist schools can be related back to her portrayal of Frado's fulfilling educational experiences (assuming their depiction to be autobiographical). Wilson's decision to name her spiritualist children's gathering a "school" rather than a "lyceum" (as such institutions were customarily called) may also be an allusion to her relatively fond memories of her own schooldays.

More likely, however, the name she chose was intended to distinguish her "school" from other spiritualist "lyceums." Once Wilson stopped writing the reports and Lord took over, the reports became briefer, but part of one in particular bears quoting: "LADIES' AID PARLORS . . . The Progressive School was visited last Sunday by several of our friends from [the Children's Progressive] Lyceum No. 1 [and this led to] a few remarks from Mr. Alonzo Danforth as to the proper teaching of children in a school of this kind."[55] This kind of monitoring (as it appears to be) is unprecedented—at least in the reports of the *Banner* concerning Boston spiritual lyceum activities—and suggests how daring Wilson's move had been in setting up her unconventionally titled progressive *school*.

Wilson also seems to have run her school in an atypical fashion. She departed from the norms chiefly by introducing into her school her teaching aid, *The Temple Within*, which she describes variously as her school's "newspaper" or "lesson sheet." Calling it a lesson sheet perhaps implies that Wilson desired to provide an education beyond the general "Sunday school" style induction into spiritualist beliefs offered by other lyceums. The *Banner* had not previously mentioned any such newspapers or lesson sheets being used in the lyceum system, though in 1893 they were to be taken up by the Children's Progressive Lyceum No. 1.[56] Despite apparently introducing such an innovation, Wilson was quickly superseded as the leader of the school, though still recognized by the school as "our best friend and worker." Wilson's school was also apparently set apart from other schools by its lack of regimentation, or division into conventionally named groups, and its avoidance of the predilection for "Banner Marches" and other formal pageants that characterized other lyceums. Apart from the mention of one "march," none of these activities ever appeared in the *Banner*'s reporting of her school.[57]

Possibly more damaging, in terms of stirring up resistance to its existence, was the way Wilson's school, like the Shawmut Lyceum where she had worked before, took the atypical step of allowing mediums under spiritual control to work with its children. When leading the children in the Progressive School, Wilson herself sometimes worked "under control of one of her Indian guides," and on at least one occasion provided "several proofs of the presence of loved ones gone before" during a session.[58] Introducing her "Indian guides" into her lyceum in this way seems to have been quite unusual for the lyceum movement, presumably because the spirits introduced by the mediums might say or do inappropriate things (so that the medium could thereby excite interest in the manifestations he or she produced). Assuming that the *Banner* reports are a reliable guide in this respect, only the Shawmut otherwise went down this road, and Wilson would certainly have been aware of this. Pertinently, in a welcoming speech to a spiritualist luminary visiting Boston, Wilson observed that she "had been called to do the work of spirits inspiring her organism for long years, and knew by sad experience the effects sometimes wrought . . . because of . . . daring to speak the words which the spirit-world demanded."[59]

These unconventional, even risky boundary-crossing propensities may have lain behind Wilson's apparent demotion in her school's hierarchy as well as her earlier restless moves from site to site within Boston's spiritualist community. These migrations may have been enforced rather than voluntary, as she sought (or followed) congenial allies ready to share her approach to lyceum teaching.

Wilson's greater liberalism—even her radicalism—is alluded to, perhaps, in a message delivered to the Progressive Lyceum No. 1 by the very well respected and prominent Boston spiritualist Mrs. Maggie Folsom in January 1884. Folsom, one of Wilson's mentors who was likely to have been instrumental in helping her set up her own school,[60] obliquely requested greater tolerance from the Children's Progressive Lyceum No. 1. She expresses a "deep . . . interest in the work progressing so finely under the motherly care of our good friend, Mrs. Hattie Wilson, at the Ladies' Aid Parlors" while also "always . . . cherish[ing] a love for the 'Old Mother Lyceum' [i.e., Lyceum No. 1]." The *Banner*'s report about Folsom then continues, "and so we occasionally hear [Folsom's] voice in defense of the right, in appeals to us to be true to our spirit guides, the old workers who march with us from Sunday to Sunday, whose spirit forms she could so distinctly see."[61] Here it seems that Folsom (or at least the person reporting her words) wishes to secure a rapprochement between the two Boston lyceums, while also intimating that, for her, like Wilson, séances should have a place in the lyceum system. Yet soon after Folsom uttered her diplomatic and carefully coded words, urging more inter-lyceum communion, the "LYCEUM UNION" event occurred that marked Wilson's school's last recorded appearance.[62] What followed is virtually a full and final withdrawal of Wilson from active lyceum involvement; the *Banner* only rarely mentions her again. She may have simply been too controversial a figure to fit in as the lyceum movement consolidated.[63]

Spiritualist Aftermaths and Issues

In total, Wilson's involvement with lyceum teaching lasted many more years than her brief platform-speaking career and waned in tandem with the decline of the lyceum system.[64] As she grew older and faded from the limelight (her death in 1900, for example, went unremarked in the *Banner*), Wilson returned to the running of trance medium sessions in her apartments. As late as 1898 the *Banner* carried a notice that "Mrs. Hattie E. Wilson, 9 Pelham street, Boston, holds circles at 7.45 P.M.," though the time had long since passed when the *Banner* regularly carried information about her (even including her current Boston address).[65]

There are several reasons for Wilson's decline from relative prominence over the decades. Firstly, spiritualism itself contracted, as the Civil War and its death toll faded from the public's consciousness. In 1896 the leading spiritualist speaker, Moses Hull, lamented this contraction, for example.[66] This perhaps helps account for Wilson's apparent loss of public speaking engagements over the decades, though for a time this was made up by her Boston lyceum involvements.

As significant was the rise in popularity of other types of spiritualism beyond Wilson's forte of "trance speaking." These changes caused Wilson, as early as July 1868, to ramp up her act, advertising herself as a "Lecturer and Unconscious Trance *Physician*" (our emphasis). By May 29, 1869, Wilson was claiming: "Chronic diseases treated with great success. Herb packs and manipulations included in the mode of treatment."[67] It is hard to believe that Wilson could cure "chronic diseases," but her audacity is as nothing compared to others' claims, accompanying the rise of so-called test mediumships. These "tests" in the postwar period involved increasingly spectacular physical manifestations of the spirit world. The more spectacular these tests, the more the "test" medium thrived. As the *Banner* noted as early as March 1870, "There seems to be a greater demand than ever all over the country for test mediums." By September 10 the tone had become drier: "Tests seem . . . to be in the ascendancy."[68] Yet the message is clear: "test" spiritualism increasingly attracted the headlines. As Wilson did not attempt to compete with these "test" mediums, her fortunes necessarily must have waned. (In 1881 one of her sessions is pointedly described as an "*old-fashioned* healing and developing circle.")[69]

As the twentieth century approached, Wilson's reduced mobility as she aged would have further contributed to her decline. Her final appearance in the "Platform Lecturers" column in 1898 mentions only her availability for visits to her house and lists no outside engagements.[70]

Wilson's embrace of spiritualism was, we suggest, always problematic, particularly as her claims concerning her powers became more ambitious over time, though she never quite represented herself as a full-fledged "test" medium. This escalation of her spiritual powers is evident in her comments at the Haverhill gathering of the Massachusetts Spiritualist Convention on October 22 and 23, 1870. On the final day, her "deeply interesting remarks, based upon her experience as a medium, affirming the permanence of the relation between parents and children, although death might apparently divide them," suggest how spiritualism offered supportive consolation to the bereaved and why it proved so popular to Americans grieving their Civil War losses. It is important to acknowledge spiritualism's positive and constructive cultural aspects. Though dominated by white males, spiritualism also provided a means for women and members of nonwhite ethnic groups (Native Americans and African Americans in particular) to gain a public platform and even aspire to professional status. Wilson herself late in life took the title "Dr. Hattie Wilson" on occasion.[71]

Spiritualism, nevertheless, even in the nineteenth century, was regarded as controversial, as the *Banner*'s repeated and continual defenses of the institution's probity suggest. In 1866, for example, in an article in the *Banner* entitled "Mr. Gaylord on Spiritualism," the Rev. N. M. Gaylord declared: "As regards physical manifestations, he did not believe in them . . . and as regards trance mediums, it was a puzzle to find how they could talk by the hour what seemed to him a mess of twaddle." Almost fourteen years later, faced with constant attacks highlighting "FRAUDULENT MEDIUMS," the *Banner* advises that "a passive condition on the part of the sitter" was "essential" to a successful session and that too much skepticism could, as it were, generate fraud (this idea is advanced without any hint of irony).[72] Spiritualism as a movement, and the *Banner* as an important organ of this movement, could not avoid addressing such constant allegations of fakery and fraudulence. For example, it prominently featured a rebuttal of a *Boston Post* attack, in an article self-explanatorily entitled "The Recent 'Exposure' of Physical Mediumship in Mercantile Hall." Even the Fox sisters' series of "Rochester rappings," the founding phenomena of "Modern Spiritualism," were revealed on October 21, 1888, by the Foxes themselves to have been faked by the two girls loudly cracking their finger and toe joints.[73]

Spiritualism certainly had its shady side. The advertisements in the *Banner* bear testimony to this, offering not only relatively harmless remedies, such as those promised by "Hasheesh Candy," but also, more disturbingly, "antidote[s] to cancer," "Winchester's

Asiatic Cholera drops . . . an infallible remedy for Asiatic Malignant Cholera," and "Dr. Storer's Nutritive Compound," claiming to be a remedy for "Scrofula . . . Syphilis, Tuberculosis, Consumption, Ulceration of the Liver, . . . Ring Worm, Rheumatism."[74] (Storer regularly shared platforms in Boston with Wilson.) Advertisements making outlandish claims for ineffective treatments appeared alongside more benign promises to disguise graying hair ("Ring's Vegetable Ambrosia for Gray Hair").[75] Wilson, we recall, had carved out a living of sorts by making and bottling a kind of hair treatment in the late 1850s in northwestern Massachusetts and southern New Hampshire. Her entrée into spiritualism, then, may have come about through her prior engagement with its patent medicinal hinterland. "Allida" tells us that Wilson's treatment did not simply color hair but could "restore" it to its original color. Wilson's advertisements placed in newspapers around New England went even further, effectively promising to cure baldness.[76]

Our concern with spiritualism's ethics color how we read the account of the main contribution Wilson made to the Haverhill convention, back in 1870:

> *Mrs. Hattie E. (Wilson) Robinson* [she remarried in 1870] *formerly Hattie Wilson*, gave a narrative of her development as a medium, by which she had been brought into acquaintance with her father in spirit-life, who was her almost constant companion. He had told her, in detail, the circumstances of her early life, and upon inquiry of the persons named by him, still living . . . found them correct in every particular. Although opposing to becoming a medium at first, and disbelieving in the purported origin of the power that controlled her, yet she was finally convinced by seeing an old school-mate, who was dead several years, standing by her bedside, who con-

versed with her as naturally as those who appear about her in the material world. Doubting, to her is impossible, and has been for many years; and when your spiritual sensibilities are opened, you will know the spirit-world is not afar off, in space, but here in our midst; and that spirits are not bodiless beings, but with us in our homes. [Notice the slide from this second-person interlude into first-person address.] Spiritualism has aroused me from my indifference and given me an interest in life—to be something and do something for others. Her entire story was deeply affecting, and won implicit confidence in its truth, by the simple natural manner in which all its details were presented.[77]

This idealistic account, though consistent with mainstream spiritualist sentimentalism, and chiming with nonconformist beliefs in useful works as a mark of divinity,[78] is somewhat undercut by our knowledge that Wilson's engagement with spiritualism always involved making a living as well, as evidenced by her charging admission for the séances she provided to the Shawmut Lyceum's sewing circle and the fees paid by charter members of her 1883 school. More important, however, her Haverhill address brings Wilson to the threshold of test mediumship. Her claims to authenticity are supported by "tests" of the evidence—the words of her father relayed from the spirit world and the materiality of her dead schoolmate, seen "standing by her bedside."[79]

Such a claim is difficult to swallow, as is the way Wilson becomes known as a medium able to contact Native American spirits. During her Boston career she developed as her regular spirit guides several "Indian guides" that "control[led]" her and enabled her to give "proofs of the presence of loved ones gone before." Native Americans were often reduced in spiritualist circles to caricature or stereotype—involving not a little racism in its celebration of bucolic "noble savagery" á la Rousseau: "The Red Man as He Was . . . Judge Flandran gave descriptions of the scalp dance, the medicine dance, moon's day and kissing day. And he concluded by saying that there is ever an interest in wild animals, but in wild men it is greatly enhanced." W. J. Colville spoke of how "the Indian of two hundred and fifty years ago" was "very different from the so-called brute of today. . . . [A] peaceful and orderly people if maltreated for centuries can develop into well-nigh fiends."[80] Given such sentimental and nostalgic framing, "Indian guides" from the spirit world became so popular that an "Indian Peace Council" was convened, attended, ironically, mostly by white mediums, and in 1894 the annual spiritualist camp meeting at Onset Grove saw the establishment of "The Wigwam," full of "Indian bric-a-brac" and featuring representations of such spirit guides as "Rolling Thunder, Eagle Eye, Gray Eagle, White Swan, [and] Eagle Wing."[81] Wilson, by providing "proofs of the presence of loved ones" dictated to her by one of her many Native American spirit guides, comes very close to becoming a practicing "test" medium.

The chief problem thrown up by this Haverhill address, how-ever, is Wilson's claim that her father appeared before her and told her the details of her early life. She claimed in 1868 that she had only been a laborer in the ranks of spiritualism for seven years, imply-ing that her first spiritual encounters postdate *Our Nig*'s composi-tion. Consistent with this, *Our Nig* makes no suggestion that Frado possesses any abilities as a medium. Though in her book's closing paragraph she compares herself to Joseph, reader of dreams in the pharaoh's prison, she also states that, quite unlike a spiritualist medium, she can only "track" the Bellmonts until the point that they pass "beyond mortal vision" (131). Nor does *Our Nig* suggest that Frado came to know about the details of her early life by way of a spiritual appearance to her of her deceased father. This may call into question Hattie E. Wilson's truthfulness at Haverhill, unless, that is, we accept that the "autobiographical" account found in *Our Nig* is a flawed fiction, and the "truth" only revealed to her later, by her father's spirit.[82]

Wilson's turn to spiritualism might therefore be linked to Frado's long association with trickery and deceit, described in *Our Nig*. Frado's husband, a "professed fugitive" passing himself off as an escaped slave, is an exemplar of how one can contrive a living and earn acceptance in the community through deception. (Mrs. Bellmont's hypocritical professions of religion also come to mind.) "Our Nig's"/Wilson's career selling a patent hair treatment (claimed by Wilson to be a regenerator: "IT IS NO HUMBUG! TRY IT AND SEE!") is another example.[83] As a young child, Frado shows a propensity to play "sly" tricks (such as filling her teacher's desk with cigar smoke so that it appears to be on fire [38–39]). Last, the bedbound Frado is suspected of being a deceitful malingerer by Mrs. Hoggs (123). All this might suggest that Frado, Wilson's fictional (autobiographical) creation, realizes the advantages of self-invention as long as it is well acted out.

If one accepts that Wilson was a charlatan to some extent, then this opens up the possibility that, when writing her life story in *Our Nig*, she embellished the details of her life, drawing on and fictionalizing the popular slave narrative genre to sensationalize her tale, perhaps even by overstating the maltreatment she experienced in the Bellmont farmhouse. Like the melodramatic opening account of Mag's seduction, such sensationalization would have rendered her book potentially more marketable, and we know by her own admission she sought to make money from her book for herself and her child. This line of argument cannot be incontrovertibly dismissed.

Yet we do not embrace it. The book's depiction of Frado's mistreatment, and particularly the way she is silenced by propping her mouth open so wide she cannot cry out, is presented with restraint, not sensationalizing hyperbole. Nor does Wilson as a medium advance fully down the path of test mediumship, where the real money lay in spiritualist circles (if also the greatest risk of exposure, which would have been fatal to the career of a colored medium). Most likely Wilson was neither simply a manipulative fake nor truly communing with material manifestations of the spirit world that live among us. Rather, she is guilty of some manipulation but does have honestly held spiritualist convictions, which mean that, setting aside her claim to treat chronic diseases successfully, there is some legitimacy in her advertisements' claims: "HATTIE E. WILSON, Trance Physician, has taken rooms at 27 Carver street. Chronic diseases treated with great success. Herb packs and manipulations included in the mode of treatment."[84] Wilson may well have had expertise in herb packs and manipulations that provided some relief of medical symptoms.

We suggest that Wilson's most likely motivation for embracing spiritualism can be found a long way back in her life: in the death of her son, George,[85] while she was, apparently, engaged in developing her hair treatment enterprise. (Probably after her son's death, she set up a kind of business partnership with Henry P. Wilson and G. J. Tewksbury of Manchester, while she worked out of Nashua.)[86] Setting aside one possible but unpalatable explanation—namely that Wilson abandoned her child to secure for herself a profitable livelihood[87]—a much better way of understanding this sequence of events is to focus on how Wilson more probably had to work unremittingly to eke out a very modest independent income, leaving her son behind for all or much of the time[88] while perhaps she sold her "hair regenerator" door-to-door, it is understandable that she could have been consumed by an excessive sense of guilt over her son's death and not surprising that she turned to spiritualism to assuage it.

Wilson's turn to spiritualism becomes in part psychologically explicable. Maltreated by her own mother, abandoned to the cruelties of a kind of indentured servitude in a house not unlike the Bellmonts', and guilt racked over leaving her child in care and his subsequent death, she may indeed have had visionary reveries that led her into a career in spiritualism. Founded in part on belief, this career would also have been fundamentally shaped by the hostile, generally racist society rendered vividly in her novel, *Our Nig.*[89]

NOTES

1. "Spiritualist Meetings," *Banner of Light* (hereafter cited as *BL*) XXI, no. 8 (May 18, 1867): 8; "Spiritualist Convention," *BL* XXI, no. 13 (June 15, 1867): 3.

2. This is the first indication in the *Banner of Light* that Wilson's engagement with spiritualism will come to center on the children's Sunday lyceums set up by spiritualists in Boston.

3. *BL* XXI, no. 15 (July 29, 1867): 8; "Second Great Spiritualist Camp Meeting at Pierpont Grove . . . August 29th [to] Sept. 1st, *BL* XXI, no. 26 (September 14, 1867): 5; *BL* XXII, no. 5 (October 19, 1865): 8.

4. *BL* XX, no. 16 (February 16, 1867): 4; *BL* XX, no. 25 (March 2, 1867): 8; *BL* XX, no. 21 (February 9, 1867): 7; *BL* XXI, no. 12 (June 1, 1867): 5. An alternative sponsor is Isaiah C. Ray. See pages vii and xiv of this edition's appendices.

5. "The State Agent's Report," *BL* XXII, no. 20 (February 2, 1868): 1.

6. *BL* XXIII, no. 11 (May 30, 1868): 11; *BL* XXII, no. 20 (February 2, 1868): 2.

7. The *Banner* similarly espoused these causes. See, for example: "Drunkard, Stop!" *BL* XVII, no. 22 (August 19, 1865): 7. "The Master and the Slave," *BL* XII, no. 16 (January 10, 1863): 8, which speaks of "the curse of slavery"; "Women's Suffrage Convention" (a supportive announcement of the meeting), *BL* LI, no. 10 (May 27, 1882): 7. The *Banner* also always embraced the idea that women could play prominent roles as spiritualist organizers and speakers. Furthermore the *Banner*'s regular, free listings of "Spiritualist Lecturers" consistently show that well over one-third of such lecturers were female.

8. Anon., "Spiritual Camp Meeting at Cape Cod," *BL* XXIII, no. 22 (August 15, 1868): 4.

9. Hattie E. Wilson, [no title], *BL* XXIV, no. 4 (October 10, 1868): 4. Apart from *Our Nig* and the notices she wrote in the *Banner* about her school, these seem to be the only words known to have been penned by Wilson, other than the wording of her various advertisements. This makes the sentiments she expresses here particularly significant.

10. See Ann Braude, *Radical Spirits: Spiritualism and Women's Rights in Nineteenth Century America* (Boston: Beacon Books, 1989).

11. Jay Chaapel, *BL* LIV, no. 20 (February 2, 1884): 5.

12. "MRS HATTIE WILSON," *BL* XXIII, no. 21 (August 8, 1868): 5.

13. "Movements of Lecturers and Mediums," *BL* XXIV, no. 25 (March 6, 1869): 4; "Marlboro', Mass.," *BL* XXIV, no. 12 (December 5, 1868): 4.

14. "Massachusetts Spiritual Convention at Haverhill," *BL* XXVIII, no. 8 (November 12, 1870): 2. Wilson is called "Robinson" here because she remarried in September 1870.

15. *BL* XXIV, no. 4 (October 10, 1868): 4.

16. A very large proportion, circa 42 percent, of those killed in the

Civil War were never identified. See Susan-Mary Grant, "Patriot Graves: American National Identity and the Civil War Dead," *American Nineteenth Century History* 5, no. 3 (Fall 2004): 95–96.

17. "Spiritualist Lyceums and Lectures," *BL* XXVII, no. 16 (July 2, 1870): 5; "Spiritualist Lyceums and Lectures," *BL* XXX, no. 1 (September 16, 1871): 3; "Spiritualist Lyceums and Lectures," *BL* XX, no. 5 (October 21, 1871): 5; "Spiritualist Lyceums and Lectures," *BL* XXX, no. 11 (November 25, 1871): 8.

18. See, for example, "Spiritualist Lyceums and Lectures," *BL* XXX, no. 26 (March 9, 1872): 8; "Spiritualist Lyceums and Lectures," *BL* XXXII, no. 1 (September 14, 1872): 5.

19. "Spiritualist Lyceums and Lectures," "Temple Hall," *BL* XXXII, no. 26 (March 29, 1873): 5; "Spiritualist Lyceums and Lectures," "Temple Hall," and "Eliot Hall," *BL* XXXII, no. 26 (April 5, 1873): 5.

20. Just after this Lyceum moved to John A. Andrew Hall from Eliot Hall. See *BL* XXXIII, no. 23 (September 6, 1873): 8.

21. The Temple Hall lyceum at this same time re-formed as the Children's Independent Lyceum Association, *BL* XXXIII, no. 23 (September 6, 1873): 8. This may have had something to do with her switch.

22. *BL* XXXIV, no. 12 (December 20, 1873): 8; see also "Children's Lyceums," *BL* XVII, no. 15 (July 1, 1865): 4. See Geoffrey K. Nelson, *Spiritualism and Society* (London: Routledge and Kegan Paul, 1969), 11.

23. See Conductor Hatch's address, Paine Hall, as recorded in *BL* LIII, no. 6 (April 28, 1883): 1.

24. *BL* XXV, no. 22 (August 29, 1874): 5.

25. "Spiritualist Lectures and Lyceums," *BL* XXXV, no. 24 (September 12, 1874): 5; "Spiritualist Lectures and Lyceums," *BL* XXXV, no. 21 (August 29, 1874): 5; *BL* XXXIV, no. 22, (February 28, 1874): 4.

26. See Bridget Bennett, *Transatlantic Spiritualism and Nineteenth Century American Literature* (New York: Palgrave Macmillan, 2007), 5–6.

27. "Twenty-Sixth Anniversary [of Modern Spiritualism] . . . at New Fraternity and the Parker Memorial," *BL* XXXV, no. 2 (April 11, 1874): 1; "Spiritualist Lectures and Lyceums," *BL* XXXV, no. 17 (July 25, 1874): 4; "Silver Lake Camp Meeting," *BL* XXXV, no. 18 (August 1, 1874): 4.

28. *BL* XXXV, no. 26 (September 26, 1874): 8; "Freeloveism," *Religio-Philosophical Journal* XVII, no. 4 (October 10, 1874): 6. Victoria Woodhull's dramatic impact upon the politics of sexuality are explored by Molly McGarry, "Spectral Sexualities: Nineteenth Century Spiritualism, Moral Panics, and the Making of U.S. Obscenity Laws," *Journal of Women's History* 12, no. 2 (Summer 2000): 8–29. Woodhull's radical interventions helped galvanize Anthony Comstock to draw up his postal bill—the Comstock Act, passed in 1873. See ibid., 9–10. Woodhull was part of a larger, controversial movement in radical spiritualist circles advocating "Free Loveism," one opposed by others within spiritualism. For a contemporary account of all this, see Emma Hardinge Britten, *Nineteenth Century Miracles; or, Spirits and Their Work in Every Country of the Earth* (New York: William Britten), 427–29. See also Joan D. Hedrick, *Harriet Beecher Stowe: A Life* (New York: Oxford University Press, 1994), 368–77.

29. *BL* XXXV, no. 26 (September 26, 1874): 8.

30. *BL* XXI, no. 26 (September 14, 1867): 5.

31. See *Spiritual Scientist* II, no. 5 (April 8, 1875): 58; II, no. 14 (June 10, 1875): 166; and III, no. 3 (September 23, 1875): 34.

32. *BL* XXXVIII, no. 26 (March 25, 1876): 4; "The Twenty-Eighth Anniversary of the Advent of Modern Spiritualism; Commemorative Exercises at Paine Hall, Boston; . . . The 31st March, 1876," *BL* XXXIX, no. 1 (April 8, 1876): 8.

33. "Gathering at Highland Lake Grove," *BL* XXXIX, no. 26 (September 23, 1876): 3.

34. "Spiritual Meetings in Boston . . . Amory Hall Meetings," *BL* XLV, no. 5 (April 26, 1879): 5; "Spiritual Meetings in Boston . . . Amory Hall Meetings," *BL* XLV, no. 8 (May 17, 1879): 5; *BL* XLV, no. 9 (May 24, 1879): 5; *BL* XLVI, no. 14 (December 27, 1879): 8. *A Love of a Bonnet* can be described as a ten-page play satirizing vanity written for amateur productions. Perhaps this is given away by the fact it features only female characters. See George M. Baker, *A Love of a Bonnet: A Farce in One Act for Female Characters Only* (Boston: George M. Baker, 1872). Somewhat better known is H. Elliott McBride's Courtship under Difficulties, also a one-act play, made into a silent film in 1898 by James Williamson. See H. Elliott McBride, *Courtship under Difficulties, Oliver Optic's Magazine*, 3, no. 238 (May 1873): 343–52.

35. James B. Hatch b. circa 1851 and "known wherever Spiritualism is heard" (Mary T. Longley, *Teachings and Illustrations as They Emanate from the Spirit World* [Chicago: The Progressive Thinker Publishing House, 1908], 5) was a clerk and gas fitter in his weekday occupations. This can remind us how spiritualism was remarkably cosmopolitan in its progressive makeup. Our thanks to Rhonda McClure and the New England Historic Genealogical Society for this and other information.

36. See *BL* XLVI, no. 4 (October 18, 1879): 5.

37. See *BL* XLV, no. 12 (June 14, 1879): 5; *BL* XLV, no. 25 (September 13, 1879): 5; *BL* XLVI, no. 4 (October 18, 1879): 5; *BL* XLVI, no. 26 (March 20, 1880): 1; *BL* XLVII, no. 1 (March 27, 1880): 1; *BL* XLVII, no. 2 (April 3, 1880): 1; *BL* XXVII, no. 3 (April 10, 1880): 8; *BL* XLVII, no. 4 (April 17, 1880): 2, quoting the words of "Mrs. Shelhamer."

38. "The Thirty Third Anniversary in Boston," *BL* XLIX, no. 1

(March 26, 1881): 5; "The Spiritual Easter," *BL* XLIX, no. 3 (April 9, 1881): 1; "The Thirty Third Anniversary," ibid., 4; "Children's Progressive Lyceum No. 1," ibid., 8; "The Spiritual Easter," ibid., 1.

39. "PAINE HALL," *BL* XLIX, no. 8 (May 14, 1881): 5 (our italics).

40. *BL* XLIX, no. 4 (June 11, 1881): 8; ibid., 12; "NEW ERA HALL . . . Shawmut Spiritual Lyceum," *BL* XLIX, no. 22 (August 20, 1881): 5.

41. Mrs. Carlisle Ireland, quoted in *BL* XLVII, no. 7 (October 30, 1880): 8. Moore argues that mediums were "extremely reluctant to accept personal responsibility . . . the spirits . . . controlled . . . [and] forced their wills into compliance." R. Lawrence Moore, "The Spiritualist Medium: A Study of Female Professionalism in Victorian America," *American Quarterly* 27 (1975): 203.

42. *BL* L, no. 16 (January 7, 1882): 12 *BL* LI, no. 4 (April 15, 1882): 7; *BL* LII, no. 6 (October 18, 1882): 7; LII, no. 8 (November 11, 1882): 7; *BL* LII, no. 12 (December 16, 1882): 5; *BL* LII, no. 14 (December 23, 1882): 5.

43. *BL* LI, no. 26 (September 26, 1882): 7. Such evidence of disharmony within the lyceum movement virtually never emerged in the *Banner*, so its appearance here suggests a considerable rift. In this respect it is surprising that Maud E. Lord now emerges as a very prominent player in the Shawmut, while very soon her husband will become the secretary to the Progressive School set up by Wilson in February 1883.

44. *BL* L, no. 14 (December 24, 1881): 10; *BL* L, no. 15 (December 31, 1881): 10.

45. See *BL* LI, no. 7 (May 6, 1882): 12.

46. *BL* L, no. 16 (January 7, 1882): 12. Moore observes that one sign of a medium's receptivity was taken to be "a light complexion" (Moore, "Spiritualist Medium," 215).

47. *BL* LII, no. 21 (February 10, 1883): 5. Possibly, a reception that Wilson held at her home in January 1883 had been intended to lay down preparation for the establishment of her school; if so, the *Banner* made no mention of it in its report of the occasion. See *BL* LII, no. 18 (January 20, 1883): 5.

48. *BL* LII, no. 26 (March 17, 1883): 5.

49. *BL* LII, no. 22 (February 17, 1883): 5; *BL* LII, no. 23 (February 24, 1883): 5; *BL* LII, no. 24 (March 3, 1883): 5; *BL* LII, no. 25 (March 10, 1883): 8; *BL* LII, no. 26 (March 17, 1883): 8; *BL* LIII, no. 1 (March 24, 1883): 8.

50. *BL* LIII, no. 2 (March 31, 1883): 8; *BL* LIV, no. 8 (November 10, 1883): 8. Lord was the husband of Maud E. Lord, who had in late 1882 been heavily involved with the Shawmut. A splintering from the Shawmut seems to have occurred.

51. *BL* LIII, no. 1 (March 24, 1883): 8.

52. *BL* LIV, no. 4 (October 13, 1883): 5; *BL* LIV, no. 8 (November 10, 1883): 8. The last dedicated notice about the Progressive School appeared in January 1884—a notice signed only by the initial "G." See *BL* LIV, no. 16 (January 5, 1884): 8. It is never made explicitly clear at any time what Wilson's position in the school was. J. C. Street seems to have emerged very quickly into prominence in the spiritualist lyceum movement, following a visit to the *Banner* offices, reported in *BL* LI, no. 2 (June 3, 1882): 7, which converted him to the cause.

53. *BL* LV, no. 4 (April 12, 1884): 8.

54. Apart from the text of *Our Nig*, and reports in the *Banner* by others reporting her words, the only other writing by Wilson (excluding the wording of her various advertisements) seems to be her letter in the *Banner* of October 10, 1868, reporting upon her positive experience at the Cape Cod camp meeting at which she spoke (4).

55. *BL* LIII, no. 8 (May 12, 1883): 8.

56. See "Children's Progressive Lyceum No. 1," *BL* 73, no. 4 (April 1, 1893): 8. See also "Children's Progressive Lyceum No. 1," *BL* 76, no. 15 (December 8, 1894): 8, which names a new series of "lesson sheets" used by the "old mother" lyceum, "The Lyceum Messenger." The Children's Progressive Lyceum No. 1 did, however, publish "books" to bolster its activities. See *BL* LI, no. 15 (December 30, 1882): 5, which mentions a title, too: the "Lyceum Instructor."

57. In this respect, it should be noted that one of the visits made by the Children's Progressive Lyceum No. 2 was to "the Soldier's Home, in Chelsea," in November 1882, where the children mounted a display of marching. See *BL* LII, no. 9 (November 18, 1882): 7.

58. "THE PROGRESSIVE SCHOOL," *BL* LIV, no. 18 (January 19, 1884): 5.

59. "Public Reception to Ed. S. Wheeler," *BL* LIV, no. 9 (November 17, 1883): 8.

60. One of the meetings of the association, for example, was held in Folsom's home. See *BL* LIII, no. 3 (April 7, 1883): 8.

61. *BL* LIV, no. 19 (January 26, 1884): 5.

62. "LYCEUM UNION," *BL* LV, no. 2 (March 29, 1884): 5.

63. By 1882, for example, the Shawmut Lyceum was beset by money problems. See *BL* LII, no. 4 (October 14, 1882): 6. Interestingly, however, the Children's Progressive Lyceum No. 1 does seem eventually to have embraced using medium contacts with the children. See, for example, Children's Progressive Lyceum No. 1, *BL* 76, no. 16 (December 5, 1894): 8.

64. By May 1886 the Children's Progressive Lyceum No. 1 was also expressing concern about its financial situation. See "Children's Progressive Lyceum No. 1," *BL* LIX, no. 9 (May 15, 1886): 8.

65. "Movements of Platform Lecturers," *BL* LXXXIII, no. 12 (May 21, 1898): 8. Looking at the *Banner*'s listings is also a way of establishing where Wilson lived. For example, from its free listings of "Platform Lecturers" in the 1860s we know she relocated from (apparently) a temporary location, "for the present" in East Cambridge in 1867 to "70 Tremont street" in Boston that same year, thence to West Garland, Maine (in October 1868), where she stayed while on speaking engagements in Maine, then back to 70 Tremont Street, then (in late 1868 or early 1869) to 27 Carver Street, and from there to 36 Carver Street (in the spring of 1869), then in April 1877 to the Hotel Kirkland, Kirkland Street, thence to Village Street. It is not quite clear when this move occurs. The *Banner* is still listing her as living in the Hotel Kirkland as late as January 7, 1882. The *Boston City Directory*, however, records her as living at Village Street as early as 1880. Finally she moved to Pelham Street in the 1890s (the *Boston City Directory*'s first mention of this address is 1897) until a short time before her death, when she moved to Quincy, Massachusetts, to the house of the Cobb family (perhaps to work as a nurse or as a family friend), where she was to die on June 28, 1900. See Wilson, *Our Nig*, ed. Foreman and Pitts, 2009, xiii–xiv. See also the chronology in this edition.

66. "Movements of Platform Lecturers," *BL* LXXX, no. 12 (November 21, 1896): 5.

67. "Boston Mediums," *BL* XXIII, no. 17 (July 11, 1868): 5 (our emphasis); *BL* XXV, no. 11 (May 29, 1869): 7.

68. "Test Mediums," *BL* XXVII, no. 1 (March 12, 1870): 4; "Spiritualist Lyceums and Lectures," *BL* XXVII, no. 26 (September 10, 1870): 5.

69. "NEW ERA HALL . . . THE SHAWMUT SEWING CIRCLE," *BL* L, no. 14 (December 24, 1881): 12; (our italics).

70. "Movements of Platform Lecturers," *BL* LXXXIII, no. 12 (May 21, 1898): 8.

71. *BL* LXVI, no. 3 (September 21, 1889): 8. See Mary Farrell Bednarowski, "Outside the Mainstream: Women's Religion and Women Religious Leaders in Nineteenth–Century America." *Journal of the American Academy of Religion* 48, no. 2 (June 1980): 213. One way of thinking about spiritualism is to note an inherent tension within it, with one more conservative side, as it were, wrapped in nostalgic sentimentalism, looking to recover past relationships (to pine for loss), while the other more progressive side (remember the way that spiritualist lyceums are routinely entitled "progressive lyceums") looking to embrace revision, change, and reform (to desire union). Perhaps we can do no more than quote from an advocate of the progressive lyceums writing in 1867:

> The very name of the *Progressive* Lyceum . . . strikes with its teaching directly at the roots of sectarian bodies, and carries with it the elements of swift and sure destruction to such institutions.
>
> Thus it becomes an engine of terrible power when brought to bear upon the ramparts of the old theology.

(C. A. E., "An Appeal in Favor of Establishing Children's Lyceums," *BL* XXI, no. 10 (May 25, 1867): 3.

72. *BL* XIX (June 9, 1866): 4; *BL* XLIV, no. 20 (February 8, 1879): 4. Recent studies have consistently emphasized, just as we would wish to do, the significance and in many respects the radical liberalism of the spiritualist movement, but this should not mean that, as was the case for its nineteenth-century contemporaries, doubts cannot be raised. See, for example, the *Banner*'s column "Discussing Spiritualism," attacking *The Atlantic Monthly*

for its "one-sided, prejudiced and inconsequential arguments" seeking to debunk spiritualism. Despite such "ridicule," the *Banner* proclaims, "the development went forward" (*BL* XVII, no. 12 [June 10, 1865]: 4). The issue was so hotly debated that Emma Hardinge Britten needed to spend pages of her review of spiritualism in America addressing this issue. See Emma Hardinge Britten, *Nineteenth Century Miracles; or, Spirits and Their Works in Every Country on Earth* (New York: William Britten, 1884): 425–30.

73. *BL* XXVI, no. 12 (December 4, 1869): 4; Moore, "Spiritual Medium," 219; Nelson, *Spiritualism and Society*, 3–9. The sisters' confession was later recanted.

74. *BL* XIX, no. 13 (July 16, 1866): 5; *BL* XVII, no. 25 (September 9, 1865): 7; *BL* XIX, no. 15 (July 21, 1866): 5; *BL* XXVIII, no. 15 (December 31, 1870): 8. See also, for example, *BL* XVII, no. 16 (July 8, 1865): 5, "Dr. Harrison's Peristaltic Lozenges . . . Piles, Falling of the Rectum . . . Palpitations, also Headaches, Dizziness, Pain in the Back, Yellowness of the Skin and Eyes . . . Liver Complaints, Loss of Appetite, . . . and all Irregularities."

75. *BL* XVIII, no. 26 (February 3, 1866): 7.

76. "Who Wants a Good Head of Hair? / Mrs. Wilson's / Hair Regenerator," *Farmer's Cabinet* (January 15, 1859): 4. See also Wilson, *Our Nig*, ed. Foreman and Pitts, 2009, 85.

77. *BL* XXVIII, no. 8 (November 12, 1870): 2–3.

78. See Bennett, *Transatlantic Spiritualism*, 18 et seq.

79. The term "test" in the oft-repeated phrase "test medium" is a slippery one. It seems above all to refer to mediums who were prepared to allow the ways they claimed they enabled manifestations to appear to be tested by observers to ensure no trickery. But, at a less demanding level, it seems also to refer to the way that some mediums put to the test the existence of an accompa-

nying spiritual world that manifested itself, and through their powers discovered it to be real, whether or not others were independently testing this at the same time. Such mediums thereby "attested" to the spiritual world. Wilson's testing out her father's words moves along the boundary between these two types.

80. "THE PROGRESSIVE SCHOOL," *BL* LIV, no. 18 (January 19, 1884): 5; *BL* XLVIII, no. 23 (February 26, 1881): 5; "Berkeley Hall Meetings," *BL* LVIII, no. 12 (June 6, 1885): 5.

81. "Onset Grove," *BL* 75, no. 2: (August 11, 1894): 2. In December 1893 the *Banner* reports how more than one hundred persons attended an "Indian Peace Council" at Hollis Hall, "most of them mediums through whom the Indians manifested" ("Hollis Hall," *BL* 74, no. 13 (December 2, 1893): 8.

82. On the other hand, if we do buy into part of her Haverhill story, that which says she investigated her Milford family past, then this might provide a reason why she at some time changes her maiden name from Adams to Green. This would mean that her account in *Our Nig* is more likely to be a fiction, however.

83. "Who Wants a Good Head of Hair? / Mrs. Wilson's / Hair Regenerator," *Farmer's Cabinet* (January 15, 1859), 4.

84. *BL* XXV, no. 11 (May 26, 1869): 7.

85. See Ellis, *Harriet Wilson's "Our Nig,"* 25.

86. Foreman and Pitts propose this business period as stretching from 1855 to the early 1860s. See Wilson, *Our Nig,* ed. Foreman and Pitts, 2009, xxxiii, xliii, lii–liii, 85; and P. Gabrielle Foreman and Kathy Flynn, "Mrs. H. E. Wilson, Mogul?" *Boston Globe,* February 15, 2009. http://www.boston.com/bostonglobe/ (accessed 8 June 2010). See also "Use Mrs. Wilson's Hair Regenerator and Hair Dressing," *Methodist Quarterly Review* 42, ed. D. D. Whedon (New York: Carlton and Porter, 1860), 714.

87. P. Gabrielle Foreman claims that "tens of thousands" of bottles marked with Wilson's name were produced. See Wilson, *Our Nig*, ed. Foreman and Pitts, 2009, xxxiii.

88. Foreman and Pitts suggest Wilson suspended her business to care for her ailing son (2009: xliii), but it is not clear this was the case.

89. An alternative explanation is to note that a small but active group of spiritualists in Milford invited William Lloyd Garrison, who had swung over to a sympathy with spiritualism, to come and speak to them in September 1864. See "NOTICE OF MEETING . . . MILFORD," *BL* XV, no. 26 (September 17, 1864): 6. Possibly Wilson was attracted to this meeting by Garrison's name and experienced some form of epiphany while there. Equally it should be noted that there was a large and very active spiritualist group in Worcester, Massachusetts, where Wilson possibly went for a while upon quitting Milford. See, for example, *BL* XVI, no. 26 (March 18, 1865): 8.

APPENDIX 2:

Hattie E. Wilson in the *Banner of Light* and *Spiritual Scientist*

A list of references to Harriet E. Wilson, known as Hattie [E.] Wilson and Hattie [E.] Robinson, in the *Banner of Light: A Weekly Journal of Romance, Literature and General Intelligence* (retitled the *Banner of Light: An Exponent of the Spiritual Philosophy of the Nineteenth Century* in March 20, 1869, XXIV, no. 1: 1) and *Spiritual Scientist: A Weekly Journal Devoted to the Science, Philosophy and Teachings of Spiritualism*.

N.B. This list will not be exhaustive, since it has not proved possible to retrieve a complete print run of either the *Banner* or the *Spiritual Scientist*, and the microfilms consulted were slightly damaged. The majority of the references to Wilson are to be found in the *Banner;* consequently the references to this journal are not prefixed; references to the *Spiritual Scientist* are prefixed *SS*. We have found no earlier mention of Wilson in any spiritualist newspaper or journal that we have consulted than the ones that now follow.

1867: May 18. XXI/10: 8. "Spiritualist Meetings": "Mrs. H. E. Wilson, (colored)" is listed as one of the "speakers engaged" under the subheadings "Chelsea" for the dates "June 2, 9 and 16" and "Charlestown" for "May 19 and 26."

1867: May 25. XXI/11: 8. "Spiritualist Meetings": The Chelsea appointments are restated and under the subheading "Cambridge," "Mrs. Wilson" is listed as engaged for June 23 and 30.

1867: June 1. XXI/11: 5. "Meeting and Lyceums" column, entry for Chelsea: "Mrs H. E. Wilson speaks for us the first three Sundays in June and Mrs. C. Fannie Allyn the last two" and lists the dates: "Mrs. H. E. Wilson (colored), June 2, 9 and 16." Columns in subsequent weeks list these dates until Wilson has spoken in Chelsea on all three occasions.

1867: June 15. XXI/13: 3. A report entitled "Spiritualist Convention . . . Friday May 30th and 31st, 1867" describes Wilson as "the earnest and eloquent colored trance medium" and notes that "the President [of the Convention], on taking the Chair, called upon Mrs Wilson, the colored speaker, to occupy the platform . . . She improved the opportunity, or rather the intelligence controlling her, by delivering a fluent speech in favour of labor reform and the education of children in the doctrines of spiritualism."

1867: June 29. XXI/15: 8. The *Banner*'s regular column "Lecturers' Appointments and Addresses" lists for the first time the address of "Mrs. Hattie E. Wilson, (colored)" as "East Cambridge, Mass., for the present." Subsequent columns very regularly record her address in this "gratis" column, and from henceforth we only note this when a change of address occurs.

1867: August 3. XXI/20: 4. "Meeting and Lyceums" column announces that "Mrs. Hattie E. Wilson will lecture at Hartford, Conn., August 4th."

1867: September 14. XXI/26: 5. A report on the "Second Great Spiritualist Camp Meeting at Pierpont Grove, Melrose, August 29th, 30th, 31st and September 1st, 1867" noted the presence of "Miss Hattie E. Wilson, the colored medium" and observed that her "address excited thrilling interest, and was at once an eloquent appeal for the recognition of the capacities of her race, the sentiment and philosophy of progress, under the figure of a moving camp tenting each night 'a day's march nearer home.'"

1867: October 19. XXII/5: 8. "Lecturers' Appointments and Addresses": "Mrs. Hattie E. Wilson (colored) will lecture in Lynn, Mass., Oct. 20 and 27; in Hartford, Conn., Nov. 3 and 10, in Stoneham, Mass., Nov. 17 and 24; in Stoughton, Dec. 1. Would be pleased to make arrangements for the Winter." Subsequent issues of the *Banner* confirm these appointments until they are fulfilled.

1867: November 23. XXII/10: 8. "Lecturers' Appointments and Addresses": Adds Groveland, December 6 and 13, to Wilson's list of appointments.

1867: November 30. XXII/11: 8. "Lecturers' Appointments and Addresses" changes Wilson's address to "70 Tremont street, Boston," and, as an alteration, notes that Mrs. Hattie E. Wilson will lecture in Groveland, Mass., December 8 and 15; it also adds both Newport, December 22 and 29, and "East Boston, Dec. 22"—an erroneous date duplication.

1867: December 7. XXII/12: "Lecturers' Appointments and Addresses" still records that Mrs. Hattie E. Wilson will lecture on

December 22 in both Newport, N.H., and East Boston, in error. Groveland, Mass., December 8 and 15 confirmed.

1867: December 14. XXII/13: 8. "Lecturers' Appointments and Addresses" changes the date of Wilson's East Boston booking to February 2 and 9.

1868: January 11. XXII/17: 8. The *Banner*'s "Lecturers' Appointments and Addresses" adds an "East Wilton, N.H." appointment for Wilson on January 12 to the two East Boston bookings. Subsequent issues of the *Banner* confirm these appointments until they are fulfilled.

1868: February 1. XXII/20: "1, 2, 8. The State Agent's Report" on the "Third Annual Convention of the Massachusetts Spiritual Association, Held in the Mercantile Hall, Boston, Jan. 7th and 8th, 1868" notes that Hattie E. Wilson was elected onto the Massachusetts Spiritual Association's "Finance Committee to look after the monetary matters of the Convention" (1); Wilson also volunteers to lecture "gratuitously" for the Association (2). The *Banner*'s "Lecturers' Appointments and Addresses" column (8) adds appointments for Wilson to speak in Randolph, Mass., April 5 and May 3. Subsequent issues of the *Banner* confirm these appointments until they are fulfilled.

1868: February 8. XXII/21: 8. The "Lecturers' Appointments and Addresses" column adds appointments for Wilson to speak in Portsmouth, N.H., February 16 and 23.

1868: February 29. XXII/25: 8. "Lecturers' Appointments and Addresses" adds dates for Wilson in East Bridgewater, Mass.,

March 1; Randolph, April 5 and May 3; and changes the Portsmouth, N.H., dates to April 12, 19, and 26. Subsequent issues of the *Banner* confirm these appointments until they are fulfilled.

1868: March 14. XXII/26: 8. "Lecturers' Appointments and Addresses" adds a date for Wilson in Leominster, Mass., on March 22.

1868: May 30. XXIII/11: 2. The "State Agent's Report" notes that "Mrs. Wilson" attends an executive committee meeting of the Massachusetts Spiritual Association.

1868: July 11. XXIII/17: 3. Listed as "(colored) trance speaker" in "Lecturers' Appointments and Addresses." In the "Mediums in Boston" advertising column (5), Wilson has paid for a small advertisement to appear: "HATTIE E. WILSON, Lecturer and Unconscious Trance Physician, Rooms 70 Tremont street, Boston, Mass."

1868: August 8. XXIII/21: 5. An anonymous note under the heading: "MRS HATTIE WILSON" records: "We learn that our valued friend, Mrs. Hattie E. Wilson, the colored medium, will probably visit Maine and the West during the Summer. She has been constantly and successfully engaged the past year in the vicinity as a healing medium and trance speaker and now has a host of friends. We cordially commend her to the hospitality of the spiritual brotherhood everywhere."

1868: August 15. XXIII/22: 4. An article, "Spiritual Camp Meeting at Cape Cod," records that Wilson spoke three times at the camp. First she addressed the theme "Who and what is God, and in

whom and how are His powers and goodness most manifest?"
Her speech is described as "spirited and contain[ing] many
good points" and as being delivered "through" her, as a trance
medium. The second, addressed to an audience of "twenty-five
hundred," addressed the "practical uses of spiritualism," while the
last, a "short and pithy" speech took as its subject "the general theme of spiritualism, its teachings and lessons, and especially . . . the power of love to conquer and subdue all the evil
passions of the world." Among those present was C. Fannie
Allyn, who also spoke.

1868: September 5. XXIII/25: 5. The editor notes that "several letters are in our office, addressed to Mrs. Hattie E. Wilson, which
are subject to her order."

1868: October 10. XXIV/4: 4. "Mrs. Hattie Wilson, writing from
Garland, Maine . . . says: 'I have been a labourer in the spiritual
ranks for seven years, and if their platform is known to me, it
is no bond, no sect, no creed, no dogma and no caste. Never
have I seen it so practically illustrated, either in public or private, as at the Cape Cod Meeting. May the Gods of Knowledge
and Wisdom protect that spirit gained until another year, when
the principles that inspired us may have become eighteen carats
more refined, spiritually.'"

1868: October 17. XXIV/5: 3. "Lecturers' Appointments and
Addresses": Wilson is listed as located in Maine: "Mrs. Hattie E.
Wilson, W. Garland, Maine."

1868: November 7. XXIV/8: 3. Listed as booked to speak in Marlboro', Mass., November 22 and Putnam, Conn., "during December."

1868: December 5. XXIV/12: 4. The *Banner* noted: "Marlboro', Mass. Mrs. Hattie E. Wilson, the colored trance speaker, has recently lectured in Marlboro' to the very general satisfaction of her audience, we are informed by a correspondent. She gave utterance to many great truths of Spiritualism in a manner that reached the comprehension at once. Our correspondent says her lecture was superior to the efforts of the reverend-divines in that place, and that people are anxious to have her visit them again."

1868: December 12. XXIV/13: 3. Listed as relocated in Boston (and therefore no longer in Maine): "Mrs. Hattie E. Wilson, 70 Tremont street, Boston."

1869: January 2. XXIV/16: 3. Listed as booked to speak in Marblehead, Mass., January 10 and 17. Wilson pays for another advertisement, in semi-display format: "**MRS. HATTIE E. WILSON** / Trance Physician and Healing Medium No. 70 Tremont street, Boston. Office Hours from 9 A.M. to 3 P.M. After office hours will visit patients in their own homes, if desired" (7).

1869: January 23. XXIV/19: 5. Advertisement appears announcing "MRS. HATTIE E. WILSON, / TRANCE PHYSICIAN / Has returned to this city, and will be happy to meet her friends in her rooms, No. 27 Carver street, four doors from Boylston street, Boston." This advertisement also appears the following week.

1869: February 6. XXIV/21: 3. The *Banner* erroneously lists Wilson as still living at 70 Tremont Street—an error repeated the following week.

1869: February 13. XXIV/22: 3, 4. Despite listing her address incorrectly on page 3, the *Banner* also carries the correct address in its "Lecturers' Appointments" column: "H. E. Wilson will speak in East Boston, Feb. 4th; in Marblehead, the 21st and 28th; in Putnam, Conn. through the month of April. Letters directed to No. 27 Carver street, Boston" (4). This address and the information about her appointments, as before, are regularly repeated until the listing needs to change.

1869: March 6. XXIV/25: 4. In its "Movements of Lecturers and Mediums" column, the *Banner* notes: "Mrs. Hattie E. Wilson will speak for the Boston Christian Spiritualists, March 7th and 14th."

1869: May 29. XXV/11: 7. A further advertisement is placed by Wilson: "HATTIE E. WILSON, Trance Physician, has taken rooms at *27 Carver street*. Chronic disease treated with great success. Herb packs and manipulations included in the mode of treatment." This advertisement appeared for several weeks, up to and including June 19 (XXV/13: 7).

1869: July 3. XXV/16: 3. Address listing notes change of address to 36 Carver Street.

1869: July 10. XXV/17: 7. Advertisement appears: "HATTIE E. WILSON, Trance Physician, No. 36 Carver street, Boston," to publicize the address change. This advertisement continues to appear up to and including August 28, 1860 (LXV/24: 7).

1869: August 14. XXV/22: 3. Listed as booked to speak in "Willimantic, Conn., Aug. 15, in Salem, Mass., Aug. 22, in Marblehead through the month of January."

1870: July 2. XXVII/16: 5. In the column "Spiritualist Lyceums and Lectures," Wilson is noted as addressing the Boston Mercantile Hall Lyceum. This seems to be the first occasion that the *Banner* notes involvement by Wilson in the spiritualist lyceum movement, rather than on the spiritualist lecture circuit. Her name in this reference is wrongly printed as Hattie A. Wilson.

1870: November 12. XXVIII/8: 2–3. A report on the "Massachusetts Spiritual Convention at Haverhill" makes extended references to Wilson's involvements. She participated three times. On the first occasion "Mrs. Hattie E. Wilson Robinson" was merely "called upon, and, coming upon the platform, was entranced and spoke briefly." The remaining two contributions were more fully reported: "*Mrs. Hattie E. (Wilson) Robinson, formerly Hattie Wilson,* gave a narrative of her development as a medium, by which she had been brought into acquaintance with her father in spirit-life, who was her almost constant companion. He had told her, in detail, the circumstances of her early life, and upon inquiry of the persons named by him, still living . . . found them correct in every particular. Although opposing to becoming a medium at first, and disbelieving in the purported origin of the power that controlled her, yet she was finally convinced by seeing an old school-mate, who was dead several years, standing by her bedside, who conversed with her as naturally as those who appear about her in the material world. Doubting, to her is impossible, and has been for many years; and when your spiritual sensibilities are opened, you will know the spirit-world is not afar off, in space, but here in our midst; and that spirits are not bodiless beings, but with us in our homes. Spiritualism has aroused me from my indifference and given me an interest in life—to be something and do something for others. Her entire story was deeply affecting, and won implicit confidence in its truth, by the simple natural manner in which all its details were presented" (2–3). Later on in the event, "Mrs. Hattie Robinson [Wilson] followed in deeply interesting remarks, based upon her experience as a medium, affirming the prominence of the relations between parents and children, although death might apparently divide them. Invisible to you, fathers and mothers, are the children, given to you to educate, and your influence affects them spiritually, after they have gone out of your sight, as truly as though they had remained upon the earth. You may be angels to them as well as they to you. If your spiritualist eyes could be opened, as mine frequently are, you would *know* this to be true. In our homes and in our midst are our children, our parents, our friends, and we mutually act upon each other" (3).

1871: September 23. XXX/1: 3. The *Banner*'s "Spiritualist Lyceums and Lectures" column notes that Hattie Wilson "occupied the platform" to the "general acceptance of those attending" the Boylston Street Association's meeting.

1871: November 18. XXX/10: 8. The column "Spiritualist Lectures and Lyceums" notes, "The meetings at Temple Hall still continue with unabated interest. Mrs. Hattie Robinson [i.e., Wilson Robinson] gives general satisfaction." The wording of this probably alludes to the way Wilson Robinson has recently replaced the former Boylston Street Association of Spiritualists, Temple Hall resident medium, Mrs. Bowditch (see October 21, 1871, XXX/5: 3).

1872: March 9. XXX/26: 5. The "Spiritualist Lyceums and Lectures" column notes a large audience at Temple Hall "greeted" Mrs. Hattie Robinson on "Sunday, February 18th."

1872: September 14. XXXI/1: 5. The "Spiritualist Lyceums and Lectures" column notes two forthcoming contributions by Wilson Robinson to the Boylston Street Association of Spiritualists, Temple Hall gathering.

1873: March 29. XXXII/26: 5. The "Spiritualist Lyceums and Lectures" column notes that Wilson is one of several speakers at Temple Hall.

1873: April 19. XXXIII/3: 5. Hattie Wilson is named as having been elected as one of the "Leaders" of one of the groups of students forming part of the Temple Hall Independent Children's Progressive Lyceum.

1873: April 19. XXXIII/3: 5. The *Banner* notes that Mrs. Hattie Robinson is one of the speakers at the wedding of the conductor of the children's lyceum at Boston's Eliot Hall.

1873: April 26. XXXIII/4: 5. "Spiritualist Lectures and Lyceums" notes that Hattie Wilson is one of those "Speaking and Reading" at a meeting of the Temple Hall Children's Lyceum.

1873: September 6. XXXIII/23: 8. A report on a highly controversial spiritualist camp meeting, begun in August 23, 1873, issue (XXXIII/21: 8), continues. The earlier report explains that this camp meeting, the "Fourth Annual Spiritualist Camp Meeting . . . 16,000 People Assembled, Silver Lake, Plympton," on August 16, witnessed Victoria Woodhull speaking out against marriage as "sexual slavery," only to be opposed by the prominent Spiritualist, Lizzie Doten. This September 6 continuation of the report details how Harriet Wilson Robinson (named as Hattie C. Robinson in error) join Woodhull and others on the stage to speak during the evening "Concluding Session."

1873: September 13. XXXIII/24: 5. Wilson is elected as a "Supplementary Leader" at a meeting of the organizers of the Children's Progressive Lyceum and Library Association No. 1, on September 2, 1873 (just after this lyceum moved to John A. Andrew Hall from Eliot Hall).

1873: October 11. XXXIV/2: 5. At a wedding at John Andrew Hall, Hattie [Wilson] Robinson is named as one of the wedding guests "contributing a good offering." This is the last time the name "Robinson" is used to refer to Wilson.

1874: February 28. XXXIV/22: 4. The *Banner* notes that "Mrs. Hattie E. Wilson, the well-known trance lecturer, gave an anniversary in honour of her spirit father, on the evening of Friday Feb. 13th, which was attended by a goodly number of friends. The exercises were preluded by a supper at her residence, 46 Carver street, Boston, after which the company adjourned to John Andrew Hall, where remarks appropriate to the hour were offered by Dr. H. B. Storer, George A. Bacon and Dr. A. H. Richardson, the hostess (entranced), making due reply. . . . The occasion was pleasant to the participants, and one long to be remembered."

1874: March 21. XXXIV/25: 5. The "Spiritualist Lectures and Lyceums" column notes that at John A. Andrews Hall "on Sunday morning, March 15th, the session of the Children's Progressive Lyceum No. 1 was well attended. . . . Mrs. Hattie Wilson participated in the exercises by reading."

1874: April 11. XXXV/2: 1. The *Banner* covers the "Twenty-Sixth Anniversary Celebration of the Advent Day of Modern Spiritualism: Exercises at John A. Andrew Hall, Boston . . . and . . . at New Fraternity Hall and the Parker Memorial," which included not only speeches by prominent Boston spiritualists, including Miss Lizzie Doten, I. P. Greenleaf, and Dr. H. B. Storer, but also, on "Children's Day" (the second day), "speeches . . . to the children by Dr. A. H. Richardson, Hattie E. Wilson and Mrs. Tabor."

1874: June 27. XXXV/13: 5. The "Spiritualist Lectures and Lyceums" column reports that "the session of Children's Lyceum No. 1 at [John A. Andrew Hall] on the morning of Sunday 21st was one of extraordinary interest and pleasure . . . readings were offered [among others] by Mrs. Hattie Wilson.

1874: June 27. XXXV/13: 5. The *Banner* reports, under the heading "A Pleasant Reunion," that "a number of the friends of Hattie Wilson, the Spiritualist Medium and lecturer, assembled at John A. Andrew Hall on Friday evening, June 12th, to join in friendly converse, listen to speeches, etc. . . . [and] remarks by Drs. H. B. Storer and A. H. Richardson, the hostess of the evening, who spoke both normally and in trance condition, and others."

1874: June 27. XXXV, no. 13: 5. The *Banner* reports on both a reading given by Wilson at the June 21 meeting of the Children's Progressive Lyceum No. 1 and a gathering in Wilson's honor at the John A. Andrew Hall on June 21, 1874.

1874: July 25. XXXV/17: 4. The "Spiritualist Lectures and Lyceums" column notes that Wilson delivered "an excellent lec-

ture ... given by the influences through her organism" at
Nassau Hall, July 19, upon the subject "Now and Then."

1874: August 1. XXXV/18: 4. The *Banner* reports ("Silver Lake Camp
Meeting") that Wilson made a "vigorous and entertaining"
contribution "under direct spirit control" at a camp meeting
sponsored by the Children's Progressive Lyceum No. 1. In this
speech she "analyzed the mental production of the three doc-
tors who had just spoken [Drs. H. B. Storer, A. H. Richardson,
and H. F. Gardenr] and very happily recognised the fitness of
the special work assigned to them as conductors of this people's
meeting."

1874: September 5. XXXV/23: 5. The "Spiritualist Lectures and
Lyceums" column, noting that the Children's Progressive
Lyceum No. 1 had increased its attendance, also observed that
"Hattie Wilson ... made some sensible remarks."

1874: September 10. *SS* I/1: 10. At a dedication of Rochester Hall,
the new home of the "Children's Progressive Lyceum No. 1 ...
Dr. Storer was the first speaker, and was followed by Dr. Currier,
Mrs. Hattie Wilson, John Wetherbee and others. ... Mrs. Hattie
Wilson was controlled to speak by one who, in years long ago in
the spirit-world, had on one occasion with others vowed, by the
strongest of vows, to devote years of their existence there to the
education of children in this sphere to a proper knowledge of
the laws and conditions which governed them. They had since
been working with others of our great teachers in the lyceums,
and tonight they were present at the dedication of the hall to
spiritualism. It might be said re-dedication, for it had been dedicated by years of free thought, until the very floors, the very

walls, gave out the influences which should last until there was not one stone left on another. They rejoiced that, in spite of theology, and in spite of all the denunciation, the Lyceum lived, and was doing good in educating the little ones—not cramming them with that which would check their growth intellectually and spiritually, but teaching them those laws which, when obeyed as they would be in times coming, would give a race strong [sic] morally, intellectually, physically, and spiritually, which would glorify the perfect image of that Infinite Creator."

1874: September 12. XXXV/24: 5, 8. The column "Spiritualist Lectures and Lyceums" notes that "Mrs. Hattie Wilson" was elected as the leader of the "Lake" group in the Lyceum No. 1 (5): At a "Dedication of Rochester Hall, Boston" ceremony, Wilson participated twice: by singing in a quartet (a rare mention of her performing other than as a trance medium or lyceum leader) and, then, "entranced, [with] the influences controlling adding the good wishes of the disembodied attendants in the dedicatory exercises" (8).

1874: September 24. SS I/3: 46. "Notes and Notices": "Children's Progressive Lyceum No. 1—William A. Williams, Corresponding Secretary, writes . . . [a] question by the Conductor [of the lyceum], 'How can we best promote the interest of the Lyceum?' [was] very ably answered by . . . Mrs. Hattie Wilson [among others], and eloquently by the assistant conductor, Mr. J. B. Hatch."

1874: September 26. XXXV/26: 8. At a meeting called by Victoria Woodhull, the radical spiritualist reformer and sexual liberationist—a "National Mass Meeting of Radicals, Socialists, Infidels, Materialists, Free Religionists and Free Thinkers," described by the *Banner* as a "mass meeting of radicals and reformers"—Wilson was to speak, offering "an address of great vigor and enthusiasm upon the conduct of Spiritualists to each other, founded upon personal experience."

1874: October 3. XXXVI/1: 5. "Rochester Hall": "Mrs. Hattie Wilson" was one of three speakers "ably" answering the question, "How can we best promote the interests of the Lyceum?"

1874: October 22. *SS* I/6: 6. "Children's Progressive Lyceum No. 1 . . . had the usual session . . . [including] Readings [by] Misses [*sic*] Hattie Wilson [and] Frank Wheeler."

1874: October 24. XXXVI/4: 5. "Rochester Hall": Lyceum session the Sunday before included a "reading" by "Mrs. Hattie Wilson."

1874: October 31. XXXVI/5: 5. "Rochester Hall": Lyceum session the Sunday before included a "reading" by "Mrs. Hattie Wilson."

1874: November 7. XXXVI/6: 5. "Spiritualist Lectures and Lyceums" column announces a "Grand Spiritualist Fair" and the formation of a "Soliciting Committee." The contact address is given as "Miss [*sic*] Hattie E. Wilson, 46 Carver st., Boston."

1874: November 26. *SS* I/11: 142. "Notes and Notices": "A PLEASANT CELEBRATION. . . . In response to an invitation, a number of gentlemen and ladies assembled in the spacious parlors, 4 Concord Square, to celebrate the ninth anniversary of the public mediumship of Mrs. Mary M. Hardy. . . . Among those present, and making short addresses were . . . Mrs. Hattie Wilson."

1874: December 12. XXXVI/12: 5. "Spiritualist Lectures and Lyceums" column confirms the "Grand Spiritualist Fair" at Rochester Hall and again names Hattie E. Wilson on the "Soliciting Committee."

1874: December 19. XXXVI/13: 8. "Spiritualist Lectures and Lyceums" column again confirms the "Grand Spiritualist Fair" and again names "Hattie E. Wilson."

1874: December 26. XXXVI/15: 8. "Mrs. Hattie Wilson" delivered a "reading" in the Children's Progressive Lyceum No. 1 the Sunday before.

1875: January 14. SS I/19: 226. "The Red Man's New Year": "An anniversary celebration, complimentary to the spirit guides of Mrs. Hattie Wilson, was given by the lady at Rochester Hall, Wednesday evening. J. B. Hatch presided, and introduced the speakers of the evening, among whom were John Wetherbee, Dr. Storer, Dr. Richardson, and also Messrs J. J. Morse and Robert Cooper of England. Mrs. Wilson also spoke, under control, for a few moments. At intervals there was introduced a varied programme of songs, declamations & c. the Alpha Glee Club, of Cambridge, Mr. Sullivan, Miss Edson taking part. After a distribution of presents from the large tree, the exercises closed with a supper and dance,—Carters Band furnishing music for a well arranged order. The conception of this novel and unique entertainment, and the successful manner in which it was carried out, reflect great credit on Mrs. Wilson, whose enterprise and generosity was the subject of commendation among those who were fortunate enough to participate in the enjoyment."

1875: January 30. XXXVI/18: 5. "Mrs. Hattie Wilson" delivered a "reading" in the Children's Progressive Lyceum No. 1 the Sunday before.

1875: February 6. XXXVI/19: 4. "Surprise Party at the Spiritualist's Home": The "friends of Mrs. N. J. Morse" who assembled at her residence included "Mrs. Hattie Wilson."

1875: February 20. XXXVI/21: 5. "Rochester Hall": Lyceum session the Sunday before included a "reading" by "Mrs. Hattie Wilson."

1875: April 3. XXXVII/1: 5. At a testimonial to Dr. John H. Currier, Hattie C. [*sic*] Wilson was among those making speeches of congratulation.

1875: April 8. *SS* II/5: 51. "Mrs. Maud E. Lord": "At the residences of Mrs. Maud E. Lord . . . a social gathering of her friends [occurred] to express their appreciation of her many pleasing qualities . . . Dr. H. B. Storer . . . Mrs. Hattie Wilson . . . and many others spoke during the evening."

1875: April 8. *SS* II/5: 58. "THE PROPOSED SPIRITUAL INSTITUTE. . . . A meeting was held at Rochester Hall, Sunday afternoon, on a call issued by some of the leading Spiritualists of Boston 'for the purpose of opening the way for establishing in this city a conservatory of spiritual philosophy.' . . . H. S. Williams as Chairman, E. Gerry Brown as secretary . . . Messrs S. P. Morse, M. Miller and Mrs. Hattie E. Wilson were appointed as a committee to retire and nominate. *Voted.* That the committee, when reported [by the committee to retire and nominate], be an Executive Board for temporary organization; and that they be instructed to draw up a plan of organization." Wilson was not elected to this executive board. The *Spiritual Scientist* followed this institute's attempts to establish a "Spiritual Temple" closely, until its apparent fractious collapse, accompanied by a welter of resignations, with "only $45 in the Treasury," as reported in September 1875 ("THE AMERICAN SPIRITUAL INSTITUTE," *SS* III, no. 3 [September 23, 1875]: 34).

1875: April 10. XXXVII/2: 4. At a meeting held in honor of Maud E. Lord, "Hattie Wilson" was among those delivering speeches.

1875: May 1. XXXVII/5: 4. At a "Testimonial to Sarah A. Byrnes," "appropriate words" were spoken by "Hattie Wilson," among others.

1875: May 8. XXXVII/6: 4. At a "Farewell Testimonial to Mr. and Mrs. Hardy," leaving for Europe, the speakers included "Hattie Wilson."

1875: May 15. XXXVII/7: 5. "Rochester Hall": "Mrs. Hattie Wilson named as one of those in attendance at the Children's Progressive Lyceum No. 1."

1875: May 29. XXXVII/9: 4. "Meetings at Rochester Hall": At a meeting of the Boston Spiritualists' Union aimed at establishing the "American Spiritual Institute," "Mrs. Hattie Wilson" was selected as its "Director—Educational Department." See *SS* April 8, 1875, above.

1875: June 12. XXXVII/11: 5. At a party at Rochester Hall, "to surprise Dr. Samuel Grover on his birthday, congratulatory remarks" were delivered by "Hattie Wilson," among others. At the Children's Progressive Lyceum No. 1 the Sunday before, a speech is delivered by "Hattie Wilson" at a Civil War memorial event.

1875: June 26. XXXVII/13: 5. "Rochester Hall": "Mrs. Hattie Wilson presents bouquets to the members of the school [lyceum] in commemoration of the anniversary of the birth of her child into spirit-life"; Wilson also makes "remarks" to the lyceum.

1875: September 25. XXXVII/26: 8. "Mrs. Hattie Wilson" is one of those "furnishing readings" at the Children's Progressive Lyceum No. 1 the Sunday before.

1875: November 13. XXXVIII/7: 5. "Rochester Hall": "Mrs. Hattie Wilson" delivered a "reading and [or] recitation" in the Children's Progressive Lyceum No. 1 the Sunday before.

1875: November 20. XXXVIII/8: 5. "Rochester Hall": "Hattie E. Wilson" elected "leader" of "Lake Group," Children's Progressive Lyceum No. 1.

1875: November 27. XXXVIII/9: 5. "Rochester Hall": "Mrs. Hattie Wilson" delivered a "reading and [or] recitation" in the Children's Progressive Lyceum No. 1 the Sunday before.

1875: December 4. XXXVIII/10: 4, 5. "Social Celebration": At the wedding anniversary celebration for Mr. and Mrs. C. C. Hayward, "Mrs. Hattie Wilson" is one of those delivering a speech. (4) Wilson appointed to collect money for the Christmas tree

and presents for Children's Progressive Lyceum No. 1 (5). Her
address is given as "46 Carver st."

1875: December 18. XXXVIII/12: 3. A further appeal, giving Wilson's name and address, is made for the Christmas tree and
presents fund for Children's Progressive Lyceum No. 1.

1876: January 1. XXXVIII/14: 8. "Rochester Hall": Julia M. Carpen-
ter, "Christmas Festival." This note records the success of this
Children's Progressive Lyceum No. 1 Christmas event, organized by "Mrs Hattie Wilson," and that Wilson "spoke a few
appropriate words, thanking the Soliciting Committee of which
she was Chairman, for their efficient labor, and also the people
who had so nobly responded to the call."

1876: March 25. XXXVIII/26: 4. "The residence of Hattie E. Wilson,
(trance lecturer) was the scene on the evening of Wednesday
March 15, of a large gathering of friends, who met to express
their good wishes at the attainment by their hostess of another
birthday in the form. Speeches by Dr. A. H. Richardson, Dr.
John H. Currier, J. B. Hatch and others, songs by Misses Cora
Hastings and Maria Adams, instrumental music by Miss Annie
Folsom, the reading of an original poem by Dr. Grover, social
conversation and the partaking of refreshments, comprised the
order of exercises."

1876: April 8. XXXIX/2: 8. "The Twenty-Eighth Anniversary of the
Advent of Modern Spiritualism; Commemorative Exercises
at Paine Hall, Boston. . . . The 31st March, 1876": This item
included a report of an address that Wilson delivered. "Dr.

Richardson next called upon Hattie Wilson to address the audience. The intelligence controlling her said it was the duty of the adherents of Spiritualism to endeavour so to live that on the passage of each year they might perceive with their spiritual senses that they had ascended another round in the ladder which led upward to the heavenly heights—that they occupied a position in advance of what they previously held; but it really seemed to the speaker that too many of the Spiritualists were halting just where they were twenty-eight years ago—they were 'halting on the old camp ground,' where they had established themselves when the knowledge of the possibility of spirit communion first reached them. The debris of the years passed were not removed from their souls, and how could such Spiritualists expect the angels to endeavour to make their way through to reach them, when it was a plain duty to clear the pathway and extend to them a pure fresh welcome? The spiritual world and those who dwelt therein were only of a finer order of materiality, and spiritual defilement met with in the minds of mortals was just as repulsive to the returning Spirit, as any marked degree of uncleanliness would be to the dweller in the mortal. The process of decease was but the gaining of a new tent in the camp ground of the Infinite, and the character of that tent and its location as to desirability or otherwise depended on the efforts made in this sphere of life to gain knowledge of higher things and to clothe it with deeds done for the good of humanity. The spirit controlling prophesied that great as had been the trials of the spiritual media in the past, there were still more serious ones in store for them and the cause they represented.

"Isaiah C. Ray of New Bedford referred in a highly complimentary manner to the work accomplished by the previous speaker [Wilson], and called attention to the fact that years ago it had been his privilege to introduce her to a Spiritualist audience at her first public lecture."

Ray had been a prominent Massachusetts abolitionist in the antebellum era, and had been in correspondence in 1843 with Asa Hutchinson of the Hutchinson Family Singers. He may have helped Wilson obtain her entrée into spiritualism by way of these connections.

1876: April 29. XXXIX/11: 5. At Rochester Hall "Hattie E. Wilson" is one of those giving an "address" at the funeral of Luther Stone.

1876: June 24. XXXIX/13: 4. At a picnic at Silver Lake Grove organized by the Children's Progressive Lyceum No. 1, "speeches" are made by Lizzie Doten, Dr. H. B. Storer, and Hattie Wilson.

1876: August 26. XXXIX/22: 4. In an advanced notice of a Children's Progressive Lyceum No. 1 meeting to be held at "Highland Lake," September 3, it is announced that "Mrs. Hattie Wilson will lecture."

1876: September 2. XXXIX/23: 5. Wilson's speaking engagement at Highland Lake Grove is confirmed: "Mr. Linton of England, Mrs. Hattie Wilson and others will furnish the speaking."

1876: September 9. XXXIX/24: 6. "Gathering at Highland Lake Grove": Wilson delivers a "trance address mainly upon freedom of thought, showing how this had been upheld or violated in the events of American history, since the landing of the pilgrim fathers."

1877: February 10. XL/21: 5. *"The Women's Amateur Dramatic Club"* announces a production of *The Spirit of Seventy-Six,* in which "Mrs. Hattie Wilson, the well-known medium, will appear in her fine impersonation of "Tom Carberry." *The Spirit of Seventy-Six* was a popular parlor farce at the time, first published in 1868 and probably written by Ariana Randolph Wormeley Curtis (though possibly with her husband, Daniel Sargent Curtis).

1877: February 17. XL/23: 5. *"The Women's Amateur Dramatic Club"* notes a production of " 'The Spirit of 76,' in which Mrs. Hattie Wilson, the well-known medium, appeared in her fine impersonation of 'Tom Carberry.' "

1877: April 14. XLI/3: 3. Gives the address of "MRS. HATTIE E. WILSON" as "Hotel Kirkland, Kirkland st, Boston, Mass."

1877: May 5. XLI/6: 5. "Rochester Hall": At a "Complimentary Testimonial tendered to Misses Lizzie J. Thompson and Florence Danforth," "recitations of the highest merit were delivered," one of these being by "Hattie Wilson."

1877: May 12. XLI/7: 5. "Rochester Hall": "The Lyceum Association will meet in the residence of Mrs. Hattie Wilson, Hotel Kirkland, (corner of Kirkland and Pleasant streets) at 7½ o'clock, in the evening of Friday May 11th."

1877: May 19. XLI/8: 5. "Rochester Hall—The Spiritualist Association connected with the Children's Progressive Lyceum will meet at the house of Mrs. Hattie Wilson, Hotel Kirkland . . . on Monday evening, May 21st, at 8 o'clock. It is earnestly hoped by the officers that every member will be present, as business of *importance* will come before the meeting."

1877: June 2. XLI/10: 4, 8. "A number of the friends of Mrs. Nellie Nelson—so we are informed—tendered her a testimonial at Rochester Hall, Boston, Friday evening, May 25th, in acknowledgement of her many years of mediumship. . . . Speeches, songs, recitations and readings, participated in by . . . Mrs. Hattie Wilson [among others] (4)." Another entry noted "the Children's Progressive Lyceum": reading by Mrs. Hattie Wilson (among others) (8).

1877: June 9. LXI/11: 4. *"Children's Lyceum"*: "[At a] Reception to Mr. Hatch . . . [t]he popular conductor of the Lyceum . . . [e]xcellent readings were given [by, among others,] Mrs. Hattie Wilson."

1877: June 16. XLI/12: 5. "Rochester Hall . . . Children's Progressive Lyceum No. 1": A reading is given by "Mrs. Hattie Wilson [among others]."

1877: September 1. XLI/23: 5. "Children's Progressive Lyceum No. 1": "The annual meeting of the Lyceum for choice of officers will be held at the house of Mrs. Wilson, Hotel Kirkland, on Tuesday evening next, Sept. 4th."

1877: October 20. XLII/4: 5. "Children's Progressive Lyceum No. 1": Wilson is appointed to a committee to draw up "an appropriate resolution" for the retirement of Mrs. Sarah Hartson "from the guardianship of the school."

1878: January 26. XLII/18: 5. "A Complimentary Testimonial to J. B. Hatch, Conductor of Children's Progressive Lyceum No. 1 of Boston took place in Paine Hall on Thursday evening, Jan. 17th," with "Mrs. Hattie E. Wilson" among those giving readings.

1878: March 2. XLII/23: 5. "Amory Hall": "At the opening of the Children's Progressive Lyceum, on Sunday A.M., Feb. 24th, an eloquent bouquet of flowers was presented to George A. Downes, the Assistant Conductor, by his friends, through Mrs. Hattie Wilson." Following this, "Mrs. Hattie Wilson" was among those delivering "select readings."

1878: March 23. XLII/26: 5. "On Friday evening, March 15th, Mrs. Hattie E. Wilson was the recipient of a complimentary benefit at Amory Hall . . . during the time occupied, an array of selections, musical and rhetorical, was brought out to the evident satisfaction of a fine audience . . . [with] readings [among others] by Mrs. H. E. Wilson."

1878: April 13. XLIII/6: 5. At a complimentary testimonial for Miss Suzanna Adams, formerly a well-known and hard-working member of the "Children's Progressive Lyceum of Boston . . . Mrs. Hattie E. Wilson" was among those giving readings.

1878: April 20. XLIII/4: 5. "AMORY HALL": "Remarks by Mrs. Hattie E. Wilson . . . contribute to add interest to the session of the Children's Progressive Lyceum."

1878: June 15. XLIII/12: 8. "Children's Progressive Lyceum No. 1": "Mrs. Hattie E. Wilson arranged . . . [a] dialogue, which was a very attractive feature in honor of the day [Memorial Day]. The groups were represented by delegates bearing in their hands bouquets of flowers; these representatives taking up their line of march to the platform, faced to the front, on reaching it, and after each had recited an appropriate verse, they countermarched, and as they passed a little mound erected on the stage bearing the inscription, 'In memory of our ascended officers and pupils,' they dropped upon it their offering of flowers. / At this point, while the band performed a selection, Miss. Lizzie J. Thompson was seen to enter the hall at the rear accompanied by two little misses arrayed in white as aids. Upon reaching the rostrum, Miss. T. recited a poem entitled 'Heaven.'"

1878: August 3. XLIII/19: 8. "Lake Walden Camp Meeting": "Following opening words by Dr. Currier and J. B. Hatch remarks [were made by] . . . Mrs. Hattie Wilson and others."

1878: August 17. XLIII/21: 1–2. "Closing Days at the Lake Walden Spiritualist Camp-Meeting": "Brief closing remarks were also made by Mrs. H. E. Wilson," among others.

1878: September 28. XLIV/1: 5. "Amory Hall," "Children's Progressive Lyceum No. 1": During the elections for officers, "Mrs. Wilson" is elected both to the "Entertainment Committee" and as a "Group Leader."

1878: October 5. XLIV/2: 5. "Amory Hall": "Mrs. Wilson" is named as one of those involved with the "Lyceum Sewing Circle."

1879: April 12. XLV/3: 5. "Spiritual Meetings in Boston . . . Armory Hall Meetings": The formation of a new lyceum, the "Chil-

dren's Progressive Lyceum No. 2 Charleston District, Boston,"
is announced at Armory Hall, where, during its first meeting,
"remarks" were made by Mrs. Hattie E. Wilson.

1879: April 26. XLV/5: 5. "Spiritual Meetings in Boston . . . Armory
Hall Meetings": The lyceum also announced the inauguration
of "a course of Saturday evening lectures and concerts under
the direction of Mrs. Hattie E. Wilson."

1879: May 3. XLV/6: 5. Details are provided of the Children's Progressive Lyceum No. 2 Charleston District, Boston's "organization," naming J. B. Hatch as "Conductor," C. F. Rand as secretary,
and, on the "Standing Committee," Mrs. Hattie Wilson.

1879: May 10. XLV/7: 5. The new "Children's Progressive Lyceum
No. 2 Charleston District, Boston" claims an attendance of "over
200 children" at its May Day celebration.

1879: May 24. XLV/9: 5. *"An Entertainment* given by the Ladies
Amateur Dramatic Class for the pecuniary benefit of Lyceum
No. 2 . . . took place at Armory Hall [Charleston] . . . Thursday
evening, May 15th, being carried out under direction of Mrs.
Hattie Wilson. The exercises consisted of two farces, 'Love of
a Bonnet' and 'Courtship under Difficulties,' characters were
sustained by [among others] Hattie E. Wilson."

1879: June 14. XLV/12: 5. "Armory Hall," "Children's Progressive Lyceum No. 2": "Decoration Sunday . . . Mr. J. B. Hatch,
president, made a few remarks appropriate to the occasion
and closed by introducing Mrs. Hattie E. Wilson, who offered

a feeling invocation" (5). Another entry, under the heading "Armory Hall," gave details of a letter of invitation from the Children's Progressive Lyceum No. 2 to the Children's Progressive Lyceum No. 1, "to invite you as guests, and extend to you the hand of love. . . . [L]et us show to the world that our actions can be in harmony with our words . . . [we invite] you to participate with us in our exercises on the occasion of Decoration Day, Sunday June 8th." The letter was signed by "Conductor F. Rand, Mrs. Hattie Wilson and Mrs. Josephine Stevens / Committee." The report then notes that this invitation was declined, but that the Children's Progressive Lyceum No. 1 wished the Children's Progressive Lyceum No. 2 "unbounded success" (5).

1879: September 13. XLV/25: 8. "Ivanhoe Hall [Charleston]," "Children's Progressive Lyceum No. 2": A move of the Lyceum No. 2 to Ivanhoe Hall in Charleston, Boston, occurs for the first meeting after the summer break. At this meeting, "Mrs. Hattie E. Wilson" offered "words of encouragement."

1879: October 11. XLVI/3: 5. "Ivanhoe Hall," "Children's Progressive Lyceum No. 2": "Mrs. H. E. Wilson" delivered a recitation, "Great Heart and Giant Despair," the previous Sunday. The recitation derived its title from John Bunyan's much reprinted *The Pilgrim's Progress* (London: Nathaniel Ponder, 1678).

1879: October 18. XLVI/4: 5. "Ivanhoe Hall," "Children's Progressive Lyceum No. 2": "Mrs. Hattie E. Wilson" delivered a recitation, "Outward Bound," the previous Sunday. A move to Amory Hall within Boston itself is announced.

1879: November 1. XLVI/6: 8. "Amory Hall [Boston]," "Children's
Progressive Lyceum No. 2": Mrs. Wilson delivered a "select reading," "Think and Do This," the previous Sunday.

1879: November 15. XLVI/8: 8. A special meeting of the Children's
Progressive Lyceum No. 2 committee, including its conductor,
J. B. Hatch, and "Hattie E. Wilson" compose a resolution offering condolences to Mrs. C. Fannie Allyn following the death of
her son, Lovernest Allyn.

1879: December 20. XLVI/13: 5. Children's Progressive Lyceum No.
2 reports that "Hattie E. Wilson" delivered a "recitation" the previous Sunday.

1880: January 17. XLVI/17: 5. Children's Progressive Lyceum No. 2
reports that "Hattie E. Wilson" gave a "reading" the previous
Sunday.

1880: February 7. XLVI/20: 5. Children's Progressive Lyceum No. 2
reports a visit by its committee, upon which Wilson at the time
served as treasurer, to New York. The committee visited spiritual
lyceums in New York and Brooklyn. It seems probable Wilson
traveled to New York on this visit.

1880: March 20. XLVI/26: 1, 5. Under the headline "A Gala Week
for Spiritualism," the *Banner* features the first of three front-
page reports of the two-day return visit by the spiritual lyceums
of New York and Brooklyn to the Children's Progressive Lyceum
No. 2 in Boston, which had ended on Sunday, March 7. Hattie
E. Wilson, named as Lyceum No. 2's treasurer, was one of those

who provided "choice flowers" to celebrate the delegation's arrival on Saturday March 6 (1). In another notice, Children's Progressive Lyceum No. 2 reports that "Hattie E. Wilson" gave a "recitation" at their meeting on Sunday March 14 (5).

1880: April 3. XLVII/2: 1. In its final front-page report of the three-day return visit by the spiritual lyceums of New York and Brooklyn to the Children's Progressive Lyceum No. 2 in Boston, under the headline "A Gala Week for Spiritualism," the *Banner* details how "Mrs. Hattie E. Wilson made an informal speech, in which she declared she was heart and soul with all who were interested in advancing the interests of the Children's Lyceum cause."

1880: April 10. XLVII/3: 8. A report is given of the decision of the Children's Progressive Lyceum No. 2 to rename itself the Shawmut Spiritual Lyceum as from the following week, the anniversary of its foundation as Children's Progressive Lyceum No. 2. The Lyceum No. 2 also reports that Hattie E. Wilson "gave a select reading."

1880: May 1. XLVII/4: 8. The Shawmut Spiritual Lyceum reports that "Mrs. Hattie E. Wilson" gave a "recitation" at their previous Sunday's meeting.

1880: October 30. XLVIII/7: 8. "NEW ERA HALL . . . Shawmut Spiritual Lyceum": "Mrs. Carlisle Ireland . . . advocated mediums hold seances whereat the children can be present and can hold converse with the spirit world. . . . Assistant Conductor Rand and Mrs. Hattie Wilson together with Conductor J. B. Hatch, offered remarks in commendation of the project."

1881: January 8. XLVIII/16: 5. "NEW ERA HALL . . . Shawmut Spiritual Lyceum," "Election of Officers": Hattie E. Wilson elected "Leader" of "Banner" group.

1881: March 26. XLIX/1: 5. A celebration of "The Thirty Third Anniversary in Boston," organized by the Shawmut Spiritual Lyceum, is announced. Hattie E. Wilson is named as one of the organizing committee, along with J. B. Hatch, C. Frank Rand, and J. B. Hatch, Jr.

1881: April 2. XLIX/2: 5. Announcement of Shawmut "Thirty Third Anniversary" celebration repeated.

1881: April 9. XLIX/3: 4, 5. "The proprietors of the *Banner of Light* return thanks to Mrs. Hattie E. Wilson and others of the Shawmut Spiritual Lyceum for floral offerings recently tendered to themselves and the Free [Spiritualist Medium] Circle Department" (4). In another notice, Harriet E. Wilson is named as one of the speakers who, "unwilling to extend the limits of the evening session" of "The Thirty Third Anniversary" after it had overrun, surrendered the opportunity to speak. She is then named as one of the "Committee of Arrangements on the part of the Shawmut," praised for its role in "mak[ing] the enterprise a success" (5).

1881: April 23. XLIX/5: 2. "The Spiritual Easter": The continuation of the report of the Shawmut thirty-third anniversary celebration again thanks the Committee of Arrangements, including "Hattie E. Wilson."

1881: June 4. XLIX/11: 8. "NEW ERA HALL": "Hattie Wilson" named as one of those offering "kind words" to the Shawmut Spiritual Lyceum.

1881: June 11. XLIX/12: 12. "The Shawmut Lyceum at Music Hall": "Harriet E. Wilson" named as one of the "Floral Sunday . . . Committee of Arrangements."

1881: July 23. XLIX/22: 8. A report of the "Shawmut Lyceum Picnic, Highland Lake" on Friday, July 15, noted that "the acting chairman seemed to be well provided with tongues, and he began by introducing Mrs. Hattie Wilson, who made an interesting speech, with a supplement."

1881: August 20. XLIX/25: 5. "NEW ERA HALL . . . Shawmut Spiritual Lyceum": "As customary upon the opening Sunday [after the summer break], remarks were made by Conductor Hatch, Assistant Rand, Mrs. H. E. Wilson, Mrs. Maggie Folsom [and others]."

1881: October 1. L/2: 7. "NEW ERA HALL . . . Shawmut Spiritual Lyceum": During a ceremony to note the death ("transit to the spirit-life") of President Garfield, "Mrs. H. E. Wilson and Mrs. Maggie Folsom . . . spoke in eulogistic terms of the departed ruler," who was believed to be a spiritualist sympathizer (see L/7 [November 5, 1881]: 6, "President Garfield with the Invisibles").

1881: December 24. L/14: 12. "NEW ERA HALL . . . THE SHAWMUT SEWING CIRCLE": "Spirit Dr. Hammond, through the mediumship of Mrs. H. E. Wilson, will give one of his old-fashioned healing and developing circles (admission 10 cents) on the evening of Jan. 11th."

1881: December 31. L/15: 12. The date of "Dr. Hammond['s] . . . old-fashioned healing and developing circle," "through the mediumship of Mrs. H. E. Wilson," is changed to "Jan. 4th."

1882: January 7. L/16: 10. "On the evening of Monday Jan. 2d. a large delegation of the friends of Mr. and Mrs. J. A. Hatch—including among others representatives of the board of officers and the members of the Shawmut [Spiritualist Lyceum]—assembled at their residence . . . to observe the birthday of Mrs. Hatch . . . brief remarks [were made] by [among others] Hattie Wilson."

1882: April 15. LI/4: 7. "NEW ERA HALL . . . Shawmut Spiritual Lyceum": At a lyceum meeting "remarks" were made by, among others, "Hattie Wilson."

1882: May 6. LI/7: 12. "NEW ERA HALL . . . Shawmut Spiritual Lyceum": "Mr. Hatch remarked on the passing away from earth-life of Aunt Mary Sterns and Mrs. Addie C. Perkins. He was followed by Mrs. Maggie Folsom and Hattie Wilson, who made some impressive remarks upon the loss sustained by us in the departures of these two sisters, and alluded to the noble work they had done on earth as small as in comparison with what they will do now that they have passed to the higher life; that though we miss them here in the mortal form they will soon make known their presence in our midst."

1882: June 10. LI/12: 7. "NEW ERA HALL . . . Shawmut Spiritual Lyceum": On "Floral Sunday," "Mrs. Hattie Wilson" made a

"presentation of a beautiful basket of flowers to Miss. M. T. Shelhamer . . . [and to] Mrs. [Maggie] Folsom, Mrs. Biggs and Mrs.
Stevens. In closing [Mrs. Wilson] stated it was to be understood
that the presentations were sent to the parties receiving them
from their friends, who had commissioned her to present them.
Miss Shelhamer expressed her sincere thanks to Mrs. Wilson
and friends."

1882: November 18. LII/9: 7. "Visit to the Soldier's Home, in Chelsea by the Shawmut Lyceum on Wednesday evening, Nov.
8th . . . remarks were offered by [among others] Hattie Wilson,
Maud E. Lord . . . and President Hatch."

1883: January 20. LII/18: 5. "Mrs. Hattie Wilson's Reception": "On
the evening of Jan. 10th a complimentary reception was given
by Mrs. Hattie E. Wilson to her friends. The Indian guides of
this gifted medium assembled in force with others to celebrate
the coming of the New Year. Though the day was stormy some
two hundred assembled. The exercises opened with an address
of congratulation by Eben Cobb, which was responded to by
Hattie Wilson, after which her Indian guides, one after another,
controlled [her] and made brief remarks. They were followed
by John Wetherbee and Haskell Baxter, and Mrs. Wilson was
presented with numerous gifts. At 10 o'clock the hall was
cleared for dancing, in which those who wished participated.
Refreshments were served during the entire evening. At 12
o'clock the friends adjourned to their homes, well pleased with
the evening's entertainment."

1883: February 10. LII/21: 5. "Notice. The first meeting of a Progressive School for children which is being formed in the Ladies' Aid

Parlors, met Sunday morning, February 4th, and will continue to meet there every Sunday morning. The children's friend, Mrs. Hattie E. Wilson, with a few others, have undertaken to form a school that will aim to be both pleasing and instructive to the children, and hope to have the assistance of all liberal minded people to help them carry on the work. Children and friends of the children are cordially invited to meet with us next Sunday morning, and those who would like to take an active part or feel an interest in the undertaking, are invited to meet at the residence of Mrs. H. E. Wilson No. 15 Village street, next Friday evening, to offer any suggestions they may have to offer or express their views as regards the best mode of instructing the children that may favour us with their attendance. MRS. HATTIE E. WILSON."

1883: February 17. LII/22: 5. "LADIES' AID PARLORS": The "First Spiritual Progressive School met in this hall this morning and not withstanding the inclemency of the weather, we had quite an interesting meeting. We are not fully organized, but hope to be able next Sunday to begin our work in good earnest. The exercises this morning consisted of local and instrumental music, remarks by Mrs. H. E. Wilson and Mr. Street, and readings by the children. We shall endeavor to have a teacher of elocution, also one of music. After the readings of the children, remarks were made by Mrs. M. J. Folsom, which were heartedly responded to by the audience. Mrs. Maud E. Lord favored us with some very pleasing remarks, which were enthusiastically received. In conclusion Mr. Cherrington gave us some very flattering predictions for our school, which we all hope will prove true.

"This week we shall issue the first number of a little paper, or lesson sheet called 'The Temple Within,' to appear once a month. It is to be the property of the school, and no doubt will prove a benefit to it.

"In closing, the thanks of the school are tendered to those who favored us with their services on this occasion. Our sessions will be held every Sunday morning. Let our work show that we merit the confidence and good will of our many friends. MRS. HATTIE E. WILSON."

1883: February 5. LII/23: 5. "LADIES' AID PARLORS": "The First Spiritualist Progressive School met Sunday morning, Feb. 18th as usual. The first number of our newspaper, '*The Temple Within,*' made its appearance and met with a hearty welcome. It needs no recommendation from me; its golden lessons and bright thoughts will make friends for it wherever it goes. Besides our exercises for the children this morning we were favored with short speeches from Mr. J. C. Street, Mrs. A. M. H. Tyler, Mr. David Brown and Mrs. J. Folsom, after which a generous contribution was made to our funds by the audience, for which the donors will please accept our thanks. We shall always be pleased to meet the children's friends and hear a kind word for them. MRS. HATTIE E. WILSON."

1883: March 3. LII/24: 5. "LADIES' AID PARLORS": "At the Spiritual Progressive School we are pleased to see many additions to our ranks. The time was occupied with lessons from '*The Temple Within,*' music lessons and a march. Our school aims to teach the children those spiritual truths that will be of lasting benefit to them, and we cordially invite all to pay us a visit, and lend us a helping hand in the work we have undertaken. We expect uphill work at first, as others have had before us; but if we are not successful it shall not be our fault. On this occasion we listened with

pleasure to kind words from Mr. J. C. Street and Dr. Wyman, and
hope to hear from them and many more of our friends often.
MRS HATTIE WILSON Boston, Feb. 25th, 1883."

1883: March 10. LII/25: 8. "LADIES' AID PARLORS": "The Spiritualist Progressive School was attended on Sunday last by a goodly
number of children, all of whom took an active interest in the
lessons, as well as what was said to them. Mr. Street's talk about
their Lesson Sheet or Paper formed a pleasing feature and
held the attention of the pupils to the subject. Dr. Richardson
favored us with an interesting speech, and was followed by Mrs.
M. J. Folsom and Mrs. H. E. Wilson. All who have the interest of
the school at heart, and wish to become charter members, will
please meet at the residence of Mrs. Wilson, 15 Village street,
next Friday evening at 8 o'clock. We hope to hear from many
old workers who have expressed a wish to help us. MRS. HAT-
TIE E. WILSON."

1883: March 17. LII/26: 8. "LADIES' AID PARLORS": "The Progressive School held a very interesting session last Sunday.
All expressed themselves much pleased with the exercises,
which consisted of singing, a short march, and a lesson from
our paper. The question, 'What does Spiritualism Teach?' was
responded to by nearly every scholar. A lesson in vocal music
and one on elocution were given, with which all were very much
pleased. After a few recitations from the children, we listened
to a few able remarks from Father Locke. The school will hold
an Easter Festival this afternoon and evening of the 24th, and
we hope our friends will help us to make it a success. Next Sunday the particulars will be given and tickets for sale. HATTIE E.
WILSON."

1883: March 24. LIII/1: 8. "LADIES' AID PARLORS": "The Progressive School is fast increasing in numbers. Last Sunday the lessons, in which all were deeply interested, occupied all the time, giving no opportunity for recitations or speeches. This week the second issue of *The Temple Within* will appear. Next Saturday the children will hold an Easter Festival in this place. The children meet in the afternoon for social recreation and supper. In the evening a public entertainment will be given. Admission: adults, ten cents; children not belonging to the school, five cents. All interested in the school, and wishing to become members of the association, are invited to meet in the residence of Miss Hartwell, no. 24 Dover street, Friday evening, March 23d, at eight o'clock. / MRS. HATTIE E. WILSON / Boston, March 18th, 1883." This was the last entry in the *Banner* to be penned by Wilson.

1883: March 31. LIII/2: 8. A note about the "Progressive School" announces the success of the Easter festival and calls another meeting at the "room" of Mrs. M. J. Folsom, "No. 2 Hamilton Place, Room 6." It is signed by "Albert A. Lord, *Secretary*"; Lord was to write such notices from then on, until November 1883.

1883: April 7. LIII/13. "Spiritualist Lecturers": For the first time Wilson's address is given as 15 Village Street, though, according to the Boston directories, she had moved there considerably earlier, starting in 1880. The *Banner* frequently complained about the way those on its listings failed to update their details.

1883: April 28. LIII/6: 8. "LADIES' AID PARLORS": Albert A. Lord, secretary, reports that in a meeting of the Progressive School "remarks were made by Mrs. M. J. Folsom . . . and Mrs. H. E. Wilson."

1883: May 19. LIII/9: 5. "LADIES' AID PARLORS": Albert A. Lord reports that Mrs. Wilson was one of those offering "fine remarks" to the Progressive School.

1883: May 26. LIII/10: 8. "Before closing the [Progressive] school [for the summer recess] Mrs. Hattie E. Wilson (our best friend and worker) had a few words to say and distributed flowers amongst the children."

1883: November 17. LIV/9: 1, 8. At a "Public Reception to Ed. S. Wheeler," "MRS. HATTIE E. WILSON" was a speaker: "MRS. HATTIE E. WILSON was then introduced. She had been called to do the work of spirits inspiring her organism for long years, and knew by sad experience the effects sometimes wrought on a medical instrument because of that medium's daring to speak the words which the spirit-world demanded of him or her. Therefore she was happy to meet on the present occasion Bro. Wheeler, a man who was pre-eminently noted or his fidelity to his unseen mentors. She expressed her high appreciation of Mr. Wheeler and his labours, and hoped the angels would speed him on in the future as in the past."

1884: January 19. LIV/18: 5. "THE PROGRESSIVE SCHOOL": "Miss [sic] Hattie Wilson, under control of one of her Indian guides, made some very interesting remarks, and gave several proofs of the presence of loved ones gone before."

1884: January 26. LIV/19: 5. "Paine Hall," Children's Progressive Lyceum No. 1: "Mrs. Maggie Folsom, who is deeply interested in the work progressing so finely under the motherly care of our good friend, Mrs. Hattie Wilson, at the Ladies' Aid Parlors, always will cherish a love for the 'Old Mother Lyceum': and so we occasionally hear her voice in defence of the right, in appeals to us to be true to our spirit guides, the old workers who march with us from Sunday to Sunday, whose spirit forms she could so distinctly see."

1884: March 29. LV/2: 5. At a "LYCEUM UNION," "our spirit friends" are described as represented by, among "a host of others," "Mrs. Hattie Wilson."

1884: April 12. LV/4: 8. At a "Lyceum Union Anniversary, Paine Hall, Boston," "Mrs. Hattie Wilson" was among the guests, and "aided by her good controls, delivered an address full of practical truths, and in conclusion said may harmony ever exist between the two schools represented here today. Allow me to thank you, on behalf of the officers and members of the Progressive School, for your cordial invitation and warm reception."

1886: November 27. LX/12: 8. "Paine Memorial Hall," "Boston Spiritual Lyceum": "Among our guests," Mrs. Hattie E. Wilson is named.

1887: February 26. LX/24: 8. "Paine Memorial Hall," "Boston Spiritual Lyceum": Mrs. Hattie Wilson, attending the lyceum, is described as "a past member . . . once more gathered with us."

1889: September 21. LXVI/3: 8. "Paine Hall": At a meeting welcoming the veteran spiritualist lecturer Moses Hull back to Boston from "his absence in the West for nearly ten years," "Dr. Hattie Wilson" [sic] was "present in the audience."

1889: December 7. LXVI/13: 3. At a meeting in "America Hall," mention is made of the use of the services of Mrs. J. E. Wilson, who after this date is, for a while, frequently mentioned in the *Banner*. This is not Mrs. H. E. Wilson but Jennie E. Wilson. Jennie E. Wilson sings frequently; Wilson is rarely noted as singing.

1898: May 21. LXXXIII/12: 8. The "Movements of Platform Lecturers" column carries a notice that "Mrs. Hattie E. Wilson, 9 Pelham street, Boston, holds circles at 7.45 P.M.," though the time had long since passed when the *Banner* regularly carried information about her (including her address).

1899: December 20. LXXXVI/15: 6. "Dwight Hall": "Mrs. Dr. Wilson said the spirit world is to her as real as this, and that many clairvoyants see and converse with their dear friends there the same as in earth-life." This would seem to be Wilson, especially as her sentiments chime closely with previous ones expressed by her.

APPENDIX 3:
Documents from Harriet Wilson's Life in Boston

**Document title: Deaths Registered in the City of Quincy
for the Year Nineteen Hundred**

No.: 192

Date of Death: [ditto mark] 28 [meaning June 28, 1900]

Date of Record: [ditto mark] [it is not completely clear that
this ditto mark indicates June 28 and not December
31]

Name and Surname of the Deceased. If a married or a
divorced woman or a widow, give also maiden name
and name of husband: Hattie E. Wilson [two ditto
marks] Green [i.e., maiden name is Hattie E. Green]

Sex (and color if other than white): F. [no mention of race]

Condition (single, married, widowed or divorced): W.
[widowed]

Age: Years: 75 Months: 3 Days: [blank]

Disease, or Cause of Death (primary and secondary cause):
Inanition

Residence: Boston, Mass

Place of Death: Quincy

Place of Burial: [ditto mark] [i.e., Quincy]

Occupation: Nurse

Place of Birth: Milford, N.H.

Names and Birthplace of Parents:

Names (give maiden name of mother): Joshua Green [no
    entry for mother]

Birthplace [of parents]: [no entry for either parent][1]

There are a number of problems with this entry. Wilson's color
is recorded as white (the default assumption in these New England
records): "Sex (and color if other than white): F [no mention of
race]." Secondly, her father's name is given as Joshua Green and
her maiden name as Harriet Green, even though previously she had
always given her maiden name as Harriet E. Adams (or, at least, that
is the name recorded), when living in New Hampshire. However,
since she gives her birthplace as Milford, New Hampshire, and her
age is approximately correct, and since no Harriet Adams (or Harriet Green) has been traced, apart from Harriet E. Adams Wilson,
living in Milford during the correct period and of the correct age-
range and color, the balance of probabilities weighs down on the
side of recognizing this Hattie E. Wilson to be Harriet E. Wilson.
After all, her death certificate ("Return of a Death") gives her "color"
as "African" though her death record does not.[2]

Document title: Commonwealth of Massachusetts
Return of a Death

No.: 192

Name: Hattie E. Wilson

Sex: F[emale]

Color: African

Date of death: June 28 1900

Age: 75 Years, 3 Months, 13 Days

Maiden Name: Hattie E. Green

Widowed

Occupation: Nurse

Residence: Boston Mass. 9. Pelham St.

Place of Birth: Milford, N.H.

Place of Death: Quincy Mass. 93. Washington St.

Name and Birthplace of Father: Joshua Green

Place of Interrment: Quincy Mass. Mt. Wollaston

Dated at Quincy Mass. On June 3 1900

Physician's Certificate [part of the death certificate]

Name and Age of Deceased: Hattie E. Wilson Age, 75 Years,
     3 Months, 13 Days

Disease or Cause of Death: Inanition incident to old age.

This death certificate lends significant support to identifying the Boston Hattie E. Wilson as Harriet E. Wilson. It details her color as "African," gives her birthplace as "Milford, N.H.," and confirms her address as 9 Pelham Street, which suggests she had not been resident in the Cobb household for very long. That both the death record and the death certificate give her name as Hattie E. Wilson might be slightly surprising, since she had remarried (in 1870), but her marriage did not last that long (seemingly it terminated some time in 1877), which can explain well enough why she reverted to Harriet Wilson in her later life. The Boston Hattie E. Wilson married John G. Robinson, as the next piece of evidence shows—namely her second marriage certificate.

Document Title: Marriages Registered in the City of Boston for the Year Eighteen Hundred and Seventy

No.: 2319

Date of Marriage: September 29

Names, Surnames and Color of Groom and Bride: John G. Robinson, Harriet E. Wilson [In the column relating

to the race of Robinson and Wilson, there is a tick by
each of their names. Some of the other names on the
page (from other marriages) do not have ticks placed
here, so the ticks possibly mean 'black.']

Residence of Each at Time of Marriage: [two ditto marks]
[meaning Boston]

Age of Each in Years: 26 [John], 37 [Harriet]

Occupation of Each: Physician [John] [there is no entry
for Harriet]

Place of Birth of Each: Woodbury, Ct. [John]
Milford, N.H. [Harriet]

Names of Parents: Albert G. [ditto mark], Jane S. [John]
Joshua [ditto mark], Margaret Green [Harriet]

What Marriage, whether 1st, 2nd, 3d &c: [ditto mark]
[meaning first marriage for John] Second [for Harriet]

Name and Official Station of Person by Whom Married:
Rev. J. L. Mansfield of Mansfield[3]

There are again problems with this marriage record, as there
are with the death record. Common practice among registrars would
mean that the ticks relating to color indicate the couple were not
white (the color white was indicated usually by the column being left
blank). The problem with this deduction is that John G. Robinson,
an apothecary, was white, not African American.[4] Since both names
are checked in the column relating to color, it would imply they were
both nonwhite. Confusion might be said to reign, though the reasonable assumption in this instance would be that this particular reg-
istrar, on this occasion at least, unusually chose to use check marks to
indicate the category white, mistaking Wilson as white. Furthermore,
this Harriet E. Wilson's age is markedly wrong. However, the listing
of Milford, New Hampshire, as Wilson's birthplace might (again) be

convincing enough to reassure us that this Boston Harriet E. Wilson and our Harriet E. Wilson are one and the same.

Census Record: 1870 Census

Schedule 1.—Inhabitants in Ward 8 West of Washington
      Street, Boston, Suffolk County, Massachusetts
Enumerated on the 7th day of July 1870
Dwelling #71 [46 Carver Street]
Family #111
Line 3 Name: Robinson, John G.
Age: 26
      Sex: Male
      Color: White
      Occupation: Physician
      Value of Real Estate: [blank = none]
      Value of Personal Property: $500
      Birthplace: Connecticut
Line 4 Name: Wilson, Hattie E.
      Age: 38
      Color: White
      Occupation: Physician
      Value of Real Estate: [blank = none]
      Value of Personal Property: [blank = none]
      Birthplace: New Hampshire

Again, Wilson's color is recorded as white. It is possible that in this instance she was seeking to pass as white. However, she always advertised herself as a "colored trance medium" in the pages of the *Banner of Light*. Alternatively, Robinson may have dealt with the census taker and may not have wanted to admit he was living with a nonwhite person. This is not likely, since Wilson ran a business as a

colored medium from the house they shared. A third possibility is
that the person who recorded the entry may have assumed Wilson
was white from her appearance, without asking. This judgment call
may have been made because the census taker assumed she must
be white because her husband was white. Perhaps, even, the census taker only interviewed Robinson, and assumed his wife must be
white without asking. The last and perhaps most unlikely possibility
is that a simple slip of the pen occurred.

Census Record: 1880 Census

Boston Ward 16, Precinct 1, Suffolk County, Massachusetts
Enumeration District 703, Page 10B, Lines 43-45
Taken the 3rd day of June, 1880
Dwelling Number: 48 [15 Village Street]
Family Number: 126
Line 43

> Name: Hattie E. Wilson
>
> Color: Mulatto [first entered as "W" (white) but this
>   was crossed out and "Mu" substituted]
>
> Sex: Female
>
> Age: 40
>
> Relation to Head of Household: [blank]
>
> Marital Status: Widowed
>
> Occupation: Keeping House
>
> Birthplace: Maine
>
> Father's Birthplace: Maine
>
> Mother's Birthplace: Maine

This census entry, in which the letter "W" for white has been
crossed out and the letters "Mu" for mulatto have been substituted,
strongly suggests Wilson was of mixed race but of a very light com-

plexion. Wilson is here recorded as a housekeeper though she was at this time still quite active in spiritualist circles. This suggests that her income from her spiritualist work was generally very modest and at this time at least needed to be supplemented.

Death Notices of Hattie E. Wilson in *The Boston Globe*

The Boston Globe carried two notices concerning the death of Hattie E. Wilson in its edition of June 29, 1900. The first appeared in the news section:

QUINCY

Mrs Harriet E. Wilson of Boston died yesterday at the residence of Mrs Catherine C. Cobb on Washington st. (9)

The second appeared in its death notice section:

WILSON—In Quincy, June 25, Mrs Harriet Wilson of Boston. Funeral from the residence of Mrs Catherine C. Cobb, 93 Washington st. Quincy, Saturday, June 30, at 3 o'clock. Train leaves south terminal station at 2.28 p. m. Relatives and friends are invited. (12)

City of Quincy, Massachusetts Mount Wollaston Cemetery Lot No. 1337 Record (n.d.).

This burial lot cemetery record shows that Hattie E. Wilson is buried in the Cobb family grave. She was the third person to be interred there, following Frank H. Cobb (1897) and then Silas H. Cobb (in March 1900), in whose family home she had died. Whereas the Cobb family members are all buried in front of the large gray granite memorial marking the plot, Wilson is buried in the rear, to the north, where she lay in isolation until 1985. Wilson's name appears on the family memorial, but on its back, at the foot of the memorial. Wilson's interment in the Cobb family grave suggests a degree of closeness with the Cobbs that perhaps transcends that

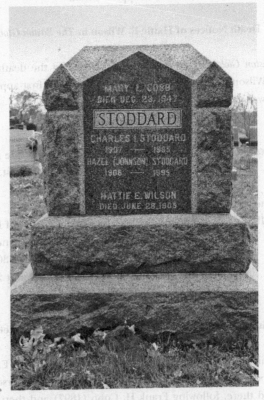

The back of the Cobb family grave memorial in Mount Wollaston Cemetery, Quincy, Massachusetts. Harriet (Hattie) E. Wilson's name appears at the bottom beneath those of members of the Stoddard family, close friends with the Cobbs, who came to share the plot after Wilson's death. Though Wilson's name was the first to be added to the back of the memorial it was deliberately placed at the bottom. (Photo by Marcus Halevi.)

which is likely to accrue from having served merely as the Cobbs' nurse, and more likely results from a long-established intimacy to do with Wilson's mediumistic practice: she had possibly served as the family's (or at least Catherine Cobb's) medium for a number of years. The Cobb family lore after her death, which came to identify her as a Native American, supports this suggestion.

NOTES

1. Our thanks to Fatin Abbas, Johni Cerny, and Donald Yacovone for assistance with the transcriptions. See *Massachusetts Deaths*, 506: 95, Massachusetts Archives, Columbia Point, Boston, Mass.
2. "Commonwealth of Massachusetts/Return of a Death," under the name of Hattie E. Wilson, June 29, 1900. Other details match those found on her death record, by and large. It also tells us she died of "inanition" and that she died in the house of the family of Silas Henry Cobb, whom she had been nursing. See Wilson, *Our Nig*, ed. Foreman and Pitts (2005), xvii, 86.
3. See *Massachusetts Marriages*, 228: 129, Massachusetts Archives, Columbia Point, Boston, Mass.
4. It is possible that this John Robinson also became involved in spiritualism (it was a common pattern for husband and wife teams to operate in spiritualist circles). On January 7, 1871, the *Banner* noted that "a young 'Indian trance speaker,' (Roy St. Francais) of Canada spoke in Vineland N.J. . . . He is very elo-

quent, rather radical, but altogether one of the best speakers in the field. He was in company with Dr. Robinson, of Boston." *BL* XXVIII, no. 17(January 7, 1871): 4.

APPENDIX 4:
A Note on the Penguin Edition

Professors P. Gabrielle Foreman and Reginald Pitts, in their Penguin edition of *Our Nig*, have uncovered remarkably valuable information about the identity of the Hayward family and Harriet E. Wilson's life, especially following the publication of her novel in 1859 and the death of her son, George Mason. Their research has extended our knowledge of Wilson's life span to the turn of the century, dramatically expanding what we know about the first female novelist in the African American literary tradition, as she pursued a career as a spiritualist during the final third of the nineteenth century. Unfortunately, however, some of their claims about Wilson's early life, prior to her departure to Boston, are sometimes overly speculative, with little or no supporting evidence provided. This dearth of convincing evidence and a certain troubling overenthusiasm for claiming definitive identifications between characters in the novel and individuals found in public records (through what we might call the biographical equivalent of false cognates) also serves to create doubt about their conclusions regarding her later life, underscoring the sometimes troublesome relationship between genealogical research and the more conservative and rigorous standards demanded of historical scholarship. When we attempted to duplicate their research, unfortunately we found that many of their claims were entirely or largely speculative and could not be supported adequately by the facts. We offer a summary here of several of their assertions that are deeply problematical and in need of reassessment (page numbers refer to the 2009 Penguin edition):

- The identity of Wilson's father remains uncertain. The claim that Harriet E. Wilson's father's name was "most certainly Joshua Green" (xxxi), advanced on the basis that this is the name given on her second marriage certificate, and, after she had passed away, the name recorded on both her death certificate and the record of her death, neglects to take full account of the way her maiden name is recorded as Harriet Adams on four occasions: in both the 1850 and the 1851 "Report[s] of the Overseers of the Poor for the Town of Milford"; in the 1850 U.S. census; and in the record of her first marriage on October 6, 1851, to be found in the April 1852 "return" of the Reverend E. N. Hidden, fifth pastor of Milford's Congregational church. There is plainly a discrepancy in the record. Wilson's father's last name remains uncertain. It is not "most certainly" Green.

- No record has yet been discovered that a Mag Smith or a Mag Adams lived in Milford, New Hampshire. To claim that Wilson's mother was called Mag Smith is both speculative and unlikely, given Wilson's consistent use of pseudonyms throughout her novel (vii).

- The drunken "Margaret Ann Smith who died in Boston," and whose death was reported in the Milford *Farmer's Cabinet,* was almost certainly not Wilson's mother, though Foreman creates the false impression that she was. There is no evidence that this Portsmouth-born Smith ever visited Milford. She is also described as black in the account of her death in the *Cabinet,* whereas Wilson's mother was almost certainly white (or just possibly a light-skinned "mulatta," unlikely to be described as black). Foreman's subsequent discovery that the sensational story of Smith's death had been widely syndicated in newspapers across New England and that in some versions Smith's color is given as white actually weakens her argument. As many papers throughout New England picked up this "shocking" story, there is no reason to believe that the *Cabinet* ran it because the Portsmouth Mag Smith had local connections. Further, if this speculative identification is true, then why did the *Cabinet*'s editors misleadingly leave Mag Smith's color wrongly recorded as "black" in its account, when presumably those in Milford who remembered Harriet's mother would have known her to be white? The *Cabinet*'s readers would be unlikely to recognize the black Mag Smith of Portsmouth as the white Mag Smith known in Milford. And both "Mag" and "Smith" were common names. In all probability, the *Cabinet* simply ran this story as another cautionary, pro-temperance tale (that Mag was "black" added an extra, racist, spice).

- There is no conclusive evidence that Wilson ever formally became an indentured servant, though it is probable she did.

- The identification of Harriet Wilson's teacher in Milford as Abby A. Kent is not supported by any concrete evidence. Kent is never named as a teacher in the official records that survive in the Milford Historical Society.

- The identifications of Mrs. Hale as Mrs. Sarah Dexter Kemball; the "two maids (old)" as Fanny and Edna Kidder; Mrs. Hoggs as Mary Louisa Boyles; Mrs. Mary Wrigley Walker as the Mrs. Walker mentioned by "Allida"; "Allida" as Jane

Chapman (Maslen) Demond; "Margaretta Thorn" as Laura
Wright Hutchinson; "C.D.S." as Calvin Dascomb, Sr.; and
Wilson's landlady as Sophia W. Young are all not supported
by any definitive evidence.

- The identification of the town or village (it is described as
  both) to which Wilson moves as "almost surely" Ware, Massachusetts, is not supported by sufficient evidence (106).
  Westborough, Walpole, and, above all, Worcester remain
  possible contenders.

- There is no evidence apart from the author's pseudonym
  that the poem "Fading Away" by "Hattie" is by Harriet Wilson (see viii, xiii). The style of this *Cabinet* poem is nothing
  like the poem quoted on pages 135–36 of *Our Nig,* which
  is quite likely to have been penned by Wilson, since at this
  point in her testimonial, "Allida" is quoting from a letter by
  "the author of this book."

- The claim that the Thomas Wilson who died on the sloop
  Cabassa in Cuba was Harriet Wilson's husband is not supported by any documentary evidence, especially as *Our Nig*
  (which Foreman and Pitts usually accept as autobiographically accurate) represents him as dying in New Orleans.

- Though one might assume that people in spiritualist circles in New England knew one another, there is no basis
  for claiming that Wilson was involved with either Laura
  Hutchinson or spiritualists in the Milford environs. Worcester had a large and active spiritualist community; Ware a
  very much smaller one, while Nashua possessed one as well.
  Wilson may even not have turned to spiritualism until her
  arrival in Boston.

- No reason is offered for the unlikely claim that G. W. Cook, who is quoted in an epigraph to chapter 10 of *Our Nig,* is a pseudonym for George Washington Light (94).

- There is no reason to prefer the attribution Charlotte Elizabeth [Brown] over that of Charlotte Elliott when seeking to identify "C. E.," the author of the epigraph at the head of chapter 11 of *Our Nig* (101).

NOTES TO THE TEXT

Compiled by R. J. Ellis with Henry Louis Gates, Jr.,
David A. Curtis, and Lisa Rivo

PAGE

TITLE   1. *OUR NIG:* The title of the book, by including the word
"nig," which in 1859 was well recognized as a derogatory
and abusive term, is perhaps one of the reasons why the
book sunk into obscurity for so long. The bookseller William French, in 1981, in conversation with Henry Louis
Gates, Jr., explained that booksellers debated whether the
book was written by a white or African American person
(the latter perhaps being unlikely to include the word
"nig" in the title). The book's recurrently fierce critique
of Northern abolitionism (see our introduction, page xx
and passim) even suggested the remote possibility that a
white Southerner might have been the author. Corrobo-
ratively, Gates also discovered that the book was largely
unrecorded in reference works on African American writing up until that time, other than a handful of exceptions,
notably: John Herbert Nelson, who mentions the title only
(*The Negro Character in American Literature,* 1926); James
Joseph McKinney ("The Theme of Miscegenation in the
American Novel to World War One," 1972 Ph.D.); Geral-
dine Matthews (*Black Writers, 1773–1949,* 1975), and Carol
Fairbanks and Eugene A. Engeldinger (*Black American*

Fiction—A Bibliography, 1978)—these rehearsing what was written in Lyle Wright's three-volume listing of American fiction (*American Fiction 1774—1900,* II, 2767); and Daniel Mott (in a Howard S. Mott Company catalogue, 1980). By contrast, in two other reference works, Wilson is taken to be white: Herbert Ross Brown's *The Sentimental Novel in America* (1940) and Monroe N. Work's *A Bibliography of the Negro in Africa and America* (1928). The title *Our Nig* should be recognized as offering an ironic commentary on blacks' difficulties in laying uncontested claim to both sole authorship and copyright. White American families at this time commonly appended the pronoun "our" before their servants' names. See, for example, Julia Caroline Ripley Dorr's *Farmingdale,* in which the white family decide to name their new, adolescent servant "Our Mary" (Caroline Thomas [Julia Caroline Ripley Dorr], *Farmingdale* [New York: Appleton Company, 1854], 231). Given the substantial allusions in Wilson's *Our Nig* to the sentimental novel tradition, she perhaps intends an intertextual reference here. While Dorr's Mary is being taken into the bosom of a loving family who are rescuing her from her impoverishment, almost the opposite is happening to Frado, as the Bellmont family give her the racist labeling, "Our Nig."

TITLE   2. The book's title and subtitle are loaded with complexities, generated by the ironic circularity of "*Our Nig . . .* by 'Our Nig,'" which underlines the way Frado is trapped by her racial identity. The description of the farmhouse uses the ambiguous terms "two-story" (suggesting that double, racist, standards operate) and "white house" (suggesting these double standards pervade the antebellum United

States). See our introduction, page xxv and passim. Harriet E. Wilson's adoption of a pen name was probably driven by expediency. The Hayward family, models for the abusive Bellmonts, still had prominent New England connections though they had dispersed from Milford, New Hampshire, by the time *Our Nig* was published. Wilson would therefore welcome the anonymity provided by a pseudonym. (See Barbara A. White, " 'Our Nig' and the She-Devil.") Ironically, a further motive might have been a desire to buffer herself from criticism for having the effrontery to write as a female—a role still not always accepted by either white or black communities at this time. See, for example, Marilyn Richardson's introduction to her *Maria W. Stewart, America's First Black Woman Political Writer: Essays and Speeches* (Bloomington: Indiana University Press, 1987).

TITLE   3. Epigraph: The quotation on the title page occurs in Josiah Gilbert Holland's *Bitter-Sweet: A Poem.* In the fifth edition of *Bitter-Sweet* (New York: Charles Scribner, 1859), these lines appear on pages 35–36. Holland (1819–81) was a Massachusetts writer. Wilson's quotation is largely, but not wholly, accurate. The quotation in the 1859 edition reads:

> . . . I know
> That care has iron crowns for many brows;
> That Calvaries are everywhere, whereon
> Virtue is crucified, and nails and spears
> Draw guiltless blood; that sorrow sits and drinks
> At sweetest hearts, till all their life is dry;

That gentle spirits on the rack of pain
Grow faint or fierce, and pray and curse by turns;
That Hell's temptations, clad in Heavenly guise
And armed with might, lie evermore in wait
Along life's path, giving assault to all—

These lines form part of the twenty-second speech of the
"First Movement," spoken by "Ruth." The next two lines
continue: "I know the world is full of evil things, / And
shudder with the consciousness." Often the pertinence of
Wilson's chapter epigraphs is enhanced when these are
read in their full context. In this case, even the poem's
title, *Bitter-Sweet,* is ironically apposite. Like the subtitle,
this reflexivity suggests that Wilson was well read and
underlines how sophisticated *Our Nig*'s narrative is.

TITLE   4. *Geo. C. Rand & Avery:* The printer, George C. Rand &
Avery, was not known as a regular publisher of novels,
though the firm had been involved in the printing of
abolitionist materials. George Curtis Rand was a friend of
and worked with William Lloyd Garrison. Possibly Rand
was carrying out the printing in part (or even wholly) as
a charitable endeavor (see Gardner, " 'This Attempt of
Their Sister,' " 226). The first edition therefore contains
many minor errors or irregularities. Other errors may
derive from the fact that this printing firm did not usually
handle novels, and may therefore have been unfamiliar
with the conventions that existed.

Page 2   5. *Mrs. H. E. Wilson:* This identification on the copyright
page helped identify the author lying behind the pseudo-

nym "Our Nig." The copyright date was August 18, 1859; the publication date, September 5, 1859.

PREFACE

Page 3 6. *failing health . . . feeble life:* Wilson's "failing health" and impoverished circumstances are confirmed by the three letters appended to the text (133–40). Wilson gave birth to her son, George, at the Hillsborough County Farm in Goffstown in 1852. Her son was to die within six months of *Our Nig*'s publication.

Page 3 7. *I would not . . . palliate slavery . . . [nor] provoke shame in our good anti-slavery friends at home:* Wilson's immediate assertions that she would not "palliate slavery at the South, by disclosures of its appurtenances North," and that she has "purposely omitted what would most provoke shame in our good anti-slavery friends at home" make plain that she was aware of the risk that, by denouncing Northern racism and abolitionist hypocrisies, she was echoing the arguments of Southern apologists for slavery. See our introduction, pages xxiii–xxiv.

Page 3 8. *I sincerely appeal to my colored brethren:* Wilson here seems to indicate that her novel was aimed at a "colored" audience. However, the copies of *Our Nig* that have survived seem to have been owned by white Americans, including the son of the abolitionist leader William Lloyd Garrison. See Eric Gardner's research (Gardner, " 'This Attempt of Their Sister' "). Perhaps Wilson is not so much indicating that she expects her readership to be black as suggesting that only African Americans will be prepared to attend fully to her message concerning the prevalence of racism in the "two-story" North, or be moved sufficiently to lend her financial or other material support. We are, however, not sure that the text does solely orient itself to a "colored" readership, and these doubts are fuelled by the preface itself: why would Wilson "purposely omit" from her novel "what would most provoke shame in our good anti-slavery friends at home" if she did not expect at least some white readers? See also notes 19 and 109.

Page 3   9. *H. E. W.:* These correspond to the initials in the name Mrs. H. E. Wilson, by whom the book was copyrighted.

CHAPTER 1

Page 5   10. *MAG SMITH, MY MOTHER:* The use of the first-person pronoun ("me"; "my") in the titles of the first three chapters does not mesh with the third-person narrative voice used in the rest of the book. While these uses of "my" and "me" might suggest an autobiographical origin (presupposing that these first-person usages are a sign of poor editing by Wilson during a hypothetical recasting of her text into the third person), they may alternatively be seen as a device to dramatize Frado's humanity—by personalizing her, giving her an immediate, first-person voice, addressing the reader through these chapter titles. "Mag Smith" is the first of many pseudonyms used in the book. See note 15 and passim.

Page 5   11. Epigraph: This is taken from "The Veiled Prophet of Khorassan," part of Thomas Moore's then famous Romantic, Orientalist long poem *Lalla Rookh*. Moore (1779–1852) was at the time often identified as Ireland's national poet. The poem can be found in Moore's frequently reprinted *Poetical Works of Thomas Moore, Collected by Himself*. See for example the Philadelphia edition (J. B. Lippincott, 1858, 257). Wilson's quotation is not wholly accurate. The version in the 1858 edition reads:

Oh, Grief, beyond all other griefs, when fate
First leaves the young heart alone and desolate
In the wide world, without that only tie
For which it lov'd to live or fear'd to die;—
Lorn as the hung-up lute, that ne'er hath spoken
Since the sad day its master-chord was broken!

The poem then continues:

Fond maid, the sorrow of her soul was such
Ev'n reason sunk,—blighted beneath its touch;
And though, ere long, her sanguine spirit rose
Above the first dead pressure of its woes,
Though health and bloom return'd, the delicate chain
Of thought, once tangled, never clear'd again.

It is possible that Wilson also encountered Moore's blistering attacks on U.S. slavery and upon Jefferson for keeping a slave mistress in his *Epistles, Odes, and Other Poems* (1806). See, in particular, Moore's epistles in *Poems Relating to America*, which denounce "the present demagogues of the United States" for allowing it to become a country containing both "the vilely slav'd and madly free— / Alike the bondage and the licence suit, / The brute made ruler

and the man made brute." Consequently, to Moore's
eyes, visitors to Washington see "Naught but woods and
J_____n . . . see, / Where streets should run and sages
ought to be." Moore's satire here bitterly reflects upon
how the United States was no reservoir of freedom: "Freedom, Freedom, how I hate thy caste" (Thomas Moore,
Poems Relating to America, in *Moore's Poetical Works,* vol. 1
[London: Longman, Orme, Brown and Longman, 1840],
30, 266, 292, 291). Lines from Moore's "Weep Not for
Those" (1816) stand at the head of "Death," the chapter
in *Uncle Tom's Cabin* describing the death of Little Eva.

Page 5   12. *Early deprived of parental guardianship:* The cloying sentimentality of this overwritten opening is derived from the
then-dominant sentimental mode of writing also found,
for example, in Harriet Beecher Stowe's *Uncle Tom's Cabin.*
In the body of *Our Nig,* however, the writing becomes
crisper and more direct.

Page 6   13. *She surrendered to him a priceless gem:* While drawing upon
the conventions of sensation literature, in which women
are seduced and lose the "priceless gem" of their virgin-
ity (see Wilson, *Our Nig,* ed. Foreman and Pitts, 2009:
xxxiv) this outburst of feeling may also be an outlet for
Wilson's frustrations over the unpalatable legacy left to her
by her mother. The "damned mob of scribbling women,"
preeminently led by E. D. E. N. Southworth in the terrain
of sensation literature, of which Hawthorne famously and
almost contemporaneously complained, provided plenti-
ful examples of such plot trajectories in the decades preceding the Civil War. These influences help account for

the strange vocabulary in the closing paragraph of this first chapter, concerning "amalgamation" and "infamy," which again adopt the phraseology found in such gothic sensation writing.

Page 9   14. *How much you earn dis week:* The contrast here between the speech of "Jim" and "Mags," as one speaks in dialect and the other more formally, echoes the sort of stereo-typical differentiations found in white writing at this time (particularly in minstrel ventriloquism), but uncommonly in African American works. This provides another reason why Wilson was not infrequently taken to be a white writer passing as African American by scholars and foreshad-ows later debates among African American artists about whether writing in dialect was a viable mode for African Americans, given its commonplace appearance in black-face minstrel performances.

Page 9   15. "Bellmont": This is the pseudonym for the Milford, New Hampshire, Hayward family, as Barbara A. White has shown. Our table in the introduction, page xliv, shows which members of the Hayward family correspond with the Bellmonts in *Our Nig.* Here Mr. Bellmont is Nehemiah Hayward, Jr.

Page 9   16. "I have barrels to hoop": That Jim is a cooper suggests, by extension, that the household of the cooper, Timothy Blanchard in Milford, New Hampshire, may have been Wilson's early or first home. See Ellis, *Harriet Wilson's "Our Nig,"* 34–35.

Page 10   17. *Singleton:* The pseudonym for Milford, New Hamp-shire. The naming is ironic: all of "Singleton" does not speak with a single voice. Many in the town had developed strong abolitionist sympathies, but others remained unsympathetic and racism remained commonplace. The Congregationalist church that Wilson probably attended reflected such division, which ensures Singleton possesses no such implied unity. See our introduction, p. liv. See also Ellis, *Harriet Wilson's "Our Nig,"* 88 et seq., and passim.

Page 10   18. *his efforts in Mag's behalf told also of a finer principle:* Despite many counterindications in the opening pages, which seem to suggest the author embraces a "white = good" and "black = bad" cosmology, Wilson often highlights how such a divide is damaging, as she does here. See also notes 19 and 21.

Page 12   19. *I's black outside, I know, but I's got a white heart inside:* Wilson here refers to the unfortunate and intentional conjunction of Christian eschatology and skin color distinctions (in which black is equated with bad and white with good), which was also conventionally drawn upon, in different ways, by proslavery and antislavery advocates to justify their antagonistic positions. Wilson advances an argument commonly adopted by antislavery exponents, who argued that appearance could belie reality, and that to rely on a black appearance was superficial and should not deflect attention away from a person's inner purity— in particular that made manifest by Christian belief. This black-white eschatology has been frequently attacked for supporting racism via its demarcations, but it is easy to see why Wilson uses this argument strategically here in order to establish the principle of human beings' common humanity—an Enlightenment principle that many of her later observations will rely upon. These sentiments also suggest Wilson anticipated a white readership.

Page 13   20. *the evils of amalgamation:* The term "amalgamation" had been popularized by proslavery advocates seeking to frighten whites away from the abolitionist cause by the racist suggestion that the abolition of slavery would lead to prolific, lascivious interracial liaisons diluting whites' inherent superiority. This, for all proslavery proponents, would be an infamous development, which also explains the chapter's closing comment about Mag's descent into "infamy": Wilson intimates that Mag has interiorized these commonplace racist values of white society.

Page 13   21. *She had descended another step down the ladder of infamy:* This gothic-toned passage, another outburst of negativity about Frado's mother, might seem to indicate *Our Nig* is written by a white writer from the way it adopts the Christian eschatology employed both by white racists and white sensation literature, but any careful reading should easily gainsay this. See notes 18 and 19. See also note 13.

CHAPTER 2

Page 14   22. Epigraph: This is taken from Percy Bysshe Shelley, "Misery—A Fragment." This can be found in *The Poetical Works of Percy Bysshe Shelley*, vol. 2, edited by Mrs. Shelley, with a memoir (New York: Little, Brown and Co., 1835), 399. Wilson's quotation is not quite accurate. The quotation in the 1835 edition reads:

Misery! we have known each other,
Like a sister and a brother
Living in the same lone home,
Many years—we must live some
Hours or ages yet to come.

The quotation consists of the poem's third stanza. Stanza 4 commences, pertinently: "'Tis an evil lot, and yet / Let us make the best of it." Shelley himself was an apposite poet to quote, as he famously championed liberty and attacked religious conservatism.

Page 14   23. *proud of his treasure:* That Jim regards Mags as a commodity (a "treasure") that can enhance his social standing can remind us that black males are negatively represented in this text, so anticipating many later depictions of them by black women writers. *Our Nig* here stands in sharp contrast to much early male black writing's positive emphasis on male action, intended, at the time, to counter the frequent racist white depictions of black male passivity (if somewhat at the expense of granting female black agency its necessary recognition). See note 70 and introduction, page xxi.

Page 15   24. *consumption:* Common term for tuberculosis.

Page 17   25. *when in the right position:* This acute little satire on black posturing is part of the attack Wilson makes on black patriarchy. Note how Seth calculates the worth of Frado as if she were a commodity: "She'd be a prize somewhere." See also note 23.

Page 17   26. *a beautiful mulatto:* This is one of only two points in
the book where Frado is described as beautiful, the other
occurring on page 47 (though page 14 mentions "two
pretty mulattos," while on page 17 Seth describes Frado
as "six years old, and pretty" and on page 47 she is again
described as "pretty"). It is also one of only five places in
the novel where her skin color is drawn to the reader's
attention. Described in passing as a mulatta on page 124,
we are also told on page 21 that she is "yeller" and on page
25 that she is "not very black." More particularly, on page
39, the text describes Mrs. B.'s determination to keep
Frado in the sun to ensure her skin darkens, and so better
distinguish her from her daughter Mary. This comparative
reticence about Frado's beauty and hue somewhat militates against viewing *Our Nig* as just another sentimental
fiction focusing on a "tragic mulatta" falling prey to white
male predation. Though the text plainly draws on this subgenre's gothic conventions, her story diverges from the
characteristic pattern of these "tragic" (or, rather, pathetic)
tales by departing from the customary focus upon white
seduction and rape. Thus, though Jim's lingering over
"the pleasing contrast between her [Mag's] fair face and
his own dark skin" (11) raises issues of gender, race, and
sexuality, any such exploration remains secondary to Wilson's more immediate concern to focus on the interac-
tions of race, class, and sadism, as when Mrs. B. threatens
to spoil Frado's beauty (47). The "dangerous passion"
exciting Mrs. B. in chapter 8 (82) hints at the way *Our
Nig*'s focus on two white females' mistreatment of a black
female carries a quite untypical charge of perversity—

namely female sadism—one far more complex to handle than the more conventional emphasis on rape, seduction, and miscegenation residing at the core of most other writing dealing with the theme of interracial violence upon the female mulatta taken from this period.

Page 21   27. *Black, white and yeller!:* The schoolchildren's cry provides the only way that the reader can confidently establish that Seth Shipley is black. Their cries also underline how much skin color is kept to the forefront in Singleton's community.

Page 21   28. *a large, old fashioned, two-story white house, environed by fruitful acres:* See note 2 concerning the resonances that cluster around this idyllic description.

Page 22   29. *John [Bellmont]:* A fictionalization of Nehemiah Hayward, Jr. See introduction, page xliv.

Page 22   30. *Mrs. Bellmont:* Also referred to as "Mrs. B." A fictionalization of Rebecca S. Hayward, née Hutchinson. See introduction, page xliv.

CHAPTER 3

Page 24   31. Epigraph: This is taken from Eliza Cook, "The Future." The lines can be found in *The Poetical Works of Eliza Cook*, (London: Frederick Warne and Co.; New York: Scribner, Welford and Co., 1870), 187. Eliza Cook (1818–89) was a prolific English sentimental versifier. Wilson's quotation is slightly inaccurate. The quotation in the 1870 edition reads:

Oh! did we but know of the shadows so nigh,
The world would indeed be a prison of gloom;
All light would be quenched in youth's eloquent eye,
And the prayer-lisping infant would ask for the tomb.

For if Hope be a star that may lead us astray,
And "deceiveth the heart," as the aged ones preach;
Yet 'twas Mercy that gave it, to beacon our way,
Though its halo illumes where we never can reach.

The quotation consists of the fourth and fifth stanzas of the poem. Stanza 6 runs: "Though Friendship but flit, like a meteor gleam, / Though it burst, like a moon-lighted bubble of dew; / Though it passes away, like a leaf on a stream, / Yet 'tis bliss while we fancy the vision is true." These sentiments are particularly appropriate to Frado's condition in the Bellmont family, since her ostensible "friends" in this family repeatedly fail her.

Page 25   32. *Mary [Bellmont]:* A fictionalization of Rebecca S. Hayward; John, a.k.a. Jack Bellmont, is probably a composite fictionalization of Nehemiah Peabody Hayward and Charles S. Hayward. See introduction, page xliv.

Page 25   33. *the County House:* Paupers of whatever age at this time in New Hampshire were lodged in one of a network of county pauper houses. The nearest to Milford at this time was the Hillsborough County Poor Farm in Goffstown, New Hampshire.

Page 26   34. *train up in my way from a child:* As Foreman and Pitts point out, "train up in my way from a child," a twisted paraphrase of Proverbs 22:6 ("Train up a child in the way he should go: and when he is old, he will not depart from it"), emphasizes Mrs. B.'s hypocrisy. Frado will be "trained up" in Mrs. B.'s way rather than the Lord's.

Page 26   35. *the L chamber:* In New England the farmhouses commonly possessed a gabled wing at right angles to the main section, and an attic in this wing's roof could just about accommodate a small servant's bedroom: hence its description as "the L chamber."

Page 27   36. *Mary . . . had just glided into her teens:* That "Mary" had "just glided into her teens" seems to suggest a date of 1833 for Frado's arrival in the Bellmonts' household, and by extension, Wilson's in the Haywards', assuming that, by "teens," Wilson means Mary had reached the age of eleven.

Page 29   37. *Frado was called early in the morning:* The description that follows of Frado's duties while still only seven years old (30) exposes how hard her life was as a farm servant. See our introduction, pages xxxvi–xxxix.

Page 30   38. *she* should *go to school:* New Hampshire state law required its communities to provide education for their children.

Page 32   39. *one who looks not on outward appearances:* See 1 Samuel 16:7, "Man looketh on the outward appearance, but the Lord looketh on the heart." The kindness of Frado's teacher is a first reminder that not all of Milford is irremediably racist, and that it had a large and active abolitionist faction. See also note 53.

Page 35   40. *propping her mouth open:* Frado's mouth is propped open wide to prevent her crying out. When a person's mouth is forced open wide enough, hardly a sound can be made. This technique, along with gagging, is used more than once, and Mrs. B. even threatens at one point to cut off Frado's tongue (72). Such propping open assumes a particular iconographic significance in this text, epitomizing the silencing of the black voice and how Wilson overcomes this "O" by resisting the Haywards and, in a climactic act, publishing *Our Nig* itself, so giving voice to her otherwise silenced suffering, as did the publication of slave narratives.

Page 39   41. *she was never permitted to shield her skin from the sun. She was not many shades darker than Mary now; what a calamity it would be ever to hear the contrast spoken of:* A reminder of how contingent interpretations of skin color necessarily must be; Mrs. B. is worried that her slightly dark-skinned daughter will be compared in terms of her skin tone with the light-skinned mulatta, Frado, thereby calling into question, at least implicitly, her daughter's racial purity.

CHAPTER 4

Page 40   42. Epigraph: The quotation is taken from Lord Byron's poem "Childish Recollections." This can be found in *Hours of Idleness: Series of Poems, Original and Translated* in *The Poetical Works of Lord Byron: Embracing His Suppressed*

Poems, and a Sketch of His Life (London: John Murray, 1845), 405. George Gordon, Lord Byron (1788–1824) was a famous advocate of liberty, and his *Childe Harold's Pilgrimage* was often quoted by American antislavery writers. Wilson's quotation from "Childish Recollections" is slightly inaccurate. The quotation in the 1845 edition reads:

Hours of my youth! when, nurtured in my breast,
To love a stranger, friendship made me blest;—
Friendship, the dear peculiar bond of youth,
When every artless bosom throbs with truth;
Untaught by worldly wisdom how to feign,
And check each impulse with prudential reign;
When all we feel our honest souls disclose—
In love to friends, in open hate to foes;
No varnish'd tales the lips of youth repeat,
No dear-bought knowledge purchased by deceit.

This comes from the second stanza. The poem continues: "Hypocrisy, the gift of lengthen'd years, / Matured by age, the garb of prudence wears." Brought to the mind of those familiar with the poem, this continuation could stand as a barbed and ironic reference to the shortcomings Wilson perceives in "professed abolitionists" (69).

Page 42   43. *James [Bellmont]:* A fictionalization of George Milton Hayward. See introduction, page xliv.

Page 44   44. *Abby:* A fictionalization of Sally Hayward, the sister of Nehemiah Hayward, Jr. See introduction, page xliv. Though her model, Sally Hayward, had been married, Abby is described as "a maiden sister" to Nehemiah (22).

Page 45   45. *a professor of religion:* This description of Mrs. Bellmont as a "professor of religion" is deeply ironic and helps make the point forcibly that often the antebellum church played a seminal role in supporting not only the practice of slavery in the States but also the racism that underpinned it. See also note 84.

Page 46   46. *Jane [Bellmont]:* A fictionalization of Lucretia Hayward. See introduction, page xliv.

CHAPTER 5

Page 52   47. Epigraph: This comes from Martin Farquhar Tupper's "Of Life," the second section of *Proverbial Philosophy* in *Tupper's Complete Poetical Works* (Boston: Phillips, Sampson and Company, 1850), 192. An English poet, Tupper (1810–89) was famous at the time and his *Proverbial Philosophy* became a best seller. The lines occur in the poem's final stanza. Wilson's quotation contains some minor punctuation differences from this 1850 edition, which reads:

Life is a strange avenue of various trees and flowers;
Lightsome at commencement, but darkening to its end
    in a distant, massy portal.
It beginneth as a little path, edged with the violet
    and primrose,
A little path of lawny grass, and soft to tiny feet:
Soon, spring thistles in the way, ...

This final stanza from "Of Life" continues appositely: "Soon, spring thistles in the way, those early griefs of school, / And fruit trees ranged on either hand show holiday delights: / Anon, the rose and the mimosa hint at sensitive affection, / And vipers hide among the grass, and briers are woven in the hedges." For those familiar with the poem, this continuation would suggest how the New England pastoral is darkened for Frado by endemic racism.

CHAPTER 6

Page 62   48. Epigraph: This is taken from Laetitia Elizabeth Landon, "Success Alone Seen," in *Life and Literary Remains of L. E. L.*, authored and edited by Laman Blanchard (London: Henry Colburn, 1841), 261. Landon (1802–38) was a popular English writer at the time. The passage is reproduced as prose (when it should be presented as verse) and is slightly inaccurate. The quotation in the 1841 edition reads:

Hard are life's early steps; and, but that youth
Is buoyant, confident, and strong in hope,
Men would behold its threshold and despair.

Page 62   49. *Fido became . . . a more valuable presence than the human beings:* This estimation of the dog, Fido, as more valuable to Frado than the human beings around her represents the climax of the ironic Frado/Fido motif, which began in chapter 3 and which suggests that Frado's life is little better than a dog's (36–37). See our introduction, pages xxxiv–xxxvi.

Page 65   50. *There rushed on Mary's mental vision a picture:* The recurrence of essentially novelistic moments of omniscient narration, such as this detailing of Mary's "mental vision," militates against viewing the text as an autobiography, rather than as autobiographical.

Page 66   51. *the manifest enjoyment of Mrs. B.:* This "manifest enjoyment" exhibited by Mrs. B. when abusing Frado economically yet eloquently intimates how sadism underlay many of the excesses visited upon servants and, above all, slaves.

CHAPTER 7

Page 73   52. Epigraph: This is taken from Henry Kirke White, "Time: A Poem." It appears in *The Poetical Works of Henry Kirke White* (London: Bell and Daldy, 1830), 20. The quotation comes from the fourth stanza:

What are our joys but dreams? and what our hopes
But goodly shadows in the summer cloud?
There's not a wind that blows but bears with it
Some rainbow promise:—not a moment flies
But puts its sickle in the fields of life,
And mows its thousands, with their joys and cares.

Page 74   53. *I feel like grasping time until opinions change, and thousands like her rise into a noble freedom:* Here, James's reflections constitute the text's most prolonged allusions to abolitionist sentiment in Singleton, the fictionalization of Milford, and New England more generally. Chapter 11 of George A. Ramsdell's *The History of Milford* (Concord, N.H.: The Kumsford Press [published by The Town], 1901), tells of the antislavery "Come-Outer" movement's development in Milford, beginning in December 1842. Certain prominent residents of the town where Harriet E. Wilson grew up organized a series of "come-outer" meetings to enlist the support of the town's residents in the antislavery cause. These meetings were just one sign of the way that, following passage of the Fugitive Slave Act in 1850 in particular, abolitionist sentiments rose to gain ascendancy in the North. Wilson's point is that such a stance was often attended by hypocrisy.

CHAPTER 8

Page 78   54. Epigraph: This is taken from Henry Kirke White, "Written in the Prospect of Death," *The Poetical Works of Henry Kirke White* (London: Bell and Daldy, 1830), 79. White (1785–1806) came from common stock, though he was not quite a peasant poet, and died young, after being taken up by Robert Southey. White became somewhat famous as an archetypal example of the Romantic poet languishing to death from melancholy. Wilson's quotation from the closing lines of "Written in the Prospect of Death" contains some inaccuracies. In the 1830 edition the lines read:

Now other cares engross me,
And my tired soul with emulative haste,
Looks to its God, and prunes its wings for heaven.

The lines immediately preceding this quote read: "No more of Hope; the wanton vagrant Hope! / I abjure all,"— sentiments that bear directly on Frado's plight. This was evidently a favorite poem of Wilson's, as she also quotes from it at the head of chapter 9.

Page 78 55. *Lewis [Bellmont]:* A fictionalization of Jonas Hayward. See introduction, page xliv.

Page 80 56. *Susan:* Since "Susan" is a fictionalization of George Hayward's wife, Nancy Abbot, "Charlie" would seem to be a fictionalization of their daughter, Caroline Frances Hayward (though of a different sex). See introduction, page xliv.

Page 82 57. *so much indulgence of a dangerous passion:* Here Mrs. B.'s sadism openly emerges. See also note 26. There was an established tradition of suggesting that white females could lose all restraint in a dangerous way when placed in control of slaves. Marie St. Clare in *Uncle Tom's Cabin* is of course the preeminent example of this line of thinking. See, for some related considerations, Michelle A. Masse, "When the Personal Doesn't Become Political," *Yale Journal of Criticism* 12, vol. 1 (Spring 1999): 154–61.

Page 84 58. *all for white people:* One of the more remarkable features of this autobiographical novel is its failure to conform closely to a predominant convention existing in contemporary slave narratives and many other writings by African Americans: that a conversion narrative be centrally incorporated, in which the African American hero reaches Christ (usually through the tutelage of white benefactors). From this point in the novel, where Frado doubts if African Americans have a place in a heaven "all for white people," through to its end, the text depicts an uneasy alternation in which Frado keeps approaching but, finally, never fully embraces the Church. She is seen to be "serious" but never sloughs off her doubts about what the Church offers to African Americans. This is quite distinct from a conventional, decisive conversion. Given the predominance of the conversion narrative model that Wilson at best half matches, Frado's constant ambivalence can be seen as quite subversive.

Page 85   59. *Come to Christ . . . all, young or old, white or black, bond or free:* Undoubtedly Wilson heard ministers in Milford, like the Reverend Humphrey Moore (pastor of the Congregationalist church in Milford from 1801–36), preaching an antislavery message, based upon blacks' and whites' common humanity. See Ellis, *Harriet Wilson's "Our Nig,"* 2004, 88–89. However, as the text ironically goes on to note immediately, "this was the message she longed to hear." Frado's oscillations continue as she wrestles with her "veil of doubt and sin" (87).

Page 90   60. *I'll beat the money out of her, if I can't get her worth any other way:* Frado appears to be a type of indentured servant, and, therefore, Mrs. B. would normally have received public money from the town of Singleton for her keep until she came of age. This seems likely to be what happened in the case of Wilson herself, as Barbara A. White suggests (White, " 'Our Nig' and the She-Devil," 34), though this is not certain. However, the text here suggests the opposite: that the Bellmonts need to "beat the money out" of Frado to get her "worth." On the face of it, what seems to be implied is that either the Bellmonts very unusually pay the town for her services (which would seem to be an inversion of normal New England practice, whereby families who accepted paupers into their care were paid by the town), or, more brutally, that, since slavery is abolished in the North and Frado cannot now be sold as a slave for profit, she must work to earn her "value," which would be lost to the Bellmonts otherwise. A last possibility is that Mrs. B. felt that any money she receives from the town (if at all) is insufficient to cover Frado's keep and that she was therefore entitled to work Frado as hard as she could. Whatever reading is preferred, this resolution by Mrs. B. once again dramatizes the economic issues lying at the heart of this text. For example, we have just been told Frado's labor can be of "much profit" (90).

Page 90   61. *God be merciful to me a sinner:* This is taken from Luke 18:13. The lines Wilson quotes are part of a parable:

And he spake this parable unto certain which trusted in themselves that they were righteous, and despised others: Two men went up into the temple to pray; the one a Pharisee, and the other a publican. The Pharisee stood and prayed thus with himself, God, I thank thee, that I am not as other men are, extortioners, unjust, adulterers, or even as this publican. I fast twice in the week, I give tithes of all that I possess. And the publican, standing afar off, would not lift up so much as his eyes unto heaven, but smote upon his breast, saying, God be merciful to me a sinner. I tell you, this man went down to his house justified rather than the other: for every one that exalteth himself shall be abased; and he that humbleth himself shall be exalted.

The few words Wilson includes from this parable are therefore highly loaded. They refer to Frado's humbly downcast eyes and so to the fact that "he that humbleth himself shall be exalted" (Luke 18:14), unlike the "professor of religion," Mrs. B., or the disciples in the verses that follow in Luke: "And they brought unto him also infants, that he would touch them; but when his disciples saw it, they rebuked them. But Jesus called them unto him, and said, Suffer little children to come unto me, and forbid them not: for of such is the kingdom of God" (Luke 18:15–16). This surely relates to Wilson's later angry outburst concerning the refusal of whites to associate with African Americans (see note 85). Few Christian readers of *Our Nig* at that time would have failed to grasp these ironies.

CHAPTER 9

Page 91   62. Epigraph: This is taken from Henry Kirke White, "Written in the Prospect of Death," in *The Poetical Works of Henry Kirke White* (London: Bell and Daldy, 1830), 79. In this edition the lines read:

> —We have now
> But a small portion of what men call time
> To hold communion; for even now the knife,
> The separating knife, I feel divides ,
> The tender bond that binds my soul to earth.

Page 93   63. *Mrs. B. was too weak:* This is perhaps the passage in *Our Nig* that best illustrates Wilson's artistic restraint, as

Mrs. B.'s hypocritical recovery of strength is economically described: one minute she is "too weak" to help lift her invalid son, the next she is thrashing Frado so vigorously that the sound of the beating can be clearly heard. This incident invites sensationalization. Yet the text resolutely declines to do this, to telling effect. The concision and matter-of-fact tone that prevail enable the cruel silencing of Frado to be represented all the more damningly.

Page 94 64. *If she minded her mistress, and did what she commanded, it was all that was required of her.* See Colossians 3:22: "Servants, obey in all things your masters." Mrs. B.'s words, as Foreman and Pitts point out, echo those used by proslavery advocates justifying slavery on the basis of this scriptural reference.

Page 98 65. *a black dress and a pink ribbon!:* A well-established convention in sentimental novels depicts an impecunious protagonist's struggles to secure appropriateness of dress, with bonnets not infrequently being a case in point. See, for example, Mary's odd bonnet in Mary Jane Holmes's *English Orphans* (New York: Appleton, 1855), 64.

CHAPTER 10

Page 102 66. Epigraph: We have been so far unable to identify "G. W. Cook" with any conviction. A very long shot could be George W. Cook, a maritime doctor, who signed himself Geo. W. Cook in his book *The Mariner's Physician and Surgeon; or a Guide to the Homeopathic Treatment of Those Diseases to Which Seamen Are Liable, Comprising the Treatment of Syphilitic Diseases, &c.* (New York: J. T. S. Smith, 1848). Given the topic of the three lines of verse quoted by Wilson, this attribution has a shred of plausibility. Cook might just have written hymns with a nautical reference.

Page 102   67. *bruised reed:* The phrase "bruised reed" appears three times in the Bible. In 2 Kings, the image figures, perhaps most pertinently, in the story of the fall of the Kingdom of Judah (18:21): "Now, behold, thou trustest upon the staff of this bruised reed, even upon Egypt, on which if a man lean, it will go into his hand, and pierce it: so is Pharaoh king of Egypt unto all that trust on him." The image appears also in Isaiah 42:1–3: "Behold my servant, whom I uphold; mine elect, in whom my soul delighteth; I have put my Spirit upon him: he shall bring forth judgment to the Gentiles. He shall not cry, nor lift up, nor cause his voice to be heard in the street. A bruised reed shall he not break, and the smoking flax shall he not quench: he shall bring forth judgment unto truth." These lines are reworked in Matthew 12:14–20:

Then the Pharisees went out, and held a council against him, how they might destroy him. But when Jesus knew it, he withdrew himself from thence: and great multitudes followed him, and he healed them all; And charged them that they should not make him known: That it might be fulfilled which was spoken by Esaias the prophet, saying, Behold my servant, whom I have chosen; my beloved, in whom my soul is well pleased: I will put my Spirit upon him, and he shall show judgment to the Gentiles. He shall not strive, nor cry; neither shall any man hear his voice in

NOTES TO THE TEXT

the streets. A bruised reed shall he not break, and smoking flax shall he not quench, till he send forth judgment unto victory.

Page 102 68. *he resolved to start on the narrow way:* See Matthew 7:14; "Because strait is the gate, and narrow is the way, which leadeth unto life, and few there be that find it." The "celestial city" (heaven) to which the gate leads is likely to be a reference to John Bunyan's endlessly reprinted *Pilgrim's Progress* (1678; 1684).

Page 104 69. *her mistress was a professor of religion:* A second ironic reference to Mrs. B. as a "professor of religion." See note 45.

Page 105 70. *stood like one who feels the stirring of free and independent thoughts:* The phrasing here alludes to the Declaration of Independence, but Frado's declaration as she makes her stand by the woodpile is only "like" its predecessor, for Frado remains in servitude. See our introduction, pages xxix–xxxi.

Page 107 71. *She got into the* river *again:* The way Frado greets the news of Mary's death is complex and contradictory: it refers back to the dunking Mary inflicted upon herself when trying to bully Frado ("She got into the *river* again"), but also shows how Frado has internalized the abusive references to blacks made by many whites (by calling Mary a "nigger," her body now blackened by hell-fires, as Frado imagines). The river Jordan is the divide between life and death in Christian eschatology, and its crossing a "big"

event for everyone of whatever color bound for heaven or
hell in the final judgment. No wonder then that her claim
to know of Mary's hell-fire destination is unacceptable to
the "pious" Aunt Abby.

Page 109 72. *her period of service:* The term "period" here suggests a
fixed term was involved, which would appear to confirm
Frado's status was similar to that of an indentured farm
servant, hired out by a typical New England town's overseers of the poor. However, see note 60.

CHAPTER 11

Page 111 73. Epigraph: The prolific religious poet Charlotte Elliott
(1789–1871) is the probable author of these lines. She
commonly signed herself C. E. What militates against this
attribution is the fact that the lines lack the consolatory
note usually found in Elliott. However, Elliott makes frequent use of anaphora (in this case, "love" is the recurrent
word). Elliott also recurrently wove references to Christ's
sacrifice into her verse (see, for example, her *Hours of
Sorrow*, 1836). Thus this quotation is reminiscent of her
work in both style and content. Foreman and Pitts suggest
another possible source: Charlotte Elizabeth Brown[e]
Tonna (1790–1846), who published under the name Charlotte Elizabeth, and whose *Collected Works* (which does not
include this verse) were edited by Harriet Beecher Stowe
in 1849. Charlotte Elliott remains the more likely attribution, not least because her large, scattered poetic output
has not been fully collected together.

Page 113 74. *Jenny [Bellmont]:* Probably a composite fictionalization of Prudence S. Carmen and Sophia Nagel. See introduction, page xliv.

Page 114 75. *Mrs. B. and Henry had a long interview:* The appearance of the name "Henry" here is at first surprising since it has not appeared since chapter 5. It may be an error, surviving from a redrafting. If this reading is embraced, the name "Lewis" would be the one intended. However, there may be a reason for bringing "Henry" back into the story in order to remind the reader how pervasively this New England family's motives are dominated by pecuniary considerations. See for example how earlier Mrs. Bellmont championed the wealthy Henry over George Means as a suitable partner for Jane (55–61). Finding Henry plotting with Mrs. B. at this point therefore makes good sense, suggesting as it does, once again, that Mrs. B. always puts economic considerations first. See note 60.

Page 115 76. *Her school-books were her constant companions:* Harriet E. Wilson's frequent references to Frado's industrious reading habits as a release from her social isolation may help to explain how Wilson's own literary background and abilities developed.

Page 116 77. *we mustn't put ourselves in the way of temptation:* An allusion to the Lord's prayer: "And lead us not into temptation, but deliver us from evil" (Matthew 6:13).

Page 124 78. *how should she, black, feeble and poor, find any one to teach her:* Wilson well understands that not to be white is to be black in a racist society, which is why she depicts the light-skinned mulatta, Frado, as black at this point.

CHAPTER 12

Page 126   79. Epigraph: Slightly misquoting, this is taken from Ecclesiastes 1:9: "The thing that hath been, it is that which shall be; and that which is done is that which shall be done: and there is no new thing under the sun." The verses continue: "Is there anything whereof it may be said, See, this is new? it hath been already of old time, which was before us. There is no remembrance of former things; neither shall there be any remembrance of things that are to come with those that shall come after." (Ecclesiastes 1:10-11). These are disturbing reflections, given the themes of this novel. However, Wilson's misquote also replicates that to be found in Sarah Josepha [Buell] Hale's poem "Nothing New" in her poetry collection *Three Hours* (Philadelphia: Carey and Hart, 1848), 106–8, which takes as its epigraph " 'There is nothing new under the sun.'—Solomon." The final lines of this poem read: ". . . who would be a slave and dwell / For ever in a dungeon cell, / Counting the links that form his chain? / —Such is the soul that would retain / The fetters forged by Time, to bend / To this poor world, th' immortal Mind" (108). This poem is possibly the more likely source for Wilson's epigraph.

Page 126   80. *there appeared often in some of our New England villages, professed fugitives:* The phrase "professed fugitives" ushers in a series of disconcerting reflections in Wilson's final chapter that successively complicate the Manichean representation of good abolitionists/bad slavers dominating contemporary debates concerning slavery. The word "professed" signals that in Northern society, which had by 1859 largely come round to favoring gradual, if not immediate abolition, a potential now existed for a new set of hypocrisies and oppressions to take root, as individuals exploited the growing antislavery consensus by trading on the money to be gained by joining this good cause. Such incidents of "professed" abolitionism were common enough by this time to be causing concern in abolitionist circles. Several of the following notes explore these reverberations.

Page 126   81. *brother Pro:* A reference to proslavery whites; the use of the term "brother" in the phrase is a disturbing reminder of the prominent role that many in the white Christian church still played in legitimizing the continuation of slavery. At this time church members still commonly called one another "brother" or "sister."

Page 127   82. *She removed to Singleton . . . and there was married:* Harriet Adams, of Milford, married Thomas Wilson, of "Virginia," on October 6, 1851, according to the records of the Milford, New Hampshire, town clerk. See our chronology, page clxi.

Page 128   83. *his illiterate harangues were humbugs for hungry abolitionists:* Samuel, now Frado's husband, stands revealed as one of the "professed fugitives" referred to on page 126. Plainly, Samuel is exploiting the dominant ideological climate in the North. A particular example in contem-

porary history would be the factitious narrative of James
Wilson, which was "so compelling, so gripping, so useful"
that "abolitionists decided to publish it and distribute it
widely, sending copies to every state and to every congress-
man" before it was exposed as a fake and retractions were
broadcast (see Henry Louis Gates, Jr., "From Wheatley to
Douglass: The Politics of Displacement," in *Frederick Douglass: New Literary and Historical Essays,* ed. Eric J. Sundquist
[New York: Cambridge University Press, 1990], 59).

Page 128 84. *Then followed the birth of her child:* That Harriet E. Wilson
had a son and that her "birthplace" was Milford is con-
firmed by George Mason Wilson's death record. See our
chronology, pages clxi–clxii.

Page 129 85. *Watched by kidnappers, maltreated by professed abolitionists:*
This mention of "kidnappers" is most probably a further
reference to the consequences of the Fugitive Slave Act of
1850, which effectively gave license to unscrupulous slave
hunters to try to lay hands on any African Americans they
encountered, under the pretence that they believed them
to be runaways. See our introduction, pages xviii–xix.
African Americans seized in this way had then to be taken
before a magistrate, who was provided with a financial
incentive if he found the African American to be a runaway. The danger of kidnap that this law therefore generated is here twinned with another danger: that of being
"maltreated by professed abolitionists" (Frado already having been maltreated by a "professor of religion"). Perhaps
the most damning phrase in the novel, "professed abolitionists" charges that racism is a deep-rooted problem in

the North, even among abolitionists. Thus George's earlier claim that "thousands upon thousands favored the
elevation of her race, disapproving of oppression in all its
forms" (75–76) is substantially undercut by Wilson's quite
different verdict upon abolitionists and their hypocrisy. As
Wilson puts it, they "didn't want slaves at the South, nor
niggers in their own houses, North" (129).

Page 129 86. *Faugh! . . . to sit next one; awful!:* This bitter outburst by
the otherwise largely implied concealed third-person narrator paradoxically mimics the viciousness of some Northern abolitionists' racism and refers to the widespread
practice in Northern churches of arranging their congre-
gations in pews segregated by color.

Page 129 87. *Traps slyly laid by the vicious to ensnare her:* By now the
reader understands that "traps" is another reference to
the consequences of the Fugitive Slave Act of 1850, or a
comment on the dangers created by Northern hypocrisy
and racism, or a signal about how vulnerable to abuse
impoverished black females could be, or (most probably)
all three at the same time.

Page 129 88. *a friend . . . provided her with a valuable recipe:* In the
first of three testimonials at the end of the book, "Allida"
describes this as "a recipe . . . for restoring gray hair to its
former color" (137). In and around Milford, Wilson was
to sell also "hair regenerator," more dubiously. See *Wilson,
Our Nig,* ed. Foreman and Pitts, 2009, 85.

Pages 130–31 89. *Jane . . . has the early love of Henry still, and has never*

regretted her exchange of lovers: It is most likely that Wilson
makes a slip here, as was possibly the case earlier (see
note 75). Jane clearly chose George, and rejected Henry
in chapter 5. However, it is possible that what is intended
is the fleeting implication that even the least materialistic
members of the Bellmont family, like Jane, at the last can
reconcile themselves to the dictates of New England business acumen. Simply put, the alliance of Henry Reed and
Jane Bellmont remains a desirable outcome, unifying as
it would the wealth of two Singleton families, so Jane may
have at the least held open the possibility of a relationship with Henry, by still retaining Henry's love, despite
his earlier villainy. Henry's second surprise reappearance
here can thus just possibly be read as one further signal of
Singleton's one main arena of single-mindedness (for all
its other double values): the pursuit of profit. The word
"exchange" might be held to point to this reading.

Page 131 90. *Frado has passed from their memories, as Joseph from the*
butler's: The reference is to Genesis 40:23, in which the
Pharaoh's butler fails to remember his promise to Joseph
to "shew kindness . . . unto" Joseph (Genesis 40:14). The
Pharaoh has imprisoned his butler and baker, in the jail
where Joseph already languishes. Both men have dreams,
which Joseph interprets. Joseph tells the butler that his
dream means the Pharaoh will release him in three days,
and then continues, "But think on me when it shall be well
with thee, and shew kindness, I pray thee, unto me, and
make mention of me unto Pharaoh, and bring me out of
this house: For indeed I was stolen away out of the land of
the Hebrews: and here also have I done nothing that they

should put me into the dungeon" (Genesis 40:14–15). However, "Yet did not the chief butler remember Joseph, but forgat him" (Genesis 40:23). This biblical quotation reminds the reader of the way that those in servitude cannot be forgotten, since their services are omnipresent, but that they can be overlooked—not recognized as human or deserving of reciprocity of feeling. It is striking that the majority of the relatively scattered direct biblical sources in the body of Wilson's novel are either to the Old Testament or, when (more rarely) to the New Testament, in references steeped in irony. This lends weight to our contention that Frado remains uneasy about Christianity (see note 39 and our introduction, pages liv–lv), particularly since the appendix is, by contrast, replete with biblical allusions, much more often referring to the New Testament (including Frado's own "letter" quoted by "Allida"). See also note 91. If Wilson did indeed become a spiritualist medium in later life, as seems probable, then it is possible that in 1859, when these words were most likely to have been written, she was already beginning to embrace spiritualism, which may help explain how it is Frado feels some spiritual affinity with the Bellmonts, despite their treatment of her. See our introduction, pages xlix–l and passim.

APPENDIX

Page 133 91. *Appendix:* The appendix consists of three testimonials. None of the authors of these "testimonials" can be confidently identified; the attributions made by Foreman and Pitts are speculative. It is possible that all three were written by Wilson herself, as Elizabeth Breau has suggested in her article "Identifying Satire: *Our Nig*," 455–65. There are some stylistic congruencies between each of the testimonials and the preface, which is initialed as her own by Wilson. For example, "Allida" 's phrase in the first testimonial, "he left . . . and embarked for sea" closely echoes Wilson's earlier words "he left her . . . embarked at sea" (127). See also notes 110 and 115. Similarly, if one reads "Allida" 's testimonial without reference to the fact it is presented as such, the common ground it shares with sensational sentimental writing becomes obvious. Such an affinity does not increase our confidence that the testimonial is genuine. Nor does the fact this first testimonial is signed by "Allida." It is very unusual to find testimonial writers using pseudonyms. In this instance, if Wilson is the author of these testimonials, she may have chosen the name "Allida" because it conveys how "Allida" is *allied* to Wilson's cause. If "Allida" did exist, then she was most likely to be a worthy citizen of W____, Massachusetts, or (less probably) Milford. The other two testimonial writers are named Margaretta Thorn and C.D.S. Nothing is known about either of them, but it is quite likely that if they ever existed they were also citizens of Milford or its environs. C.D.S. might be an abbreviation of "Colored Indentured Servant," since this was then a common legal abbreviation in parts of the United States. Wilson, however, quite probably appended these testimonials in order to gain authority and suggest authenticity—and both are generic conventions of slave narratives of the time. See also note 114.

Page 133 92. *Truth is stranger than fiction:* John Ernest, in his notes to his edition of *Our Nig* (in *Shadowing Slavery*, 508) makes the point that this adage is frequently cited in works by and/or about African Americans, in order to convey the cruelly perverse strangeness of the system of slavery and its consequences. So, for example, the 1858 version of the life story of Josiah Henson, who became famous (not quite correctly) as the self-proclaimed inspiration for "Tom" in Harriet Beecher Stowe's *Uncle Tom's Cabin*, carries the title *Truth Stranger than Fiction: Father Henson's Story of His Own Life*. The phrase appears in canto 14 of Lord Byron's 1823 poem *Don Juan:* "'Tis strange,—but true; for truth is always strange; / Stranger than fiction: if it could be told, / How much would novels gain by the exchange! / How differently the world would men behold!" (Halifax: Milner and Sowerby, 1823).

Page 133 93. *"black, but comely":* When "Allida" speaks of the face of "the author of this book" as "black, but comely" she is reinforcing the novel's message that, in the end, all nonwhites are always seen as black—a message underlined by the fact that the phrase "black, but comely" derives from the Song of Solomon 1:5, "I am black, but comely, O ye daughters of Jerusalem, as the tents of Kedar, as the curtains of Solomon."

Page 133 94. *"My cup runneth over. What shall I render to the Lord for all his benefits?":* Psalm 23:5, "thou anointest my head with oil; my cup runneth over." This psalm is famous, particularly for verse 4 ("Yea, though I walk through the valley of the shadow of death, I will fear no evil: for thou art with me; thy rod and thy staff they comfort me"). Later

in "Allida"'s testimonial "the author of this book," in her
letter, quotes from this same psalm (see note 98), which,
despite the psalm's fame, might provide further evidence
to support the claim made about Wilson's possible authorship of these testimonials (see note 91). The phrase "what
shall I render to the Lord for all his benefits" comes from
Psalm 116:12. Verses 6–13, pertinently, maintain: "The
Lord preserveth the simple: I was brought low, and he
helped me. . . . I said in my haste, All men are liars. What
shall I render unto the Lord for all his benefits toward me?
I will take the cup of salvation, and call upon the name of
the Lord." In turn, these verses are referred to in Matthew
22:21: "Render therefore unto Caesar the things which
are Caesar's; and unto God the things that are God's."
This verse has long aroused theological controversy and
was often cited by both pro- and antislavery campaign-
ers in support of their arguments. See also Isaac Watts,
"What shall I render to my God / For all his gifts to me?" in
"Praise for Mercies, Spiritual and Temporal" in *The Works
of the Reverend and Learned Isaac Watts* (London: Printed by
and for John Barfield [etc.], 1810), 4: 394.

Pages 133–34 95. *"it is not in man that walketh to direct his steps"*: Jeremiah 10:23, "O Lord, I know that the way of man is not
in himself: it is not in man that walketh to direct his steps."
The preceding verses run: "For the pastors are become
brutish, and have not sought the Lord: therefore they shall
not prosper, and all their flocks shall be scattered. Behold,
the noise of the bruit is come, and a great commotion out
of the north country, to make the cities of Judah desolate,
and a den of dragons" (Jeremiah 10:21–22).

Page 134   96. *that class who are poor in the things of earth, but "rich in faith"*: This is derived from James 2:5–6: "Hearken, my beloved brethren, Hath not God chosen the poor of this world rich in faith, and heirs of the kingdom which he hath promised to them that love him? But ye have despised the poor."

Page 134   97. *there was nothing to save her from the "County House"*: During her lifetime, Wilson was sent to the Hillsborough County Poor Farm in Goffstown, New Hampshire. See also note 33.

Page 135   98. *"The Lord is my shepherd,—I shall not want"*: Psalm 23:1. See also note 94.

Page 135   99. *"My room was furnished some like the 'prophet's chamber,' except there was no 'candlestick'"*: 2 Kings 4:10. The irony becomes clear in a fuller reference: "And it fell on a day, that Elisha passed to Shunem, where was a great woman; and she constrained him to eat bread. And so it was, that, as oft as he passed by, he turned in thither to eat bread. And she said unto her husband, Behold now, I perceive that this is a holy man of God, which passeth by us continually. Let us make a little chamber, I pray thee, on the wall; and let us set for him there a bed, and a table, and a stool, and a candlestick: and it shall be, when he cometh to us, that he shall turn in thither" (2 Kings 4:8–10). Without a candlestick, Frado will be passed by; she herself encounters no such charity.

Page 135   100. *"I am poor and needy, yet the Lord thinketh upon me"*: This comes from Psalm 40:17, "But I am poor and needy; yet the Lord thinketh upon me: thou art my help and my deliverer; make no tarrying, O my God."

Pages 135–36 101. *"O, holy Father, by thy power"*: These verses, written in hymnal long measure, seem most likely not to have been plagiarized but to have been written by "the author of this book" (in "Allida"'s phrase) and pay further tribute to her creative abilities. Their unambiguously Christian sentiments stand as something of a contrast to Frado's more dubious and (at best) semiconsummated conversion to Christianity in the novel itself. While it is true that the final chapter sees Frado "reposing on God" (130), this "devout and Christian exterior" (125) seems to cover enduring doubts about whether Christianity was "all for white people" (84). The switch of tone here, in these verses' much more conventional piousness, and their biblical framing (see note 88) may be aimed at persuading *Our Nig*'s readers of the author's good Christian standing after all, making her a deserving charitable case. See also note 110. The "lines" the author includes here echo some phrases in common with the work of Isaac Watts and others. For example "My heart shall not repine / The saint may live on earthy unknown / And yet in glory shine" echoes phrases in Isaac Watts's "Psalm 73 . . . The Mystery of Providence Unfolded": "And felt my heart repine / While haughty fools with scornful eyes / In robes of honour shine" (Isaac Watts, *The Psalms and Hymns of Dr. Watts . . . in one volume* [Philadelphia: David Clark, 1839], n.p. [Psalm 73].) Similarly, "He came unto his own, but lo! / His own received him not" echoes one of John and

Charles Wesley's hymns, "Arise, my soul, arise,/Thy Saviour's Sacrifice": "His own on earth He sought/His own received him not" ([John Wesley], *A Collection of Hymns for the Use of the People Called Methodist by the Rev. John Wesley* [London: T. Crodeaux and T. Blanshard, 1820], 190–91.) In this latter case, this phrase has, of course, a common source, namely John 1:11: "He came unto his own, and his own received him not." That both the poems in the appendix, one ostensibly written by the "author of this book" and one by "Allida," perhaps share common debts to Watts and Wesley might again suggest their common authorship.

Page 136 102. *A kind gentleman and lady took her little boy into their own family, and provided everything necessary for his good:* Barbara A. White discovered that the "kind gentleman and lady" taking Harriet E. Wilson's son into their house were remunerated under Milford's provisions for the destitute, since "Wilson boy" appears in its register of paupers. See our chronology page clxiii.

Pages 136–37 103. *they shall be "recompensed at the resurrection of the just":* This comes from Luke 14:14: "For thou shalt be recompensed at the resurrection of the just."

Page 137 104. *another method of procuring her bread—that of writing an Autobiography:* Plainly, "Allida" considers *Our Nig* sufficiently true to life to describe it as an "Autobiography."

Page 137 105. *"I will help thee, saith the Lord":* This comes from Isaiah 41:14.

Page 137–38 106. *"I will help thee," promise kind:* It is unclear whether these verses are being presented as being written by "Allida" or as being quoted by her. If the latter, then the "source" would be a hymn or a related devotional verse. However, the first four stanzas are composed in long measure and the last three in common measure. Hymns did not make this sort of switch partway through. It seems probable, therefore, that "Allida," or Wilson (if she herself wrote these testimonials—see note 88), is offering a pastiche here. Much of the phrasing in this poem is reminiscent of that of John and Charles Wesley. For example, the phrase "supplicating cry" appears three times in *The poetical works of John and Charles Wesley: reprinted from the originals, with the last corrections of the authors; together with the poems of Charles Wesley not before published.* Collected and arranged by G. Osborn, 13 vols. (London: The Wesleyan Methodist Conference Office, 1868). Similarly, the phrasing of William Cowper and Isaac Watts are echoed in the first two stanzas. See, for example, both Cowper's "Light Shining Out of Darkness," "God moves in a mysterious way / His wonders to perform; / He plants his footsteps in the sea, / And rides upon the storm" (*The Works of William Cowper* [London: Baldwin and Cradock, 1835, 1837], 8: 82) and Watts's "Our God, our help in ages past / Our hope for years to come, / Our shelter from the stormy blast, / And our eternal home" ("Psalm XC" in *The Works of the Reverend and Learned Isaac Watts* [London: Printed by and for John Barfield [etc.], 1810], 4:191). Finally, there are substantial overlaps with the closing stanzas of Sir John Bowring's hymn "Siste, Viator!":

Look above thee—there indeed
May thy thoughts repose delighted;
If thy wounded bosom bleed,
If thy fondest hopes be blighted;
There a stream of comfort flows,
There a sun of splendour glows:
Wander, then, no more benighted!

Look above thee—ages roll,
Present, past and future blending;
Earth hath nought to soothe a soul
'Neath affliction's burthen bending;
Nothing 'gainst the tempest's shock;
Heaven must be the pilgrim's rock,
And to heaven his steps are tending.

Look above thee—never eye
Saw such pleasures as await thee;
Thought ne'er reach'd such scenes of joy
As are there prepared to meet thee:
Light undying,—seraphs' lyres,—
Angel-welcomes,—cherub-choirs
Smiling thro' heaven's doors to greet thee.

See John Bowring, *Matins and Vespers: with Hymns and Occasional Devotional Pieces* (Boston: Hilliard, Gray, Little and Wilkins, 1827), 214–17. The sentiments that "Allida" and Bowring share are stock ones, of course.

Page 138 107. *Allida:* A pseudonym. See note 90.

Page 138   108. *To the friends of our dark-complexioned brethren:* Apparently, "Margaretta Thorn," the writer of this second testimonial, envisages a white as well as an African American readership for Harriet E. Wilson's work. See note 91.

Page 139   109. *She was indeed a slave, in every sense of the word:* The parallel drawn here between Frado's life and that of a slave is the most explicit in the book; that it comes in an appended testimonial makes it all the more telling. As Foreman and Pitts point out, "Margaretta Thorn" is effectively charging the Bellmonts retrospectively with a crime, since in 1857 New Hampshire had passed an act outlawing slavery.

Page 139–40   110. *Do good as we have opportunity; and we can always find opportunity, if we have the disposition:* Many examples of this sort of sanctimoniousness lurk in mid-nineteenth-century writing. If, as we suggest, this testimonial may be the work of Wilson, then the Franklinesque tone of Margaretta Thorn's words is being used satirically ("Therefore we should do with all our might what our hands find to do. . . . Therefore, let us work while the day lasts, and we shall in no wise lose our reward" [140]). It is, perhaps, reasonable to suggest that this sort of unreflective religiosity is, precisely, a "thorn" in the side of Frado, making this testimonial a subtle commentary on the shortcomings of white Christian benevolence and a sign that the testimonials are penned by Wilson (see also note 89).

Page 140   111. *I hope those who call themselves friends of our dark-skinned brethren, will lend a helping hand:* See note 8 regarding colored brethren. "Margaretta Thorn" is echoing Wilson's earlier words, in her preface, "I sincerely appeal to my colored brethren universally for patronage" (3). This might lend weight to the idea that these are the words of Wilson, not a testimonial writer, for these sentiments handily expand the potential audience to include a white readership. See notes 8 and 19.

Page 140   112. *inasmuch as ye have done a good deed to one of the least of these my brethren, ye have done it to me:* This comes from Matthew 25:40.

Page 140   113. *even a cup of water is not forgotten. Therefore, let us work while the day lasts, and we shall in no wise lose our reward:* "Margaretta Thorn" could have picked up this pat nostrum from many a sermon. Certainly George Ware Briggs, in his *The Bow in the Cloud* (Boston: Joseph Dowe, 1846, 135), uses the words "let us work while the day lasts" as a chorus in one long devotional passage. The other part, "even a cup of water is not forgotten . . . we shall in no wise lose our reward" may be taken from Mark 9:41 ("For whosoever shall give you a cup of water to drink in my name, because ye belong to Christ, verily I say unto you, he shall not lose his reward") or Matthew 10:42 ("And whosoever shall give to drink unto one of these little ones a cup of cold water only in the name of a disciple, verily I say unto you, he shall in no wise lose his reward"). Within a decade, Charles Kingsley was drawing on these sources, too, in his "Sermon IX: Ruth," in *The Water of Life and Other Sermons,* 1867 (London: Macmillan and Co., 143–57). See note 109.

Page 140   114. *Margaretta Thorn:* "Margaretta Thorn" is likely to be
           another pseudonym. Certainly the way Margaretta Thorn's
           self-help nostrums (see notes 109 and 112) promote a ver-
           sion of the white American creed of self-reliance would
           make her a sharp "thorn" in the side of the systemically
           disadvantaged Frado. See also note 90.

Page 140   115. *Milford:* It was this single word at the head of C.D.S.'s
           testimonial that enabled Henry Louis Gates, Jr., and, sub-
           sequently, Barbara A. White to track down the historical
           identity of Harriet Wilson.

Page 140   116. *I hope no one will refuse to aid her in her work, as she is
           worthy the sympathy of all Christians:* C.D.S.'s words here
           echo those of Wilson earlier: "reposing on God . . . she
           asks your sympathy, gentle reader. . . . Enough has been
           unrolled to demand your sympathy and aid" (130). Once
           again, the idea that Wilson authored the testimonials is
           reinforced.

Page 140   117. *C. D. S.:* A pseudonym. See note 90.

CHRONOLOGY OF HARRIET E. ADAMS WILSON

Compiled by R. J. Ellis

This chronology draws on the research of Henry Louis Gates, Jr., Richard J. Ellis, David A. Curtis, Barbara A. White, P. Gabrielle Foreman, Reginald H. Pitts, Johni Cerny, and Donald Yacovone.

1825? 1827? 1828?: Birth of Harriet E. Wilson, née Adams or Green. Her birthplace is recorded as "New Hampshire" in the 1850 Milford, New Hampshire, federal census, which gives her name as "Harriet Adams." She would have been born in 1827 or 1828, based on the 1850 census, which recorded her age as twenty-two years on August 24, 1850, and her race as "B[lack]." The 1851 marriage record of Harriet Adams and Thomas Wilson also records her birthplace as Milford, New Hampshire. Examinations of census details have so far identified an Adams family that fits the deducible details in *Our Nig*. If the fictionalized autobiography is accurate concerning Wilson's life—including her natural father's early death—it is possible that, although there was no free black head of household in New Hampshire in 1830 named Adams, Harriet could have been living with her mother in a family headed by her mother's common-law husband. In Milford itself, the Timothy Blanchard household, on the Shed[d] farm, as it was marked on a contemporary map (see introduction, page xlii) contained both colored and white residents and young children in the 1830 census, making it the most plausible candidate for Wilson's childhood household in Milford. Blanchard ran a cooperage, and Frado in *Our Nig* notes her father was a "hooper of barrels," "boarding cheap" with a cooper. It is possible Wilson was born earlier, on the basis of the death certificate of Hattie E. Wilson, issued in 1900, who in all likelihood is the same person. On this death certificate, her father and mother are named as Joshua and Margaret Green— an alteration to her last name that cannot be readily explained, though the cooper in *Our Nig* is given the pseudonym "Pete Greene." If Hattie Wilson is Harriet E. Wilson, she is possibly recalling this pseudonym, or just possibly she may, as she claims in the *Banner of Light* on December 12, 1870, have at some time in the 1860s pursued enquiries about her background that suggested "Adams" was not her surname.[1]

1834? 1835? 1836?: Frado "was taken from home so young," according to "Margaretta Thorn," one of the three people providing a testimonial for *Our Nig*. Harriet E. Adams spent her early life living with and in service to the Nehemiah Hayward family.[2]

1840 July: The 1840 census lists a female "free colored person" between the ages of ten and twenty-four living on July 1 alongside the Hayward family of "free white persons," in the Hayward household at the Hayward family farm in Milford. Nehemiah Hayward is the only person referred to by name, as the head of the household. This is also the only reference to a female "free colored person" living in Milford in the 1840 census, which suggests it was indeed Harriet E. Adams.[3]

Many of the characters and circumstances of the Hayward family parallel the Bellmont family in *Our Nig*, further suggesting Harriet E. Adams was associated with the Hayward family:

- Nehemiah Hayward, Sr., (1738–1825) was born in Hardwick, Massachusetts, to a family who had emigrated from England to Massachusetts in the 1640s. After amassing considerable property in New Brunswick, he bought 118 acres of land between Milford and Wilton, New Hampshire, in 1781. Like *Our Nig*'s "Sire," Nehemiah Sr. bought land that was unincorporated and therefore untaxed. Also like "Sire," he left his holdings to his son, with the stipulation that his daughter, Sally (like "Aunt Abby"), owned a "right in the homestead" and had the right to occupy part of the house.

- Nehemiah Hayward, Jr., (1779–1849), like "Mr. John Bellmont," inherited this farm from his parents.

- Rebecca S. Hutchinson Hayward (1780/81–1850) married Nehemiah Jr. in 1806. A direct descendent of the Pilgrim Anne Hutchinson and the granddaughter of one of Milford's earliest settlers, she bore nine children, seven of whom lived to adulthood. Like "Mrs. Bellmont," Rebecca Hayward seems to have possessed a difficult personality.

- The Hayward farm, like the "Bellmont farm," had orchards, sheep flocks, and was located above the fast-flowing Souhegan River in a steep-sided valley.

- The youngest Hayward daughter, Rebecca Hayward, like "Mary Bellmont," died in her teens while visiting Baltimore.

- Lucretia Hayward, the family's other daughter, like "Jane Bellmont," married a man from Vermont and eventually moved West.

- George Hayward, Nehemiah's eldest son, like "James Bellmont," worked in Baltimore and returned home with his
  wife and child after falling ill. He died early and was buried
  in Milford. Wilson's son, George Mason, may have been
  named after George Hayward's son George M. Hayward.
  Some of the Hayward family had abolitionist ties. Rebecca
  Hayward was related to the Hutchinson Family Singers,
  who gained international acclaim in the late 1840s and the
  1850s as progressive supporters of women's rights, temperance, and the abolition of slavery. Rebecca's son Jonas Hayward, a Baltimore businessman, who seems to have been
  an abolitionist, aided the Hutchinson Family Singers when
  they visited Baltimore in 1844. The Reverend Humphrey
  Moore, whose strong abolitionist sentiments aroused controversy in Milford, officiated at the marriage of Nehemiah
  Hayward, Jr., and Rebecca and served as the Hayward family pastor (they owned a pew in his church) until he was
  elected by antislavery men to the New Hampshire House of
  Representatives in 1840 and the state senate in 1841.[4]

1832? 1834? – 1836? 1838?: Attends a Milford public school, probably in District School Number 2, where the Hayward farm was
  located, according to C. E. Potter's 1854 map of Milford.[5]

1842? 1845? 1846?: Leaves the Hayward household, most probably
  aged eighteen.

1850: Harriet Wilson appears as Harriet Adams in the "Report of the
  Overseers of the Poor for the Town of Milford, for the Year Ending Feb 15th 1850." "Harriet Adams" is listed as a "Pauper Not

on the Farm," her cost to the town being $43.84. She does not
appear in the "Report of the Overseers of the Poor" for the years
1839 through 1849. Clearly during the year 1849–50, Harriet E.
Adams was unable to support herself. She would have been
placed with a local family, who would have been reimbursed by
the town.[6]

1850: In the August 24, 1850, census, Harriet Adams is listed as
twenty-two years old, black, and resident in the household of
Samuel Boyles.[7] Presumably this was the family with whom she
was placed as a pauper at that time.

1851: Harriet Adams is again listed as a Milford "Pauper Not on the
Farm" for the year ending February 15, 1851.[8] Clearly she was
still unable to support herself.

1851: "Allida," in her testimonial at the end of *Our Nig* reports that,
most probably in early 1851, an "itinerant colored lecturer"
took "Our Nig" (Harriet E. Adams) to W_____, an "ancient
town" possessing a straw hat industry. There she became an
"inmate" of Mrs. Walker's household in W_____ and began
working as a "straw-sewer" (133). However, so weakened by
her "hard treatment" in the Hayward family that her "constitution [was] greatly impaired," she soon becomes Mrs. Walker's domestic help instead (133). It is unclear whether Walker
is or is not another pseudonym, though *Our Nig* consistently
uses pseudonyms. W_____ is likely to be Ware, Westborough,
Walpole, or Worcester, in an area of Massachusetts where straw-
sewing industries were concentrated. Arthur Chase describes the
"manufacture of straw goods" as "an important industry of the

village [of Ware] in former times." He reports that this industry "was commenced in 1832" but "besides the work done in the shops, straw-sewing was done largely in the houses about town." A common household industry, "the sewing of hats by hand," according to Herman DeForest, "was for a long time confined to this part of Massachusetts," meaning that "a large number of sewers were required." Braid, brought to Westborough sewers by "stock-carts" from Upton—where the industry began in 1825— was "sewed into straw hats by women in this town." Isaac Newton Lewis refers briefly to the straw-goods manufacturers of Walpole in his section on the industry of the town. The other W_____ town in this part of Massachusetts is the larger town of Worcester, where again straw goods were produced in quantity, and a town where spiritualism would take a strong hold, supported by Thomas Wentworth Higginson. The 1850 federal census reveals there were approximately two dozen Walker families living in Walpole, Ware, Westborough, and Worcester in 1850. A significant proportion of these Walker families lived in Worcester. There is no sure way of narrowing the list of Walker families, based on available evidence.[9] Walker may, of course, be yet another pseudonym.

1851 September/October: Harriet E. Adams had by this time returned to Milford, New Hampshire, to marry Thomas Wilson, whom she met in W_____, according to the testimonial writer "Allida" in the appendix to *Our Nig.* "Allida" reports that "months passed" between Adams's being transferred by the "itinerant colored preacher" to "W_____" and his return in the "early Spring" (this seems be an unlikely date; it is more likely to have been some time in the summer). This second encounter, according to *Our Nig,* saw the preacher accompanied by a man representing himself as a fugitive slave (a house servant): "Suffice it to say, an acquaintance was formed, which, in due time, resulted in marriage.... In a few days, [Frado] left W_____,... and took up her abode in New Hampshire." Given that "Allida" attests in 1859 to knowing Harriet E. Wilson for only about eight years (i.e., from 1851/52), the dates in the early 1840s that she gives in her testimonial are likely to be errors, considering that Thomas Wilson married Harriet Adams in 1851.

1851: Thomas Wilson marries Harriet Adams on October 6, 1851, in Milford, New Hampshire. No details of age or race are listed. This information was "returned" in April 1852 by Rev. E. N. Hidden, the fifth pastor of Milford's Congregational church, for the years 1849–58. The records show that Thomas Wilson was from "Virginia" and Harriet Adams from "Milford." [10]

1852?: George Mason Wilson born, probably in late May or early June of 1852 (approximately nine months after Thomas Wilson of Virginia married Harriet Adams of Milford). The birth occurred in Goffstown, New Hampshire, a few miles north of Milford in Hillsborough County—where the Hillsborough County Farm was located at the time. Margaretta Thorn reports that the son was born on the "County Farm" while Wilson was "in her sickness" and unable to "pay his board every week." The county farm was an undesirable, disease-ridden place to live. George Plummer Hadley recounts that "in 1853 some of the inmates were stricken with smallpox, and it was necessary to build a pest-house for the proper care and segregation of the smallpox patients" and concludes, "What tales of sorrow could some of the unfortunates unfold."[11]

"Allida" reports that "for a while" the couple settled down, but that the husband ran away to sea: "Days passed; weeks passed," and *Our Nig*'s author fell so ill she had to go to the "County House," where she gave birth to her child, and that "then" the husband returned. The family then moved to "some town in New Hampshire," according to "Allida," "where, for a time, the husband supported her and his little son decently well. . . . But again he left her as before." He never returned; the narrator of *Our Nig* notes that Frado's husband later died in New Orleans.

1852: In the *Farmer's Cabinet* for July 8, July 15, and July 22, Harriet Wilson's name appears in the "List of Letters in the Post Office at Milford, N.H., July 1, 1852." Possibly this letter (or these letters) came from her friends in W_____.

1855: "Harriet E. Wilson" appears on the February 1855 Milford "Report of the Overseers of the Poor" listed under "Pauper Not on the Farm" and costing the town $45.45.[12]

1855: George Wilson is admitted to the Hillsborough County Poor Farm for four weeks beginning August 19, 1855: "Wilson, George Age: 3 / Time Admitted: Aug 19, 1855 / Former Residence: Milford / Colored / Time of discharge: Sept. 11, 1855 / Place of destination: Milford to his mother / No. weeks board: 4 / No. days board: 1."[13]

1856: "Harriet E. Wilson and child" are listed as Milford "Paupers Not on the Farm" for the year ending February 15, 1856.[14]

1856? 1857? 1858?: If "Allida" is reliable, "the heart of a stranger was moved with compassion, and bestowed a recipe upon [Harriet E. Wilson] for restoring gray hair to its former color. She availed herself of this great help, and has been quite successful." Surviving bottles carrying the name "Harriet E. Wilson" have been found in the New Hampshire/western Massachusetts area, suggesting she enjoyed some success in this business. By 1859 Wilson's hair restorative/regeneration business is being advertised in the Milford *Farmer's Cabinet* and elsewhere—such as the *Methodist Quarterly Review* (in 1860).[15]

1856: In the *Farmer's Cabinet* for October 9, October 16, and October 23, Harriet Wilson's name appears twice in the "List of Letters in the Post Office at Milford, N.H., October 1, 1856" (as "Harriet Wilson" and as "Harriet E. Wilson"). Possibly these letters are connected to steps Wilson was taking to establish her hair restorative/regeneration business.

1857: "Wilson boy" appears on the list of Milford paupers "not on the farm." This curt entry, following on from the entry for "Harriet E. Wilson and child" in 1856 suggests that this is George Wilson. This is the first of three entries for 1857–59 that, taken together, seem to support the claim made by "Allida" that Wilson left her son with a family in Milford. Margaretta Thorn tells the same tale: "At length a kindly gentleman and lady took her little boy into their own family." The author of *Our Nig*, adds Thorn, "wishes to educate her son." Thorn also reports that the child "shows promise."

1858: "Wilson boy" again appears on the list of Milford paupers "not on the farm."[16]

1859: "Wilson boy" once more appears on the list of Milford paupers "not on the farm."[17]

1859: In her 1859 testimonial, "Allida" states that *Our Nig's* author's health "is again failing" and that she decided to write her "autobiography" as "another method of procuring her bread." No dates or places are given in this section of "Allida"'s account of Harriet E. Wilson's life. In the last chapter of *Our Nig*, the narrator pleads for support for herself in her present destitute condition and tells how she passed through the various towns of the state she lived in, then into Massachusetts. It is possible she was selling both her hair-care product and her book door to door during this time. However, in the preface to *Our Nig*, its author notes that writing was an "experiment" undertaken to help her "maintain" herself and her child "without extinguishing this feeble life," which is not suggestive of door-to-door selling.

1859: "C .D. S.," the third testimonial writer in *Our Nig*, reports on July 20, 1859, that he/she has been "acquainted with her [the author] for several years." He/she has a "deep interest in the welfare of the writer" and testifies that "her complexion is a little darker than my own," which may suggest that C.D.S. was of mixed descent.

1859: *Our Nig* was copyrighted on August 18. A copy was deposited at that time "by Mrs. H. E. Wilson, In the Clerk's office of the District Court of the District of Massachusetts." The novel was printed for the author by the printers George C. Rand & Avery of Boston, Massachusetts. Rand & Avery did not usually publish novels, but had published some abolitionist writings. Rand & Avery may have entered the book for copyright on the author's

behalf (a common practice by publishers in order to establish copyright, since this was in their interest as much as their
author's).[18]

1860 February 13: George Mason Wilson, aged "7 years, 8 months,"
died in Milford, New Hampshire, according to the New Hampshire Bureau of Vital Records. He was recorded as black, and
his parents are listed as Thomas Wilson of Virginia and Harriet Wilson of Milford, New Hampshire. He died of the "fever."
Because George Mason Wilson died in a census year, his death
was also recorded in the Mortality Schedule of the federal census, which lists his cause of death as "billious fever" following
an illness of twelve days and gives his "color" as "mulatto." The
Farmer's Cabinet—Milford's local paper—reports that a George
Mason Wilson died in Milford on February 13, 1860, at the
age of "7 years, 8 months," the "only son of H. E. Wilson." Harriet E. Wilson's son thus died within six months of *Our Nig*'s
publication, rendering futile what the narrator describes in *Our
Nig*'s final chapter as an attempt to raise money to support her
child by publishing *Our Nig*.[19]

1860: No blacks fitting the description of Harriet E. Wilson appear
in the 1860 federal census for Hillsborough County, suggesting
she had left the area by that time. However, an advertisement
for her hair dressing published in 1860 provides a "testimonial"
provided by a "Mrs. H. E. Wilson of Nashua."[20]

1860–61: Wilson enters into a business relationship with Henry P.
Wilson (no relation), who manufactures and sells her hair prod-
ucts, in bottles carrying her name.[21] According to P. Gabrielle
Foreman and Katherine Flynn, in the period 1860 to 1861 "at

least 1,500 ads for Mrs. Wilson's hair products appeared in a
score of papers."[22]

1863: "Mrs. Wilson" is listed in Milford's 1863 "Report of the Overseers of the Poor" under "Support of County Paupers" (in a
reorganized record system). This is possibly Harriet E. Wilson.
Though she had not previously been given a title in Milford's
town records, her advertisements for her hair-care products
had named her as Mrs. H. E. Wilson, and this may have caused
a change in her mode of address more generally. After this
1863 entry, Wilson's name does not appear again in Milford's
records.[23]

1866/1867: Wilson probably moves to the Boston area within a few
years of 1863, most probably in 1866 or 1867. This seems to
be associated with an embrace of spiritualism and the seeking-
out of a spiritualist career. The evidence for this move is the
records of a (second) marriage and a death, both of which suggest that Harriet E. Wilson is the same person as Hattie E. Wilson, a colored Boston spiritualist who emerges in the pages of
the spiritualist newspaper the *Banner of Light* in 1867 (see appendix 2). Likely sponsors of this move into a spiritualist career are
C. Fannie Allyn, who became a very prominent spiritualist at
this time and who spoke in both Milford and Worcester, Massachusetts and/or Isaiah C. Ray.[24]

1867: Hattie E. Wilson is listed in the Boston spiritualist newspaper
Banner of Light as both a speaker (from May 1867) and as living
in East Cambridge, Massachusetts (in June). She is known as
"the eloquent and earnest colored trance medium." She joins
the Massachusetts Spiritualist Association. She participates in

their conventions and gives an address in favor of labor reform. The *Banner* now begins regularly to record aspects of Wilson's involvement with Boston spiritualist activities (for full details, see appendix 2, "Harriet E. Wilson in the *Banner of Light* and *Spiritual Scientist*").[25]

1867 September: The *Banner* reports Wilson's address to a "Great Spiritualist Camp Meeting" in Pierpont Grove, Melrose, Massachusetts, which generated "thrilling interest" by its plea for both "recognition of the capacities of her race" and the "philosophy of progress."[26]

1868: Mrs. Hattie E. Wilson is listed in the *Boston Directory, Embracing the City Record* for 1867. She appears twice: in the general listing (705) and as a "Physician" (623). Her address is given as "70 Tremont." From this date onwards, Wilson regularly appears in Boston's city directory. This chronology will henceforth only pick out noteworthy directory entries.[27]

1868 February: Wilson is elected onto the Massachusetts Spiritual Association Convention's "Finance Committee," as recorded in the *Banner*.

1868 August: The *Banner* details Wilson's participations in a camp meeting in Cape Cod.

1868 September: As noted in the *Banner*, Wilson moves to West Garland, Maine, in October for a few months, while on a lecturing tour in Maine, but before the end of the year returns back to Boston (to 70 Tremont Street).

1869: Wilson moves to 27 Carver Street, as recorded in the *Boston City Directory* (652, 837).

1869 January: She begins a brief career as a successful platform speaker (as recorded in the *Banner*).

1869 July: Moves to 46 Carver Street, as recorded in the *Banner*.[28]

1870: Wilson starts the process of shifting over from platform speaking to a concentration upon the spiritualist children's lyceum movement, as is apparent in *Banner* reports.

1870: The 1870 federal census lists "Hattie Wilson" as a thirty-eight-year-old white female, born in New Hampshire, and gives her occupation as physician. She is living in the household of John Gallatin Robinson, a twenty-six-year-old apothecary born in Connecticut.[29]

1870 September 29: John Gallatin Robinson and Harriet E. Wilson marry in Boston. The record shows that "Harriet E. Wilson," born in Milford, New Hampshire, but resident in Boston, declared that she was thirty-seven years old, the daughter of Joshua and Margaret Green, and that this was her second marriage (while her husband's first). The minister in charge was the Reverend J. L. Mansfield. Despite all the substantial discrepancies with what we know about Wilson, this would still seem to be the Harriet E. Wilson who wrote *Our Nig*, not least because her death certificate provides corroborative evidence.[30] The record also contains a column for the color of the individuals marrying to be noted. In this column, check marks appear for both

Robinson and Wilson, but the meaning of these is not clear. For a discussion, see appendix 3. Following this marriage, Wilson usually continues to be referred to as Hattie E. Wilson in *Banner* news reports, though until the couple split up, most probably in 1877, she also appears as Hattie E. Robinson in the *Banner's* listings. See appendix 3, "Documents from Harriet Wilson's Life in Boston."

1870 November: The *Banner* provides a detailed report of Wilson's three contributions to a spiritualist convention in Haverhill, Massachusetts.

1871ff September: As recorded in the *Banner,* Wilson becomes involved in regular spiritualist sessions in Temple Hall, perhaps as its resident medium, and later becomes involved in its Children's Progressive Lyceum.

1873 April: Wilson is elected as one of the "Leaders" of one of the groups of children forming part of the Temple Hall Independent Children's Progressive Lyceum.

1873 August: The *Banner* notes how Wilson speaks on the same platform as the highly controversial Victoria Woodhull (a "free love" advocate) and others at the Fourth Annual Spiritualist Camp Meeting, Silver Lake, Plympton, Massachusetts.

1874 February: The *Banner* notes that "Mrs. Hattie E. Wilson, the well-known trance lecturer, gave an anniversary in honour of her spirit father"—the first of many such mentions of Wilson's involvement in the social side of Boston's spiritualist activities.

1874 circa March: Begins to become involved with Boston's Children's Progressive Lyceum No. 1, as noted in the *Banner*.

1874 August or early September: Wilson speaks at the dedication of Rochester Hall, Boston, to which the Children's Progressive Lyceum No. 1 had moved, and her address is reported at length in the *Spiritual Scientist*'s first issue, on September 10, 1874.

1874 September: The *Banner* records that Wilson was elected as the leader of the "Lake" group of Boston's Children's Progressive Lyceum No. 1.

1874 September: The *Banner* reports that Wilson speaks in Boston at a convention of the "Universal Spiritualist Association," whose president was the controversial "free love" advocate, Victoria Woodhull. This event, which Woodhull missed, is also reported extensively, and very disapprovingly, in the *Spiritual Scientist*.

1875 January 14: The *Spiritual Scientist* extensively reports upon a large celebration held by Wilson at Rochester Hall, attended by senior figures in Boston's spiritualist circles.

1875 May: The *Banner* notes that, at a meeting of the Boston Spiritualist Union aimed at setting up an "American Spiritual Institute," Wilson was selected as its "Director—Educational Department." The *Spiritual Scientist* notes that Wilson was appointed at the meeting to the "committee to return and nominate," the function of which seems to have been to arrange for the collation of nominations to the institute's Acting Executive Committee. Wilson was not on this latter committee, nor later ones. After this one mention of Wilson, the extensive reports in the *Spiritual Scientist* about how the American Spiritual Institute tried to set about funding the establishment of a "Spiritual Temple" in Boston never referred to Wilson again. This institute eventually seems to have collapsed, almost penniless, in September 1875.[31]

1876 April: The *Banner* provides an account of a speech given by Wilson the previous month at "the Twenty-Eighth Anniversary of the Advent of Modern Spiritualism Commemorative Exercises at Paine Hall, Boston."

1877 circa April: The *Banner* notes that Wilson moves to Hotel Kirkland, Kirkland Street; this is probably a consequence of breaking up with John Gallatin Robinson. (After this date her name does not again appear as Mrs. Hattie Robinson in the *Banner*.)

1879 April: *Banner* reports show that Wilson is centrally involved in the foundation of a new lyceum, "Children's Progressive Lyceum No. 2," which would soon rival the Children's Progressive Lyceum No. 1 as the leading children's lyceum for Boston spiritualists.

1879: The *Boston City Directory* lists Mrs. Hattie Wilson's address as 15 Village Street (973). Wilson is consistently listed in the *Boston City Directory* as living at this address from 1879 through 1897 (1610).

1880: The U.S. Census lists Wilson as aged forty, a mulatto and as keeping house at 15 Village Street. (Curiously, she is recorded as born in Maine.) The other family listed at this address consists of Frank J. Ellis, his wife, and their three children.[32] The *Banner* still continues to list her as resident at the Hotel Kirkland at this time. However, the *Boston City Directory* notes Wilson's address as 15 Village Street, Boston. It is unclear exactly when in 1879 she moved there, but this *Banner* 1870 listing is certainly erroneous (the *Banner* regularly complains that its spiritualists did not update their listings).

1880: Wilson serves as the treasurer of Boston's Children's Progressive Lyceum No. 2, as recorded by the *Banner.*

1880 April: The *Banner* notes that, at a ceremony marking the Children's Progressive Lyceum No. 2's renaming as the Shawmut Spiritual Lyceum, Wilson delivers a reading. Subsequent issues of the *Banner* continue to record her regular involvement until the end of 1882.

1883 January: The *Banner* reports upon "a complimentary reception . . . given by Mrs. Hattie E. Wilson to her friends," possibly as a preparation for the founding of her school the next month.

1883 February: Wilson founds a "Spiritual Progressive School" for children in Boston, her name for her spiritualist lyceum for children. This seems to cease operation early in 1884.

1897: Boston's city directory lists "Mrs. Hattie E. Wilson" as "board[ing at] 9 Pelham" in Boston (1641). This address is also listed in the 1898 directory (1660). This 1898 listing is the last listing for Wilson in the *Boston City Directory.*

1898: The *Banner* of May 21, in its "Movements of Platform Lectur-

ers" column, carries a notice that "Mrs. Hattie E. Wilson, 9 Pelham street, Boston, holds circles at 7.45 P.M." (8).

1899: The *Banner* records on December 20 that at a meeting in
"Dwight Hall" a "Mrs. Dr. Wilson" speaks of her spiritualist convictions. This may be a reference to Harriet E. Wilson; if it is, it
is the final reference to her in the *Banner,* and one of only a tiny
number in the last decade of her life.

1900: The 1900 U.S. Census does not record Hattie Wilson in Boston, or in Quincy, Massachusetts, where she is to die on June
28.[33] It is unclear why she is in Quincy at the time of her death.
P. Gabrielle Foreman and Reginald Pitts speculate that she was
employed as a nurse in the home of Silas H. Cobb. This speculation is supported by the facts that Silas Cobb was injured during
the Civil War (a cannon rolled back over him, leading him eventually to file for a disability), that Wilson's death certificate notes
her occupation as "nurse," and that Silas Cobb dies on April
4, 1900, which cumulatively might suggest Wilson had gone to
Quincy to nurse him.[34] While it is possible that she did serve
as a "nurse" of some sort for the Cobbs, we do not know how
long she had been living in Quincy before her death, though
we are told that the "inanition" that caused her death had lasted
for two months (see appendix 3). However, her place of residence on her death certificate is given as "Boston. 9 Pelham
Street." This suggests her time in Quincy may not have lasted
long. Though she is not recorded in the *Boston City Directory*
after 1898, she was in the audience at Dwight Hall in December
1899 and she may simply have become too old to bother or be
able to arrange for any listing in the directory after 1898. She
may therefore have just been visiting Catherine Cobb's house-

hold, or Catherine Cobb may have fetched her from Boston to
Quincy after her illness set in, perhaps because Catherine Cobb
was a long-standing client of hers or an admirer of her spiritualist talents. This speculation is supported by Cobb family lore,
which for a long time held that Wilson was a Native American,
a mistake that can best be explained not by supposing she was
attempting to pass as a Native American (her listings in the *Banner,* for example, always listed her as a "colored" medium) but
by the fact that her fame as a medium chiefly resided in the
access she claimed she could gain to "Indian" spirit guides (the
assumption here being that over the years the Cobbs' family narrative came to misremember that she was a medium accessing
Native American spirits). Since Wilson's "inanition" is recorded
as "incident to old age" and lasting for "two months," it seems
a little unlikely she was nursing Silas Cobb a few weeks before
her terminal decline, and much more likely that the Cobb family rescued her from a situation of some need in Boston. This
would also explain her burial in Quincy in the Cobb family plot:
the Cobbs take upon themselves the task of arranging for Wilson's burial because Wilson's estate could not support the cost
of transporting her body back to Boston (Wilson's spiritualist
career seems to have long been almost dormant, as detailed in
appendix 2). Cobb family lore explicitly supports this idea, as it
holds that Walter Cobb, Silas H. Cobb's son (and a prominent
Quincy newspaperman), generously arranged for her burial in
the Cobb family plot because she died in poverty. Notices of her
death appear in late June in the *Boston Herald, Boston Globe,* and
Quincy Patriot, along with details of her funeral. The *Globe*'s June
29 notice details how the funeral will be held from the residence
of Mrs. Catherine C. Cobb, 93 Washington Street, Quincy, Saturday, June 30. Wilson is buried in Mount Wollaston Cemetery,

Quincy, in plot 1337 (the site of the Cobb family grave). Her
name is recorded at the bottom of the back of the Cobb memorial, under the names of deceased members of the Stoddard
family (close family friends of the Cobbs who came to share the
same burial plot).[35]

NOTES

1. See U.S. Federal Census, Milford, N.H., 1850; U.S. Federal Census, Milford, N.H., 1830; Milford Town Hall Vital Records, "copy
of marriages returned by Rev. E. N. Hidden, Apr. 1852." No
Adams families are listed as living in New Hampshire in Carter G.
Woodson's *Free Negro Heads of Families in the United States in 1830*
(Washington, D.C.: The Association for the Study of Negro Life
and History, Inc., 1925). There are, however, well over thirty
Adams families fitting the description provided in *Our Nig* listed
as living in other states. There is probably no way to determine if
one of these black Adams families is the family of Harriet Adams,
since the 1830 federal census, upon which Woodson's book is
based, only lists the names of the heads of households. See also
Massachusetts Deaths 506: 95, Massachusetts Archives, Columbia
Point, Boston, Mass.; and *Banner of Light* (hereafter cited as *BL*)
XXVIII, no. 8 (November 12, 1870): 2–3.

2. See Barbara A. White, "'Our Nig' and the She-Devil," 19–52.

3. U.S. Federal Census, Milford, N.H., 1840. See also White, "'Our
Nig' and the She-Devil," 21–22.

4. See White, " 'Our Nig' and the She-Devil," 19–52; R. J. Ellis, *Harriet Wilson's "Our Nig,"* 19–46. The depiction of the Haywards in *Our Nig,* the Bellmont family, was adapted to fit the requirements of a fictional tale. Consequently the chronologies do not match exactly, the Bellmonts have fewer children than the Haywards (five instead of seven), the sequence of arrivals and departures in and out of the family home of the Haywards does not match that found in *Our Nig,* and Sally Hayward was not Nehemiah Hayward's "maiden sister," since at some point she married, becoming Mrs. Sally Blanchard, though she did come to live with the Haywards. See Ellis, *Harriet Wilson's "Our Nig,"* 39.

5. Based on the information provided in *Our Nig.* There is some dispute over this; C. E. Potter's map, however, does seem to show the divide between school districts two and three as the Souhegan River. See C. E. Potter, [Map of] Milford (Milford: n.p. 1854).

6. The 1850 overseers for the poor report, and all others, are still located in the Town Clerk's Office in Milford. White and Ellis have viewed reports from the years 1839 through 1869.

7. U.S. Federal Census, Milford, N.H., 1850.

8. See the overseers' report for the poor, 1851, located in the Town Clerk's Office in Milford.

9. Arthur Chase, *History of Ware, Massachusetts* (Cambridge, Mass.: University Press, 1891), 224; Herman Packard DeForest, *The History of Westborough, Massachusetts* (Westborough: The Town, 1895), 364; Isaac Newton Lewis, *A History of Walpole, Massachusetts* (Walpole: First Historical Society, 1905); 1850 U.S. Federal Census, Accelerated Indexing System: Massachusetts. See also D. Hamilton Hurd, ed., *A History of Worcester County, Massachusetts* (Philadelphia: J. W. Lewis and Co., 1889).

10. Milford Town Hall Vital Records, "copy of marriages returned by Rev. E. N. Hidden, Apr. 1852."

11. George Plummer Hadley, "Hillsborough County Farm," in *The History of the Town of Goffstown, 1733–1920* (Concord, N.H.: Published by the Town, n.d. [1924?]), 424–37.

12. Overseers' report for the poor, 1855, located in the Town Clerk's Office in Milford Town Hall.

13. "Paupers Received and Discharged, 1853–1855," Hillsborough County Nursing Home (formerly Hillsborough County Farm), Goffstown, N.H.

14. Overseers' report for the poor, 1856, located in the Town Clerk's Office in Milford Town Hall.

15. Wilson, *Our Nig*, ed. Foreman and Pitts, ix; "Who Wants a Good Head of Hair? / Mrs. Wilson's / Hair Regenerator," *Farmer's Cabinet* (January 15, 1859), 4. See also "Use Mrs. Wilson's Hair Regenerator and Hair Dressing," in *Methodist Quarterly Review* 42, ed. D. D. Whedon (New York: Carlton and Porter, 1860), 714.

16. Overseers' report for the poor, 1858, located in the Town Clerk's Office in Milford Town Hall.

17. Overseers' report for the poor, 1859, located in the Town Clerk's Office in Milford Town Hall.

18. Some critics insist Harriet E. Wilson must have copyrighted the novel. See also Eric Gardner, " 'This Attempt of Their Sister' ": 226–46.

19. February 15, 1860, death record from the New Hampshire Bureau of Vital Records. This record enables George Wilson's birth date to be deduced. Mortality Schedule of the Federal Census for Milford, 1860. "Death Notices," *Farmer's Cabinet,* (February 29, 1860): 3.

20. U.S. Federal Census, Hillsborough County, N.H., 1860; *Methodist*

Quarterly Review 42, ed. D. D. Whedon (New York: Carlton and Porter, 1860), 714.

21. See Wilson, *Our Nig,* ed. Foreman and Pitts, x.

22. Foreman and Flynn, "Mrs. H. E. Wilson, Mogul?, rpt. at http://www.harrietwilsonproject.org/news/Mogul_Boston_Globe_Feb09.pdf.

23. Report of the overseers of the poor, 1863, located in the Town Clerk's Office in Milford Town Hall.

24. See appendix 2, "Hattie E. Wilson in the *Banner of Light* and *Spiritual Scientist.*" All future references to the *Banner of Light* can be cross-referred to this section. See also our introduction. See *Massachusetts Marriages,* 228: 129, Massachusetts Archives, Columbia Point, Boston, Mass.; and *Massachusetts Deaths,* 506: 95, Massachusetts Archives, Columbia Point, Boston, Mass. See also appendices pages iv, xxxvi, and clxx–clxxi of this edition.

25. See Wilson, *Our Nig,* ed. Foreman and Pitts, x; see also appendix 2, "Hattie E. Wilson in the *Banner of Light* and *Spiritual Scientist.*"

26. *BL* XXI, no. 26 (September 14, 1867): 5.

27. *Boston City Directory, Embracing the City Record* (Boston: Sampson, Davenport and Co., 1868), 623, 705. Wilson is listed in the following directories published by Sampson, Davenport: 1869 (652, 837, with the second listing recording her as a physician); 1870 (706, 809, with the second listing recording her as a physician); 1873 (798); 1874 (971); 1875 (946); 1876 (950); 1878 (940); 1879 (973); 1880 (1022); 1881 (1070); 1882 (1104); 1883 (1139); 1884 (1149); 1885 (1163); 1886 (1234); 1887 (1289); 1888 (1335); 1889 (1343); 1890 (1371); 1891 (1402); 1892 (1446); 1893 (1471); 1894 (1479); 1895 (1532); 1896 (1610); 1897 (1610); 1898 (1660).

28. The 1870 *Boston City Directory* records her address as still 27

Carver Street, probably erroneously. In 1872, this directory also records a Mrs. Hattie Wilson living at 5 Fayette Street (764). This is probably not Harriet E. Wilson, who by this time had moved into John Gallatin Robinson's household in 46 Carver Street and is listed in the *Banner* as living there in 1872.

29. U.S. Federal Census, Ward 8, Boston, 1870. On more than one occasion, Wilson is recorded as white in the official records. There are a number of possible reasons for this. She may have been seeking to pass as white (though it must be noted that she always advertised herself as a "colored . . . medium" in the *Banner*). Her husband may not have wished it to be known he had married a nonwhite person (again unlikely, since she ran a business as a colored medium from the house they shared). The person who recorded the entry may have assumed she was white from her appearance. Or perhaps here the census taker only interviewed Robinson and assumed his wife must be white without asking. Finally, the bare possibility exists that a simple error or slip of the pen occurred. See also appendix 3.

30. See *Massachusetts Marriages,* 228: 129, Massachusetts Archives, Columbia Point, Boston, Mass. See also appendix 3.

31. See "Meetings at Rochester Hall," *BL* XXXVII, no. 9 (May 29, 1875): 4.

32. U.S. Census, Population Schedule, Ward 16, Boston, 1880.

33. The 1900 Boston census, however, does record a Hattie Wilson living as a lodger at 15 Cortes Street. She is recorded as white, female, born in December 1850, a seamstress, born in Maine, with a father and mother both born in Maine. This record cannot simply be ignored. Though it is exceedingly unlikely that this Hattie Wilson is Harriet E. Wilson, nevertheless the coincidences stack up: Harriet E. Wilson was more than once taken to be white in official records, she had previously probably worked

in a sewing job, in W_____, Massachusetts (sewing hats), and in the 1880 census she had been recorded as born in Maine with both parents also born in Maine. There is an age discrepancy of more than twenty years, but the 1880 census had recorded an age discrepancy of more than ten years. What Wilson could be doing in Cortes Street, Boston, a matter of weeks before her death in Quincy is unclear, especially as her death certificate records her as not only living in Quincy at the time of her death but also as (usually) resident in Boston, in 9 Pelham Street. The likelihood, then, is that the Hattie Wilson in Cortes Street from the 1900 census is not the same Hattie Wilson. However, the Cortes Street Wilson's existence does remind us just how common the names "Hattie" and "Wilson" were in Massachusetts at this time.

34. See Wilson, *Our Nig,* ed. Foreman and Pitts, xiv.

35. *Massachusetts Deaths,* 506: 95, Massachusetts Archives, Columbia Point, Boston, Mass. See also Wilson, *Our Nig,* ed. Foreman and Pitts, xiii–xiv; notice of Wilson's death, *Boston Globe,* June 29, 1900, 12. See also appendix 3. The details of the Cobbs' family history and family lore derive from an e-mail sent by Russell Cobb to R. J. Ellis, December 13, 2010.

SELECT BIBLIOGRAPHY

Baker, Houston A., Jr. "In Dubious Battle." *New Literary History: Literacy, Popular Culture, and the Writing of History* 18 (Winter 1987): 363–69.

Bassard, Katherine Clay. "Gender and Genre: Black Women's Autobiography and the Ideology of Literacy." *African American Review* 26, Women Writers Issue (Spring 1992): 119–29.

———. "'Beyond Mortal Vision': Harriet E. Wilson's *Our Nig* and the American Racial Dream-Text." In *Female Subjects in Black and White: Race, Psychoanalysis, Feminism,* edited by Elizabeth Abel, Barbara Christian, and Helene Moglen. Berkeley: University of California Press, 1997, 187–200.

Boggis, JerriAnne, Eve Allegra Raimon, and Barbara W. White, eds. *Harriet Wilson's New England: Race, Writing, and Region.* Durham: University of New Hampshire Press, 2007.

Borrego, Silvia P. Castro. "Harriet Wilson's *Our Nig*: Towards the Development of the 'Woman Question' and the Problem of 'The Color Line' into XX Century America." In *Actas III Congreso de la Sociedad Espanola para el Estudio dos Estados Unidos/Spanish*

Association for American Studies (SAAS): Fin de Siglo: Crisis y nuevos principios/Century Ends, Crises and New Beginnings, edited by Maria Jose Alvarez Maurin, Manuel Broncano Rodrigues, Camino Fernandez Rabadan, and Cristina Garrigos Gonzalez, Leon, Spain: Universidad de Leon, 1999, 49–55.

Breau, Elizabeth. "Identifying Satire: 'Our Nig.'" *Callaloo* 16 (Spring 1993):455–65.

Carby, Hazel V. "'Hear My Voice, Ye Careless Daughters': Narratives of Slave and Free Women before Emancipation." In *Black Women's Intellectual Traditions: Speaking Their Minds,* edited by Kristin Waters and Carol B. Conaway. Hanover, N.H.: University Press of New England, 2007, 91–112.

Cole, Phyllis. "Stowe, Jacobs, Wilson: White Plots and Black Counterplots." In *New Perspectives on Gender, Race, and Class in Society,* edited by Audrey T. McCluskey. Bloomington: Indiana University Press, 1990, 23–45.

Davis, Cynthia J. "Speaking the Body's Pain: Harriet Wilson's *Our Nig.*" *African American Review.* 27, Women's Culture Issue (Autumn 1993): 391–404.

Doriani, Beth Maclay. "Black Womanhood in Nineteenth-Century America: Subversion and Self-Construction in Two Women's Autobiographies." *American Quarterly* 43 (June 1991): 199–222.

Dowling, David. "'Other and More Terrible Evils': Anticapitalist Rhetoric in Harriet Wilson's *Our Nig* and Proslavery Propaganda." *College Literature* 36 (Summer 2009): 116–36.

Doyle, T. Douglas. "'A Two Story White House': *Our Nig* and the Catechization of Northern and Southern Slaves." *MAWA Review* 15 (December 2000): 22–26.

Drews, Marie. "Catharine Beecher, Harriet E. Wilson, and Domestic Discomfort at the Northern Table." In *Culinary Aesthetics and Practices in Nineteenth-Century American Literature,* edited by Monika Elbert and Marie Drews. New York: Palgrave Macmillan, 2009, 89–105.

Ellis, R. J. "What Happened to Harriet E. Wilson, nee Adams? Was She Really Hattie Green?" *Transition: An International Review* 99 (2008): 62–168.

———. *Harriet Wilson's "Our Nig": A Cultural Biography of a '"Two-Story" African American Novel.* Amsterdam: Rodopi, 2003.

———. *"Our Nig*: Fetters of an American Farmgirl." In *Special Relationships: Anglo-American Affinities and Antagonisms, 1854–1936,* edited by Janet Beer and Bridget Bennett. Manchester: Manchester University Press, 2002, 65–88.

———. "Traps Slyly Laid: Professing Autobiography in Harriet Wilson's *Our Nig."* In *Representing Lives: Women and Auto/Biography,* edited by Alison Donnell and Pauline Polkey. Basingstoke, England, and New York: Macmillan, St. Martin's Press, 2000, 65–76.

———. "Body Politics and the Body Politic in William Wells Brown's *Clotel* and Harriet Wilson's *Our Nig."* In *Soft Canons: American Women Writers and Masculine Tradition,* edited by Karen L. Kilcup. Iowa City: University of Iowa Press, 1999, 99–122.

Elwood-Farber, Lisa. "Harriet Wilson's *Our Nig*: A Look at the Historical Significance of a Novel That Exposes a Century's Worth of Hypocritical Ideology." *Women's Studies: An Inter-disciplinary Journal* 39 (2010): 470–89.

Ernest, John. *Shadowing Slavery: Five African American Autobiographical Narratives*. Acton, Mass.: Copley Publishing Group, 2002.

———. "Economies of Identity: Harriet E. Wilson's *Our Nig*." *PMLA* 109 (May 1994): 424–38.

Foreman, P. Gabrielle. *Activist Sentiments: Reading Black Women in the Nineteenth Century*. Urbana: University of Illinois Press, 2009.

———. "The Spoken and the Silenced in Incidents in *The Life of a Slave Girl* and *Our Nig*." *Callaloo* 13 (Spring 1990): 313–24.

Foreman, P. Gabrielle, and Katherine Flynn. "Mrs. H. E. Wilson, Mogul?" *Boston Globe*, February 15, 2009.

Foster, Frances Smith. *Written by Herself: Literacy Production by African American Women 1746–1892*. Bloomington: Indiana University Press, 1993.

Fox-Genovese, Elizabeth. " 'To Weave It into the Literature of the Country': Epic and the Fictions of African American Women." In *Poetics of the Americas: Race, Founding, and Textuality*, edited by Bainard Cowan and Jefferson Humphries. Baton Rouge: Louisiana State University Press, 1997, 31–45.

Gardner, Eric. "*Our Nig; or, Sketches from the Life of a Free Black*." *African American Review* 38 (Winter 2004): 715–18.

———. "'This Attempt of Their Sister': Harriet Wilson's *Our Nig* from Printer to Readers." *New England Quarterly* 66 (June 1993): 226–46.

Grasso, Linda. *The Artistry of Anger: Black and White Women's Literature in America, 1820–1860*. Chapel Hill: University of North Carolina Press, 2002.

Henderson, Carol E. "Shades of Blackness: Race, Religion and Single Parenthood in Harriet E. Wilson's *Our Nig*." *MAWA Review* 14 (June 1999): 31–42.

Ibarrola-Armendariz, Aitor. "Harriet E. Wilson's *Our Nig*: An Idiosyncratic Attempt to Locate the Color Line in Terms of Class, Gender and Geography." In *Literature and Ethnicity in the Cultural Borderlands*, edited by Jesus Benito and Anna Maria Manzanas. Amsterdam: Rodopi, 2002, 23–33.

James, Jennifer C., and Cynthia Wu. "Editors' Introduction: Race, Ethnicity, Disability, and Literature: Intersections and Interventions." *MELUS* 31, Race, Ethnicity, Disability, and Literature Issue (Fall 2006): 3–13.

Jefferson, Margo. "Down & Out & Black in Boston." *Nation* 236 (May 28, 1983): 675–77.

Johnson, Ronna C. "Said but Not Spoken: Elision and the Representation of Rape, Race, and Gender in Harriet E. Wilson's *Our Nig*." In *Speaking the Other Self: American Women Writers*, edited by Jeanne Campbell Reesman. Athens: University of Georgia Press, 1997, 96–116.

Jones, Jill. "The Disappearing 'I' in *Our Nig.*" *Legacy* 13 (1996): 38–53.

Joyce, Joyce A. "'Who the Cap Fit': Unconsciousness and Unconscionableness in the Criticism of Houston A. Baker, Jr., and Henry Louis Gates, Jr." *New Literary History* 18, Literacy, Popular Culture, and the Writing of History Issue 18 (Winter 1987): 371–84.

King, Debra Walker. "Harriet Wilson's *Our Nig.*" In *Recovered Writers/ Recovered Texts,* edited by Dolan Hubbard. Knoxville: University of Tennessee Press, 1997, 31–45.

Krah, Barbara. "Tracking Frado: The Challenge of Harriet E. Wilson's *Our Nig* to Nineteenth-Century Conventions of Writing Womanhood." *Amerikastudien/American Studies* 49 (2004): 465–82.

Larson, Jennifer. "Renovating Domesticity in *Ruth Hall, Incidents in the Life of a Slave Girl,* and *Our Nig.*" *Women's Studies: An Interdisciplinary Journal* 38 (July–August 2009): 538–58.

Lester, Neal A. "Play(writing) and En(acting) Consciousness: Theater as Rhetoric in Harriet Wilson's *Our Nig.*" *Western Journal of Black Studies* 34 (Fall 2010): 347–57.

Leveen, Lois. "Dwelling in the House of Oppression: The Spatial, Racial, and Textual Dynamics of Harriet Wilson's *Our Nig.*" *African American Review* 35 (Winter 2001): 561–80.

Lindgren, Margaret. "Harriet Jacobs, Harriet Wilson and the Redoubled Voice in Black Autobiography." *Obsidian II: Black Literature in Review* 8 (Spring–Summer 1993): 18–38.

Lovell, Thomas B. "By Dint of Labor and Economy: Harriet Jacobs, Harriet Wilson, and the Salutary View of Wage Labor." *Arizona Quarterly* 52 (Autumn 1996): 1–32.

Marfo, Florence. "Marks of the Slave Lash: Black Women's Writing of the 19th Century Anti-Slavery Novel." *Diaspora: Journal of the Annual Afro-Hispanic Literature and Culture Conference* 11 (2001): 80–86.

Mitchell, Angelyn. "Her Side of His Story: A Feminist Analysis of Two Nineteenth-Century Antebellum Novels—William Wells Brown's *Clotel* and Harriet E. Wilson's *Our Nig.*" *American Literary Realism, 1870–1910.* Special Issue on African-American Fiction (Spring 1992): 7–21.

Mullen, Harryette. "Runaway Tongue: Resistant Orality in *Uncle Tom's Cabin, Our Nig, Incidents in the Life of a Slave Girl,* and *Beloved.*" In *The Culture of Sentiment: Race, Gender, and Sentimentality in Nineteenth-Century America,* edited by Shirley Samuels. New York: Oxford University Press, 1992, 244–64.

Peterson, Carla L. "Capitalism, Black (Under)Development, and the Production of the African-American Novel in the 1850s." *American Literary History* 4 (Winter 1992): 559–83.

Piep, Karsten H. "'Nothing New under the Sun': Postsentimental

Conflict in Harriet E. Wilson's *Our Nig*." *Colloquy: Text Theory Critique* 11 (May 2006): 178–94.

Pratofiorito, Ellen. "'To Demand Your Sympathy and Aid': *Our Nig* and the Problem of No Audience." *Journal of American & Comparative Cultures* 24 (Spring–Summer 2001): 31–48.

Raimon, Eve Allegra. *The "Tragic Mulatta" Revisited: Race and Nationalism in Nineteenth-Century Antislavery Fiction.* New Brunswick, N.J.: Rutgers University Press, 2004.

Santamarina, Xiomara. *Belabored Professions: Narratives of African American Working Womanhood.* Chapel Hill: University of North Carolina Press, 2005.

Short, Gretchen. "Harriet Wilson's *Our Nig* and the Labor of Citizenship." *Arizona Quarterly* 57 (Autumn 2001): 1–27.

Stern, Julia. "Excavating Genre in Our Nig." *American Literature* 67 (September 1995): 439–66.

Stover, Johnnie M. *Rhetoric and Resistance in Black Women's Autobiography.* Gainesville: University Press of Florida, 2003.

Tompkins, Kyla Wazana. "'Everything 'Cept Eat Us': The Antebellum Black Body Portrayed as Edible Body." *Callaloo* 30 (Winter 2007): 201–24.

Warren, Joyce W. "Performativity and the Repositioning of American Literary Realism." In *Challenging Boundaries: Gender and*

Periodization, edited by Joyce W. Warren and Margaret Dickie. Athens: University of Georgia Press, 2000, 3–25.

West, Elizabeth J. "Reworking the Conversion Narrative: Race and Christianity in *Our Nig.*" *MELUS* 24 (Summer 1999): 3–27.

White, Barbara A. " 'Our Nig' and the She-Devil: New Information about Harriet Wilson and the 'Bellmont' Family." *American Literature* 65 (March 1993): 19–52.

Willey, Nicole L. "Mothering in Slavery: A Revision of African Feminist Principles." *Journal of the Association for Research on Mothering* 9 (Fall–Winter 2007): 191–207.

———. *Creating a New Ideal of Masculinity for American Men: The Achievement of Sentimental Women Writers in the Mid-Nineteenth Century.* Lewiston: Edwin Mellon Press, 2007.

Wilson, Harriet E. *Our Nig; or, Sketches from the Life of a Free Black, in a Two-Story White House, North. Showing that Slavery's Shadows Fall Even There.* Boston: printed by George C. Rand & Avery, 1859.

———. *Our Nig.* In *Three Great African-American Novels,* edited by John Ernest. Mineola, N.Y.: Dover Publications, 2005.

———. *Our Nig.* Edited with an introduction by P. Gabrielle Foreman and Reginald H. Pitts. New York: Penguin Books, 2005.

———. *Our Nig.* Edited with Introduction by P. Gabrielle Foreman and Reginald H. Pitts. Second edition. New York: Penguin Books, 2009.

————. *Our Nig.* In *Classic African American Women's Narratives,* edited by William L. Andrews. New York: Oxford University Press, 2003.

————. *Our Nig; or, Sketches from the Life of a Free Black, in a Two-Story White House, North. Showing that Slavery's Shadows Fall Even There.* Edited with Introduction by Henry Louis Gates, Jr. New York: Vintage Books, 1983, 2002.

————. *Our Nig; or, Sketches from the Life of a Free Black, in a Two-Story White House, North. Showing that Slavery's Shadows Fall Even There.* Edited with Introduction by R. J. Ellis. Nottingham: Trent Editions, 1998.

Dissertations

Bell, Sophia R. "Naughty Child: The Racial Politics of Sentimental Discipline in Selected U.S. Antebellum Texts." Ph.D. dissertation, Tufts University, 2008.

Creighton, Jane Margaret. "The Bordering Nation: Problems of American Identity in Selected Novels from *Our Nig* to George Washington Gomez." Ph.D. dissertation, Rice University, 1997.

Francis, Allison E. "When the 'Unprotected' Body Speaks: The Narratives of Nineteenth-Century Black Females in the Caribbean and the United States." Ph.D. dissertation, Washington University, 2005.

Gardner, Eric Scott. "After Uncle Tom: The Domestic Dialogue on

Slavery and Race, 1852-1859." Ph.D. dissertation, University of Illinois at Urbana-Champaign, 1996.

Green-Barteet, Miranda A. "Neither Wholly Public, nor Wholly Private: Interstitial Spaces in Works by Nineteenth-Century American Women Writers." Ph.D. dissertation, Texas A&M University, 2009.

Jefferson, Lynne T. "The Emergence of a Pioneer: The Manipulation of Hagar in Nineteenth-Century American Women's Novels." Ph.D. dissertation, Indiana University of Pennsylvania, 2008.

Jones, Jill Colvin. " 'You Don't Know about Me': The Disenfranchised Narrator in Nineteenth-Century United States Fiction." Ph.D. dissertation, Tufts University, 1995.

Lidinsky, April. "Working Figures: Discourses of Race and Class in Nineteenth-Century Working Women's Self-Representations." Ph.D. dissertation, Rutgers, The State University of New Jersey, 2000.

Murphy, Jessica Alexandra Maeve. "Nation, Miscegenation, and the Myth of the Mulatta/o Monster 1859–1886." Ph.D. dissertation, Université de Montréal, 2009.

O'Connell, Catherine Elizabeth. "Chastening the Rod: Sentimental Strategies in Three Antebellum Novels by Women." Ph.D. dissertation, University of Michigan, 1992.

Pratofiorito, Ellen C. "Selling the Vision: Marketability and Audience in Antebellum American Literature." Ph.D. dissertation, Rutgers, The State University of New Jersey, 1998.

Seldon, Tyra Lynnette. "Defining Free America: Reading Black Women's Novels as Counter, Contending, and Contested Narratives." Ph.D. dissertation, University of Rochester, 2002.

Wright, Nazera Sadiq. "Girlhood in African American literature, 1827–1949." Ph.D. dissertation, University of Maryland, College Park, 2010.

"A book of historical truth spoken loud and clear, as none of us have ever quite heard it before." —*Black Issues Book Review*

AUTOBIOGRAPHY OF A PEOPLE
*Three Centuries of African American History
Told by Those Who Lived It*
Edited by Herb Boyd

Autobiography of a People is an insightfully assembled anthology of eyewitness accounts that traces the history of the African American experience. From the Middle Passage to the Million Man March, editor Herb Boyd has culled a diverse range of voices, both famous and ordinary, to create a unique and compelling historical portrait: Benjamin Banneker on Thomas Jefferson; Old Elizabeth on spreading the Word; Frederick Douglass on life in the North; W.E.B. Du Bois on the Talented Tenth; Matthew Henson on reaching the North Pole; Harriet Jacobs on running away; James Cameron on escaping a mob lynching; Alvin Ailey on the world of dance; Langston Hughes on the Harlem Renaissance; Curtis Morrow on the Korean War; Max Roach on "jazz" as a four-letter word; LL Cool J on rap; Mary Church Terrell on the Chicago World's Fair; Rev. Bernice King on the future of Black America; and many others.

African American Studies

BLACK WOMEN WRITERS (1950–1980)
A Critical Evaluation
Edited by Mari Evans

"The most distinctive feature of *Black Women Writers* is its organization. An organization that makes it possible to present in a single volume (a) the writer's reflection on her work, her intentions, inspirations and goals, (b) a substantial evaluation by two perceptive critics and (c) the hard biographical and bibliographical data that often provide their own curb against sentimentality on one hand and excessive speculation on the other" (Stephen Henderson, Ph.D., from the Introduction). Featuring works by Maya Angelou, Toni Cade Bambara, Gwendolyn Brooks, Alice Childress, Lucille Clifton, Mari Evans, Nikki Giovanni, Gayl Jones, and many more.

Literature/Women's Studies/
African American Studies

COLORED PEOPLE
A Memoir
by Henry Louis Gates, Jr.

In a coming-of-age story as enchantingly vivid and ribald as anything by Mark Twain or Zora Neale Hurston, Henry Louis Gates, Jr., recounts his childhood in the mill town of Piedmont, West Virginia, in the 1950s and 1960s and ushers readers into a now-vanished "colored" world of hellfire religion and licentious gossip, of lye-and-mashed-potato "processes," and of slyly stubborn resistance to the indignities of segregation. A winner of the *Chicago Tribune*'s Heartland Award and the Lillian Smith Prize, *Colored People* is a pungent and poignant masterpiece of recollection, a work that extends and deepens our sense of African American history even as it entrances us with its bravura storytelling.

Autobiography/African American Studies

THE FUTURE OF THE RACE
by Henry Louis Gates, Jr., and Cornel West

Almost a hundred years ago the great W.E.B. Du Bois proposed the notion of a "talented tenth," an African American elite that would serve as leaders and models for the larger black community. In this unprecedented collaboration, Henry Louis Gates, Jr., and Cornel West—two of Du Bois's most prominent intellectual descendants—reassess that relationship and its implications for the African American future. *The Future of the Race* is a visionary work that is sure to be read and debated as long as race remains an issue in America.

African American Studies

THIRTEEN WAYS OF LOOKING AT A BLACK MAN
by Henry Louis Gates, Jr.

What does it mean to be a black man in twentieth-century America? Henry Louis Gates, Jr. suggests that the idea of a unitary black man is as illusory as the creature Wallace Stevens conjured up in his poem "Thirteen Ways of Looking at a Blackbird." In eight essays, many of which first appeared in *The New Yorker*, Gates profiles a series of unusual men who, he writes, "have shaped the world as much as they were shaped by it, who gave as good as they got." Colin Powell, Harry Belafonte, Louis Farrakhan, Anatole Broyard, Bill T. Jones, James Baldwin, Albert Murray: these men and others speak of their lives with startling candor and intimacy, and their illuminating stories reveal much about the anxieties and contradictions of our society. What emerges is an unforgettable portrait gallery of "representative" black men—which is to say, most unrepresentative ones indeed.

African American Studies

HER DREAM OF DREAMS
The Rise and Triumph of Madam C. J. Walker
by Beverly Lowry

Madam C. J. Walker is an American rags-to-riches icon. Born to former slaves in Louisiana in 1867, she went on to become a prominent African American businesswoman and the first female self-made millionaire in U.S. history. The story of her transformation from a laundress to a tremendously successful entrepreneur is both inspirational and mysterious, as many of the details of her early life remain obscure. In this superior biography, Beverly Lowry's abundant research fleshes out Walker's thinly documented story and frames it in the roiling race relations of her day.

Biography

CROSSING THE DANGER WATER
Three Hundred Years of African American Writing
Edited and with an Introduction by Deirdre Mullane

Combining an extensive selection of poetry, prose, speeches, songs, documents, and letters dating from the pre-Colonial era through today's best and most well-known writers, *Crossing the Danger Water* offers a testament to the pervasive influence of African Americans on the political, creative, and cultural development of this nation, even well before its inception. This important collection introduces readers to long-neglected and relatively unknown items, such as the rousing letters of anonymous slave rebels, or the petition for freedom from a group of Bostonian slaves to the governor of their colony—written almost a century before the Civil War. *Crossing the Danger Water* is a timeless text that no one interested in African American history can afford to be without.

African American Studies/History

RACE MATTERS
by Cornel West

As a scholar, theologian, and activist, Cornel West has built a reputation as one of the most eloquent voices in America's racial debate. *Race Matters*, his bestselling book, was first published in 1993 on the one-year anniversary of the L.A. riots; it has since become an American classic. West's subject matter ranges from the crisis in black leadership and the myths surrounding black sexuality to affirmative action, the new black conservatism, and the strained relations between Jews and African Americans. He never hesitates to confront the prejudices of all of his readers—or wavers in his insistence that they share a common destiny. Bold in its thought and written with a redemptive passion grounded in the tradition of the African American church, *Race Matters* is a work that is at once challenging and deeply healing. It represents the thinking of a man at the forefront of discussions about race and will stand for years as the book to turn to for creative insights into the problems of our multiracial democracy.

African American Studies

VINTAGE BOOKS AND ANCHOR BOOKS
Available wherever books are sold.
www.randomhouse.com